Acclaim for Charles Martin's novels

"Martin's strength is in his memorable characters . . . [his] prose is lovely."
—*Publishers Weekly* review of *Chasing Fireflies*

"[C]olorful, memorable characters; Southern regional flavor that's drop-dead accurate; and lyrical, intelligent writing make *Chasing Fireflies* an exceptionally good read."

—*Aspiring Retail*

"If I could use only one word to describe *Chasing Fireflies* it would have to be "WOW!" From the very beginning of the book I was drawn into the story and could not put it down."

—epinions.com

Chasing Fireflies, a 2007 Pulpwood Queen book club selection.

"Beautiful writing . . . offers hope and redemption without too-neat resolution."
—*Publishers Weekly* regarding *Maggie*

". . . charming characters and twists that keep the pages turning."
—*Southern Living,* regarding *When Crickets Cry*
Southern Living Book-of-the-Month selection, April 2006

"How is Charles Martin able to take mere words and breathe such vibrant life into them? Each character is drawn with an artist's attention to detail, beauty and purpose. Readers won't want the story to end because that means leaving these lovable people who have become so much more than just a name in a book."

—inthelibraryreviews.net regarding *When Crickets Cry*

"[*The Dead Don't Dance* is] an absorbing read for fans of faith-based fiction . . . [with] delightfully quirky characters . . . [who] are ingeniously imaginative creations."

—*Publishers Weekly*

"[In *When Crickets Cry,*] Martin has created highly developed characters, life-like dialogue, and a well-crafted story."

—Christian Book Previews.com

"Martin spins an engaging story about healing and the triumph of love . . . Filled with delightful local color."

—*Publishers Weekly* regarding *Wrapped in Rain*

"[O]ne of the best books I've been asked to review, and certainly the best one this year!"

—bestfiction.tripod.com regarding *When Crickets Cry*

"Charles Martin has proven himself a master craftsman. Double the story-telling ability of Nicholas Sparks, throw in hints of Michael Crichton and Don J. Snyder, and you have Charles Martin."

—Paula Parker, www.lifeway.com

"If you read any book this year, this is the one."

—Coffee Time Romance regarding *When Crickets Cry*

"Mr. Martin's writing is gifted and blessed and insightful. His prose captures the essence of the story [*When Crickets Cry*] with beauty and sensitivity. I look forward to reading more of his work, past and future."

—onceuponaromance.net

"Charles Martin is changing the face of inspirational fiction one book at a time. *Wrapped in Rain* is a sentimental tale that is not to be missed."

—Michael Morris, author of *Slow Way Home* and *A Place Called Wiregrass*

"[*When Crickets Cry*] will be a classic and this gifted author will be listed among the literary greats of our time."

—novelreviews.blogspot.com

"The American South has produced many of our finest novelists and this is the case of Charles Martin and his novel, *When Crickets Cry*."

—bookviews.com

"*When Crickets Cry* is one of the very best books I have ever read, and I am still reeling from this knock-your-socks-off story several days after finishing it."

—romancejunkies.com

Chasing Fireflies

Other novels by Charles Martin

The Dead Don't Dance
Wrapped in Rain
When Crickets Cry
Maggie

Chasing Fireflies

A Novel of Discovery

CHARLES MARTIN

THOMAS NELSON
Since 1798

NASHVILLE   DALLAS   MEXICO CITY   RIO DE JANEIRO   BEIJING

Published in Nashville, Tennessee by Thomas Nelson. Thomas Nelson is a trademark of Thomas Nelson, Inc.

Thomas Nelson, Inc. titles may be purchased in bulk for educational, business, fund-raising, or sales promotional use. For information, please e-mail SpecialMarkets@ThomasNelson.com.

Publisher's Note: This novel is a work of fiction. Names, characters, places, and incidents are either products of the author's imagination or used fictitiously. All characters are fictional, and any similarity to people living or dead is purely coincidental.

Library of Congress Cataloging-in-Publication Data

Martin, Charles, 1969–
  Chasing fireflies / Charles Martin.
      p. cm.
  ISBN: 978-1-59554-056-0
  I. Title.
  PS3613.A7778C46 2007
  813'.6—dc22

                                    2007007486

Printed in the United States of America
07 08 09 10 11 QW 8 7 6 5

For my Dad

. . . nothing compares

Prologue

Rocketing through the hazy orange glow of dawn, the green 1972 four-door Chevrolet Impala fishtailed sideways off the dirt road onto Highway 99, squealing both rear tires and billowing white smoke from bald retreads. The exhaust pipe spewed sparks some six feet beyond the bumper, and the tip of the pipe glowed cigarette-red. The engine whined, backfiring out the hole in the muffler, and then the car straightened and sped down the mile-long straightaway that paralleled the tracks. The left rear brake light was busted, and the front windshield was an indiscriminate spiderweb of cracks stretching from hood to rooftop.

A mile down the road, the speedometer bounced above ninety miles an hour, but it was a good thirty or forty off. Another quarter mile and the driver hit the brakes with both feet pressing the pedal to the carpet. Swerving from median to pavement to emergency lane and back again, the car moved like an untied balloon that had slipped from a clown's fingers. At the end of two long black lines, the driver threw the stick into reverse and gunned the small-block 400, producing more white smoke from both the rear wheel wells and the right exhaust pipe. Without signaling, the car U-turned, swung wide, and the driver pegged the accelerator.

The kid in the passenger seat stared into the side mirror, squinting so that his eyelashes touched, and studied the spray of sparks. If he closed them just right, the exhaust pipe comet transformed into a fanciful fountain of fireflies dancing along the South Georgia asphalt.

The car reached the railroad crossing in the wrong lane, finally swerving into the turn lane only to power-slide into the wrong lane again. The fountain disappeared. Steam rose from underneath the hood, swirling up and around the bulldog hood ornament. The cloth headliner had partially fallen from the ceiling and now flapped in the crosswind like a tent. All four windows were down, and only jagged corners remained of the back glass. The car sat smoking, just inches from the tracks.

These historic tracks.

The Silver Meteor was a speeding silver bullet placed into service in February 1932. Before the Second World War, boys would appear out of the woods, flag her down, and ride north to New York, where they'd hop on a steamer, float the ocean, and shoot at Germans. Her Mars lamp created a figure eight, sweeping the tracks ahead and keeping rhythm with the chatter of the telegraph at every stop. Air-conditioned in 1936, diesel powered, with reclining seats, a diner, tavern-coach, and coach-observation car, she was a modern marvel. With her all-stainless steel streamlined luxury coaches, Pullman sleepers, and white-coated porters opening doors and placing step-boxes on the platform, she was also a gateway to the world.

In her heyday from 1956 onward, she departed New York at 2:50 PM, arriving in D.C. some three and a half hours later, then promptly departed again at 7:05 en route to a 4:00 PM arrival in Miami the following day. That put her through Thalmann, a few miles west of the green Impala, sometime in the early morning.

Prior to every crossing, the conductor would check his Hamilton, gauge the time, and hang on the horn. But it wasn't always necessary. Sometimes it was just bragging. Then again, not many people had his job.

Normally, the Silver Meteor carried twenty cars and traveled between seventy-four and ninety miles per hour, meaning she would need all of five miles to stop. After she left Thalmann, she'd turn south, hug the Georgia coastline, streak into Florida, and top a hundred miles per hour on the straights between Sebring and West Palm Beach. She was a symphony of sound and a king's banquet of smell, feel, and otherworldly power. Her domed observation car would round the corner and sparkle in the distance like the Northern Star. A minute later, the caboose would reach and clear the corner, only to disappear once again behind her nose.

Barreling down the straight, the bone-jarring horn would sound every quarter mile and then constantly in the last quarter. As she neared the crossing, she sent an odd combination of sonar pings— the banging of the draft gear between the cars, the thundering engines, bells ringing, horn blowing, sparks flying in her wake. She was a panoramic display of *clickety-clack* glory, the sum of which reached out ahead of the train only to sneak around and rise up through your spine like a jackhammer exiting the earth. And when she had disappeared, her single red light tailing off into the distance, she left you with that same lover's touch, the lingering remnant and sweet aroma of spent diesel, hot oil, and creosote.

The driver of the Impala was female. Skinny fingers. Thin skin. White knuckles. A half-empty brown bag bottle pressed between her high-mileage thighs. Sunglasses dwarfed her face, covering the hollow sockets, and a purple shawl covered her ears and hair. She was screaming at someone on the other side of the spiderweb.

The boy next to her might have been eight, but his meals had been sporadic and less than nutritious. He looked like an alley cat in a ghost town. He wore only cutoff jeans—fraying across his thighs like dandelion wisps. A safety pin held together the right hinge of his glasses, and both lenses were grooved with deep scratches.

The glasses had been given to him by one of the men who was not his dad. They had been at Wal-Mart walking past the optometrist. The kid tugged on the man's leg, looked at the doctor's door, and then at the man. The man frowned and walked over to the bin where folks throw their old glasses. He looked over his shoulder, and then stuck his arm into the mouth of the mailbox, pulling out the first pair his hand touched. He turned them over in his hands, and then slammed them on the kid's face. "There. Better?" The kid looked at the scars on the man's hand, the grease under his fingernails, and nodded. That'd been two years ago.

The kid looked straight ahead, clutching a spiral-bound notebook and pen. His skin was white and covered in scars. Some new, some old, all painful. Some were circular, about the size of the head of a pencil, while others were about an inch in length and maybe half an inch wide. On his back, in the middle of his right shoulder blade, the most recent wound oozed.

The woman turned toward the kid, pointed an uncertain finger in his face, and continued screaming. In the background a hollow, distant horn sounded. The kid didn't flinch. He'd quit flinching a while ago.

She grabbed the brown bag, sucked hard on the courage, and turned her spit-filled tirade back at the windshield. In the distance, the train's headlamp appeared.

She pounded the steering wheel, sucked hard again, and then backhanded the kid, rocking his head off the right door. He picked his glasses off the floorboard but never let go of the notebook.

Her fingers tapped the seat next to her while she caught her breath. She lit a cigarette, breathed deeply, and then exhaled out the window. He watched the glow out of the corner of his eye. Two more quick puffs, one more swig, and then she ran her fingers through his hair. It had been cropped short, shorn like a sheep, and the back of his head looked like a soccer ball where patches were missing.

A half mile away, the train passed a white signal post and sounded again. She finished off the bottle, stamped out the cigarette, and then placed her hand on his shoulder. Her finger touched a scabbing scar, causing her brow to wrinkle and sending tears cascading down a face stretched taut across her skull. The temperature hovered in the eighties, but the kid shivered beneath a blanket of sweat and a trickle of puss. As if flipping a switch, she threw the bottle at the face beyond the windshield. It ricocheted off the dash and the empty carton of Winstons. Another long horn caught her attention. She turned to the boy, pointed again, and screamed from her belly—the veins in her neck bulging like kudzu vines.

The kid shook his head, his shoulders trembling. The woman banged the steering wheel, pointed at the train, and then reached across the car and backhanded the kid hard across the mouth. His head flew back, slammed into the side of the door, and sent his glasses and both lenses flying in three separate directions across the asphalt. His hands clutched the notebook, and his arms and face shook as the blood trickled out his nose. When he still didn't budge, she reached across him, threw open the car door, and then leaned against her door, raising her heel high.

The horn was constant now, as was her scream. When the rumble of the train shook the car and the *clacking* of the wheels hammered in his eardrums, she gripped the steering wheel with one hand and the seat back with the other, then let go with her foot and caught him square in the temple, rocketing him out of the car. The blow sent him tumbling like Raggedy Ann while the notebook spun through the air like a Frisbee. His limp body skidded across the asphalt, rolled across the gravel and a patch of broken glass, and tumbled down into the ditch, where his nose came to rest just inches from the water.

With the train just four car-lengths away, she redlined the tachome-
ter, threw the stick into first, ground gear on gear, and lurched forward.

Six feet later the tires stopped spinning, and several of the lug
nuts snapped off from the impact.

The hundred-plus car train, traveling nearly sixty miles an hour
and ferrying Toyotas to the port in Jacksonville, T-boned the car, which
bent in the middle like a boomerang, then arced upward like some
sick synthesis of a Harrier jet and a knuckleball. It sailed across the
tops of the seven-year-old saplings and landed like a meteor in a bed
of fresh pine straw. A hundred feet too late, the conductor slammed
the brake amidst a chorus of Mother Marys.

A half mile later, the train—nearly a mile in length—stopped.
Screaming into a radio, the conductor jumped off his engine and
ran flat-footed toward the flames. By the time he arrived, the paint
had bubbled and the tires had melted. Seeing the driver's fingers still
wrapped around the wheel, he covered his nose and averted his eyes.

Twenty minutes later the paramedics arrived, along with two fire
engines, a sheriff's deputy, and a farmer who'd seen the explosion
from his tractor more than a mile away. In the three hours they spent
dousing and talking about the fire, the explosion, and what remained
of the woman, they never saw the kid, and he never uttered a word.

Chapter 1

I stepped out into the sunlight humming a Pat Green tune, slipped on my sunglasses, and stared out over the courthouse steps. After three days of incarceration, not much had changed. Brunswick, Georgia, was like that. Discarded bubblegum, flat as half-dollars, dotted the steps like splattered ink. Lazy, blimpish pigeons strutted the sidewalk begging for bread scraps or the sprinkles off somebody's double-shot mocha latte. In the alley across the street, an entire herd of stray cats crept toward the wharf just four blocks down. The sound of seagulls told them the shrimp boats had returned. And on the steps next to me, two officers lifted a tattooed man, whose feet and hands were shackled and cuffed, up the steps and, undoubtedly, into Judge Thaxton's courtroom. Based on the mixture of saliva and epithets coming out of his mouth, he wasn't too crazy about going. No worries. Given my experience with Her Honor, his stay in her courtroom wouldn't be long.

His next short-term home would be a holding cell downstairs. These were cold, dark, windowless, and little more than petri dishes for mold and fungi. I know this because I've been in them on more than one occasion. The first time I stayed here as a guest, I scratched *Chase was here* into the concrete block wall. This time I followed it up with *Twice*. Makes me laugh to think about it. Sort of following in Unc's footsteps.

Two blocks down, rising above the rest of town like the Ferris wheel at a county fair, stood the bell tower above the Zuta Bank and Trust. Most churches-turned-banks have that. At the turn of the century, its Russian Orthodox congregation had dwindled down to nothing, leaving the priest to roam the basement like the Phantom in his catacomb.

And while the Silver Meteor was the most famous rail ever to run these woods, she couldn't hold a candle to the one that ran underground.

When the first Russian immigrants appeared in the late 1800s, they built on an existing footprint. A hundred years earlier, the local inhabitants had built their own meetinghouse. The building served several purposes: town hall, church, and shelter. Unique to the structure was a basement. Because much of South Georgia rests so close to the water table, they dug the basement into a hill, then lined the walls and floors with several feet of coquina. This did not mean it stayed dry, but it was dry enough. Through two trapdoors and one hidden stairwell, the townsfolk survived multiple Indian attacks and two Spanish burnings of the building above. Few today know about the basement. Maybe just the four of us. Sure, folks know it was there at one time, but most think it was filled in when the ZB&T was built. Scratchings on the walls show the names of slaves who knelt in the dark, listened, and prayed while dogs sniffed above.

Eventually the Phantom vacated as well, leaving the building empty for nearly a decade. Hating to see it go to waste and needing a place from which to loan money, a local businessman bought the building, ripped out half the pews, one confessional, and most of the altar, and installed counters and a vault. Local sentiment swayed in his favor. The depression was still fresh on people's minds, and in that mind-set you couldn't let a perfectly good building go to waste. If you built the church, don't take it personally. Just because folks around here don't like your brand of God doesn't mean they don't like your brand of architecture. Count your blessings. Most in Glynn County echoed this sentiment. Some of the locals proudly traced their roots to the Founding Fathers—the English prisoners sent from England to inhabit the colony back before the Revolution. Such sentiment was not unique; folks in Australia did the same. In the sticks of Brunswick, Georgia, rebellion was as hardwired into the DNA of the residents as was the love of Georgia Bulldog football.

While South Georgia found itself squarely embedded in the Bible Belt, and most churches were filled on Sundays, only Saturdays were sacred. Saturday afternoons from September to December, folks huddled around the altar of an AM station and worshipped the red and black of the Bulldogs. And while local pastors were much admired and respected, none carried the weight of the radio voice of the Bulldogs, Larry Munson. If Larry said anything at all, it was gospel. Throughout the decades, much has been written about Notre Dame and Touchdown Jesus, The Crimson Tide and Bear Bryant, and Penn State and Paterno, but from the salt marsh to the mountains, it was a certifiable fact that God himself was a Georgia Bulldog. How else did Larry Munson break his chair?

November 8, 1980. A minute to go in the fourth quarter. The Gators led the Bulldogs by a point. The Bulldogs had the ball, but ninety-three yards stood between them, the goal line, and their shot at the national title. On the second play of the game, Herschel Walker had bounced off a tackle and scorched seventy-two yards for six points and the beginnings of immortality. Now he stood on the field, having rushed for more than two hundred yards, either a target or a decoy. Buck Belue of Valdosta, Georgia, took the snap, pump faked—causing Florida Gator Tony Lilly to stumble—and dumped the ball down the left sideline to Lindsey Scott, who high-stepped ninety-three yards and joined Herschel atop Mt. Olympus. Amidst the mayhem in the press box, Larry Munson would break his folding chair, solidifying his place alongside the commentating gods and inside the heart of every man, woman, and child in the state of Georgia. *Sports Illustrated* later called it the "Play of the Decade," and many sportswriters agreed that Herschel Walker was the greatest athlete ever to play college football.

Folks in Georgia need no further argument. The State rests.

My office at the *Brunswick Daily* sat across the street, looking down on me. I could see the rolling slide show of my screen saver shining through my third-story window. My perch. As a reporter assigned to the court beat, I kept my finger on the court's pulse by watching these steps. The sign above my head read GLYNN COUNTY JAIL, but I didn't turn and look at it. Didn't need to.

After three days in jail, I was pretty sure that my editor had bitten his nails to the quick and was up there eyeing me from his perch, just seconds from walking out the double doors across the street. I looked east, toward the water and my boat. Home sounded like a good idea. I needed to get a shower, put on some deodorant, and breathe something other than dank cell stench. The paper could wait.

Uncle Willee sat in the driver's seat smiling at me from beneath his wide-brimmed palmetto leaf hat, called a "Gus." It's a cowboy hat for hot weather, a lightweight version of the hat made famous by Robert Duvall in *Lonesome Dove*. The brim was soiled and crown wrinkled, worn dirty by a farrier with a fishing addiction. It sagged a bit around the edges but curled up at the ends—a mirrored contrast to his face.

I stuffed my hands in my pockets and sniffed the salty air blowing in over St. Simons, across the marsh, and bringing with it the ripe smell of curdling salt and mud—a function of our geography. The Gulf Stream, some hundred and fifty miles due east, keeps constant pressure against the East Coast's most western edge—something akin to a hedge—causing the "Bermuda High." Thanks to it, the

Golden Isles live under a constant sea breeze that keeps both the no-see-ums—invisible gnats with an attitude—and hurricanes at bay.

The coastal rivers of Georgia, like the Satilla, the Altamaha, and the Little Brunswick, flow out of the west Georgia mountains through the Buffalo Swamp and empty into the cordgrass of the marsh flats. Like a seine made of cheesecloth, the marsh filters the flow and sifts the sediment, creating a pluffy, soft mud.

Here in this pungent muck, native anaerobic bacteria decay bottom matter and release a gaseous bouquet that smells like rotten eggs. As the tide recedes, fiddler crabs, snails, worms, and other tiny inhabitants burrow into the pluff where they hope to escape being slow-cooked at a broiling 140 degrees. As the tide rises, the critters climb from their holes, where they—like beachcombers—bask and bathe.

During peak tourist season, visitors stroll the sidewalks, sniff the same air, and wrinkle their noses. "Something die?" Technically, yes, the marsh is always dying. But then the tide returns, trades old for new, and the canvas gives birth again.

To us—those who seek the solace of the marsh—it is a stage where God paints—yellow in the morning, green toward noon, brownish in the afternoon, and blood red toward evening. It is the sentinel that stands guard at the ocean's edge, protecting the sea from the runoff that would kill it. It is a selfless and sacrificial place. And when I close my eyes, it is also the smell of home.

When I graduated college, I came back to Brunswick, bought an acre along the Altamaha and a sailboat named *Gone Fiction* at the annual police auction. She was a thirty-six-foot Hunter and had been confiscated during an offshore drug raid. The SWAT guys at the auction said they'd busted some Florida writer running drugs along the coast. When his books didn't sell, he traded his pen for a habit and joined the dark side. I didn't know a thing about sailing, but she looked cozy—had a bed, toilet, shower, small kitchen, and a bow big enough for a folding chair. Not to mention a rope railing where I could prop up my feet. I sized her up, imagined myself perched on her nose watching the tide roll in and out, and raised my hand. *Sold!* I got her in the water, motored her upriver to my acre of land, and dropped anchor in water deep enough not to ground her when the tide ran out. She sits about eighty yards offshore, which means when I tell people I live on the water, I'm not kidding.

Unc sat in a black, four-door 1970-something Cadillac hearse pulling a double-axle trailer he'd bought at a U-Haul auction. As a farrier, he uses the trailer as his workshop and his home away from home. He bought the hearse, which he calls Sally, more than a decade ago when a nearby funeral home needed an upgrade. It's the joke he plays on the world, and given the life he's lived, a joke is helpful.

A single fishing pole stuck out the back, the line tip dangling with a redheaded jig. Unc tipped his hat back, raised his eyebrows above his polarized Costa Del Mars, and smiled a guilty grin. He lifted his seat belt buckle, popped the top on a Yoo-hoo, stuffed an entire MoonPie into his mouth, and then sucked down the Yoo-hoo like it was the last on earth. I shook my head. Sometimes I wonder how a man like that raised a kid like me. Then I remember.

He dropped his glasses down on his chest. "You look like the dog's been keeping you under the porch."

Maybe I did look a bit disheveled.

I walked up to the car and began pulling on the ID tag they'd put on my wrist three days ago. It's like one of those plastic bands they give you when you check into the hospital. When they booked me, I told them, "I don't really need this. I already know my name." Problem is—that's not entirely true.

After about ten seconds, I decided that you'd have to bench-press five hundred pounds to break it. I pulled harder. It might as well have been a pair of handcuffs.

Unc shook his head. "Boy, you couldn't pour pee out of a boot with instructions on the heel."

Uncle Willee speaks his own language made up of one-liners that make sense mostly to him. Aunt Lorna and I just call them "Willee-isms," and between the two of us we can usually figure out what he's trying to say.

I stuck my hand through the window and said, "May I?"

He reached into his back pocket and handed me his Barlow pocket-knife. "Always drink upstream from the herd."

Another thing about Willee-isms—they often use just a few words to say what would require ordinary people about a hundred. In this short exchange, he was bringing notice to the fact that he came pre-pared with his Barlow—as always—while I was without mine. Hence, naked and dependant on another, i.e., Uncle Willee, who to my knowl-edge had never followed the herd. That meant he thought ahead, while I had not. But why say all that when you can talk about some herd drinking upstream from some other herd somewhere in some ethereal pasture?

He looked through the windshield and picked at a front tooth with his toothpick. ". . . like being caught with your shorts down."

I shook my head, opened the smaller of the two blades, and cut off the wristband that told the jail my name.

He slipped the knife back into his pocket and whispered under his breath, "Better to have it and not need it, than to need it and not have it."

I climbed into Sally and buckled my seat belt. "Well, aren't we just as full of wind as a corn-eating horse?"

"It ain't boasting if you done it."

"You're an embarrassment to civil society."

Unc dropped the gearshift into drive, turned up Wynonna Judd's rendition of "Free Bird," and said, "You don't know the half of it."

That, too, was true.

I was six years old, or so I'm told, when the state sent me to the home of Willee and Lorna McFarland. It would be my last stop. But after twenty-two years of living with Uncle Willee, I knew only half his story. It was the other half I'd spent most of my life trying to figure out.

Just as we were about to merge into traffic, he pulled the stick back up into neutral and pulled his glasses down to the tip of his nose. "Oh . . . Tommye's home."

Willie Nelson sings a song about an angel that skirts too close to Earth, clips a wing, and ends up sick and grounded. He mends her wing and patches her up only to watch her catch an updraft and exit the stratosphere. As the words *Tommye's home* echoed between my ears like a bell clapper in a clock tower, I remembered that tune.

Unc grabbed a fresh toothpick that'd been stuffed into the foam above the visor and laid it on his tongue, all the while studying my eyes.

I tried to mask them and nodded. "When?"

He pushed his glasses back up and adjusted his side mirror. "Few days ago."

"Where's she staying?"

He accelerated and waved at a Sea Island soccer mom driving a black Suburban, who let him merge. "With us."

After years of unanswered phone calls, "return to sender" letters, one unannounced visit, rampant rumors, and finally the ugly and public truth, Tommye had flown home.

Thirty minutes later we turned off Highway 99 and onto the dirt road that led to home. It was lined with some fifty-four pecan trees that Unc's daddy—Tillman Ellsworth McFarland—had planted almost fifty years ago. He dropped me at the barn and looked up at the loft. "I'll be up in a bit. Give you two some time."

I climbed the steps, filled my lungs, and pushed open the door. The loft was my home away from home. I'd lived up here throughout high school, during college, and for a while after. Even now, when I don't feel like driving back to the boat, I sleep here.

The window unit was set on "high," and condensation ran down the inside of the windows. Tommye stood near the refrigerator, reaching for a glass off the top shelf. She wore sweats that looked two sizes too big and a cutoff shirt exposing a sunrise tattoo on the small of her back. Her brunette hair was blonde, stringy, and tired looking. She heard the click of the door and turned slowly. Her face was thinner, her eyebrows sculpted, and the green emeralds I'd known in high school were dim, bloodshot, and burning low.

She smiled, tilted her head, and . . . have you ever seen video of melting glaciers where huge chunks, the size of skyscrapers, break off and crash into the sea? If hearts can do that, then when her hair slid from behind her ear and down over her eyes, and the right side of her lip turned up, I heard my heart crack down the middle.

I nodded toward the cabinet. "What're you looking for?"

She never took her eyes off me. "Anonymity."

Barefoot on the worn carpet, fresh red polish on her toes, she stepped across the single-room apartment. She stopped, her face inches from mine, reached for my hands, and pulled gently. A hug that said, "Meet me in the middle." Her arms and back were strong, and her tomboy's chest felt unnatural and Hollywood-firm. We stood there several minutes, her holding me. But as the minutes passed and the facade faded, she leaned on me, and the hug passed from her holding me to me holding her.

The night she left—nearly nine years ago—she had ducked in out of the rain, fear on her lips. Her hair was dripping, her clothes were soaked, she carried a light backpack with the few things she had gathered from the apartment, and crusted blood was smeared across her face. She woke me and pressed her lips hard to mine. The blood tasted bitter, and the swollenness felt strange and taut. She pressed her finger to my lips and said, "Remember, I was happy once. With you . . . here . . . I was." She fought back the tears, wiped her face on her sleeve, and her eyes narrowed. "Chase . . . never settle for less than the truth." She threw her head back, exposing the parallel bruises on her neck. "Never." Blood broke loose from her nose and dripped down off her chin. "Promise me."

I reached to wipe the blood, and she brushed me off.

Her voice echoed across the room. "Do it."

I nodded.

Another kiss, and then she disappeared back through the rain, the taillights of her Chevrolet glowing like two red eyes.

This hug betrayed her, as that one had.

She kissed me where my cheek joins my lips, and I heard the two sides of me crash into the sea. Technically, Tommye was my cousin, but since I was adopted, my family tree had been grafted in—labels didn't matter. I leaned forward and pressed my lips to the corner of her mouth. She pressed her cheek to my face, pulled away, and then touched me gently. The confident body language of the kid I knew had been hijacked by the quiet, retreating woman before me.

I opened the fridge, pulled out the milk jug, and drank from the bottle. "You been home?"

She looked around and folded her arms across her chest. "I am home."

I offered the jug, which she accepted, pouring the milk into a glass and then handing the jug back. She sipped slowly. Her skin looked like an iron canvas stretched across a cracked, wooden framework. Her body was thin but fit—like she'd been living on vegetables, Pilates, and plastic surgery.

I was about to make more small talk when Unc knocked on the door.

"Well, you never knocked before," I called. "What'd you start for now?"

He came in, kissed Tommye on the forehead, and handed her a plate covered in aluminum foil. "They're hot. Lorna'll be up in a minute. She's curling her hair."

Tommye pulled off the foil, closed her eyes, and breathed above the steam. She eyed the cookies. "Some things never change."

I looked at her. "And some things do."

She bit in, the melted chocolate chips dotting the edges of her lips, and chewed. She polished off a cookie, brushed her hand on her pants, and leaned in under Uncle Willee's big left arm, tucking her shoulder under his.

I was about to say something else stupid when the phone rang. I sat on the desk, punched speakerphone, and said, "Chase here."

"Chase!" It was Red Harrington, my transplanted New York editor. "How was your vacation?"

A forty-something, blue-blooded, ponytailed Yankee who was, as Unc liked to say, as out of place in South Georgia as a long-tailed cat in a room full of rocking chairs, Red had followed his Ivy League wife south after she tired of Manhattan, him, and his girlfriends ten years earlier. He was wifeless, houseless, and working to pay alimony. The paper was all he had left. Besides his baggage and the compromises in his own life, Red had a nose for news and an absolute and all-encompassing passion for discovering the truth hidden in any story. He was the epitome of the postmodern man—he trusted few and constantly asked, "What are you hiding?"

"It was . . . good." I looked at the phone. "Thanks for the dinner."

"Oh, don't worry. I'll deduct it from your paycheck. Listen, I know you probably want a few days off to rid yourself of whatever you picked up in prison . . ."

I looked at Tommye, who smirked at me. Her face told me she was impressed.

". . . but I need you." His tone of voice told me he wasn't lying. "What's up?"

"A train hit a car out in the boonies, some whacked-out lady on a suicide run."

"They know who she is?"

"Not yet, but DNA results ought to be in tomorrow."

"How 'bout dentals?"

"Can't do. Dentures."

"You want me to track her down?"

"Eventually, but she's backstory. The real story is the kid she kicked out of the car just before she parked in front of the train."

Unc zeroed in on the phone, and a single wrinkle appeared above his eyes. He let go of Tommye, walked over, and stood by the desk.

"They found him yesterday," Red's voice continued. "The morning after the crash. He was standing in the road, looking lost, and covered in ant bites . . . among other things."

Unc looked at me. I knew what he wanted.

"What other things?" I asked.

"Just get to the hospital. Room 316. You'll see."

"Anybody gotten anything out of him?"

"No. That's your job."

The phone clicked, and Unc looked out my window and across the pasture dotted with palm trees and a few of his Brahman cows.

I grabbed my car keys and looked at Tommye, who had lain down on my bed, pulled the sheet up, and closed her eyes. "You staying awhile?"

She nodded. "Not going anywhere."

I walked over to the bed and placed my hand on her foot. "That's what you said last time."

She rolled over and looked at me. Tired would have been an understatement.

I walked down the steps and into the barn, where I found Unc already sitting in the passenger seat of my truck, hat on and buckled in. "Where you going?"

"With you." He pointed out through the windshield. "Drive."

Is it just me, or has the world picked up speed since I stepped out of jail? The shower and deodorant would have to wait—as would the view off my bow.

My vehicle is a 1978 Toyota Land Cruiser, and her Christian name is Vicky. On my seventeenth birthday, after two years of penny-scraping and nonstop daydreaming, Unc matched my savings and helped me buy her. She's forest green, sports a black padded roll bar, large worn mud tires, winch, manual locking hubs, four-speed transmission, and front and rear pipe bumpers, and she'll go most anywhere. Judging from the freshly dried mud along her wheel wells, that remains true whether I'm in jail or not. You can take the kid out of the candy store, but not the candy store out of the kid.

One feature that allows her to do this is the snorkel intake that runs up out of the hood and along the passenger's side of the windshield. A snorkel intake feeds oxygen to the engine. Most stop at the top of the engine, while this one is about seven feet in length. It has its history in Africa, where British guides and explorers who needed to ford rivers could do so in water that rose up over the hood and steering wheel. Vicky's snorkel allows her to drive through water that would cover up the steering wheel. Though I've never done that to her, it's something to dream about.

Last month Vicky turned over two hundred thousand miles. We celebrated with an alignment, oil change, and a fish dinner on the beach. She rides a little stiff, her springs creak, she's showing rust bubbles around the rivets of her wheel wells, and she seldom sees the northern side of seventy miles an hour. Despite all this, I like her for many of the same reasons I like the marsh—when in her, I breathe deeply.

Which is something I desperately needed now. I pressed in the clutch, slipped the stick into first, and rolled out of the barn. We pulled onto the drive, and I shifted into third. The wind swirled around me— a hug from Vicky. That's when it hit me, the thing that'd been on the tip of my tongue since Tommye pressed her face to mine. I touched my face, rubbed the tips of my fingers with my thumb, and looked out beyond the dotted white line. There was no doubt about it.

She was burning up.

Chapter 2

We pulled down the drive but were intersected by the unkempt Lincoln Continental of Peter "Pockets" McQuire. He was nicknamed after the holes in his pockets—his clients discovered that no matter how much money they put into them, he always had room for more.

He waved us down and passed an envelope to Unc. "William . . . it's a copy of our appeal."

Unc nodded.

"If that doesn't work . . ."

Unc waved him off. "Pockets . . . there is no more 'if that doesn't work.' After twenty years of legal maneuvering, I'm out of money." He slipped his glasses down and looked at Pockets. "Most of which you have. If you weren't so dang good, I'd have fired you a long time ago."

Pockets smiled. "Thanks for the vote of confidence." He pointed at the envelope. "It sits with the judge now. I think we've made a good case. And I think you're in the right."

Unc looked out through the window. "That ain't never changed."

"Remember, William, I'm on your side." Pockets began rolling up his window. "Always have been."

As we drove off, Unc nodded and whispered over his shoulder, "That'd put you in the minority."

The wind rattled through the bikini top, carrying with it the strong smell of salt marsh and the train that had appeared alongside me—doubles filled with cars headed for the ports in Brunswick and Jacksonville. Hollow and haunting, the sounding horn thrust me into the only memory I had of my father.

As best I can figure, I must've been about three. I had heard the distant, hollow horn, crept out of the house, and tiptoed down the drive. I think there might have been grass beneath my feet, and maybe it was wet with dew. Somehow I made it through the station house and jumped off the loading platform to the tracks to place my half-dollar flat across the track. I remember a cat, maybe gray, possibly a tabby, brushing alongside me. Its whiskers were long. The steel rail felt cold to my fingertips, as did the shard of amber glass I did not see that sliced into my foot. I remember the sensation of falling, of hearing something crack in my rib cage, of landing on the tracks and not being able to breathe, and of warm liquid on my foot. Lastly, I remember trying to get up, but—like Gulliver—I was tied down.

I tried to scream, but when I opened my mouth all I felt was a knife in my side, and all I heard was the horn of the train. I reached behind me, trying to free the belt loop from whatever held it, but couldn't. I remember the blinding light of the train and the warmth in my shorts—I had seen what a train could do to a penny.

Like a record that's scratched, the soundtrack skips again, but I think I heard footsteps, maybe boots, because today I don't so much see them as feel them. I saw a flash, a long shadow crossed over me, big hands wrapped round about me, and I felt the belt loop pop off like a shirt button.

Another skip. I opened my eyes and saw the rusted underside of the train cars whizzing by just inches from my head. As the wheels screamed to a stop, they skidded against the steel rails and showered me with orange sparks that stung my cheeks.

Up to this point, the memory is like an Ansel Adams photograph: I feel long whiskers, hear the rib crack, see sparks, touch cold steel, and sense warm wet jeans. But here, at this moment, it blurs. Fades. Blacks out. Like the projector jammed and the lamp burned a hole in the tape. I turn to see him—the man connected to the shadow and the arms—but all I see is a hole where his face was, and when he opens his mouth all I hear is the film tab slapping the machine through the feeder.

No matter how many times I play and replay the tape, I cannot hear him and I cannot put the words back in his mouth. And yet I know, when he opens his mouth, he calls me by my name. My real name. The one he gave me.

For twenty-five years since then, through three foster homes, two boys' homes, and finally to Unc and Aunt Lorna's house, I have listened to the names people call each other and me. Hoping, somehow, to hear the whisper of my own.

I'm told that because I'm a foundling—aka a "doorstep baby"—I was given a name upon discovery. The director of the home assigned names to the nameless much as meteorologists do to hurricanes. Evidently it was a busy year, and the staff had progressed through the Vs when somebody pitched me overboard. Sometimes I wonder if Moses ever felt the same way. The story is that come Monday morning, the staff threw all the "W" names that they could think of into a hat. That done, they repeated the process for a first name—in much the same manner as people pick lottery numbers.

Even now, when someone calls me by the name on my driver's license, Chase Walker, it's as if they're asking for someone else. Like my entire life is one of mistaken identity. I know this because when they say it, it doesn't fill in the blank on the tape. If you want to know what I'm talking about, spend an entire day introducing yourself as someone you're not, and then listen when people call you by that name. You'll understand.

When I was thirteen, tired of living between hope and nowhere, I saved my money and bought a book of names, something pregnant couples flip through at night, and read five thousand names aloud. Alone in the woods I whispered, then shouted, trying to remember. But his voice, like the Silver Meteor, no longer rides these tracks.

Chapter 3

The Brunswick hospital has never been much to look at. It is the definition of function over form. Not waiting on me, Unc strode out of Vicky and was the first to punch the button for the elevator.

As a farrier, Unc spends a lot of time in barns and around horses. Given this, his uniform, if you want to call it that, is pretty simple. Dirty hat (either a Braves baseball cap or his dirty Gus hat, depending on his mood and whether or not the Braves are in the pennant race), a denim long-sleeve shirt (snaps, no buttons), faded Wrangler jeans fraying behind the heel, old boots twice resoled, leather belt with *WILLEE* stamped across the back, and either a red or blue handkerchief tied around his neck. He says it keeps the dust off, but I tell him it looks like a bib and he should use it to dab the sides of his mouth. Because the Braves are up five games, and because Chipper hit a three-run dinger last night, he's wearing his cap right now.

We stepped onto the third floor and walked down the hall to room 316. A guy in a suit sitting in a chair reading a *SWAT* magazine stood when we walked up. He looked at me. "You the reporter?"

I flashed my credentials.

He nodded, shrugged, said, "Good luck," and opened the door.

25

The room sat in the corner of the hospital where two large windows poured heavy sunlight onto the whitewashed walls. The TV was off, and the kid sat in a chair looking out the window. He was drawing in a spiral notebook. He held the pencil sideways—like an artist sketching with charcoal—and his hand made quick strokes. He heard us walk in, tucked the pencil behind his ear, closed the notebook, and folded his hands across it. He sat cross-legged in the chair and wore only long pajama pants covered in baseballs.

I pulled up a chair and sat quietly alongside him. For a minute, I said nothing. I scanned the skin on his back, looking at the random pattern of scars, while Unc circled us. When he got behind the kid, he managed a quick, short breath and sucked unconsciously between his teeth. He wiped his nose, took off his hat, and leaned against the window, shaking his head. A second later, he cussed under his breath.

The kid was skinny, pale, and covered in ant bites. Puss leaked out from beneath white gauze on his back and trickled down his spine. Unc walked out of the room to the nurses' counter, grabbed some pads, and then knelt in front of the kid. He showed the clean pad to the kid and said, "I'd like to use this to wipe off your back. That okay with you?"

The kid nodded once, but never took his eyes off the floor. He reminded me of a yellow Labrador puppy I'd once seen in a humane shelter—thick, dirty hair matted like a Brillo pad, big round eyes glued to the floor, floppy ears that hid half his face, tail tucked between his legs, and oversized paws that he was years from growing into.

Unc held out his left hand. "Here, you hold my hand."

The kid's eyes darted from the floor to the hand.

"If it hurts at all, you squeeze my hand." He paused. "Deal?"

The kid slowly placed his hand inside Unc's.

Remember that game in grammar school where one kid places both palms on top of another kid's outstretched palms and then pulls them back before the other kid slaps the top of one? And remember how, if you were the kid whose hands were on top, it was to your advantage to press ever so slightly? That's what I thought of when I saw that kid place his hand in Uncle Willee's.

Unc peeled off the yellowed gauze and gently patted the trickle. He placed two more clean pads across the festering wound and then helped the kid sit up and lean back where the pressure against the chair held the pads against his back.

The kid slid his hand back and stared at his lap.

Unc knelt next to him and said, "All done." When the kid didn't respond, Unc pulled a lollipop out of his shirt pocket and said, "You know . . . you should never take candy from strangers?"

The kid eyed the green candy, bit his lip, and then continued studying the floor.

Unc pulled off the wrapper and held it out. "Good, let's keep it that way."

The kid hesitated, like he didn't intend to fall for this trap.

Unc saw his hesitation and set the candy on top of the wrapper on the notebook. "Whenever you want it." Unc stepped back, and the kid's hand slowly cupped the lollipop.

I looked at the notebook and made a conscious decision to lower and soften my voice. "What you drawing?" Since we had walked in, I had yet to really see the kid's face. Until now, I'd only seen the top of his head and the first inch or so of his forehead.

He let go of the end of the sucker and flipped open the notebook. Spread across two pages was a sketch of the moment when the front end of a train collided with what looked like an old Impala. This was no child's stick drawing, and it was no cartoon either.

"Is that your car?"

He shook his head.

"Is that the car you were in?"

He nodded.

"What's your name?"

He pulled the pencil from behind his ear, drew a question mark, then circled it.

Seconds passed. I tried again. "Until the age of six, folks called me something different every time they shuffled me from one home to the next. I didn't know what my birth certificate said until Unc here showed it to me."

He shot a glance at Unc's boots.

"You ever seen yours?"

He shook his head.

"What do people call you?"

He turned to a clean page and wrote in block letters: SNOOT.

I studied the page. "They call you anything else?"

From the moment we had walked in, his left leg had been bouncing like Pinocchio tied to an invisible tether held by a puppeteer above the ceiling.

"What if you could pick any name . . . and you knew folks would call you by it . . . what would you pick?"

The hand stopped, Pinocchio's tap dance quit abruptly, and the kid's head slowly turned toward my feet. After nearly a minute, he turned back to center, and the puppeteer tightened the slack.

For the first time, I noticed that most of the pages in the notebook were covered in sketches. "Will you show me your notebook?"

He turned to the first page and held it open on his lap. I put my hands behind me so he'd know I wouldn't take it, and leaned in. The realism was stunning yet, based on what I had seen walking in, so was the speed with which he sketched. He flipped the pages while Unc looked over my shoulder.

We saw a rundown trailer on blocks with a fat, collared cat sunning itself on top and a German shepherd burrowed in the dirt below with two, undoubtedly pink, flamingos thrown off to one side. One of the heads had been chewed off. One high-top basketball shoe, the laces untied with a hole above the big toe, sat at an angle before the front door. Beer cans and Jim Beam bottles riddled the grass around the front door. A clothesline hung off to one side. Men's underwear, a woman's thong, a few pairs of jeans, and one pair of kid's faded jeans hung from it. A tall live oak rose up from behind the trailer and towered above it. A fifty-gallon barrel cut in half and resting on its end sat front and center, flames rising above the rim. A bag of charcoal had been tossed aside and lay crumpled nearby. On the door hung the number 27. All the windows were open, and a huge floor fan had been lodged in the bedroom window on the end.

I tried to find his eyes, but he lowered them further. "Can I turn the page?"

He nodded, and I slowly turned the page—again putting my hand behind me.

The second page contained a close-up sketch of what looked like a massive and muscled right hand, covered in grease and calluses, wrapped around a pair of pliers and squeezing like a vise. The pliers were pressed against what looked like the back of someone's arm or shoulder blade, and pinched inside the nose of the pliers was a fold of skin, maybe an inch long and half an inch in width. The next picture, or frame, showed the hand and pliers just after they had ripped the skin off the arm.

I compared the kid to his pictures. First his arms, then shoulders and back. His skin was a war-torn canvas. Including the one beneath the gauze, I counted sixteen scars. Each one was about as long as the nose on a pair of pliers.

The kid's head had been buzzed short, and entire random patches of hair were missing. They'd been pulled out. His shoulders, bony and narrow, fell off like waterfalls at the edges. His fingernails had been bitten down to the quick, and his feet were that kind of dirty that no single bath would clean.

Unc studied the pictures, the kid, and then me. His lips were sort of wrapped around the left side of his mouth, and his front teeth were chewing on the inside of his right cheek. Every few seconds, he'd spit out what looked like a dead piece of skin.

I knelt next to the kid, trying to level my eyes to his. Without touching, I pointed to his arms. "Who did this to you?"

The speed of the hand on the tether was tapping double-time and now controlled both his left leg and right hand. His head moved from Unc's feet to mine and then back to center. Finally, he shut the notebook and crossed his arms.

I sat on the floor in front of the kid and pointed. "What's his name?"

Now his head began bobbing along with his leg.

"Can you draw it?"

The hand slowed, the bouncing stopped, and a few seconds later he quit moving altogether.

I tapped the notebook. "Show me."

He pulled the pencil from behind his ear, opened the book, and in a matter of three minutes sketched a man from the waist up. Dark hair, mustache, sleeves rolled up, big biceps, beer belly, shirt untucked and unbuttoned, a cigarette dangling from his lips, tattoo of some creature with a snake's head on his right bicep and a naked woman wrapped in a much larger snake on his left forearm, long sideburns, and a name patch ironed on his chest. It read *Bo*.

I pointed at the name. "Bo did this?"

The kid didn't respond, letting the picture speak for him.

"Does Bo have a last name?"

Still no response.

"Is Bo your dad?"

The kid picked up his pencil, turned the notebook, and pressing hard on the paper wrote No.

"Did your mom live there too?"

He used the tip of his pencil to point to the word.

I pointed to the Impala on the first page. "Did your mom live in that car?"

He pointed again.

Unc reached slowly across, flipped the page to the sketch of the train intersecting the Impala and pointed to the woman behind the steering wheel. He spoke slowly. "Was that your mom?"

The kid looked back and forth between our feet five or six times like windshield wipers set on intermittent. Finally he circled the word.

I sat back, rubbed my chin, and scratched my head. Too many things weren't adding up. Without thinking, I patted the kid on the knee—which made him flinch. "You like pizza?"

The kid looked around the room, behind him, then began bobbing forward and back. He eyed the man in the suit on the other side of the door and wrote slowly in the notebook YES.

"Pepperoni?"

He pointed.

"Extra cheese?"

He circled it twice.

"Be right back."

I dialed Nate's Pizza—my late-night writer's addiction. While the phone rang it struck me that, in all of our conversation, the kid had never uttered a word, and I had yet to see the color of his eyes. I told Nate what I needed, and he promised me fifteen minutes, which meant thirty. Then I dialed Red, who flipped open his cell phone on the fifth ring.

"You at the hospital?"

"You want to tell me what's going on here?"

"That's your job. The paper has decided it is in that kid's best interests—"

"You mean 'the paper's.'"

"Right . . . to discover that kid's identity, where he's from, and what sick mutant of a human has been beating the hell out of him."

I hung up, slid the phone into my pocket, and stood in the hall considering. I needed to talk with anyone who had contact with this kid: paramedics, firemen, nurses, his doctor. I pulled a small black notebook out of my back pocket and began making notes.

Just then a doctor, maybe thirty, appeared at the door and began reading the chart. I tapped him on the shoulder and extended my hand. "Chase Walker. I'm with the paper."

He nodded and sidestepped away from the door, causing his stethoscope to sway like dreadlocks.

"Yes . . . Paul Johnson. I've read your stuff. You do good work. The drug story on the shrimp boats was fascinating."

Two years ago, I began researching a rumor that the shrimp boats located out of Brunswick were being used to run ecstasy from Miami to Myrtle Beach. Because money follows drugs, it wasn't hard to uncover. I took some late-night video, showed it to the police. They staged a sting, and Red printed my story on the front page.

"Thanks for coming." Dr. Johnson looked up and down the hall, eyeing the nurses, techs, and other doctors working there. "We thought it might help to get some media coverage. Find out who this kid is."

"What happens from here?"

"Well, as soon as I clear him, the state will come pick him up and assign him to either a boys' home or foster home. We don't have too many registered foster parents in Glynn County, and from what the DA and CFS tell me, those we do have are either top-heavy or not interested in taking in a . . . a kid like that."

The doctor turned, and Unc stuck out his hand.

"I'm Willee McFarland." He pointed at me. "I'm with him."

The doctor shook his hand and continued. "I think he likes the ice cream, and he really seems to like the quiet and . . . the guy with the gun guarding the door. If he's asked to see that gun once, he's asked to see it fifteen times. Well—he points, mostly." He turned to me. "Have you gotten him to say anything?"

"No. You?"

"He won't talk."

Unc piped in, "Won't . . . or can't?"

The doctor nodded in agreement. "You picked up on that?"

"Just because a chicken has wings doesn't mean it can fly."

The doctor looked confused. I tried to help him out. "Appearances can be deceptive."

He nodded in agreement and flipped the chart open. "Yesterday we took some pictures, and as best we can figure he suffered some tracheal trauma somewhere in the past. Damaged his voice box. It might work, might not. I don't have much experience with kids like him, but I've read in the journals where kids with a history of abuse—especially his kind—suffer permanent memory loss—and sometimes stop talking."

I flipped open my black book and probed. "What do you mean?"

"It's a defense mechanism. Their minds block it out—sort of like an intelligent hard drive in which the most horrific files have been deleted in an automatic response to protect the whole drive."

"So, he can draw like Michelangelo, but might not know his own name?"

"Exactly."

"And his voice?"

"Another mechanism. Not speaking brings less attention to themselves, meaning they are noticed less and, they hope, beaten less. They're usually told to shut up whenever they do speak. Add to that the physical damage to the voice box, and you've got a kid that for all practical purposes is mute."

"You think he'll ever speak again?"

The doctor shook his head. "Don't know. In time, if his vocal cords and voice box can repair themselves, but the rest is up to him. But that's jumping the gun. I'm no psychologist, but in order for that to happen he's got to understand there are people in this world who want to hear him. Thus far, that's not his experience, so we're rowing against the current."

"That explains his notebook."

He nodded and closed the chart. "Remarkable. I've never seen anything like it. He's got the speed of a cartoonist and the talent of Norman Rockwell."

Unc nodded. "How old do you think he is?"

Doctor Johnson squinted one eye and tilted his head. "Maybe nine. Not ten. He's still prepubescent."

We small-talked a few minutes, and I noted everything I could remember and wrote down questions to research later. About that time, I started smelling pizza.

I paid the delivery boy, and then the three of us took the pizza into the kid's room, where Unc served four plates. I was three bites into my slice before the kid lifted his to his mouth. He smelled it, studied the edges, and then looked at the door and the man wearing the suit. The guard sat half in the doorway in a folding chair, reading a Clive Cussler paperback. The kid slid off his chair, and I noticed how skinny he was. Every one of his ribs showed, and his hips looked hollow. Walking slowly and humpbacked like an old lady, he carried his plate to the door and offered it to the guard.

The guard—four, maybe five, times larger than the boy—looked at the top of the boy's head, then at the pizza. He held out a plate-sized hand. "No, thanks. I'm trying to quit."

As if bolted to a lazy Susan, the kid turned, paused, then turned back again and slid the plate below the open book and onto the man's lap.

The guard sat back, set down his book, and said, "Well . . . if you insist. Thank you."

Unc served the kid another piece, and he began to eat. He chewed slowly, swallowed as if it required effort, and looked at the box. Over the next forty-five minutes he ate four pieces and drank three small cartons of milk. When he'd polished off the last of his milk, he turned his head toward my plate and the two uneaten pieces of crust.

"You can have it." I tilted the plate toward him. "I'm done."

When I was working on the shrimp boat story, I got to know a mangy dog that used to show up not long after the boat guys had clocked out and gone home. After three months of baiting him with dog biscuits, he still would not let me pet him. He only came close enough to smell whether or not I had food. And if I did, he'd wait until I set it down and walked off. He had no collar, his hair was matted and tangled with cockleburs, and he lived beneath a warehouse porch three blocks away. One day I made the mistake of picking up my tripod to reposition my camera. It was a few days before I saw him again. Looking at the kid, I was reminded of that dog.

I set the plate down, and the kid slowly took the crust, pulling it back to his plate only after he'd looked over his shoulder. He ate and I jotted notes—those that only I could read and would make no sense whatsoever to anyone else. Based on what I saw, his skin-and-bones presentation was not a function of small appetite. The kid was a vacuum cleaner.

I set my card on top of the notebook. "You need anything, you have somebody call me. Okay?"

He slipped the card inside the accordion pocket in the rear of his notebook, but made no other movement. For all I knew, he had a hundred others just like it in the same place. His cooperation at the moment did not suggest compliance in the future.

As we walked out, I heard his pajamas sliding along the floor behind us. He stood behind Unc and tugged on his back pocket. Eye-level with Unc, the kid opened his notebook, tore out a page, and handed it up without looking at him.

Uncle Willee studied the picture for several minutes while his front teeth chewed on the inside of his right cheek. Finally, he took off his baseball cap and set it gently on the boy's head. It teeter-tottered from the center, hung well out over his ears, and dwarfed his face.

Unused to receiving gifts, he looked confused. Unc read the kid's posture and then gently reached over the top, adjusting the Velcro to fit his head. "There, how's that?"

The kid's mouth showed no expression, but when he looked into the wall-length mirror, his chin lifted ever so slightly.

As we walked down the hall, my flip-flops smacking my heels, Dr. Johnson stopped us.

"Sir?"

We turned, hanging our thumbs in our jeans—a habit of association.

"Did you say your name was Willee McFarland?"

Unc took a deep breath, slid his glasses off his nose, and let them hang over his neck. "Yes."

The doctor looked down at the floor, then back at us. He pointed west out the window—toward the Zuta. "You any relation to those two brothers?"

Unc slipped his glasses back up on his nose. "Yep."

The doctor nodded, raising both eyebrows. "Wow. Well . . . okay."

I shook my head because I knew what was coming.

"Uh . . ." He had to ask. "Which one are you?"

Unc smiled and pushed the glasses halfway down his nose, looking over the tops. "I'm the one that went to prison."

"Oh."

Unc turned, then pointed toward the kid's room. "Why haven't y'all gotten him some new glasses?"

The doctor looked toward the kid. "Didn't know he wore glasses."

Unc nodded. "The crown of his nose will tell you that he did."

We stepped into Vicky and within a few minutes were shifting into fourth. We crossed under I-95, beyond the truck stop, and passed the ten thousand rows of planted pines—parallel, equidistant, and angling toward the road. Driving through the dusk of a falling sun, each stand of pines looked like a giant hallway to some Celtic cathedral. I drove, lost in the picture of that kid.

Unc read my face and put his hand on my shoulder, something he started doing twenty years ago and something that has told me more about myself than any report card, paycheck, or job title. Despite my unanswered questions, where I came from and who I am, that hand on my shoulder spoke to a part of me few words ever reached. And to be honest, when my demons rose out of the past and reminded me that I'd been left on some street corner and that I wasn't good enough even for my own parents, that hand told me otherwise.

"Yes sir?"

He turned back to face the windshield and rested his foot up on the side of the door. "Kids are like a spring, or a Stretch Armstrong. No matter how many times they're passed around, passed off, and passed on . . . they snap back." He spit through his window. "Hope . . . it's the fuel that feeds them." He shook his head and spit something off the end of his tongue. "God forbid the day they stop eating it."

When Unc and Aunt Lorna first brought me home to their house, they sat me down and said something I'll never forget.

"Chase . . . our home is what the state calls a foster home. That means you can stay here and live with us until your parents come get you." He patted the bed. "That means, until then, this is your room."

I looked around, my feet dangling a foot above the floor.

"But we probably ought to decide what you should call us. So . . ." He took Lorna's hand and swallowed hard. "Why don't you call my wife Aunt Lorna, and you can call me . . . you can call me Uncle Willee . . . or . . . Unc . . . if you like." He was quiet several seconds. "That way . . . when your folks show up, you'll have room in your head for names like Mom and Dad."

The words "when your folks show up" sent shock waves through me that echo still. Uncle Willee did something no other adult had ever done. He gave credibility to the thought I'd had for as long as I could remember. He silently agreed with the simple notion *They might . . .*

Unc was right. Kids hope.

All they need is a reason.

Moments passed before I said anything. "When do they quit?"

He leaned his head back against the seats. "That depends . . . that depends."

Chapter 4

The story of the McFarland brothers has nearly grown to mythical status around Zuta, Georgia. And after a generation of embellishment, it changes like a chameleon in the sun. It's the cause of endless speculation, volumes of courtroom proceedings, several federal investigations, and three murders—and is the reason I spent last week in jail. It's also the reason I became a journalist.

I first heard whispers of the trouble between William McFarland and his brother in my early teens. I had felt something funny, kind of like an electric charge in the air, a few months after Unc and Aunt Lorna brought me into their house at the age of six, but they did a good job of keeping it from me and every other kid who passed through their house. Living with Unc painted one picture, while the rumors painted another. When the two didn't add up, I started digging, and pretty soon my bedroom walls were tacked with a collage made from bits and pieces of the truth.

Getting through my senior year of college was predicated on writing a passing thesis. All journalism students rowed in the same boat. In the beginning of our junior year, they sat us down and gave us the game rules. The requirements were simple: Pick a national, newsworthy story or issue that has not been solved by the gathering of information or has been put to bed by disinterest, then investigate it and contribute new information to the discussion that the previous news networks have not. Do not summarize existing material. Put your talent to work and dig up something new. This was to be an in-depth piece, and bonus points were given for finding and using primary sources. Three keys stood out: *national, newsworthy,* and *new*. Many of the students spent months agonizing over a story topic that they would then spend the next ten to twelve months investigating. For me it was never really an issue.

The story I'm about to tell you comes from local papers, court documents, interviews, hearsay, gossip, carvings found on old swamp trees, and local legend. Knowing all this, Red—while he shares my passion for the story—has never let me print a single word of it.

Tillman Ellsworth McFarland was born in 1896. But that's a bad place to start, so let's back up. A lot.

No one's really sure how the Golden Isles of Georgia got their name. Some credit the Spanish, others claim the English, who were promoting their seventeenth-century settlement. Regardless, Sea Island is the richest zip code in the country today; richer than Beverly Hills or Aspen during the ski season. Tolerable winters, breezy summers, and expansive beaches make up the isles, the westernmost shore on the East Coast. The location makes it a low-risk storm area because it's so far removed from the hurricane highway, aka the Gulf Stream. From the three-hundred-year-old oaks draped in Spanish moss swimming with chiggers and red bugs, to the white sandy beaches glittering with sharks' teeth and sand dollars, the entire region is cradled in the palms of an ecosystem we like to call the marsh. It's a no-man's-land made up of soft mud flats crested by jagged oyster beds and knife-edged wire grass that changes colors hourly and bathes twice daily in the rising tide. But the most inescapable aspect of the marsh is the smell. While tourists drive across the causeway, get their first whiff, and turn up their noses, locals wake up, walk outside, stretch their arms, inhale, and fill their fingertips. From dead and rotting organisms to new life bubbling up through the muck, the marsh—like its history—is a daily continuum of death and resurrection.

The Creek Indians settled here first. Other than a few trash and burial mounds, the only remnants of their existence are found in the words they left: names like Satilla and Altamaha. In 1540, they greeted Spanish conqueror Hernando DeSoto and his troops with curiosity. DeSoto set one foot on the beach, claimed the coast for Spain, and returned the greeting with musket balls and disease. If that bugs you, don't worry. His achievement was short-lived, as he died in a return journey in 1542.

But with limited success the Spanish returned to St. Augustine, giving the French the opportunity to brave the mosquitoes and start their own colony. Unflinching, Spanish King Phillip II sent in a party of Jesuits, who were promptly hacked to pieces by the remaining Indians. By 1570, most of the Jesuits had tired of the warfare and moved to Mexico, making room for the Franciscans in 1573.

Now fast-forward a hundred years and hop back across the ocean to the motherland. Following years of war, debtor prisons in England were overflowing with often well-respected citizens who had overextended their credit in an attempt to pay their taxes. Looking at indefinite incarceration complete with filth, damp cells, starvation, and the beginnings of a smallpox epidemic, they jumped at the chance to settle Georgia under King George II's mandate to establish a colony between South Carolina and Florida. For God and country . . . and the absolution of all debts.

In November 1732 a two-hundred-ton frigate named *Ann* carried 114 "prisoners" and their families to the New World. Led by a British hero by the name of Oglethorpe, the ship landed in "Charles Town," where the sailors found their land legs and settled in. In 1736,

Oglethorpe braved the hostile frontier, loaded his ship, and skirted the coast to Cockspur Island. With skilled blacksmiths, carpenters, and farmers, he ventured onto St. Simons and built a settlement, which they called Frederica. Knowing the flock would need spiritual leadership, Oglethorpe brought with him two brothers, John and Charles Wesley, to Christianize the Indians and build what is today Christ Church.

The Spanish, headquartered in St. Augustine, saw the colony as an attack against the Spanish crown. So they mounted an offensive and marched northward. Outnumbering the English and feeling confident of victory, they retired for the day, built fires, and stacked their rifles in clusters around the campground. The English led by Scottish Highlanders, hid like guerillas in the palmetto bushes until they could smell the hint of dinner. The next day, when the marsh ran ankle-deep with Spanish blood, England's claim to Georgia had been settled. Today the place bears the name Bloody Marsh.

In 1782, hampered by the same taxes and tariffs they sought to escape, the Georgians declared themselves a state and kicked out any sign of English authority. For God and our new country.

With Georgia on the map, a few key things occurred to cement her place in history. Because South Carolina farmers didn't understand crop rotation, and because they were almost single-handedly meeting the world's voracious cotton need, they soon depleted their soil. Finding the lands west of the Golden Isles fertile and nutrient-rich due to rivers such as the Satilla, Frederica, and Altamaha, South Carolina plantation owners acquired land, dug complicated drainage systems—which remain to this day—and began planting cotton. And not just any cotton. They developed a special, fine, long-staple cotton whose seed came from the West Indies island of Anguilla. It was an instant success. But with more yield came a greater need to separate the boll from the cotton, and human fingers could only do so much so fast. In 1786, the Georgia widow of Nathaniel Greene of Mulberry Plantation hired Eli Whitney to tutor her children. Seeing that Eli possessed mechanical skill, she asked him to invent some better way to extract the seeds from the cotton. And he did—inventing what was arguably, along with the printing press, one of the most transforming machines in human history. This came on the heels of the development of the spinning jenny in England. Eli's cotton gin now allowed the plantations of Georgia and South Carolina to satisfy England's appetite for cotton—en masse.

The former prisoners' colony soon became the talk of the States. Chasing white gold with black hands, expansive plantations arose under names like Hampton, Cannon's Point, and Retreat. So attractive were their amenities that Vice President Aaron Burr fled here after he killed Alexander Hamilton in 1804.

It wouldn't be the last time that a murderer would seek refuge in this place.

Along with cotton production, the area became a worldwide supplier of lumber. Given the intersection of so many large rivers whose mouths emptied in or near the Golden Isles, entrepreneurs mowed down entire forests and floated them to the coast, where the logs were planed at the mills and loaded onto ships bound for the Orient and the motherland. Much of the oak used in "Old Ironsides" was cut from Cannon Point. But like that of South Carolina, the soil gave out, as did people's appetite for slavery. Amidst their own opulence and the scarred backs on which it was built, somebody finally looked around and figured out that not only does slavery kill those you enslave, but it kills you, too.

For a while resourceful men tried to cultivate rice, but found that too complicated and not too profitable when the storm tide of 1898 flooded the marshes under nine feet of water. Living in the shadow of crumbling tumbleweed plantations, lumber production soared. Following the Civil War, lumber mills dotted the coastline. Toward the latter half of the nineteenth century, mills in and around Brunswick and St. Simons became a clearinghouse for lumber-laden steamers.

Much of the Brooklyn Bridge was built from wood shipped out of Brunswick.

While her natural resources had been tapped into and would one day be tapped out, the Golden Isles still had more to offer. In 1886, fifty-three members of what became known as the First Name Club bought Jekyll Island from John Eugene DuBignon. And while the members might have been on a first-name basis with each other, everyone else just called them "sir." The membership fee was set at one million dollars each, and that was just to set foot on the island. Members included men like J. P. Morgan, William Vanderbilt, John D. Rockefeller, and my favorite, Joseph Pulitzer. At the turn of the century, when the fifty-three members met on the island, it is believed they controlled one-sixth of the world's wealth. From the island they made the first transcontinental phone call and later, disguised as duck hunters, drew up a plan for what became the Federal Reserve System. The club flourished through the 1920s, survived the 1930s, and then sold the island to the State of Georgia after the imposed burden of an income tax. Funny how that works.

In the absence of the First Namers, others moved in, and with the advent of the diesel powered, stainless steel Silver Meteor, they came in droves. The allure of the Golden Isles had caught on across the country, filling to capacity a new five-star club called The Cloister. Such famous names as Charles Lindbergh—who landed his plane on a hastily organized landing strip on Sapelo Island—and Eugenia Price all signed the guest book.

In 1920, a twenty-four-year-old World War I hero named Tillman Ellsworth McFarland, carrying an honorable discharge and a footlocker full of medals, hopped off a railroad car in Thalmann, Georgia. He had packed light but was carrying all he owned: a few handsaws, hammers, and hickory-handled axes; seventy dollars; and a browfull of sweat and gumption. Not to mention a strong desire never to dig another trench. While some passengers stepped into cars that ferried them to the shoreline for a vacation, Ellsworth began knocking on doors and offering his services: cutting firewood, clearing land, building barns, whatever. Dressed in a white shirt, tie, and wool slacks, he'd shake their hands and state, "If you're not happy, don't pay me."

Locals felt the callused, muscled palms, stared into the sunken eyes, and gave him a chance. Word of his sunup to sundown work ethic spread, and within months he had bought an acre, traded a winter's worth of wood for an old horse, begun the construction of a house, and opened a logging and turpentine business. This put money in his pocket and meat on his bones, and meant that he walked most every square inch of Glynn County. For eight years his business flourished, and when men started jumping out of windows on Wall Street, Ellsworth—who had saved the first penny he ever earned—lived by the idea that had brought him south. *Buy dirt and you won't get hurt.* By 1931 he had acquired 26,000 acres in and around Zuta, Georgia—some twenty miles west of Brunswick—naming it simply "The Zuta."

To the locals, the Zuta was a messy mixture of sick pine trees and gnarly oak hammocks surrounding an immense swamp known as the Buffalo—tens of thousands of acres of virgin, uncut timber rising up out of the south Georgia gumbo that few dared venture into. Given the property's relative proximity to the Altamaha River, the Buffalo flooded whenever heavy rains in the middle of the state overflowed the riverbanks. Folks in Thalmann, Popwellville, Jesup, Darien, and Brunswick heard about his acquisition and shook their heads. *That boy ain't right.* Thing was, Tillman had spent years walking, studying, and learning what they'd forgotten. A hundred years earlier, the Zuta was the southeast quarter of a much larger plantation called Anguilla. The owners had limited success planting cotton because the soil was too wet and too sandy, and conditions were too unpredictable. Starting in 1856, in a decade-long effort to stem the floods and drain the land, slaves with mule teams erected dikes and dug drainage ditches big enough to float a canoe down. Then came 1865.

In the following years, the property festered beneath a heavy cover of its own vines, pooling waters, and Jurassic-sized mosquitoes. Due to the water, portions became inaccessible, and as a result, knowledge of the wealth contained there died with those who had seen it last. Over the next few decades, the property was sold off in small unrecognizable pieces to whoever would buy it. So undesirable was the land that in the late 1890s two competing railroads redirected their tracks and skirted the property to avoid the quagmire. This formed nearly perfect north, south, and west borders, and would prove fortuitous some thirty-five years later when Ellsworth pieced the land back together from the dozen or so fragmented owners who couldn't wait to get rid of it. With the state of the economy, they nearly gave it away.

Ellsworth assessed the dikes and drains and discovered that the previous attempt had actually made the problem worse—it now drew more water onto the property than off. He scratched his head, engineered a new solution, and rented heavy machinery. The way he saw it, the Buffalo—God's drain for the Altamaha—had become clogged with several thousand years of silt, runoff, dead trees, and beaver dams. Add to that the spiderweb of half-completed, crisscrossing drains, and Ellsworth found a twenty-six-thousand-acre bathtub that needed somebody to pull the plug, plunge the hole, and snake the pipes.

For six months, starting in 1932, he dredged, blew up the beaver dams, corrected the spiderweb, and cleared downed trees out of the deep water in the heart of the Buffalo. With the Buffalo flowing and the Zuta floodwaters receding, he got to work on the ditches feeding into and out of the Buffalo. Seeing his progress and the possibilities before him, he gambled with the remaining lumps in his mattress. Seven months later, given the advantage of dump trucks, tractors, large cranes, and eight-man crews, he laid down a road system and used it to complete what the slaves had started. Within a week, 60 per-cent of the property was dry. In another six months he rode horseback across the property and looked at the gold mine he'd uncovered.

Trees.

Given his drains, the road system, his natural access to the Buffalo, and the water highway it provided to the Altamaha, Ellsworth—at the age of forty—opened Zuta Lumber Company. The interesting thing about twenty-six-thousand acres is that if he managed it well and put back more than he took, he'd never run out of trees. Whenever he cut one down, he planted two in its place. Working day-in and day-out in such close proximity to the land, he stumbled upon six flowing wells that bubbled up through the earth and trickled into the Buffalo. The crystal water was clean, sweet, and attracted wildlife like a magnet—especially the more than one hundred wild Brahman cows long since forgotten within the Zuta borders. The same locals who'd laughed and called him Johnny Appleseed behind his back now knocked on his door, called him "sir," and asked his opinion.

By 1940, Zuta Lumber had become a powerhouse throughout the Southeast. Ships, homes, bridges, and even skyscrapers in New York City had been built with trees off the Zuta. In a decade when so many lost their shirts, Ellsworth created something out of nothing. In the process, he made a county full of friends and believers. This too proved beneficial, because when Ellsworth ran out of room in his mattress and decided to open his own bank on April 6, 1945, cus-tomers lined up around the block to make deposits.

A few doors down from the Ritz Theater, Ellsworth bought a deserted church, an oddity given its placement in the Bible Belt. The church was a huge, gray stone building with a pitch so steep that roofers had to wear harnesses. When Russian Orthodoxy failed to catch on amidst so many Baptists, the church leaders had vacated and sold the building to the city. A decade later, Ellsworth bought it, gut-ted the interior, converted the covered portico into a drive-through for his tellers, and poured a vault on the first floor. And this was no ordinary vault. The walls were three feet of concrete, reinforced with steel beams and a one-foot-thick steel door that Japan's best bombs couldn't unhinge. Word quickly spread that Ellsworth had the safest safe in Georgia, and given the climate of general distrust for anything governmental, the vault brought business. And business boomed. With the postwar economy, and the need for both new construction and loans, the Zuta First National did something unheard of in the banking world—it made a profit in its second year.

Ellsworth found he liked the banking business. He liked the interaction with the customers, liked helping people buy homes, and even more, he liked helping people who, on paper, couldn't get help elsewhere. And when those same people missed a payment or two, Ellsworth knocked on their door, gave them a side of beef, sipped a glass of tea, and worked them through their troubles. In 1948, Zuta First National had the highest loan close percentage, highest retention percentage, and lowest foreclosure rate of any bank in Georgia.

And when the space behind his banker's desk grew too tight, he slipped out the back door, drove home, and saddled his horse for an afternoon on the Zuta. For as much as he liked banking, he liked growing trees more. The bank grew and the lumber business exploded, and Ellsworth hired the right people to run both. At fifty-two, he looked at the balance sheet of his life and, for the first time, felt lonely. Maybe that's why he noticed a thirty-eight-year-old piano teacher named Sarah Beth Samuelson when she walked into the bank to open a checking account. It was summer; she wore a tan hat, carried a shade umbrella, and dabbed the sweat off her top lip with an embroidered handkerchief. Ellsworth fell hard and fast.

Three months later they married. They caught the Silver Meteor at Thalmann and rode it all the way to Grand Central Station, where they stepped off, strolled through Manhattan, and marveled at the towering buildings. After a tour that took them through the Catskills, the Finger Lakes, and the Adirondacks, then on up through New England, they returned to the Zuta. There Ellsworth built his bride a Georgian plantation house with a tin roof, wraparound porch, and a driveway lined with fifty-four pecan trees—one for every year of his life. A year later, she gave him Silas Jackson "Jack" McFarland—the first-born son of a wealthy man. Ellsworth could not have been prouder. A year later, he discovered he *could* be, when Sarah Beth gave him William "Liam" Walker McFarland. That would be the last gift she ever gave him. After her funeral Ellsworth placed a boy on each knee; Jack took one look at Liam, and that's about when the trouble started.

Ellsworth poured himself into his sons. He bought them each a pony, showed them every inch of the Zuta, and had little desks built alongside his at the bank. He even glued their names on the door. Seldom was the trio not together. But Jack and Liam could not have been more different. Physically, they were healthy, an equal match, but the similarities ended there. Jack, a quick wit and good with numbers, needed to be heard and often was, from a long way off. Further, he seldom filtered what came from his brain before it exited his mouth. He found identity and status in the possession of things. Liam was quiet, thoughtful, slow to speak, and always gave away more than he took in.

Chapter 5

Too tired to drive home, I slept in the apartment on the floor. I woke before daylight to the sound of Unc's double-axle trailer rolling out of the drive—seven-ply radials on gravel. A sound I'd heard a thousand times. Having taken yesterday off to be with me meant he had some catching up to do. Most of his clientele live in gated communities from Pawley's Island to Jacksonville. Given the amount of money they put into their horses and the stress of a weekend-to-weekend show season, they start to get itchy if you're not there to put new shoes on their horses when they want you. They might have a quarter-million in one horse, and when they want new shoes, they want new shoes.

I lay there on a hard, hastily made pallet on the floor of my room, listening to Unc disappear down the drive. My back felt good, but the sides of my hips hurt—the impact of wood floors and age. A second blanket beneath me would've been nice, but it was spread across Tommye, who was curled up in the bed. I watched her sleep. Her eyes—dancing behind her eyelids—dreaming, her hands tucked under her flushed face, the lines of her hips graceful beneath the blanket, and one foot slightly uncovered—her toenails bright red.

She owed me a conversation. At least that.

I went out and tied Unc's canoe on top of Vicky, then went back up to the loft and poured myself some orange juice. I turned around and found Tommye watching me.

She pointed. "Nice boxers."

"Yeah," I said, pulling on some shorts, "they're jail issue."

"What'd you do this time?"

"Got caught."

"You guilty?"

I nodded. "But not nearly as much as somebody else."

She smiled. "Didn't I teach you anything?"

"Evidently not." I got the orange juice out again and poured her a glass.

She shook her head and propped her chin on her knees. "You still digging around that vault?"

I smiled and pulled on my Braves cap.

Tommye stretched and looked out the window. "You're looking in the wrong place."

"I'm not so sure."

She walked to the counter and drank the juice. Refilling her glass, she opened her purse, shook a pill out of each of three separate containers, and swallowed all of them at once. She peeled a banana, ate it slowly, and then looked out the window at Vicky. She smiled, nodded, and said, "I'm gonna hop in the shower first."

"I'll meet you downstairs."

I was sifting through the barn, looking for nothing, when Aunt Lorna walked out and handed me a cup of coffee. She looked toward the sound of someone standing in the shower above our heads. "Go easy on her."

Both hands wrapped around the mug, I blew the steam off. "I will."

She wiped her hands on her apron and looked out the drive, eyeing Unc's fresh tracks around the puddles. "He had to go out there and get her, you know."

"What do you mean?"

"I mean, last week, the day you were put in jail, he got a call from her. Two hours later he boarded a plane, flew out there, and brought her back."

"From Los Angeles?"

She nodded.

I looked up at the underside of my shower and listened as soapy shower water rushed through the exposed PVC drainpipe that dropped out of the floor and then fell alongside one of the timber supports inside the barn.

"Don't forget." She began walking back to the kitchen. "Silver screen or not . . . that's just a little girl up there. Nine years doesn't change that." She reached the back porch steps and added, "Oh . . . and Red called you a few minutes ago. Wants you to call him this afternoon."

The shower water cut off, and I heard the door squeak. I cranked Vicky, slid on my Costa Del Mars, and waited.

Tommye had pulled her hair back and put on a T-shirt, baggy cargo shorts, and flip-flops—something we started wearing as kids. We seldom wore shoes, and when we did, they were something we could slip on and off with relative ease.

Thanks to Unc's Daddy Ellsworth, the road system inside the Zuta was better than that of some cities, but given the number of logging trucks hauling out timber the last year or so, the roads were in pretty bad shape. It hadn't rained much lately, so the dust was up and the gumbo down. We took it slow and eased through or around the bigger holes. Vicky was so at home on the Zuta that I almost let go of the wheel and let her drive it alone.

We drove around the pasture and up to the canal. The canal was Ellsworth's coup de grâce—the main drainage that pulled the plug on the clogged Buffalo. The water level in the canal rose and fell with the tide, and at thirty feet wide and over ten feet deep it was one of the primary reasons the Zuta was so valuable. We stopped on top of the concrete bridge that crossed the canal and watched the water.

Tommye leaned out the door of the Land Cruiser and watched the water pass beneath. Finally she sat back and shook her head. She stared up at the tall trees and then out over the gaping clear-cuts that were encroaching closer to the magnificent pines. "Jack's sure cutting a lot of timber out of here."

The sight of it disgusted me. "I'm all for cutting, but when you don't plant behind you, you're just . . . taking without giving back."

She nodded, her face expressionless. "Jack's good at that."

Sometime in high school, Tommye had begun referring to her father as "Jack." Then and now, it struck me as odd—like a piano out of tune.

"How's the appeal going?"

"Pockets filed it with the court. We're asking for a 'statutory way of necessity,' but from a legal standpoint—" I shook my head. "Well, if we were on death row, we'd be down to the twelfth hour without a governor willing to sign a stay or pardon."

"That bad?"

"Jack did his homework."

"Nobody ever said he was stupid."

"He know you're on this side of the Mississippi?"

She shook her head, lost in thoughts that stretched out across the brackish water.

On the bank below, fiddler crabs scurried from mud hole to mud hole. At the water's edge, a raccoon stood on its hind legs washing an oyster shell. We watched his hands move at lightning speed as he turned the shell over and over in the water.

"He washes that thing any more, and I'm liable to eat it myself."

She laughed, leaned back, propped her feet up on the dash, and we eased off the bridge. We drove through some of the older sections of timber, then rounded a corner and turned onto Gibson Island. I pulled down to the launch, unloaded the canoe, and we pushed off. She wanted to paddle, but I told her to sit back and relax, which she

did with little argument. The canoe slid across the top of the water as
we wove among towering cypress trees.

She looked up. "Wonder when he'll get to these."

"He's already started."

She looked at me. "He's cutting the Buffalo?"

I nodded.

"Where?"

"South. Won't be long before we'll be paddling in one huge golf
course lake."

"You seen the plans?"

I nodded and watched several wood ducks launch themselves like
helicopters, reach the treetops, then disappear like Harrier jets. "Last
county hearing I attended, he showed plans for three golf courses,
two different gated communities, a landing strip big enough to handle
a Gulfstream, a shopping center, and a K-12 school."

She laughed and placed both hands behind her on the rails of the
canoe, soaking in the sun that had broken through the trees. After a
few minutes she shook her head. "How much is enough?"

I didn't answer. We reached the landing, and I beached the canoe
and helped her out. She hooked her arm inside mine and leaned on
me as we walked on a quiet carpet of pine straw and sand. We walked
an old path, one beat down over time, where the tender bamboo shoots
reached up and brushed our thighs—it was the earth's welcoming
chorus. They were glad to see her too.

Fifteen minutes later we reached our destination.

The Sanctuary, a 250-acre virgin and uncut island of timber, sat
smack in the center of the Zuta, surrounded on all sides by the Buffalo
Swamp. On topographic maps it's called DuBignon Hammock, named
after the guy who sold Jekyll Island to the First Namers. It's accessible
only by canoe and spirals with towering virgin timber. Countless sprawling live oaks stretch out across the ground like giant octopus arms.
Some of their limbs, bigger around than a man's waist, bow down to

the ground, touch, then arch back up. Palm trees shoot up at random. Bamboo shoots grow two and three feet tall, clipped clean at the tops by the deer that feed there.

At the northern tip, planted in a neatly-orchestrated perimeter, grow trees which, when viewed from the air, look like a giant European cathedral. Ellsworth had designed and planted them some seventy years ago. During the war, he and his company lived for several months in a cathedral. The Germans had them pinned down, but they couldn't penetrate the walls of the church or its catacomb. When Ellsworth bought the Zuta, he spent a few years planting trees to match the dimensions.

To match the walls in his mind, he planted palm trees in two perfectly straight lines, each tree six feet apart and some three hundred feet between the parallel rows. Now most were nearly fifty feet tall and looked like columns at what might have been the end of each pew. Towering above the palm tops like a net are the canopy-like branches of sixteen water oaks—eight on each side—that, unlike the sprawling live oaks, shoot straight up nearly sixty or seventy feet, then mushroom at the top like a nuclear cloud. At one end, forming what might be the front wall, grow twelve Japanese magnolias and twelve Drake elms. In the middle of those, forming what one might call the narthex, are twelve orange trees butted up against eight lemon trees and then finally, two kumquat bushes. If the kumquats mark the front door, then four hundred feet away at the opposite end, forming the back wall, stand eight cypress trees, spreading at the base like a Victorian woman's dress as she bows to curtsey. In the middle of those, where the priest might stand, grows one single giant magnolia, its massive arms spreading out beyond the windows of the church, reaching out over the water of the Buffalo.

Unc said he'd started coming here with his dad when he was just a boy. When Ellsworth died, Unc kept coming. Judging by the fresh trimming of the palms, and the clearing of debris from beneath the trees and inside the borders, that hasn't changed.

Tommye looked around. "I can't understand how Jack never liked it here."

Uncle Jack was never interested in the Zuta except for what it could get him. We both knew that.

I smiled. "I'm glad Unc held onto it. It's the only hang-up left in your dad's development."

"What do you mean?"

"Well, it sits in the middle of twenty-six-thousand acres of prime development. Sticks out like a sore thumb. Unc's not selling, so your dad has to, by law, give him access. That puts a crimp in his development."

"Funny."

"What's that?"

"The thing he wanted least is now the thing he needs the most."

"It's fitting."

Some time back, Unc had created a mock campground in the middle of the Sanctuary. Two logs, touching end-to-end in an L-shape, formed benches. It was midmorning when we arrived, and I built a small fire. I made some coffee, scrambled some eggs, and even managed to not burn the biscuits. I handed Tommye a warm cup of cowboy coffee, and she leaned in and stared down into it.

"You'll make someone a fine husband one day. I could get used to this."

"It's called the comfort of necessity."

She sipped, stirred the eggs around her plate, and asked, "Got any girlfriends?"

"I got a few I go out with."

She raised both eyebrows. "You always had those. That's not what I asked."

"I stay pretty busy."

"Hmm-hmm." She wasn't buying it, her smile told me that. She eyed her watch, pulled a small silver container from her pocket, and popped another pill.

I spread some jelly on a biscuit and handed it to her. She licked the jelly spilling out around the edges and then bit into it.

Her T-shirt read *I LUV LA*. I pointed to it. "I flew out there once."

"Where?"

"L.A. . . . well, Studio City."

"When?"

"About three years ago."

She calculated. "Why didn't you call me?"

"I did."

"My roommate didn't tell me."

"That's cause I didn't talk to your roommate."

"Who'd you talk with?"

"I talked with you. Or rather *to* you. Some guy picked up the phone, then held the phone up to your ear. You mumbled a few things I couldn't understand, and then the line went dead."

She nodded, looked down into her cup, but said nothing.

I prodded. "Is that what all the pills are about?"

She shrugged, the honesty painful. "You do enough of the wrong kind of drugs, then sleep with enough of the wrong people, and these"—she patted her pocket—"become part of your life."

"You want to tell me about it?"

"Is this why you brought me out here?"

"It is."

She smiled, trying to lighten the air. "It's sort of refreshing to be with a guy who just wants to talk with me."

She lay back on her log-bench, a leg on either side, and spoke to the clouds. "I found a few acting jobs, nothing of note. Couple of commercials. Couple of appearances on a B-level soap opera. Then this . . . opportunity came up. Seemed harmless. I thought it might be a back door into the business . . . but it was more like a trapdoor."

I stoked the fire. "One night about three years ago, I was eating some wings at Pete's down on the water. This guy from high school came in. I knew his face, couldn't place his name. He started laughing with some guys in the next booth, then he pulls this DVD from his briefcase, slips it into his laptop, and angles the screen so his buddies could get a closer look. That angle included me. I saw your name and the title roll across the screen, and then this guy walking down the beach in his birthday suit. I knew what I was about to see, and I didn't want it in my brain. I dropped some money on the table and walked out."

She kicked off a flip-flop and ran her toes through the sand. "Did Uncle Willee tell you about coming to get me?"

I shook my head. "Aunt Lorna told me this morning."

She sat up. "I need to tell you something."

I didn't want to hear what she was about to say. "I don't have to know everything."

"I know you better than that."

"I can lie every now and then."

"I know you better than that, too." She stood from her bench and came to rest on mine alongside me. She leaned against me, resting her head on my shoulder. "I read a lot of your stories online . . . I'm surprised you haven't been picked up by one of the bigger markets."

"They've called."

She nodded. "Uncle Willee told me on the plane. Said you had one more story to tell here."

I nodded, my eyes lost in the flames.

"Can you let it go?"

I shook my head.

She probed. "Can't or won't?"

"I'm getting closer. I owe him that."

She rested her head on my shoulder again and closed her eyes. "What if you don't like what you find?"

"'Least I'll know the truth."

"Sometimes the truth can kill you."

Several minutes passed before either of us spoke. "What was it you wanted to tell me?" I asked.

She closed her eyes. "It can wait." She rested her head in my lap, and I put my arm around her, pulled the rubber band off her ponytail, and ran my fingers through her still-damp hair.

Have you ever been to the circus and seen those crazy men on motorcycles ride in small loops inside that metal spherical cage? Usually there are about eight of them, and they're always about a millisecond from killing each other.

That was a good picture of my mind at that moment.

She sat up. "There's something I need to do." She took my hand and held it in her lap. "I want you to help me."

"Want . . . or need?"

"Need . . . and want." She half-smiled, spread her hand beneath mine, and ran her thumb along the line of my knuckles.

Her emerald eyes shone green beneath the trees. And below the pain of history, I saw a sparkle. "Is that why you came home?"

A minute passed before she answered. "Partly."

Chapter 6

Being a farrier was not Uncle Willee's first career choice. When he came home with Lorna, his options were limited. The business community of Brunswick had blackballed him, so he exercised a trade that would take him beyond the borders of Glynn County and allow him to put food on the table.

Tillman Ellsworth McFarland had always shoed his own horses. Doing so taught him how to read them. Unc says he remembered many a day when his daddy pulled his horse's leg through his and began scraping the V or pulling off a shoe and putting on a new one. Before he put on a new one, he'd hold the old up to the sunshine and read it—how it wore and where it was worn. "Horses are always talking. The shoes coming off their feet are akin to a scream at the top of their lungs."

Unc took this to heart, and I guess pretty soon he was reading more than just horses.

Shortly after I realized this, I also got clued in to the contrast between Unc and his older brother, Jack. It was midsummer, hot as Hades in the shade, and a mile above us six or eight buzzards floated in wide circles, riding the heat rising off the earth. Tommye and I were swinging on the tire swing, our faces sticky with watermelon juice, trying to stay away from Unc's crazed pet turkey, Bob. Unc had just pulled into the drive, covered in horse smell, dirt, and honesty. He kissed Lorna and was repacking his trailer for the next day when Uncle Jack pulled in behind him. He drove a new dark-blue Cadillac and wore a striped silk suit, cuffed pants, Italian leather loafers, Armani tie, and gold cuff links through French cuffs. The town zero and the town hero—as different as sunshine and rain.

Unc was working paycheck to paycheck, known around town as the prodigal who'd never come home and who'd robbed both his family and most of the town blind. The pardon had done little to change that. Upon his incarceration, Unc had been fired from the bank and Zuta Lumber, removed as a junior elder in the church, and kicked out of both the Rotary and the country club. Uncle Jack was the respectable one—president of the bank, president of Zuta Lumber, elder in his church, and founding member of the Glynn County Rotary, not to mention being rather wealthy.

He'd come to pick up Tommye.

At midnight the night before, Tommye had appeared at our kitchen door. And because she was just eight, that meant she'd run across the Zuta through the dark to get to us. I stood in the bathroom, running her a hot bath and wondering, *Ran across the Zuta? What could be worse than five miles of darkness and lightning?* Whatever it was had written itself all over her face. She walked in, her hair streaking down over her face, her feet covered in gumbo clay, and her long flannel gown dirty and torn from falling.

Aunt Lorna got her bathed and fed her some soup, and Unc put her in my bed and spread a pallet on the floor for me. I lay awake most of the night watching her twitch and listening to her talk in her sleep. The next morning the police showed up, sat Tommye on the porch, and started asking her a bunch of questions. She just sat there, said nothing, and looked at me. That same morning, the front page of the paper showed a picture of her dead brother. He'd had an accident, and a bullet went up through his head. The article went on to say that medics had to give Jack a sedative to calm him down. Witnesses say he was pretty distraught. The paper described him as "inconsolable."

Pretty soon Unc built bunk beds, and for the next several years, Tommye slept in the bottom bunk more nights than not. I don't know if this heightened the strain between Unc and his brother or just brought it out of the closet, but at any rate, whenever they were in the same room you could cut the tension with a knife. I think Willee and Jack would just as soon forget each other, but the fact that Tommye spent more time at our house than her own forced an uneasy truce between them.

Short of building a prison, Jack couldn't stop his daughter from escaping their house. For some reason, the two of them were like oil and water. She—along with an older brother—were given to him by his first wife. After her, he'd courted four more—somehow escaping more children. He never made much of a fuss over Tommye not staying at home. As more and more women became his wives, matched by the number who quietly filed for divorce, he became less vocal about it. Maybe it was easier to not have to explain a little girl running around to future prospects.

If Uncle Jack ever beat her, I never saw any signs of it. He was a lot of things—mostly a mystery—but violent was never one of them. And I looked. As did Unc—and I'm pretty sure if he had found any signs, that uneasy truce would have ended.

Tommye was something special—a quiet, pug-nosed, country girl with an accent that could melt butter and make old men forget their aches and pains. She made all As without really trying, was named all-state as pitcher on the girls' softball team, played the leading role for three years running in the school drama production, and was elected homecoming queen her senior year. If her internal and private life seemed shrouded in secrecy, her public persona was touched.

Few of my childhood memories don't include her, and in truth, she was as much—if not more—Willee's daughter than Jack's.

Sometime in high school it hit us that I was a foster child in her uncle's home—so I moved into the apartment above the barn, and we quit living like brother and sister. It was never anything physical, just something that shifted in our heads—how we thought about each other. And the moment that happened, an odd distance, palpable as an anvil, wedged itself between us.

She had all kinds of offers for our senior prom, yet, for reasons I never understood, she asked me. The girl I wanted to take was already going with somebody else, so why not?

That's when I realized how many looks Tommye got from other guys. Their eyes walked up and down her as if she were an interstate highway. And while she liked it, and to some extent fed off it, she had invited me for a reason. It's a good thing I didn't know much about fighting, because that night convinced me that a man's eyes can hurt almost as much as his hands. We made an appearance, danced, and then left early and ate a sack full of Krystal burgers on the beach in our tux and evening gown.

Chapter 7

I parked Vicky, hopped into my canoe, and paddled the twenty-seven strokes from my landing to my boat. I tied up, unloaded a bag of groceries, and leaned against the mast, staring out across the marsh. At four o'clock in the afternoon, the shade was turning from dull gold to light root beer.

One of the interesting things about living on a boat is that unless you live at a dock where power and phone lines are wired in, you have to think ahead. Like getting back and forth to shore. For carrying stuff, I use the canoe. It's sturdy, stable, and minimizes the number of trips. For simple transit, I use the kayak. It's quick and, given the drop-in rudder, maneuvers better in stronger currents—which occur every time the tide turns. On board, most everything runs off propane, so hot water and cooking are never really a problem. But anything electric—like cell phones and laptops—requires a generator if you don't want to run down the battery. I cranked the generator and charged my phone while I checked my e-mail and researched a few ideas online. While my boat borders on the primitive, Red can't stand the idea of my being totally unplugged, so he splurged and bought me a wireless broadband card.

An hour later, I gave him a call. "It's me."

"You been to see the kid today?"

"I'm going now. Thought I'd call you first."

"What have you got so far?"

"I called the Georgia Department of Family Services. Based on the appearance of chronic and prolonged physical abuse—and because they don't know whom he belongs to—they've filed an Emergency Shelter Petition, which will put him in foster care as soon as his doctor releases him. It makes him a ward of the state, giving them full custody."

"When's that happen?"

"Any day. Depends on the kid."

"What clsc?" Red asked.

"The DA's office assigned one of its own to investigate, see if they can find out who this kid is and possibly look into terminating parental rights."

"Can they do that?"

"Only if they find cause."

"One look at the kid's back will give them cause."

"Yeah, well, I'm meeting her at the kid's room in an hour."

"Her?"

"The attorney."

"Keep me posted."

I stepped off the elevator and into the pediatric ward. The same guard sat outside the door, reading a Louis L'Amour novel. He looked up at me and moved his huge shoulders out of the doorway. "He's in there. Scribbling."

I walked in and pulled up that stainless steel stool that doctors use to slide around in exam rooms. He stopped drawing long enough to adjust the new glasses on the end of his nose and look up just slightly. Not at my face, but maybe at my toes. He was still wearing Unc's

Braves cap. Before I went in, I'd decided to call him something other than Snoot, "the kid," or "hey you." Every kid ought to have a name. I rolled up next to him, careful not to get too close.

"Hey, Sketch."

He paused, scanned the floor as if he was allowing the name to roll around the inside of his head, and then gave it permission to rest on him. He looked across the room and wrote in his book without looking either at me or the page. Then he turned the page toward me. It read HI.

If my handwriting were half as legible as his, I might actually write letters to people. "The hat looks good on you. You like the Braves?"

He shrugged without taking his eyes off his page.

"Where did you learn to write so . . . so perfectly?"

His hand began moving before his eyes ever looked at the page. He drew what looked like a hospital bed with an older woman lying in it. Her face was wrinkled, she had oxygen tubes in her nose and a pencil in one hand. On the other side of the bed sat a small kid. The kid was watching her draw. On the page in her hand, she'd written half the alphabet.

I pointed. "That you?"

He nodded. I noticed that his face was fuller, like maybe he'd gained a pound or two.

I pointed again. "Who's that?"

Everything he wrote was in small block caps. MISS MYRLENE.

"She related to you?"

Just then, a late-twenties, brunette female wearing jeans, running shoes, and a white oxford button-down appeared in the door. I looked up while the kid looked through the tops of his glasses at her feet.

I stood and held out my hand. "I'm Chase Walker."

"Mandy Parker." She pulled up her shirttail and flashed the DA's badge looped over the waist of her jeans but hidden from view.

I stepped out of the way so she could get a look at the kid. She walked up, leaned over, quickly took in his bare back and arms, and then placed her hands on her knees and spoke softly. "Hi."

He had flipped to another page in his notebook and was shading in the wings on what looked like a male cardinal hanging from a bird-feeder. I looked out his window and saw the birdfeeder, but no bird. He didn't look up, but stopped shading long enough to look out the corner of his eyes.

She spied a chair in the corner. "Go ahead. I don't want to inter-rupt you."

I scooted up next to the kid again just as he broke the tip of his pencil. On the nightstand behind him lay a package of new black No. 2 pencils and an electronic sharpener. He stuck the pencil in and worked it 'til he was satisfied with the point, then he began drawing detail around the cardinal's beak and eyes.

I pointed to the drawing supplies. "Somebody give you all this?"

He nodded slowly, as if unsure whether I was baiting him just before I planned to snatch it off the table.

"Somebody must like you."

He raised his head slightly, showing me the tops of the whites of his eyes. The look told me he thought I knew. He flipped to a clean page and quickly sketched the outline of Unc's face and hat.

"Uncle Willee brought you all that?"

A quick nod.

"When?"

He drew a clock face, with the hour hand pointed at six and the minute hand on the one.

I sat back and spoke to both him and me. "I thought he left a little early this morning."

The kid closed his notebook and looked over his shoulder at Mandy Parker.

I pointed to her. "Oh, she's an attorney."

He sketched the top of a pair of pants, two belt loops, and a leather-cased badge hanging over the belt between the two loops.

I studied the drawing and said, "You don't miss much, do you?"

He shrugged. I looked at the bald spots atop his head; a few of them were starting to show signs of hair.

"She's with the state. What they call the DA's office."

He immediately crossed his arms, pulled his knees up into his chest, and clung to the notebook, turning his knuckles white.

I read the body language. "But she's one of the good guys."

He pulled his knees in tighter to his chest. He wasn't buying it, and Mandy Parker saw it.

She stood and said, "I'll come back." Then she pulled a DVD out of her back pocket and quietly set it on the bed. "It's one of my favorites. Thought you might like it, too." Then she looked at me. "Coffee sounds good. I'll wait outside."

I nodded. "Yeah, give me just a minute."

I looked at the DVD. It was Disney's *Jungle Book*. I handed it to him. "You seen this one?"

He shook his head.

"You want to?"

He paused like I'd asked him a trick question. I slipped it into the DVD player below the television and pushed *PLAY*.

The second the picture appeared, he dived beneath his bed and crawled as far underneath it as he could. The guard outside heard the ruckus and immediately appeared in the room. I don't know who was more surprised—him, the kid, or me. I got on my knees and looked under the bed where the kid had balled himself into a fetal position, pulling his arms over his head.

The guard looked at me and whispered, "He did that last night. Somebody down the hall flipped on a TV, and he wouldn't come out for a couple hours."

Mandy stood outside the door, watching from across the hall.

I crawled around to the head of the bed, so I'd be closer to his ears. I spoke softly. "I'm real sorry. I should've asked. You don't have to watch it if you don't want to." I turned the TV off and laid the remote on the ground next to him. "Here. You control it, okay?"

He looked through the hole between his underarm and chest and watched me set the remote on the ground.

I backed up and said again, "I'm sorry. Okay?"

The guard stepped aside and said, "You didn't mean nothing. Just give him a little while."

It was little consolation. If I'd made any headway in two days, it was gone now. "Thanks."

I stepped out of the room and walked down to the coffee shop with Mandy Parker. In the elevator, I was the first to speak. "I'm not trained for this."

She watched the floor numbers change above our heads. "Kids who've experienced his type of abuse have triggers. We often don't know what they are until we trip one."

We ordered coffee and sat down at an outdoor table, and the salty smell of the marsh washed over us.

She smiled. "You from around here?"

"Born and raised." I paused. "Well, raised, actually. I was placed in foster care before I could remember much. I don't really know where I was born. I think it must've been somewhere in the South, and probably near the ocean, but for all I know I might be from Seattle. You?"

"Florida girl. Panhandle." She changed the subject. "Your editor called me. Said he'd assigned you to write a story about the kid."

I nodded. "Yeah, and I'd be grateful for anything you could tell me."

"What do you know?"

I told her everything I'd been able to deduce from his drawings, my interaction with him, and my conversations with the doctor and the guard. All together, it wasn't much. We didn't know his name, where he was from, who his family was, or how he got to the railroad track.

I finished, "His memory is selective. Sometimes it's photographic, at others it's nonexistent."

She nodded. "I've been with the DA for five years. Worked with maybe a hundred kids. Some of the worst ones have memories like that. The trauma blocks it out."

"How do you get anywhere with them?"

"That's tricky. Takes time."

"You been able to find out anything?"

"No. Our databases list plenty of abused kids in his age range and size, but none who show his level of abuse, and nothing describing a mute kid. And . . . given his skill with a pencil, I'd say he's been silent awhile."

"What's that tell you?"

"That no one has reported him as missing."

"What will happen from here?"

"Based on what I've seen, we'll file an emergency petition to place him in foster care. And I'll push the court to fast-track the termination of parental rights." She paused. "The State of Georgia, like every other state, assumes that no one will care for a child as his or her parents will. The goal is notification and reunification. And in every case, including those involving severe abuse, the legal system is predicated on an individual's ability to change. I agree with this . . . but there are exceptions." She pointed up. "Like John Doe #117."

"Is that what you're calling him?"

She shook her head. "No, it's what the computer labels him when it spits out his folder. I hate it, but it's the system, and I can only fight so many battles in a day."

I liked Mandy Parker; she spoke my language.

"How long does that process take?"

"Best case, a month—though that's seldom seen. Notification is a legal process, and it takes time. We put classified ads in newspapers, get his story on the news, and get in touch with military services to make sure there's not a soldier somewhere who's unaware, whatever we can. Worst case, twelve to twenty-four months. Depends on lots of factors. If the parents mysteriously show up and want their child back, we'd start a Child Welfare Case plan, which outlines how they can get their child back. That takes twelve to eighteen months, and their progress is reviewed every six."

I was familiar with this process, though I didn't tell her that. "Let's suppose for a minute that his parents never show. What happens?"

"We file an Affidavit of Diligent Search listing what we've done—in effect covering our tails, proving to the court that we did attempt to find his parents. If this is deemed acceptable, then the department gets him a social security number and gives him a name—or the child can choose his own name—and the judge puts it into order. At that point, he's declared a true ward of the state, his parents have no more rights, and he's placed in long-term foster care, possibly with the same family."

"So at that point, anyone can petition to get the kid?"

She nodded.

"And for now, you place him in short-term foster care?"

"Yes. Well, the judge can . . . *if* an approved home is willing and available. Availability in Glynn County right now is a problem, and if that weren't bad enough, most folks don't want a kid with his issues." She pulled a folder from her shoulder bag and opened it on the table. "You know this man?"

I chuckled. "That'd be William Walker McFarland. Otherwise known as Uncle Willee."

She nodded. "He came to see me this morning, asked that he and his wife be considered as foster placement."

"Well?"

"He's led quite a life."

"You could say that."

"Does he ever talk about life before prison?"

"Not really. And trust me, it's not from a lack of prying."

She flipped through the chart. "From what I can uncover, it's as if he's led two totally different lives."

"I think when you bury your father, wife, and son all in the same six months, whatever prior life you led pretty much gets buried with them."

She nodded. "They passed the DCF home inspection and the initial interview."

"They'd already had all that."

"The state wants to move on this kid. Be proactive. He's been through a lot. Also, with you covering the story . . ."

"I see."

"As a result, the McFarlands' file is pending."

"Pending what?"

She smiled. "My conversation with you." She flipped a few pages. "They've got some experience. Your home as a child must've had a revolving front door."

I nodded. "You can say that again."

"You turned eighteen a decade ago, yet you still have an apartment above the barn. How come?"

I laughed. "Free rent. I don't *have* it as much as they let me sleep there when I'm too tired to drive home."

She smiled, but waited just the same.

"You've done your homework."

She shrugged. "It's not hard. Computers do most of it, if you know where to look. And if you know how to phrase the right questions, the people on the other end of the phone do the rest."

"You'll be hard-pressed to find a better pair than those two." I wrote my number on a napkin, then stood and threw my cup in the waste can. "I better get back upstairs. Call me if anything comes up?"

"Yes, provided you do the same."

I stuck out my hand. "Deal."

She walked off, out through the sliding doors, and into a convertible Volkswagen bug, one of the new ones with the flower shooting up out of the dashboard. I walked back upstairs and found the lights off and television on. Unc was sitting on my stool, his socked feet propped up on the bed. The kid sat on the bed, his eyes wide and glued to the screen. Both were eating popcorn. On the screen, Baloo was singing "The Bare Necessities." When he uprooted the palm tree and began scratching his back, Unc laughed out loud. The kid looked at Unc, then me, then back at the screen.

I tapped Unc on the shoulder. "Thank you."

He threw a piece of popcorn at me. "Fastest way to the heart is through the stomach."

I backed out of the room and waved at the kid, who regarded me without expression. Outside, I stepped into Vicky, turned my cap around backwards, and considered what Unc had said. I chewed on it all the way home, but something didn't set right. I rolled into the barn and cut the engine. Was that true? Do you get to the heart through the stomach? Or is there some other portal? I left that hanging because there was one other question more timely, and it had to do with that kid: If you can't speak, then how do you laugh? And if you can't laugh, then how do you cry?

I had a story to write.

Chapter 8

Ellsworth McFarland raised his sons to know the value of a dollar. If they wanted one, they had to earn it. Only difference was that while Jack spent, Liam saved. But there was one benefit to Jack's gambling habit. He learned the power of leverage. Which meant he was continually making deals and continually in debt. Mostly to Liam. This does not suggest that Jack was dumb or foolish. Quite the contrary. The boy was brilliant.

The brothers spent their summers working as tellers at the bank. In each boy's senior year, Ellsworth made him a junior loan officer, so by the time they graduated high school a year apart, the boys knew more about the community banking business than most of their business professors at the University of Georgia. They studied SAE, pledged Business, and thanked God for the red and black. After graduation they married within a year of each other and joined their dad at the bank. Then came the storm of 1979.

While geography sets Brunswick out of the path of hurricanes, it has little effect on tornadoes and thunderstorms in July. At 3:00 PM the space behind Ellsworth's desk got too cramped, so he left the bank in his boys' hands and drove home for an Arturo Fuente cigar and a walk around the Zuta on his horse, Big Bubba, followed by dinner with his attorney. At seventy-five years of age, Ellsworth found that some things had become so simple. His legacy was intact. By 6:30 PM the tellers had balanced and clocked out, leaving his sons to lock the vault and turn out the lights—a nightly routine.

The door of the vault had been marred by three different robbery attempts—one with dynamite, one with various tools including a sledge-hammer, and a third that included both plus a tractor blade. None was even remotely successful, and the marred door had been left in open sight for all the bank customers to see. It was a steel badge of safety. One local billboard even showed a photograph of just the vault door. The caption read *The only place in town where your money is safe.*

Earlier that year, regulators had valued the bank at $57,000,000—making it a community bank with regional power. Also during this time, an interesting event occurred in history. Despite the fact that Jimmy Carter was a peanut farmer from Georgia, his financial policy had become a disaster, and the interest rates reflected this. By the spring of 1979, prime had reached 15 percent. Two years later it would peak at 20.5 percent. Hence, Carter became a one-term won-der. Searching for secure investments, folks all around the South had invested in bearer bonds. Second only to cash, they were sold with a fixed interest rate paid twice yearly. The bearer of the bond would clip off the coupon, send it in, and receive an interest payment that ranged from 6 to 8 percent.

There was just one problem. Unlike a stock certificate, they were issued to "Bearer." No name appeared on the bond. This meant that, if stolen, there was no way to reclaim it. No way to cancel it. It was like losing a $100 bill. Or a $100,000 bill. This explains why the govern-ment halted the issuance of bearer bonds in 1982. But, given that Ellsworth's vault was robbery proof, folks came from all across Georgia for two reasons. The first was simple safekeeping. Twice a year they'd show up, show a note, clip their own coupon, and mail it in for their interest payment. But then the interest rates went to 20 percent, and opportunity knocked. Bondholders approached the ZB&T, secured a loan, usually at 90 percent of bond value, then took the loan amount and placed it with a Savings and Loan where they could usually get a point or two better than prime on their money. That meant 16 percent. That eight-to-ten point spread was clean profit. And in 1979 this practice was running wild. This meant that on the night of the storm, the ZB&T held more than $6,000,000 in bearer bonds as collateral for loans. These bonds were kept in a file cabinet in the back of the vault.

Bottom line, folks just didn't trust the government—not with double-digit interest and American boys still missing in Vietnam. H-e-double-hockey-stick no. Folks in South Georgia were waving the Confederate flag, pointing toward D.C., hailing Ronald Reagan, and screaming stuff I can't write.

The risk was this—while the FDIC insured people's deposits, they did not insure collateral on loans. Nor did they insure "safekeeping." But given the visible and well-advertised scars on the vault door, folks from Florida to Alabama to North Carolina knew their money was safer in Ellsworth's safe than tucked under a mattress. So, to put people at ease, Ellsworth insured the vault contents. It was a no-brainer.

There was just one problem.

The brothers were locking the vault and the doors when thunder-clouds appeared on the horizon above the Zuta. Liam and Jack climbed to the third-story roof and watched the lightning lick the earth.

When Ellsworth didn't answer his phone, Liam said, "We better check on Dad."

"Not me. You. Old coot don't use much electricity anyway." Jack checked his watch. "They're cutting cards in twenty minutes." Without another thought, he hopped into his convertible and aimed the nose toward the beach, the pub, and the backroom Wednesday night poker game. Except it was only Monday. For the last several months, every night had been Wednesday.

Liam drove through the hail, down the row of pecans, and into the yard. The peacocks were all spooked and roosting in the barn away from the wind, baseball-sized hail, and coming noise. Big Bubba was in the barn, the house was empty, and Ellsworth's truck was nowhere to be seen. Hearing a radio report of a tornado in town, Liam drove back to the bank to wait out the storm. He walked up to the door to find the front glass broken and a man in black wearing a ski mask rummaging through the cash drawers.

Because Ellsworth had survived one world war, one depression, and countless attempted bank robberies, he'd become partial to carrying a Colt 1911. He had also given one to each of his sons when they turned sixteen. The pistol held more bullets than a revolver, and if you were looking at it from the business end, the sheer diameter of the barrel might convince you to do something other than what you were currently contemplating.

The boys had grown up knowing how to shoot and shoot well. So when they joined the bank after college, it was assumed they would keep their Colts close at hand when near the bank. Liam kept his in his briefcase. So when he found the man in black rummaging through his tellers' drawers, he reached into his briefcase. Liam placed the barrel to the man's head, and James Brown Gilbert put his hands in the air and confessed every crime he'd ever thought of committing.

That's about when all Hades broke loose. The tornado hit the bank, and Liam was lucky to get the vault open before the wind tore the roof off, which it did. Liam shut the door, and both men sat in the dark while the noise outside tore apart the world. Due to the portion of the roof that had fallen in front of the vault door and across every roadway in town, it was after dawn when folks found Liam locked up tight and dry in the vault with James Brown, whose rap sheet was already three pages long. They pulled away the wreckage, freeing the door and the duo inside.

Not long after, Jack showed up fresh with winnings from an all-night vigil at the poker table. The newspaper people arrived in time to take a picture of cuffed James stepping into the squad car and the police patting Liam on the shoulder. The picture ran in the afternoon paper several hours later: SON OF ZUTA SAVES BANK.

Remember how they say "glory is fleeting"?

Noticeably absent during all the chaos was Ellsworth. When he didn't show and didn't answer the phone, Liam drove to the house to check on him while Jack worked to open the bank. Despite the carnage of the storm, the bank's innards were in fine shape. People's deposits were safe with the FDIC, and on-hand cash had been kept safe in the vault. Nothing had been lost except the roof and furniture inside, so Jack ordered a circus tent, erected it in the parking lot, and set up business in the sunshine—which was glorious.

Liam arrived at the house to find the lights out. He found his dad's truck parked in the barn, then noticed a maroon Lincoln Town Car with a white ragtop parked out front. Perry Kenner had been the bank's attorney since its inception. He was not only the second highest stockholder, but also Ellsworth's best friend. He had handled the FDIC filings and handled oversight of the bank's securities. Witnesses say the two men were friends of the closest kind. They often scheduled business meetings that had little to do with business and much to do with horses, fishing, or cigars.

The amount of leaves and twigs covering the car suggested it'd been there longer than just this morning. Liam placed his hand on the hood, but it was cold. He walked up the porch steps, then pulled open the back door.

"Dad?"

No answer.

"Dad?"

The only sound was a wind chime sounding oddly muted.

He noticed the tangled chime, spent a few minutes untying the knot that the wind had tied, and then walked through the back door into the kitchen and hollered again. The front door was wide open, and rain had blown in clear through to the dining room. He closed the door, began mopping up the water, and then noticed that his dad's office door was open—and water was coming out of there too. He dried the foyer, then slid on his knees across the wood to the puddle coming from his dad's office. He began mopping it up, but it was sticky—like somebody had spilled a Coca Cola. He went outside to empty the mop bucket, but the sunlight showed something else. The water was red.

Liam found his father facedown on his desk, shot in the head. Across from him lay Perry Kenner—his blue hand still gripping the pistol that had killed them both. Spread across the desk—apparently the subject of last night's work—lay Ellsworth's last will and testament.

But Liam's heartaches were just beginning. On the floor behind Ellsworth's chair lay another body. Perry's gun had killed one more. Liam rolled over the body and stared into the face of his young wife, Suzanne.

Liam and Jack buried Ellsworth and Suzanne alongside Sarah Beth on a grassy hill in the Sanctuary where their tombstones would face the rising sun.

Between the storm and the murders, questions abounded. So following the funeral, Liam swallowed his grief long enough to do what his father would have done—he asked that auditors be brought in to set the customers at ease. Two days later, auditors came in. Three days later, the bank was shut down and taped off. Two weeks later, a flashlight awoke Liam in the middle of the night in his bed, where his three-year-old son was tucked in alongside him. He was arrested and cuffed. This time the caption on the front page read SON OF ZUTA STEALS MILLIONS. Seven million to be exact. Seven million in untraceable bearer bonds.

Because his alleged crime was federal, the district attorney placed Liam in Fulton County Federal Penitentiary, where he awaited trial in

Atlanta. Ellsworth McFarland's last will and testament called for the
orderly disposition of his estate, granting an even split between the
two sons with managerial control of both the bank and Zuta Lumber
left in the hands of the firstborn. While Liam got used to daylight
filtered by prison bars, Jack became the uncontested Managing
Director of Zuta Properties.

During the months preceding the trial, Jack did two things: he
publicly distanced and disowned Liam, and he rolled up his sleeves
and learned how to become a banker. From newspaper to television,
the rift between the two grew like the Grand Canyon. Because Liam
was damaged goods, no one stepped forward to care for his three-
and-a-half-year-old child. They said it had something to do with the
sins of the father being carried down on the son. So, making sure that
sin didn't go unnoticed, his three-year-old quickly became a ward of
the state.

Following the robbery, folks got itchy to know about their bonds.
'Course, when they heard that every single one of them was gone,
they started screaming. To prove their point, a lynch mob gathered
outside the bank screaming Liam's name. Technically, Jack could have
folded his arms and closed the doors, leaving the town to wrestle with
their own debts.

Not many would have blamed him. In the absence of the bonds,
regulators found the bank woefully underfunded and unsecured.
They told Jack that he either had to come up with several million or
shut the doors. Given that most of the bonds were held as collateral
for loans, Jack looked at the balance sheet, rolled up his sleeves, and
took a long, honest look at his options.

Option one was to close the doors and walk away. Sure, he wouldn't
be too welcome in church, but what did he care? He wouldn't be
broke. Second option was to fund the bank himself. But where could
he get the money? That's when he surprised most of South Georgia.
Jack traveled to Atlanta and found a Savings and Loan that gave him

a $10,000,000 line of credit using the Zuta as his collateral. With the line of credit in his back pocket, he met personally with every bond-holder, forgave their debt to the bank if they had one, and then paid any outstanding difference out of his own money. That meant, if some-one had secured a $90,000 loan with a $100,000 bond, he forgave the ninety and paid the extra ten out of his own checkbook—or rather the S&L's. When folks heard, they said, "Boy's got his dad's character. It's a good thing too, 'cause the other one sure didn't get it."

Word of an honest banker spread, and pretty soon cars with out-of-state tags were parked out front. Around town, perception changed. Where once folks had seen nothing more than a footloose card shark who was a little too thick in the middle, those same people began tip-ping their hats on the sidewalk.

Jack was no dummy. It required work, but he turned his misfor-tune into the bank's fortune. Within two years, his loan balance had nearly doubled and his bank was making cash hand over fist. He couldn't have printed it any faster. For each of the next twenty-five years, the ZB&T had its best year ever. The path of the bank's success was a moon shot taking its cue from the American-Soviet space race. Within a few years, people were whispering Jack's name and *mayor* all in the same sentence. A few even whispered *governor*. Jack seemed unfazed, content to work hard and make good on the bad his brother had caused.

Six months after the robbery, William Walker McFarland was put on trial for stealing more than $7 million in bearer bonds. The wit-ness stand was chock-full of unhappy people—including Jack and every other customer of the bank, which included most every inhab-itant in Brunswick, Sea Island, St. Simons Island, and Glynn County. Six different tellers placed their hands on a four-inch Bible and swore "So help me God" that the bonds were in the vault that afternoon before closing. Four different police officers and two plainclothes investigators swore on the same Bible that the bonds were gone when they inspected the vault the morning after the storm. As the DA laid out his case, it became clear that the only two people in or near the vault who had access or any hope of getting into it were Liam and his new best buddy, James Brown Gilbert. The only other person who knew the combination was Jack, but his alibi was a hard nut to crack. Six people, including two exposed church elders who did not like facing their fellow congregants in the jury, swore under oath that Jack had been sitting at the card table with them.

The DA put James Brown Gilbert on the stand, but they soon discovered what most in town already knew. James Brown was about ten cards shy of a full deck. When he said, "I don't know nuffin' 'bout no bombs," the jury looked at Liam and frowned. Then they swore.

The jury made a simple decision. Called it a crime of association. Liam, and only Liam, was in the vault, and so were the bonds. By the time he left, they were gone. Given the storm, no one else had access or could have gotten away with it. This alone explains why the trial was short and sentencing severe: forty-seven years in prison—and 200 percent retribution. The courtroom cheered when the verdict was read. Liam's ownership in the bank was spread among the current shareholders. But that only paid half his debt to the bank, and because it was early in the seventies and interest rates were on their way to 20 percent, cash was in low supply—meaning few to no buyers existed who could fork out several million for timberland. To pay the remainder of his debt, Liam sold half his ownership in the Zuta to Jack who, with his own S&L line of credit, paid him fifty cents on the dollar. The result did two things: it gave Jack 61 percent of the bank and 75 percent of the Zuta, and it gave Liam forty-seven years to think about it.

Funny thing, no one ever found the bonds.

Somewhere about this time, the reality of Liam's life began to sink in. Looking at a clean mirror, only one issue remained. Given the climate at home, the absence of family willing to step up and raise his son, and the fact that most of the town wanted his head on a platter, Liam decided he could help his son most by distancing him from his name and the stigma of his incarceration. Somewhere in a jail cell in Atlanta, he made the second hardest decision of his life. He signed over power of attorney for his three-year-old son to the State of Georgia. Further, he asked the state to seal the file—forever. That done, he lay in his cell and refused to eat or drink for nineteen days. When they took him to the medical ward and attempted to put an IV in his arm, he fought until he passed out, at which time they inserted the needle and fed him. When he awoke two days later under the heavy fog of sedation, he wiggled his fingers and toes, saw the ceiling instead of God, and realized that he was healthy and still in hell.

The local incarcerated population learned of the silver-spoon kid gone bad, and to heap insult atop injury, they collectively renamed William Liam Walker. Within days, he was affectionately referred to as "Wil-Lee."

Five months into Liam's jail sentence, Jack arrived at the prison for an unannounced visit—the first time the two had seen each other or talked since the courtroom. The guards brought Willee in and sat him down. The room was cold, concrete, and dotted with hard, dull steel tables and chairs painted battleship gray. Every profane word in the dictionary, and some not, had been etched into the thick paint.

Beyond the glass, the guards watched a game show and ate pork rinds.

"William . . ." Jack rubbed one hand with the other. "Something's happened."

Liam leaned in and listened as though his ears were plugged with cotton.

"It's your boy . . . somebody . . . somebody found out . . . and well . . ."

Like a dog studying something he didn't understand, Liam's head tilted, weighing what he heard.

Jack spread a letter on the table. "They left this . . ."

A typewritten letter read simply: $4 MILLION IN UNMARKED $100s. WATERTIGHT. LEAVE ON TOP OF CLIFFORD WILLOWS CSA GRAVE, CHRIST CHURCH CEMETERY. MIDNIGHT, TOMORROW. NO FEDS. OR WE'LL SEND YOU YOUR SON IN A BOX CUT FROM YOUR OWN LUMBER.

The only asset Liam had left was his 25 percent ownership in the Zuta. His 6,500 acres were estimated at $7,000,000. Five minutes later, he had sold it to Jack for $4,000,000. He kept two things—neither of which Jack wanted: the house in which he grew up and where his father and wife were killed, and DuBignon Hammock.

Using his connections in the banking industry, Jack acquired the cash, noted the serial numbers, packed two duffels to overflowing, and dropped both on top of the grave. To protect himself and defend against foul play in case the deal went bad, Jack brought in the sheriff and a local attorney to witness both the packing of the duffels and the drop. They placed the money on top of the grave, sat with the engine running in the parking lot, and waited.

The kidnappers never showed.

An hour later, the three spread out looking for the boy, but there was no sign of him—or the money.

The following day, somebody dropped the boy's burnt body on the courthouse steps, and the following day one of the prison guards slid the news article through Liam's prison bars. The State of Georgia let Liam out of prison long enough to bury his son. He was driven to the morgue, given fifteen minutes with the body, then driven to the Buffalo, where he canoed across to DuBignon and dug a 4x2x6-foot grave next to his wife's. A few hours later, they drove him back to Atlanta to serve the remaining forty-six-and-a-half years of his prison term.

Walking back into prison, Liam shut off his mind, cut away his heart, and wrote "Willee McFarland" inside the collar of his shirts and the waist of his shorts. For two years, he existed. He read books, studied orchids, and talked to the hands that fed him food behind the cafeteria line. The glove-covered hands belonged to a female voice, and while she could see him, he never saw her. Until a year later, that is, when for no logical reason I can uncover, the governor of Georgia signed a full pardon. Willee McFarland walked out of prison—fatherless, wifeless, childless, penniless, and free.

The pardon reads ". . . for hardship, time served, and evidence that has since surfaced that was not available during trial." Seems sort of weak, doesn't it? And no, I've never been able to find that piece of evidence either.

Willee had walked almost a mile down the road when a ragtopped Mustang pulled up alongside. The driver stuck out a gloved hand, and for the first time he saw the face attached to it. Lorna Sanchez was a Mexican bombshell who looked like a cross between Madeline Stowe and Elizabeth Taylor.

Before meeting Uncle Willee, Aunt Lorna was a twice-divorced waitress and part-time housecleaner working the cafeteria line at the Fulton County Penitentiary. So when Unc tells you he met his wife in prison, he's not kidding. They met sometime in his first month and spent the next three years getting to know one another across the glass. Lorna says he wooed her with his charm and the way he holds his mouth when he talks. Unc says she seduced him with her spaghetti. If that's true, then she seduced a couple hundred men.

"You can get in this car if you tell me the truth and only the truth, every time you open your mouth. From now 'til forever."

He squatted next to the car and threw his bag over his shoulder. "Lorna, my daddy told me that at the end of the day all I've got, the only thing I can control is my word—" He looked back at the prison. "And to this day, I've kept it."

Unc promised her a rather certain life of poverty, hardship, and endless hounding rumors. The two married and moved to his child-hood home back in Brunswick.

Lorna walked through the front door, saw the red stain in the foyer, and asked, "What's that?"

"It's a long story, but it doesn't start here." He took her to the Sanctuary, sat her down next to the graves, leaned against his daddy's marble tombstone, and started at the beginning. A year went by, but Lorna's body would not give them children, so they jumped through some hoops and registered as a foster home.

After all my research—and the writing of my thesis—three questions remain: First, who stole the bank securities, and where are they? Why would William Walker McFarland steal them? What did he have to gain?

Second, the coroner said Perry Kenner didn't appear to have powder residue on his right hand. If he'd shot a .45-caliber revolver, chances are good there'd have been some type of residue. So if Perry Kenner didn't shoot Ellsworth and Suzanne, who did? And if he did, then who shot Perry Kenner?

Lastly, who kidnapped William Walker McFarland Jr., and how'd they find out his real identity if the documents were sealed? How did the swap go bad, who killed him, and what happened to the cash? In twenty years, shouldn't some of those serial numbers have been circulated through?

Oh yeah . . . and what was the evidence that brought about the pardon, and where is it?

Chapter 9

I showered and shaved in the dark, but it's hard to hide in my old apartment, and Tommye had always been a light sleeper. I finished shaving and splashed on some aftershave, and she sat up in bed and rubbed her eyes. She looked pale.

She stretched. "I love that smell."

"Yeah." I smiled. "It's hard to beat Old Spice." I slapped my face again. "Nothing but the best for my face."

She held a rubber band between her teeth, did that thing only girls can do with their hair to push it into a ponytail, then grabbed the rubber band and did the one hand flip, wrap, and flip. Half-awake, she hobbled out of bed, brushed her teeth, popped a handful of pills, and walked across the room where, with no warning whatsoever, she stripped down to absolutely nothing.

I was not expecting that.

I guess my mouth was pretty far open, because when she turned and began walking to the closet where I kept the ironing board, she saw me, and a look of confusion spread across her face. Two seconds later, she saw herself. She stopped short, closed her eyes, and said, "Sorry. Old habits—" She shook her head.

I grabbed my keys, threw on my cap, and slipped into my flip-flops.

Pulling the door behind me, I said, "The rain over the last couple of nights has probably raised the water level in the swamp. Thought maybe I'd go down to Gibson Island this afternoon and see if the warmouth have come in. You want to go?"

I heard the pitter-patter of feet, then she stuck her head around the door. "Yeah, I'd like that."

"Aunt Lorna and Unc'll probably go."

"Even better."

I smiled and pulled my cap down. "I don't know how they fish in L.A., but down here we cover up a bit. Keeps off the sun and the mosquitoes. Although I doubt the mosquitoes have ever seen anything like you either."

She nodded and tried to rub the sleep off her face. "I suppose I had that coming. See you later."

Unc and Aunt Lorna had one phone in their house. It hung in the kitchen, its dial worn and yellowed. It was not unusual for Unc to get calls from customers this early. I sat closest, so when it rang I answered it. In the background I heard someone being paged over an intercom, followed by a series of dings, and then somebody tapped the phone.

I added powdered creamer to my coffee and asked again, "Hello?"

More tapping. That's about when I woke up. "Sketch, is that you?"

Several taps.

That confused me. "Wait, wait. One is yes. Two is no."

A second passed. One tap.

I sipped and burnt my lips. "Are you okay?"

One tap.

"You want to talk with me?"

One tap.

"Can it wait a day?"

Silence, followed by one tap.

"I'll get there soon as I can."

I hung the phone back in the receiver as the first hint of sunshine was breaking the treetops in the distance. One of Aunt Lorna's peacocks strutted across the shadows beneath the kitchen window. In the pasture out beneath the setting moon, several Brahman cows grazed quietly and three or four turkeys marched single file along the fence-row. Unc cleared his throat and raised his eyebrows, bringing me back inside the house.

"Oh," I said, pointing my mug toward the phone. "That was the kid. Said he wanted to talk with me." I shook my head. "Actually, he tapped the phone." I turned up my cup, rinsed it in the sink, and then headed for the door. I pushed it open, then turned. "I met a friend of yours yesterday."

Unc raised his eyes but not his head. "Yeah."

I smiled. "Mandy Parker . . . she works with the DA's office." I waited for a reaction, but didn't get one. "She had an old picture of you." I paused, letting the effect set in. "The kind where your hair is messed up and there's that big ruler on the wall behind you." I smiled. "She said they'd be placing the kid in a day or so."

Unc looked at Lorna, and then both looked up at me. He folded the paper. "That okay with you?"

"You never needed my permission before. Why now?"

"This one's different."

"How so?"

He sat back, tilted his hat, and stared out the same kitchen window. "Twenty-seven years, five months, and six days ago, my three-year-old son faced a real similar thing . . . He sat all alone with people he didn't know, waiting for somebody to rescue him from a world that scared him." He folded his napkin and wiped the corners of his mouth. "No kid should ever have to know that." The creases in his face showed, like they did whenever the sun got bright. "Lorna and I

. . . we just thought we'd sit in while all of you work to figure out that kid's story."

Aunt Lorna reached across the table and held his hand. I shut the screen door and then looked back through the screen at a man who'd carried the weight of the world on his shoulders for most of his adult life. I once thought maybe that weight was a chip. As I got older and could see the forest for the trees, I saw that it was more like a yoke.

"Yes sir. It's all right with me."

I idled Vicky down the drive to the hard road, where the glisten off the train tracks caught my eye. For a moment I sat there like a man staring into a campfire—seeking the ghost of the Silver Meteor.

I thought about young Tillman McFarland unloading here with nothing but a box of tools and hope. And thought of what he started. But it wasn't the sound of tires on gravel, the four wood ducks jetting overhead at nearly forty miles an hour, the train in the distance, or the lost sound of my father's voice that gave me pause. It was Tommye's laughter. There was no getting around it. Tommye was a pretty woman—some would say "drop-dead gorgeous," and they'd be right—but it was her laughter that was beautiful.

Chapter 10

In the hospital, the guard was gone, but his chair remained. Outside the door, a male nurse stood over a rolling cart filled with prescriptions. The newspaper was spread across the top of the cart, open to the sports page. I motioned to the paper. "Smoltz pitch last night?"

He shook his head. "Some new guy. Gave up only two hits. Chipper hit a three-run dinger in the sixth. Braves won by five."

"He's a shoo-in for Cooperstown."

He nodded.

"Something told me this would be a good day."

I walked into the room, but it was empty. The bed was made and the kid was gone. I looked around for some sign that he was still here, then turned back to the nurse. "Where's the kid?"

He shook his head. "They checked him out this morning."

No wonder Sketch had called me. "Where'd he go?"

He shrugged. "Don't know."

"He leave anything?"

"You might check with the doctor."

"Thanks."

I walked across to the nurses' station and spoke to a lady who seemed to vaguely recognize me. "The kid that was in that room . . . where'd he go?"

She pointed down the hall toward the elevator with her pen. "Doctor sent him home this morning."

"Home?"

She nodded.

"Where's that?"

"Are you related to the boy?"

I shook my head. "No, I'm with the paper. We're trying to—"

She held up her hand. "Can't help you."

"Thanks."

On the first floor, I called Mandy Parker. "Mandy, this is Chase Walker."

"Thought you might be calling. You at the hospital?"

"Yeah. Where's the kid?"

"Glynn County Boys' Home."

"Please don't tell me that. When?"

"Early this morning."

I took a deep breath. "Thanks. I'll be in touch."

By the time I turned six, I'd lived in half a dozen foster or group homes. Seems like somebody was hell-bent on moving me around as much as possible. About the time I got my sheets warm, somebody came in, loaded me into a car, and drove me someplace else. Don't get me wrong, homes for children are needed, but it's a lot like purgatory. Why prolong the suffering; why not just get it over with?

Your entire life is consumed with two opposing ideas: On the one hand, you know you've been abandoned, rejected, thrown out on the street. Otherwise, you'd be with your parents. The flip side tells you that they could come to their senses, change their minds, and come barging through that door at any second. For that reason, you learn to sleep with one eye open. Because when they do, you want them to know that you've kept up the vigil. That you believed. That you hoped. Problem is that around the age of six, your eyelids grow heavy.

I walked into the GCBH and signed in with the receptionist. "I'm here to see a little boy who was brought in this morning from Southeast Georgia Regional Medical Center. Goes by a John Doe name at the present."

She checked what looked like a logbook, then pointed behind her. "Second hallway on the right, third door on the left."

"Thanks."

The door was cracked and a fluorescent light flickered on the other side, so I knocked lightly and pushed gently. The room was small, about the size of a broom closet. If it had been gray at one time, age had turned it an off-shade of mildew green. No books, no TV, no radio, and no window. The only color in the room was the red ink on the poster that gave escape instructions in case of a fire.

I took a shallow breath as a host of memories flooded over me that I had no desire to recall. I shook them off.

Sketch sat at a small desk opposite the bed. A single-bulb, green-shaded banker's light was on, and he sat huddled over his note-book. He was dressed in new jeans, a baggy T-shirt, and flip-flops. When I walked in, he looked up and showed absolutely no reaction whatsoever.

"Hey, Sketch." I sat on the bed and looked around the room. "Looks like they moved you to a new place."

He looked around as if the obvious was obvious to him too.

"How you feeling?"

Just then, a janitor pushing a dolly loaded with several cases of empty soda pop bottles passed in the hallway. Sketch saw the dolly pass, looked off into space, then slid from his chair and walked into the hall. He followed the janitor a ways, his little flip-flops smacking his heels, turned left, and stopped when the dolly stopped outside the men's bathroom. When the janitor walked inside, the boy knelt next to the empty bottles.

Evidently, between the nurses and the antibiotics, his back had quit oozing and was no longer soaking through his shirt. And his glasses seemed to fit his face. He leaned in close, read a bottle, and then pointed. I leaned in and saw nothing but a swallow of backwash that remained in the bottle. He pointed again. I felt like we were playing charades.

I held my hands wide like I was telling a fish story, then narrowed them to just a few inches apart. "Big or little word?"

He shook his head like he didn't have time for all that foolishness and pointed again.

I looked again, but still nothing caught my eye. I put one finger in the air. "First word. First letter. What's it start with?"

He rolled his eyes and opened his sketchpad. In two seconds, he drew the outline of a shape and held it up for me. It looked like a soda bottle. I reached into my pocket and pulled out two quarters. "You want a soda?"

He shook his head again, smacked the paper with pencil as if he were saying *Pay attention!,* and drew another picture. He held it up, and this time I saw a truck—the kind with roll-up doors on the side that delivers cases of beer or soda.

This time I shook my head. "I don't understand."

He looked into the men's bathroom, and when he didn't see the janitor, he slid the bottle from its blue plastic container and held it out, motioning me to look closer. He turned it slightly and pointed at the name of the bottler stamped into the glass.

I read it aloud. "Jesup Brothers Bottlers." I looked at the kid, who was looking at me. I read it again. "Jesup Brothers Bottlers?"

He nodded.

I held the bottle. "Does this have something to do with you?"

He pointed at the bottle, then opened his sketchpad and pointed at the picture showing the man from the waist up.

I put two and two together. "Does Bo drive that truck?"

He shook his head, flipped a page, and pointed to the hand holding the pliers.

I picked up the bottle. "Does Bo work on those trucks?"

He looked over each shoulder, then nodded quickly and darted back down the hall to his room.

Jackpot.

I followed him to his room, where he was trying to climb up onto the bed. His right foot was slipping on the double sheet, and all he was doing was pulling the sheet off the bed. I knelt down and held out two hands like you do to help somebody up on a horse. He hesitated.

I nodded at my hands. "Go ahead. I've got some experience with this sort of thing."

He put his feet in my hands as if they were a lion's mouth, and I gently lifted him up. I propped him up with some pillows and then pointed back out the door. "You want a soda?"

He shook his head.

"You sure?" I held out the quarters again. "My treat."

He nodded.

"Coke?"

He shook his head and scribbled quickly without looking at the page. He held it up. MOUNTAIN DEW.

I smiled. "A kid after my own heart."

I bought a couple of Dews and two MoonPies. He sat on his bed and ate carefully, not spilling a crumb. I sat on the chair at his desk, spilling crumbs all across the floor. When we finished, I stood and headed for the door. When I did, he stopped chewing and watched me closely—which told me more than a smile would have.

"I'm going to check in with the administrator here, and then I've got to get to work. You going to be okay?" I should've known better.

He drank the last sip of Mountain Dew and set the bottle quietly on the table beside the bed. As he did, it struck me how much we both had in common with that bottle.

I tried to smile. "I'll come back . . . tomorrow. Maybe bring a game of checkers."

He frowned.

"You don't like checkers? How 'bout cards? We could play slapjack or 21."

He flipped to a clean sheet. His hand flew across the page, then he held it up to show me what looked like matching king and queen chess pieces.

"You play chess?"

One quick nod.

"You any good?"

A second quick nod.

"But I don't play chess."

He thought for a moment, then both sides of his mouth turned up slightly. I read his face.

"Okay, tomorrow. Chess it is."

I turned to walk out, but he tapped the bottle with his pencil. When I turned around he was holding up his notebook. It read BYE, CHASE.

"Bye."

When I said that, his right hand came up, pushed his glasses up on his nose, and took the right side of his mouth up with them even farther. I walked out of the room and down the hall—my own flip-flops slapping my heels. The echo of my gait brought to mind the picture of Sketch, his room, and this place. I looked around, read the signs for the office of the administrator, and shook my head. This whole thing had just gone from bad to worse. I had done the one thing you never do to a kid like that. I'd offered false hope. His face told me that. And false hope is worse than no hope at all.

Mandy Parker picked up her office phone and sounded busy. "District Attorney's Office."

"Mandy . . . Chase Walker. I've got some information that might help you with our little friend. You got a minute?"

"Yes. Let me drop some stuff off at the courthouse, and I'll meet you at Starbucks in fifteen minutes. I'm in desperate need of caffeine."

I arrived early, ordered two double shot lattes, and didn't have to wait two minutes before she arrived. She wore a gray striped suit—the kind with a skirt—high heels, a white blouse, and nylons. When I stood up to offer her a seat, I had to look up. She was about an inch taller than me. "You been in court today?"

"Yes . . . a couple of different hearings."

I told her about my visit to the boy's home and how we'd played ring around the Coke bottle until I figured out what Sketch was trying to tell me.

She sipped her coffee and tried to read my face. "What're you going to do?"

"Thought I'd drive over to Jesup Brothers Bottlers and see if I can find anyone who knows Bo."

"Want some company?"

Chapter 11

After bouncing around the state from home to home, I landed in Augusta in a boys' home where the walls were lined with bunks, smelly socks, and too many pairs of the same kind of shoes. I remember waking up to the smell of cut grass and the sound of mowers. I could look out my window and watch those men in green suits and yellow earmuffs zip across the fairways on red machines. Between them and me stood a really tall chain-link fence.

About twice a day I would imagine myself hopping that eight-foot containment fence and riding one of those mowers home. There were only two problems with this. First, the other boys told me I was too short to crank it, but I told them that if I could get across that fence, I'd figure a way. My second problem was a little harder to fix.

It was a Tuesday morning when a man in denim signed me out and took me home. I studied him and thought he was just one more stop on the streetcar called my life. He was different from a lot of the men I'd been around. He was tall and skinny, his boots were dirty, and his jeans were faded and fraying at the ends. His sunglasses looked like the kind the baseball players wear that flip up and down. His baseball cap was old, and whenever he was inside he carried it in hands that were knotty and hard. He wore a gold ring on his left hand, a white T-shirt beneath his button-up, and his hair was cut real short around the sides and back—like you could see his skin— and the top was cut just long enough to comb over. Unlike most of the other men I'd been around who were always telling me what to do, he didn't talk much, but always seemed to be pointing his ear at me. The first time he shook my hand, I thought he smelled like a horse.

When we got in his truck he said, "You hungry?"

I nodded.

"You like Krystal?"

I shrugged.

"Well"—he flipped on his blinker and eased out of the parking lot—"we'll try Krystal, and if you don't like it, we'll go someplace else."

I looked in the rearview mirror, saw a cloud of white smoke, and smelled what I would later learn was burning oil.

He turned to me and flipped his glasses up. "That okay with you?"

In one fell swoop, he'd done something that no man had ever done before: he asked me twice in the same minute what I liked. And he listened for the answer.

We ate a sack of Krystals and then pulled into a convenience store for dessert. He left the truck running and reappeared a few minutes later carrying two brown bottles and two circular things that looked like huge hockey pucks wrapped in plastic.

He popped the top on a bottle and handed it to me. "It's a Yoo-hoo." He swigged his own and said, "It's like chocolate milk . . . only better." Then he broke open one of the hockey pucks and shoved about three bites' worth into his mouth. Barely able to talk, he motioned for me to do the same.

I pulled on the bag, which broke and sent crumbs flying across the cab of the truck. I tried to catch them, but doing so spilled my drink. I looked at the crumbs and at the chocolate stain on the seat and braced for the backhand. And the U-turn.

I'd seen it happen before. A couple picked up a little girl, and before they got out of the parking lot, they were back dropping her off.

But he just took another bite and said, "It's called a MoonPie." He chuckled. "Don't really know why." He looked out the windshield in a moment of measured pleasure. "I guess if you ate enough of them, you'd get big as the moon."

We rode three or four hours and then turned into Brunswick, Georgia. He glanced at me. "You want a tour?"

I nodded.

"You thirsty?"

Another nod. Then I shook my head.

He thought for a minute. "You got to pee?"

I nodded several times.

"If you pee, you think you'll be thirsty again?"

I smiled and looked at the plastic wrapper on the floor.

He stood outside the stall while I did my business, and then we bought two more Yoo-hoos and just as many MoonPies. We loaded up and stuffed our faces while he gave me a tour of the town that has been my home ever since.

We drove past the funeral home, where there must have been a viewing going on, because he took his hat off. Next came the movie theater. "That there's the Fox. Run by two brothers named Ronald and Rupert. Ronald keeps the books while Rupert tears the tickets. Ronald . . . he's pretty sharp, but Rupert . . . well, the engine's running, but there ain't nobody home."

I looked at him, a wrinkle above my brow.

"Oh, he, uh . . . he got kicked in the head by a horse when just a kid." He swirled his finger around his ear. "Sort of scrambled his thinker. But he's strong as an ox, and he's the smilingest kid I've ever seen."

Further down the street we passed a house with a white sign out front that read SMITH AND SMITH. He pushed his hat down tighter and tipped it back just a bit. "Attorneys." He shook his head and spit out the window. "The Smith brothers died years back. Now it's run by a couple of Buddha-bellies who are all hat and no cattle."

He peered into the window where a large man in a white shirt was leaning back in his chair, his feet on the desk, the phone pressed to his ear. "Uh-huh, there he is now, giving somebody a handful of howdy and a mouthful of much-obliged." We passed, and he tilted his hat further back. "He's probably talking to my brother."

I looked at him.

"Oh, yeah, I got a brother. Name's Jack. Year older. He doesn't claim me, but we're still blood." He laughed. "He thinks the sun comes up just to hear him crow." He waved his hand across the dashboard. "Unfortunately, most folks around here tend to agree with him." He pointed at a big, huge castle-looking thing on our left. "He owns that bank, but"—he pointed at a large white church on our right—"folks over here say he's still tighter than the bark on a tree." He talked, to himself and to me. "I used to work at that bank, and . . . I used to go to that church . . . funny how life works."

The confusion grew thicker across my face. He saw me and nodded again. "Yup . . . my brother's taught me a couple things . . . the first is that meanness don't just happen overnight, and the second . . ." He got quiet and flipped his glasses back down over his eyes. "Well . . . it don't take a very big person to carry a grudge . . . so, forgive your enemies"—he chuckled—"it messes with their heads." Then he laughed louder and patted the seat. "Oh, and maybe there's one more." His laugh was deep, easy, and told me he did it a lot. He poked himself in the chest. "Never judge someone by their relatives." He looked at me. "You want to see where he lives?"

I shrugged, and we turned east down the causeway. It would be my first time smelling the marsh.

We drove through the security gate. He waved at the guard, the gate lifted, and we passed through. He tapped the windshield. "I got this sticker up here that lets me in whenever I want. Makes it easier for me to get to these people's horses. But, in truth, I'm about as welcome around here as a skunk at a lawn party."

We drove past a huge country club, and I heard a strange sound on my right. After another mile or so we came upon a huge house, built up high and facing east. He pointed. "He lives there. Married to this woman who . . . well, we've howdied but we ain't shook yet." He shook his head. "Word around the barn is that she's got enough tongue for ten rows of teeth." He nodded. "And they ate supper before they said grace."

That one really stumped me.

"Oh, um . . . she moved into his house, stayed awhile, and then they got married. She's the second one to do that. And I doubt she'll be the last."

I nodded.

We U-turned, drove back south, and headed back toward the security gate. The sound, now to our left, kept drawing my attention. I couldn't place it.

He noticed, studied me a minute, and then said, "Ohhhh." He slowed, turned left down a dead-end street, and parked in front of some tall grass and a sand dune that was taller than the top of the truck. We climbed the hill, pulling on the grass to get over, and when I looked up, the world got a lot bigger.

That's one thing Unc did from the start—he made the world a lot bigger.

I stood there, the ocean at my feet, and listened as the waves broke on the shore. Finally he sat down, pulled off his boots and his socks that had holes in one heel and one toe, and offered me his hand.

"You don't really know what it's like 'til you step in it."

He led me down the dune and into the water. I stood knee-deep as the waves crashed into my legs. I'll never forget the power. It took my breath away.

Unc did that too. And then he gave it back.

He reached down, cupped the water in his hand, and sipped it. He swished it in his mouth and then spat it out in a long stream out over the waves. "Go ahead. Won't hurt you. But you probably don't want to swallow it. 'Cept maybe a little."

I did likewise. It was salty, swimming with sand and bubbles. I spat it out in more of a spray than a stream.

He laughed. "Yeah, me either. But sometimes you need to be reminded."

We stood in the water, nearly thigh deep. His pants were soaking wet, but he didn't seem to mind. And he didn't seem bothered that mine were wet too. We looked out across that expansive blue, and he pointed. Enormous black clouds moving fast from left to right climbed high into the sky with smaller clouds that looked like cats and dogs.

Lightning flashed behind them. He nodded. "Gonna be a real frog-strangling turd-floater." Thunder clapped and spread out above us. He looked up, unafraid.

I jerked, crossed my arms, and looked toward the sand.

"Oh . . . never mind that. It's just God moving the furniture."

I smiled.

"Besides"—he looked out over the water, talking to someone other than me—"once you've been dead, everything else is gravy."

We jogged back through the water, up the sand, and through the grass just as the first few tablespoon-sized drops began to fall. He grabbed his boots and held my hand, and we slid down the back of the dune. When we reached the truck, he lifted his head high to heaven, took off his hat, and opened his mouth wide. The rain pelted his face and wet his tongue. He shook his head, opened my door, and smiled. "Free water. Never pass it up."

We sat in the truck, drying off as the rain came down in sheets. It was the hardest rain I'd ever seen. The wipers made no difference. We could barely see the front of the truck through the glass. He smiled and leaned his head back against the glass. He had to speak above the roar of the rain on the roof. "It's raining like a cow peeing on a flat rock."

Lightning flashed close to the truck, the thunder echoing inside. I jumped, grabbed the door handle, and my knuckles turned white. He stared out the window, studying the underside of the clouds, and whispered over his shoulder, "Sort of makes your butt feel likes it's dipping snuff."

I wasn't quite sure what he meant, but his tone of voice and the laughter that followed told me what I needed to hear.

Minutes later, as quickly as it had come, the rain let up and then stopped altogether, letting the sun out where it immediately burned the water off the road. We drove through the swirling steam, past the country club, out the gate, and back down the causeway.

Twenty minutes later, we turned off the hard road and onto what would become the driveway of my life. It was dirt, patched with gravel, and lined with pecan trees that were draped in Spanish moss and chattering with territorial fox squirrels. Ryegrass—green as the ripe meat of an avocado—swayed in the breeze, forming the carpet that spread from the highway to the house. I counted six huge birds with long tails and more colors than the rainbow perched in the limbs of the trees.

"Those are Lorna's peacocks." He shook his head. "They make more noise than a roomful of women."

Beyond the trees was a pasture spotted with huge cows that had horns as big as an easy chair. We eased down the drive, skirting the potholes. Midway down, Unc stopped the truck, walked into the middle of the road, and picked something up. He walked it over to my side of the car, cracked it between his viselike hands, and handed me a piece. It was the first pecan I'd ever seen taken out of the shell. Until then, I thought they came in cellophane bags.

It was sweet.

I stepped out of the car and saw a white house with two stories, a porch that wrapped around the bottom, and enough room underneath for a dog to sleep.

A tall, slender woman met us in the driveway. Her hair was jet black, combed straight, and hung down to her waist. She wiped her hands, knelt down, and kissed me on the cheek. I remember because her lip was fuzzy, and while her hair was black, her lip was blonde.

"Hi . . ." She looked at the man in denim, then back at me. "I'm Lorna."

She held my hand and walked me into the kitchen. The table was covered with coupons and sweepstakes entries. She handed me a plate, led me over to the Crock-Pot, and picked up a big spoon. I held out the plate, and she covered it with brisket, mashed potatoes, field peas, and biscuits. We sat down, and she pointed at my plate with her fork.

"I didn't know what you liked, so I asked Liam, and he said he thought maybe you'd like what he liked." She tapped her plate. "Which is this."

I looked from her to him, unsure.

"Him . . . I call him Liam. Everybody else calls him Willee."

He smiled, but his face looked pained and his eyes were wet. He reached both his hands out; she grabbed one, and I did likewise. Then they bowed their heads, but no words came. He tried several times, but couldn't get them out. His hand trembled, tears dripped off his nose, and his shoulders shook one time. Finally she said, "Amen."

He pulled a handkerchief from his back pocket and wiped his face. Then he refolded it and slid it back into his pocket.

It was the first time I'd ever seen a grown man cry.

After dinner she slid a small bench up against the sink, where I stood with a towel and dried the dishes he washed. She led me out onto the porch, where we sat in rockers while he dug something out of the bottom of the fridge. He walked out on the porch carrying three cups of Jell-O chocolate pudding. He peeled off the lids and handed one to each of us. We rocked and ate chocolate pudding, and he showed me how to squeeze it through my teeth so it made your teeth look all brown and dead.

Lorna said, "Liam . . . that's gross. Don't teach him that."

He laughed that deep laugh, tossed his head back, and began licking the inside of his cup.

It was glorious fun.

At bedtime they led me to my room on the second floor; it sat on the front of the house just across the hall from theirs. It had a small bed and one dresser. Above hung a ceiling fan, and you could see the underside of the tin roof.

I didn't want to go to bed, but they tucked me in, turned out the light, and pulled my door half-shut. He must've known or talked to somebody at my last home. Us foundlings never slept much. You could get through the days okay, but nighttime was the hardest. It's when you remembered and wondered.

I heard the front door shut, so I climbed over to the window and looked out. He walked out beneath the moonlight into the yard, grabbed the sprinkler, and connected it to the hose. Then he turned the water on and aimed the sprinkler at my corner of the house. The water rose in a high arc over the porch and above my window, and fell lightly on the tin roof above.

Three minutes later I was asleep. And ten hours later, I woke up having slept like the dead.

Chapter 12

I spent the rest of the afternoon tucked away in my office perch overlooking the courthouse steps, the phone glued to my ear, working my own sources. By suppertime I had enough for my column. Red eyeballed it, made three corrections, gave me the nod, and said, "Get back to work. I want part two next week."

The following morning in the predawn darkness, I slipped out of my apartment where Tommye lay sleeping and walked across the yard and into the kitchen where Unc sat with Aunt Lorna, drinking coffee. He was dressed for work while she wore her slippers and a tired robe. The checkbook was open, Lorna was licking a stamp, and Unc was spreading cinnamon roll crumbs across the newspaper. He shoved the rest of a roll into his mouth, turned the paper 180 degrees, pushed it toward me, and raised his eyebrows.

MUTED JOHN DOE: A MARVEL AND A MYSTERY

Four days ago local fire department personnel found a young boy—now labeled John Doe #117—in a ditch off Highway 99 near the Thalmann railroad crossing. Naked except for a pair of cutoff jeans, he was disoriented and covered in ant bites.

Hours before, the local fire department was called to the scene of a car fire caused when a southbound train T-boned a green 1972 Chevrolet Impala. Authorities are not citing the car wreck as a suicide, as no note has been found. The boy was found the following morning, standing in the middle of the highway. Apparently he had been thrown from the car only seconds before the driver drove in front of the train. Doctors believe he is between the ages of eight and ten.

He has numerous body markings that would identify him, but his doctor states, "His most striking characteristic is that the boy cannot speak." To compensate for the inability to communicate, he utilizes a sketchpad, drawing pictures with a cartoonist's speed and an architect's detail. One nurse states, "He's a prodigy. The most remarkable thing I've ever seen. That kid can draw like DaVinci."

The sheriff, working in conjunction with the district attorney's office, has determined that the woman driving the car was not his mother and is investigating her identity. Mandy Parker, who works with the DA, says national databases have produced nothing of note. "They tell us that no one has reported him missing. Which, after a week, tells us a lot." The Department of Children and Families, along with the DA's office, has filed an emergency petition to place the boy in temporary foster care.

Scars, cigarette burns, and other markings cover the boy's body, suggesting years of severe and chronic abuse. That trauma has also apparently affected his memory, as the boy does not know his name, where he's from, or anything that might help authorities find his home or family. When asked his name, the boy scribbles in his pad, Snoot.

Medical tests confirm tracheal damage, suggesting his muted existence is not a choice. His doctor adds, "That further complicates any hope of ever recovering the ability to speak." A local law enforcement officer, speaking on condition of anonymity, states, "Somebody's been beating the heck out of this kid. And it ain't been just once. It's been many times over a long period of time. I pity the fool if we ever find him, because prison ain't friendly to people that do stuff like this."

Near the bottom of the page, Red had written an editor's note saying that the paper would continue to follow this story, and that part two would appear next week.

Chapter 13

Highway 25/341 passes out of the northern tip of Brunswick, through Sterling, and straight into Jesup—a drive of maybe thirty minutes. There's usually no traffic, other than logging trucks, heading either way. When Uncle Jack gained control of the Zuta and the bank, he built a house on the northern tip of the property—if you can call it a house. I've never been in it, but I'm told it has ten or fifteen bedrooms and enough space to house a small African tribe. Though he doesn't ride, he owns about fifteen horses and had a nice-enough stable built to board a Triple Crown winner. Case in point—the horses' stalls are air-conditioned.

I downshifted at the light at Sterling, caught the green, and brought Vicky back up to sixty. Mandy didn't seem to mind. Only problem with a bikini-topped vehicle is that it makes it difficult to talk at highway speeds. So we drove in silence, letting the wind mess up her hair. We soon began passing the Zuta on the left. After twelve months of nonstop clear-cutting, the earth looked like it'd been napalmed. That monstrous thing Uncle Jack once called a house sat off on our left, a half mile off the road. Surrounded by nothing but burn piles, it stood out like a sore, opulent thumb.

Mandy pointed. "Seems strange to have such a pretty house nestled in all those trees, and then cut the trees."

I nodded but said nothing. The truth would take too long.

Jesup Brothers Bottlers was a hole-in-the-wall place on the outskirts of town, hemmed in by chain link and razor wire. Several unwashed and unmaintained delivery trucks sat parked along the fence next to a long, nondescript warehouse. Sometime long ago the company name had been hung in large letters above the door to the office. Now all that remained was SUP BOTTLERS. On the gate hung a sign that read FORGET DOG. BEWARE OF OWNER.

The gate was closed, but the chain hung loose. I bumped it with Vicky's nose, and it swung open. I parked in front of the office door and knocked, but no one answered. I walked around to the one open bay door of the warehouse and whistled. Still no one showed. Finally I honked twice and stood next to Vicky.

Mandy looked at me and said, "Maybe nobody's here."

I looked around and shook my head. "I doubt it."

About two minutes later a shaggy, white-haired guy who was probably fifty but looked seventy walked out of the bay and into the sunlight. He was wiping his greasy hands on an orange rag and squinting in the sunlight. He wore blue pants and a lighter blue shirt with his name ironed on the front. He looked a lot like the man in Sketch's picture, but then any mechanic in a rented uniform would.

I read his nametag and waved. "Hi . . . Mr. Ruskin."

He kept wiping his hands. "Ruskin's my first name. Skinner's my last. Momma called me Rusky. And my kids don't call me at all anymore."

I stuck out my hand. "I don't have kids, never knew my mom, and my friends call me Chase."

He took my hand and shook it. At one time he'd had strong hands, but now the skin was loose, and softness had taken the place of calluses. "What can I do for you?"

I thought about lying but decided to try the honest approach. "Mr. Skinner, I'm looking for a fellow I think once worked here. All I know is that his name was . . . is . . . Bo, and that he might have lived in a trailer."

He squinted an eye. "You with the police?"

"No sir."

"The government?"

"No sir."

"Well, it's a dang shame. Wish you were. That boy owes me money. If'n we're talking 'bout the same person." He held up his hand to about my ear level. "'Bout this tall?"

I shrugged. "Don't know. All I've ever seen is a picture of him."

"Had a bunch of tattoos on his back."

"Don't know—I never saw it."

"You don't know much, do you, boy?"

I shook my head and smiled. "Guess not. I'm trying to do somebody a favor, and that's all I've got to go on."

He pointed at me. "What you do, boy?"

"I'm a journalist. I work with the *Brunswick Daily*."

"You writing a story on Bo?"

I shook my head. "No sir. But I think he might have known a little kid I've gotten to know."

Ruskin nodded. "I never saw the kid, but he used to talk about him. If'n it's the same kid." He flipped over a five-gallon bucket, dusted off the top, and sat down, leaning against the warehouse in the shade. He flipped the rag over his shoulder and looked through the gate. "He had this woman living with him. They were both drinkers. Bad for each other. He only worked here a short time. Maybe a year. Not too dependable, rarely showed up on time, but"—he held out both hands—"he could fix anything. That Bo did know diddly when it came to engines and anything mechanical."

"You know where he is now?"

"Sure." He nodded and took his time. "Prison."

That didn't surprise me, and to be honest, I was glad. "You know where?"

"Florida, I think. Somewhere in the panhandle. But it's been awhile."

I turned, took a few steps toward Vicky, and then turned again. "You don't happen to know where he lived, do you?"

He nodded. "Sure." He pointed down the dirt road that ran behind the warehouse. "'Bout a mile that way. Can't miss it. Only thing back there."

"Did he own it?"

Ruskin shook his head. "No." He pointed toward the office door. "Owner let him live there for"—he held up his hands and made quotation marks with his fingers—"security."

"You mind if I take a look?"

"Suit yourself."

Mandy and I idled down the dirt road until a white single-wide trailer came into view. Poison ivy had grown up over the porch railing, and kudzu was making its way along the pitch of the roof. A charcoal grill was overturned in the yard, along with three pink flamingos, a kid's bike with no rear tire, and the tireless rear end to some car. The grass was a foot tall, and Coors Light cans dotted the yard like seashells. Three cars stood on blocks beneath the shade of a scrub oak. Each was missing at least one tire, most of its windows, and even a door or two. All of the trailer's front windows had either been shot out or broken, and the front door was hanging from one hinge.

Mandy saw me shaking my head and said, "Pretty bad."

"Can you imagine being a kid and living here?"

She spoke softly, as if saying it any louder would make it hurt that much more. "Not really."

I pushed the front door aside and walked in. The squeaking noise of the door scared a herd of cats. They ran in eight different directions, and then the smell hit me. Evidently, they didn't leave the house much. The trailer had one bedroom, a bathroom, a living room, and a kitchen—all of which needed to be torched. Other than the bike out front, there was no sign inside the trailer that any kid had ever been there, much less lived there.

Mandy followed me, holding her nose and looking disgusted.

I stood in the living room, where one of the kittens eyed me with that take-me-home look. "You ready?"

She nodded.

Standing at the front door, I turned and eyeballed the place one last time. I spoke to both Mandy and myself. "If you were a kid living here, and you were told not to touch anything—ever, except you had this insatiable need to draw stuff all the time, where would you draw so that it'd never be noticed?"

She looked around the room. "Good question."

We spread out and began thinking like a kid who didn't want to get beat. It didn't take me long. Wedged into the corner of the den sat a five-legged table. A lamp sat on the floor next to it. *Why the floor?*

I grabbed my flashlight out of the console between Vicky's seats, returned to the table, knelt, and shined upward. One thing immediately came to mind—the Sistine Chapel. The underside of the table was a collage of thoughts or things seen by the kid. From a man throwing a beer can to a woman crying to a cat chasing a mouse . . . it was all there.

Back on Highway 341, the fresh air felt good and smelled even better. Neither of us said much for a while. We passed through Mt. Pleasant, through the light at Everett, over the railroad tracks, and to the northwest corner of the Zuta. Two more miles and we passed the northern gate on the main road. It was open, which was unusual, but given the number of logging trucks going in and out every day, not surprising.

"You in a hurry to get back?" I asked.

"I don't have to be in court. What've you got in mind?"

I U-turned and cut across the highway and through the main gate, which was marked by an enormous sign that read NO TRESPASSING. TRESPASSERS WILL BE SHOT ON SIGHT.

Mandy pointed. "You saw that sign, right?"

I nodded. "My uncle's father bought this property some seventy years ago." I waved my hand across the dashboard. "Unc and his brother Jack used to own everything from those tracks back there, south to Thalmann, east to Sterling, and west again to Everett."

Mandy calculated. "That's a lot of land."

"Twenty-six thousand acres."

"Who owns it now?"

"Jack."

She thought for a minute. "There's probably a story there."

I nodded. The thought of losing the Zuta and, more importantly, the Sanctuary, to Uncle Jack dug at me. I hated the idea. He didn't appreciate it, never had, and didn't deserve it. He was going to strip it of any value, drain it of its beauty, and leave it naked as he had every other property he'd ever owned. Then he'd sell it off to developers, who'd come in and build condos or golf courses or retirement villas.

When I get to this place in my thinking, where the anger burns and messes with my head and heart, I remember that life is not fair and was never promised to be so. But that does little good, and I still hate Uncle Jack. My hatred for him is simple: I hate him because he wants to take from Unc the one thing that means the most to him. The one thing he held onto. The only thing he's got left.

And some things are sacred. No matter how much money you have.

We passed beneath the major power lines that ran from the coast to central Georgia, cutting through the northern corridor of the property in its path. The main road snakes through the middle of the property, more or less cutting it down the middle, minus a big westerly turn to cut around the Buffalo. Vicky rumbled along, at home on the dusty roads.

With every corner, I filled Mandy in on more of the history. I told her about how Ellsworth had gambled with the money in his mattress, pulled the bathtub drain, made a fortune, and begun cutting the timber, which was then used from America to the Orient.

Her face told me she liked hearing the story. The all-business attorney even leaned back and propped her right foot up on the side of the door. In the middle of the property the road turned right, or west, and began following the outline of the Buffalo. On our left we could see the towering treetops rising up out of the pines. A mile or so later the road turned left again, crossing the Buffalo and putting DuBignon Hammock on our right.

When Ellsworth drained the property, he had to build a road across the Buffalo without hindering the water flow. A bridge was too expensive, and a dam defeated the purpose. So he sat up on his horse, scratched his chin, and asked himself, *What is strong enough to drive across but will let water flow through?*

It took him a few days, but somewhere in the Zuta the idea hit him. One of the railroad lines had abandoned three rail cars on an unused section of track on the western boundary. The two-mile-long track had been laid so that trains could pass each other if they planned it right. Sometime back, they quit using it as a passing lane and began using it to dump old cars. Three freight cars had been sitting there long enough to get rusty, so Ellsworth "borrowed" them. He dredged a section of swamp, slid the train car doors off the cars, dropped the three cars end-to-end in the water and—using a welding rod and cutting torch—snugged them together using the doors to close the gaps between each. He then covered the top with fill-dirt and sand so when you drove across you couldn't see the train cars. Actually, it was pretty ingenious. And for seventy years, water has flowed through, and horses, carts, and vehicles have driven on top.

We stopped on top of the train cars and watched the Buffalo silently slip beneath us. Tall cypress trees sprouted up out of the water on either side, along with purple irises that were just starting to bloom. Because of the rain, the water level was high, as was the fish activity around the bridge.

We eased off the bridge, through Arnette Field, around the Turpentine Shack—an old shack where they used to sleep while working the turpentine trees, down past the picnic grounds, and finally through Gibson Island, across the canal, and around the back pasture of the house and barn. Unc's Brahman cows were milling around our end of the pasture, and in the distance I heard Aunt Lorna's peacocks raising a ruckus.

Mandy, who'd been silent a long time, said, "Is that a peacock?"

"Yeah, my Aunt Lorna thinks they're pretty."

"I thought those things only lived in zoos."

I drove into the clearing, the house in view, and smiled. "Welcome to McFarland's Zoo."

"Please tell me it's okay for us to be here. I don't feel like getting shot today."

I laughed. "Unc and Aunt Lorna live there." I pointed at the barn where the light was on and the window unit was running, dripping water on the roofline below. "And that's my second home. I stay here when I'm too tired to drive out to my boat or just feel like hanging out."

Two hundred yards down the road, Bob the Turkey strutted into the middle of the road, fanned his tail feathers, walked a big, bragging circle around a peacock, and then hopped up on the fence rail and clucked.

Mandy watched in amusement, then waved her hand across the landscape. "You all got any elephants or giraffes?"

"Not yet, but I wouldn't put it past Uncle Willee."

The sun was going down, my nose told me that Aunt Lorna was

cooking pot roast, and lunch had been a long time ago. "You hungry?" I asked.

"I can eat."

"You eat meat?"

She smiled. "Yeah, when it's dead."

We walked into the kitchen where Aunt Lorna, wearing an apron, was standing over the stove stirring mashed potatoes. She came around the counter, wiping her hands on a towel, and I introduced them.

"Aunt Lorna, this is Mandy Parker. She's with the district attorney."

Aunt Lorna nodded. "Liam was telling me about you."

Mandy looked confused. "Liam?"

"Sorry." She pointed out the door at Unc, who was just then walking up the back porch. "Willee."

Unc walked in, hung his hat on a hook next to the back door, kissed Aunt Lorna, and shook Mandy's hand. "Ms. Parker. Good to see you. You hungry?"

Mandy nodded. "Yeah, I think so."

I set the table while Unc washed up and combed his hair. About the time we sat down at the table, Tommye walked in the back door. She had showered, dressed in jeans and running shoes, and looked like she was going somewhere. She waved her hand across the room. "Hi, everybody."

Unc stood up and kissed her on the cheek. "Hey, sweetheart." He placed his palm to her cheek and then sat back down.

"Tommye," I said, "this is Mandy Parker."

Tommye extended her hand. "Tommye McFarland."

Aunt Lorna stood up and began fixing another plate, but Tommye stopped her. "No, thanks, I'm not all that hungry. I'm just stopping in to ask—" She noticed the lemon pie on the cake stand on the counter. "But I'd love a bite of that." She lifted the glass top and cut a thin slice of pie. "Ouch."

Tommye had nicked her finger, and blood dripped off onto the counter. I grabbed a paper towel and was reaching out to mop it up when Tommye's other hand grabbed mine with conviction.

"I got it." She wrapped her finger in the paper towel and stopped the bleeding.

I reached in Lorna's junk drawer and pulled out a box of Band-Aids. I peeled the sticky end off one, and again Tommye's hand took it from me.

She smiled and tried to speak beneath the dinner table conversation. "Really, I got it."

I brushed her off. "Get lost. I can put a Band-Aid on a finger."

She smiled and held the bleeding finger behind her back. "Eat your dinner."

Mandy spoke from across the table. "Tommye, did you grow up knowing Chase?"

Busy with her finger, Tommye nodded. "Yeah, he was my date to the senior prom." She laughed. "He was pitiful. I felt sorry for him 'cause the guy couldn't get a date no matter how much he begged."

Mandy laughed, and I threw my napkin across the kitchen. "You can fix your own finger."

"You live around here?" Mandy continued.

Tommye finished cleaning the countertop and sat down at the table with her pie. "Sort of. At the moment, I live above the barn. I'm just home for a little while."

Mandy was just looking for conversation, but I could feel it coming. "Do you work around here?"

Tommye opened her mouth, but I interrupted. "She's an actress."

Mandy's eyes grew wide. "No kidding?"

Tommye nodded. "Yes, but—"

I broke in again. "She's been in L.A. about ten years and came home for a much-needed vacation."

"You been in anything I've seen?"

Tommye shook her head. "I doubt it. Early in my career, I made a few commercials, shot some underwear ads, but for the last eight years, I've been working in the adult film business."

Mandy's head tilted sideways while the words *adult film business* looked for a landing inside her brain. "Oh."

Tommye smiled. "When I was a kid, Uncle Willee and Aunt Lorna took me in and gave me my own room." She looked around the house. "So when I decided to come home, this is where my heart led me."

Unc smiled and nodded.

Mandy looked at Unc. "You've done that for a lot of kids."

Unc stirred his mashed potatoes around his plate and then looked up. "Years ago, I lost a son. He was kidnapped and . . . killed. Prison gave me a lot of time to think about that boy, being scared and wishing his father would show up and rescue him." Unc's eyes glassed over. "So when I got out, I decided—we decided—that we'd just open our house to kids, no matter their background or condition. We read an article about him"—he pointed at me—"about him getting older, passed over. And try as we may, we just can't get rid of him."

"Thanks. You can do the dishes by yourself."

Tommye tapped me on the knee and whispered, "Hey, can I borrow Vicky for about an hour?"

"Sure."

She said good night to the others, and we walked out onto the drive where night had fallen and the moon had replaced the sun. I grabbed Mandy's leather briefcase and my notepad from the backseat.

Tommye hooked her arm inside mine and whispered in my ear, "She's pretty."

I turned. "She's with the D.A. She's been assigned to this kid I'm writing about. And she probably carries a gun in this bag."

"And she's pretty."

I shook my head and pointed at the clutch. "She's gotten a little sloppy, so be easy."

She nodded, did that ponytail-rubber-band-flip-thing with her hand and hair, and then eased off down the driveway and out onto the hard road. I watched the taillights disappear and walked slowly back into the kitchen.

Mandy was standing over the sink, an apron tied around her waist and her arms covered in soapsuds. Unc was sitting at the table sipping his coffee. He looked at me and nodded at Mandy. "Hey, Chase, you can have her back anytime."

Mandy rinsed a plate and slid it into the dish drainer. "Well . . . if Judge Thaxton gives us a favorable decision, that could be tomorrow afternoon."

Unc let me borrow Sally, and I drove Mandy home. She sat in the front seat, looked around, and said, "I thought my first ride in one of these would be my last."

"Well—" I aimed toward a tree, swerved into the grass, then corrected back onto the drive. "You haven't seen me drive yet."

"Does he really drive this thing?"

"Yeah . . . this is Uncle Willee's way of laughing."

"At what?"

"His past, mostly. He quit caring what the world thought about him a long time ago."

Chapter 14

Two blocks off Main, down near the docks, the shrimp boats, and the seagulls who dine there, sits Kilroy's—an old militaria store that caters mostly to tourists. Half museum and half retail, the entire place is decked out like a World War II headquarters complete with Willys Jeeps, a Sherman tank, ham radios, and leafy, netted camouflage draping hanging down from the ceiling. They sell everything from hard to find surplus like flak jackets, empty mortar casings, and German wool clothing to full sets of armor for knights and their horses. In addition, they sell miniature collectibles. I saw what I wanted in the window, so I stopped in, bought the display, and then drove out to see Sketch.

His room was empty when I got there. I heard some boys playing and screaming out beyond the building, so I set the package on the bed and walked toward the double doors that led outside.

The janitor saw me and said, "He ain't out there." He leaned on his mop and pointed toward the cafeteria. "That boy . . . the one that don't talk . . . he ain't real social."

I waved, said "Thanks," picked up my brown paper package, and walked down the hallway to the cafeteria. Sketch sat alone at a table. He was still wearing Uncle Willee's Braves hat and was putting together a jigsaw puzzle. It was one of those puzzles with five thousand pieces, each one smaller than a quarter.

I set the box on the table, sat down across from him, and smiled when he looked up. He eyed the box and then me. "Go ahead," I said.

He set down the puzzle piece in his hand and studied the package. He slid his finger under one piece of tape, then another, and slowly unwrapped the paper. When he pulled off the bubble wrap, exposing the box, he looked at it, then at me, then back at the box. He flipped open the clasp that locked the lid, slowly lifted it, and his eyes grew wide when the fluorescent light from above began glistening off the pewter pieces.

Slowly he pulled each piece out, examining the detail. First something that looked like a castle tower, then something with a horse's head, and then two pieces that must have been the king and queen. He shut the lid, grabbed a paper towel from the wall above the water fountain, and wiped off each piece. Then he set the pieces in their proper places atop the board and looked at me.

I shrugged. "I've never played this . . . ever."

He raised one eyebrow, reached across the board, and moved a pawn one space toward me. That done, he pulled his feet underneath his butt, raising him up higher, then reached again and slid my outside pawn one space toward his. When he'd done that he looked at me, then back at the board. I caught on, copying his moves, making a few of my own, and as a result, he had me at checkmate in about three minutes. When his rook captured my king, he placed it on the table in front of him and raised both eyebrows twice. I looked at his side of the table, decorated with most of my pieces, and said, "You're a good teacher."

He flipped open his notebook, wrote without looking, and slid the paper toward me. YOU STINK.

I laughed. "Thanks."

It was quiet in the cafeteria. I saw some women busy in the kitchen, but for the most part we were alone. The kid was competitive—he liked winning, but he'd also grown comfortable with me.

After he'd captured my king for the fifth time, I asked, "How's your back feel?"

On the table in front of me lay one of his few pawns that I'd captured. He reached across, stood it up, set it in front of me, and crossed his arms. I had learned that while his mouth didn't work, he could talk just fine. Knowing what he said meant learning how to listen.

"Can I ask you something?"

He shrugged.

I looked around the room. "You like it here?"

He looked at me like I was from Mars.

"Okay, bad question." I paused, gauging my words. "If you could leave here and go to a foster home, would you?"

Again he wrote without looking, using his left hand as a straightedge guide for his right. He turned the paper toward me. THAT DEPENDS.

"On what?"

He wrote while looking over his shoulder. ON WHO'S DOING THE FOSTERING.

The kid was smart. "You remember my Uncle Willee?"

He tipped his hat at me.

"What if Uncle Willee took you to his house, just until they try and find out where you live and who you belong to?"

He pointed at me.

I nodded and said, "I don't live there anymore, but I'm around a good bit. I think they're gonna put you in my old room."

He looked at the chessboard and pointed.

I smiled. "It's yours. It goes where you go."

He wiped each piece again, placed them back into their fitted forms inside the box, locked the lid, and placed both it and his note-book under his arm like a stack of books. As we sat waiting on each other to speak, the only sound was his heels tapping like machine guns underneath the table.

Chapter 15

I sat on the bow of my boat looking out across the marsh. My boat had at one time been a seaworthy vessel, but after the shootout that nearly sank it, it needed more money than I had to get her back on the ocean. Automatic gunfire has a way of bursting more than just your bubble. This did not mean she couldn't putter up and down the inland waterways or float in one place for a guy who wanted to sleep in her. She floated just fine.

After I patched all the bullet holes, I spent enough money to get the mechanics working. That means that mechanically she works fine, but aesthetically she leaves much to be desired. This point did come to mind as I sat on the bow in my swim trunks watching the sun go down. And it was this thought swirling around my head when I heard my name being called from shore. I turned and saw Mandy Parker standing on the bank waving some papers overhead.

I stood up. "Wait a minute, I'll be right there." I paddled to shore, pulled up into the salt grass, and wondered how she'd found me.

She read my face. "Your Uncle Willee. And Google Earth."

"Oh."

She had to stand on her toes because her high heels were sinking into the mud. She laughed. "You weren't kidding when you said you lived on the water." She held out the folder in her hand. "The judge okay'd them. He can move tomorrow."

"You told the folks that?"

"Just got off the phone. They said they'd have his room ready first thing tomorrow morning." She paused and raised both eyebrows. "I thought maybe you'd like to go with me to take him over there."

"I would. Thanks."

She studied the view, noticed the fact that I had no neighbors anywhere, and looked at me. "How do you live out here? Don't you go nuts?"

"Come on, I'll show you."

She looked at my canoe. "What, in that thing?"

"Well . . . unless you can walk on water."

She stepped into the boat, sat facing me, and said, "If you flip this over and get my new suit wet, I'll . . ."

"What?"

She looked at the water around us and then at the shore getting farther away and placed her hands on the gunnels. "Send you the dry cleaning bill."

We tied up, I helped her aboard, and she looked across my home. That's when she noticed the view. "Well . . . it's hard to beat that."

It was sundown, and the light reflecting off the marsh had turned from root beer gold to fire red, swirled with violet and light patches of yellow and black. She sat on the bow, kicked her shoes off, and just shook her head.

"You hungry?"

She ran her finger over several of the patched bullet holes. She did not look impressed. "You can actually cook out here?"

"Well . . . there are some limitations. But as long as you like grilled fish . . ."

"I'll try most anything once."

The mullet were coming up river, churning the top of the water like

tiny swimmers in a race. Huge schools, three and four times the size
of the boat, fed through the grass beds, which brought them within casting distance. I coiled the rope in my hand, bit one lead sinker to help
it expand, then threw the cast net off the stern. I let it sink, pulled hard
on the rope, and pulled up an entire net full of finger-sized mullet. She
watched wide-eyed as I emptied the net onto the back of the boat.

"I guess you've done that before."

I put a dozen or so in a floating bait bucket and pushed the rest
back into the water. I grabbed two poles, baited both the hooks,
stretched the bobber knots to about six feet, and threw both lines off
the bow. The lines landed, the current caught them, and the bobbers
danced with the current.

Within a few seconds, both bobbers disappeared. I set both hooks,
handed her a pole, and said, "Okay . . . reel." In order not to get us
tangled, I walked to the bow and gave her space to work the fish from
the stern. This meant that, for a second, I turned my back on her.
Unc had done this with me a thousand times. It's how I learned to
fish. While I thought I was helping, giving her some space, hindsight
says something different.

She grabbed the reel, pulled like me, hard against the fish, and
the fish pulled back. There were just three problems with that. The
fish she was reeling was bigger than mine—a good bit bigger; her
drag was set too strong; and her nylons didn't grip the boat all that
well. That meant when the fish pulled back, it pulled her. And she,
with bad footing and not wanting to let go of the reel, followed the
reel—over the railing and into the water.

I heard the splash, and my first thought was *Please tell me that she
did not just go overboard.*

I slammed my rod in a holder, opened the bail to let the fish run
freely, and found Mandy struggling to stay afloat on the other side of
the boat. I dove in, grabbed her hand, and we pulled against the current toward the stern ladder. The depth beneath the boat at high

tide was twelve to fourteen feet, but at low tide, like now, it was closer to six. And the oyster beds beneath the boat rose a good three feet off the bottom. If she kicked too hard and in the wrong place, she'd slice her foot in half.

Somehow in the process of going over and under she had gotten tangled in the fishing line. This meant that every few seconds the fish would pull on her other arm, submerging her just briefly. She reached the ladder, pulled herself up, and stood soaking wet and wide-eyed in the back of my boat. I grabbed a towel and sat her down, checking her feet to make sure she hadn't sliced them all to pieces. When I didn't see blood on her feet, hands, or legs, I stood back and waited for her to lambaste me.

That's when she started laughing. Not only that, but that's when I noticed she still had the rod in her hand. I was wrong. It wasn't that she'd gotten caught in the line—she'd just never let go of the rod. After about three minutes, she was laughing so hard she was crying. Finally she handed me the broken pole and said, "That better be one really big fish." And to her credit, the line was still taut.

By now the fish was exhausted. I netted him next to the boat, laid him on the deck, and shook my head. A thirty-inch red fish that weighed probably eight or nine pounds. That might not sound like much to the non-fisherman, but an eight-pound red can fight like a thirty-pound trout.

I reeled in my fish and held it next to hers. By then, Mandy had caught her breath. She pushed the hair out of her eyes, rubbed her smeared mascara off her cheek, and said, "Mine's bigger." She measured with her hands. "About twice as big."

I dropped the fish into the live well, opened the hatch, and led her downstairs. "There's the shower. It gets pretty hot, so test it before you step in. And in that closet you'll find some sweats and stuff that might fit." I shook my head. "It's a good thing your fish is bigger than mine . . . otherwise I'd really feel bad."

I filleted the fish and sparked the gas grill. By the time she surfaced ten minutes later, I'd made cheese grits, sliced a tomato, and was nearly finished cooking the fish.

She climbed out of the hole, followed her nose, and sat opposite me, eyeing my work. "Wow, you really can cook."

I looked around at the mess I'd made and handed her a plate. "More of Uncle Willee's influence."

"He seems like one of a kind."

"Well, I'd hate to think there was more than one of him walking around. I'm not sure the world could handle it."

She eyed the two pieces of fish on the grill and said, "Which one's mine?"

I pointed with my fork. "The smaller one."

She flicked a forkful of cheese grits at me. "Get out of town."

I ducked and laughed.

I pulled up a folding chair for her, and we propped our bare feet on the rope railing and rested our dinner in our laps. We ate and chewed, watching the seagulls ride the breeze. Toward the ocean, ten or twelve porpoises swam upriver, flashing their fins like dolphins while hunting the mullet farther upstream.

Mandy eyed my right foot. "Is that a scar?"

I showed her the scar that ran from the bottom center of my foot and up the side of my arch. "Yeah . . . I stepped on a piece of glass when I was about three."

She studied the six-inch scar. "That must have been some glass."

"I used to wish it'd go away, but now that I'm older . . ." I trailed off. "If it weren't for this . . . I might forget."

"Forget what?"

"My dad. I only have one memory of him, and this scar reminds me that it was real."

I retold the memory for the ten thousandth time. When I'd finished, we were quiet awhile.

She pointed out into the water where I'd cast for our bait. "Is it always that easy to catch fish there?"

"Not always. Below us, it's pretty level. Maybe six to eight feet now. But out there it drops off like a shelf to maybe fourteen, even at low tide. So the fish hang out right there. It's safe, and there's usually an abundance of bait moving through in the rapid water."

"How'd you learn all this stuff?"

I shrugged. "Everything I know about fishing I learned from Uncle Willee."

"He's pretty good?"

"I swear, sometimes I think that man has gills."

"You know, most of the guys I work with don't ever talk about the men in their lives—and when they do, it's not to speak well of them. Seems like they're always fighting, trying to outdo one another or get away from each another."

"We've had our fights."

"Yeah, but I can hear it in the way you talk about him. You respect him. You spend time with him. And you seem to enjoy it."

I nodded. "When I was a kid, Unc had a boat. More of a big canoe really. Little 5-horse hanging off the back. If you leaned too far one way, it'd take on water. I remember one of the first times he brought me out here. He woke me long before the sun rose, handed me a biscuit, lathered me in sunscreen, baited my hook, and taught me patience. Since then, we've caught a lot of fish together."

"That seems to be the missing ingredient . . . *together*." She shook her head. "In my line of work, I'm surrounded with men who don't care . . . and it's the boys they spawn who pay the price for it."

I looked at her out of the corner of my eye, trying to figure out how we just went from jumping overboard like Jonah to dissecting the world's problems like Dr. Phil. I motioned with my fork. "Bad day at the office?"

She looked down and stirred the grits around her plate. "Sorry.

There ought to be a decompression chamber for DAs at the bottom of the totem pole."

"How'd you get assigned to the kid's case?"

"Oh . . . I asked my boss if he'd let me in on it."

"Florence Nightingale?"

She smiled. "No . . . it was just that picture of the kid. Sitting alone, in the back of that ambulance. No clothes, his body cut up, shaking, shivering, whatever. I just wanted to know who would do that to a kid. And why. And then I wanted to make sure they spent forever looking out through an iron grid."

"So, you're bent on vengeance?"

She shook her head. "No, justice. There's a difference."

"You learn that in law school?"

"No . . . the grammar school playground."

"You want to walk me through that?"

"Somewhere around fourth grade, we were playing on a jungle gym. You know, the kind that looks like a geodesic dome. Anyway, I was hanging, my feet dangling, and this bully ran up and yanked my underwear down and completely off my feet." She shrugged. "All I could think of the rest of the day was how to get him back. He sat behind me, and as the weeks went by I realized that his grades were a lot like mine."

I smiled. "Good eyes?"

She nodded. "Near the end of the year we had those standardized tests coming up that determine whether you're fit to progress to the next grade. I went to my teacher, told her that I'd be out the day of the test, and asked if I could take them a day early. I did, and when his tests came back . . . well, he repeated the fourth grade."

I sat back. "Wow . . . remind me never to come up against you in court."

"Of course I was mad, but I was fair. He sank his own ship. Should've studied more." She paused to finish her fish. "So . . . when

I see pictures like that kid in the back of that ambulance, scared out of his mind, I remember the school yard, and that every bully gets his due."

"Let's hope so. Speaking of bullies, any leads on Bo?"

"I think so. If it's the same one, he's already in prison. I'm going to pay him a visit tomorrow." She looked at me. "You want to go?"

I didn't even have to think about it. "Sure . . . as long as you promise not to tell Uncle Willee about our first fishing adventure. I'll never hear the end of it."

When Mandy gave Sketch the good news about moving to Unc's, the kid didn't seem all that impressed. A lot of people worked really hard and fast to make that happen, and based on what little I did know of him, I knew that he knew that. His reaction told me a lot. It said he'd been moved around more than once and he'd stopped getting his hopes up with each new move. I knew because I'd done it too.

Before Willee and Lorna took me in, I'd bounced around a good bit. The first couple of times, I'd go into a new home and open up my heart, and then they'd beat me, or stick me in a corner and collect state money, or feed me food and nothing else. So I turned cold, too. Why? Because you can't hurt cold. If you get all warm and fuzzy for each new set of arms, you learn that most, if not all, are just as cold as the last. So you learn that if you turn cold, they can't hurt you.

At least that's the lie you tell yourself.

As I sat on the bow of my boat, I realized the lie that Sketch was telling. His facade was just as fake as mine had been.

Something told me this kid had been taken, and somewhere out there was somebody who wanted him. They might not be able to keep him, or even to voice it, but somebody wanted this kid. My nose told me that.

I remember my first summer with Unc and Aunt Lorna. We celebrated my birthday on July 31, and Unc gave me two things: a Timex waterproof wristwatch that glowed in the dark and the promise to take me fishing.

He doused us in Muskol bug repellant, and we stepped out the back door at 5:01 AM. I know because I looked. I carried a knapsack filled with lunch, and Unc carried the poles and a flashlight. We walked out the back door, through the back pasture, and skirted the Zuta. There was no moon that I can remember, and it was as dark as I'd ever seen it in the woods. We stepped in under the cover of the canopy of the swamp, and I remember asking, "Shouldn't we wait 'til it gets light?"

Unc shook his head and stepped into the swamp. I remember this, too, because he did the one thing I won't ever forget. He clicked on the flashlight, but rather than pointing it in front of him so he could see, he held it behind him so that I could. We walked nearly a mile, skirting cypress stumps and bog holes and skipping over ditches. Midway through, I tugged on his pant leg. He stopped and waited.

I said, "Unc, how can you see?"

He looked around, shrugged, and said, "Don't need to."

"Why?"

He smiled and leaned over, whispering a secret. "'Cause I know where I'm going."

He turned to walk, and I tugged on his pants again. "But . . . but aren't you scared?"

He stood up, looked around, and shrugged again. "Of what?"

"Just . . ." I looked over my shoulder and out into the blackness. ". . . of stuff."

He knelt down and pointed through the swamp with the tips of the two fishing rods. "Ain't nothing out there gonna hurt you."

"How do you know?"

"'Cause I grew up out here."

"What about snakes?"

"Well . . . sure, there're snakes. But, they're a lot more scared of you than you are of them."

"And spiders?"

"Yup, there're spiders too. But they're little and squish easily."

"What about . . . monsters?"

"What, you mean like the boogeyman?"

I nodded.

"Listen . . . you might as well learn this now." He pulled me close to him. His breath smelled like coffee and his skin smelled like Muskol. "The only monster you need to worry about in this life is the one that stares at you from the mirror each morning. You tame him, make friends with him, and the rest of life is nothing you can't handle."

"Yes sir."

By the time we made it to the canoe, I was thoroughly convinced that he had X-ray vision. We loaded into his canoe and paddled out into the Buffalo. We were just downstream from Ellsworth's Sanctuary. Little pink blooms from the crepe myrtle tree were floating on the water. Every time Unc took the paddle out of the water, they stuck to it, only to wash off as soon as he slipped it back in. By 10:30 AM we'd caught nearly fifty bluegills and a dozen warmouth. Our stringer was full and trailing behind us like a ribbon off a lady's hat.

We fished until 11:37 AM, when he opened the knapsack and served lunch. Peanut butter and jelly sandwiches, with Oreo cookies for dessert. We tied the stern rope to a cypress and let the current pull against us. There had been a lot of rain lately, so the Altamaha was running pretty quick. Little swirls would appear in the water where the current bounced off the sandy bottom and created an undertow.

Unc pointed to them and said with his mouth full, "Be careful of those. Keep your head above them when you're swimming. They're not too strong, but if you're trying to come up and get a breath, it'll give you enough pause to make you wish it wasn't there."

I watched the swirls zigzag around the hull of the canoe. "Unc? How long can you hold your breath?"

"Oh, I don't know. Maybe a minute." He eyed the swirls again. "If you ever get caught in one, don't worry. They disappear as quickly as they appear. Just let it carry you down. It'll set you on the bottom, where it'll dissipate and let you go. It's just the way they work. My brother Jack and I . . . back when things were different . . . used to ride them just for fun."

We finished lunch, and Unc said, "Let me see your line."

I held out my pole, and he cut off my bobber and hook and replaced it with a little spinner bait called a Beetle Spin. He smiled, spit on the bait, and said, "The afternoon sun makes the fish kind of lazy so you have to rouse them out of their slumber. This"—he jiggled the spinner—"is too good to pass up. Fish just can't stand to let it go by. I'm not sure if it makes them hungry or mad, but either way they hit it with a vengeance."

He was right. We caught fish on our first three casts.

He pointed at ten or twelve huge stumps off in the distance. "See those? Back when my daddy first cut this property, he'd cut those huge trees, clear the limbs, then float them down this river to Brunswick and the sawmill. There, they'd cut them into timber and ship them all around the world. He used to tell me that parts of the Brooklyn Bridge came out of this swamp."

"What's the Brooklyn Bridge?"

"Oh . . . it's a bridge in New York City."

I dipped my hand in the water, testing the pull of a swirl that had surfaced just outside the hull. "Where's this water go?"

"Atlantic Ocean." He swallowed and tilted his gaze toward the invisible horizon. "If you're man enough, you can canoe all the way from here to anywhere in the world."

"Really?"

"Sure. You might need a bigger boat once you get to the ocean, but barring that, the only limits you face are those you place on yourself."

"Have you ever done it?"

"What?"

"Paddled from here to the ocean?"

He looked off into the distance again. "Yep . . . many times."

We were floating again, the current carrying us along at a pretty good clip. Unc turned the paddle, using it as a rudder, and steered us toward an arm-sized piece of wood that was lying half out of the water. It was dead and waterlogged. He tied the stern rope to it and tossed it behind us. It sank and dragged in the water about five feet off the stern.

"We're moving a little faster than I'd like," he said. "The log will give us a little extra drag. Slow us down a bit." He smiled. "'Cause there's good fishing in here, and we don't want to miss it."

I watched the swirls, saw the log tugging at our stern, and didn't feel quite as comfortable in the boat as I had earlier that morning.

At 3:07 PM we rounded a corner to find that a huge pine tree had fallen across the river. It would have made a good bridge if we were on foot and trying to cross.

Unc turned the paddle again and said, "I want you to lean forward and keep your hands in the boat. I'll tell you when you can sit up. Got it?"

I nodded and leaned forward. The only problem was that I had left my fishing pole sticking up too far into the air. Unc tillered us beneath the tree, but the hook on my Beetle Spin caught on the bark and began pulling against my drag. Without thinking, I stood up and reached for it.

Unc said, "Nope, Chase, I got it."

But it was too late.

My shifting weight dipped the up-current side of the canoe down into the water where the current, and increased flow of the river, caught it. Within a second we were upside down and swimming. The current grabbed me like a huge hand and shoved me to the bottom, where it spun me like a top. Then all at once, just as suddenly as it grabbed me, it let go. I looked up through the rust-colored water and saw sunlight. I reached out my feet, kicked off the bottom, and started soaring to the surface like Superman. Unc was right. It was fun.

Problem was, the current carried me downstream and into a chaotic mass of downed trees and limbs. It looked like an underwater beaver dam, but looking back, it was just a logjam. The trees were jammed up against an enormous cypress whose hollowed-out stump reached down into the water and spread out like the tentacles of a giant squid. Some were fat, some slender, but all fanned out and tied themselves into the river bottom. There in its arms, the logs piled up.

I drifted into the roots of the tree, where the jumbled mass swarmed around me, grabbed my clothes, and pinned my left foot into the V-notch of a root. I pulled at my foot, but only made things worse. I tried to scream, but the water wouldn't let me. I grabbed a limb above me, pulled as hard as I could, and lifted myself into what must have been a waterfall inside the stump. Given the rain and the increased water in the river, the level of the water had risen above the normal level on an old stump and created a small waterfall that would last only as long as the water level remained this high.

I poked my head in behind it where a cavity had formed and sucked in as big a breath as it would let me. I choked and sputtered, and the current began pulling against me. That's when I felt Unc's hands on my foot. The wood was cutting into my shin and the pain was growing, but I was more worried about my arms giving out. It was all I could do to hold on. I pressed in hard against the back of the stump and took another breath. I rested my head against my left hand, my eyes pressing against the face of my watch.

I watched thirty seconds pass as Unc pulled on the logs that had latched their viselike grip on me. At one minute, my arms were shaking. At two minutes, my left foot was numb, yet Unc hadn't let go. Two and a half minutes passed, and I felt myself slipping further into the water. Finally, at three minutes, when the waterfall covered my face and closed off the air, I let go.

When I woke up, I was lying on the riverbank, Unc beside me. He was coughing and sputtering like an old outboard motor. His face and lips were blue, and his eyes were bloodshot. He was sucking in huge gasps of air. I looked down at my ankle, which was cut and bleeding, but my foot was still attached. I wiggled my toes inside my shoe and lay back down. That's when I started crying.

Unc put his arm around me and pulled me toward his chest. His heart was pounding unlike anything I'd ever heard, and he had yet to catch his breath.

"Unc . . ." I tugged on him and cried again. "Uncle Willee . . . you . . . you could have died."

He tried to laugh, but doing so brought up more water and deeper coughing. "Nah . . . I've already been dead once. Can't die a second time."

"But . . . you stayed under for over three minutes."

"Really?"

I held up my watch and nodded.

"Well—" He wiped the spit off his mouth with his shirtsleeve that was torn and frayed. "That'd definitely be a new record for me."

In a half dozen foster and boys' homes, many men had been my caretakers or guardians. They had come in differing sizes, shapes, and sounds, and those that made promises broke them before they had time to take root. In general, they came and went, gave me as much notice as the gum stuck to their shoe, and never said or did much. Until now.

"But . . . why?"

He pulled me across his chest, his face a few inches from mine. He pushed aside my hair and wiped the tears out of my face with a muddy hand. He tried to smile, but his breathing was still difficult and raspy. He coughed, blew out more water, and behind his eyes I saw a broken, shattered man. Finally he said, "'Cause, Chase, nothing . . . not one thing . . . compares to you."

There, on that bank, soaked in that water, basking in that sunshine, lying on that man's chest, I hoped for the first time that my real dad would never show up and take me home.

Chapter 16

From inside my boat I can hear distant automobile traffic, the waves lapping the sides, and the wind rattling the rigging, but other than that, it's pretty quiet. So the sound of someone climbing aboard my boat at five in the morning got me up quickly.

I stepped out of bed, pulled my Remington 870 shotgun from the shelf above my head, and hunkered down next to the engine compartment, giving myself a fish-eye view of the hatch. Shadows appeared over the glass, then a hand rattled the latch, lifted it, and laid it down. A long leg slid into the hole and stepped onto the ladder. I clicked the safety off and waited. A second leg. A set of running shoes was coming down the ladder. Finally the person stepped off the ladder, and I looked down the barrel.

When she whispered, "Chase!" my knees went weak and I nearly peed all over myself.

I flicked on the light and saw Tommye standing in the middle of my boat. I lowered the shotgun and clicked the safety back on. "Do you know I nearly blew your head off?"

She pulled the hood of her sweatshirt down and said, "Well . . . that would certainly beat death by Alzheimer's."

"What are you doing here?"

She was bundled in sweats even though it was June in the Golden Isles. Probably seventy-five degrees outside.

"And aren't you hot?"

She looked around my boat. "I once made a movie in a boat like this. But . . . it was a bit nicer. Belonged to a Beverly Hills plastic surgeon. Everything was leather and—"

I shook my head and put the shotgun back in its cubby. "That's too much information."

She shrugged. "Another life. One I'm glad not to be living." She pulled a shoestring from around her neck and crumpled it into her hand. Then she pulled me by the arm and sat me down. She placed her hand over mine and dropped the lace. "I want you to keep this for me."

Two keys dangled from the shoestring. I eyed them, then her. "What're you up to?"

She leaned against me. Her heart was beating real fast, she was pasty with sweat, and yet she didn't seem bothered by the three layers of clothes. "Not now." She breathed deep and then placed the shoestring necklace over my head. It looked like something kids wore in high school. The keys came to rest in the center of my chest. She patted them against me and said, "Perfect, right there in your bird's chest."

"Thanks."

She hopped up, climbed the ladder, and looked back down through the hole. "Well . . . come on."

"I'm not going anywhere until you tell me about these keys and whether I'm now an accessory to some crime."

She laughed and stood looking out over the bow as the sun broke the horizon. "Not now. But soon."

I climbed up next to her. "What am I supposed to do until then?"

She looked at me, shrugged, and crossed her arms, looking back out across the marsh, which was yellow and light green. "Just keep them for me, Chase . . . just do this for me." Her eyes glistened, the corners turning wet, and her voice fell to a whisper. "I need you to do this for me."

Tommye had her own timing and her own reasons. I knew digging at her wouldn't unearth them. She'd talk when she was ready. She pulled a MoonPie out of her sweatshirt pocket, tore open the wrapper, and began to eat. She was spilling crumbs across the deck of my boat.

"Breakfast of champions," I said with a smirk.

She motioned toward the shore, where Sally was parked next to Vicky. "It was sitting on the front seat." She swallowed the last bit, stuffed the empty wrapper into her pocket, and climbed back down to my kayak, which she'd used to paddle from shore. "I'd better get back. I told him I'd only be gone an hour."

"I'll be over sometime today. I'll check in on you."

She paddled across, beached the kayak, and disappeared out of my drive.

I got to my office early—which meant about seven. I rarely get there any earlier, because I seldom have anything to say or write before about ten in the morning. It's not that I can't, it's just that Red rarely prints it, so I've learned to let my mind engage first and then start writing—usually somewhere shy of noon. I made some phone calls, sent a few e-mails, and joined an Internet chat room for novice chess players. One of the options allowed new users to view real-time, online chess games. I watched some guy in Portugal beat the pants off somebody in the States, and then someone in Australia barely get by a guy in England. Both matches convinced me that I spent way too much time goofing off in college.

I learned a few basics, like chess is played on an 8x8 board comprising sixty-four squares. As you face the board, the lower left square is black. There are two teams, white and black, and each has a rook, knight, bishop, king, queen, and eight pawns. It's not checkers, where every piece only moves one way; each piece has its own prescribed movement. Some move forward, some diagonally, and some can hop around. Lastly, if your opponent ends a move by uttering the word "checkmate," that's bad.

When I shut off my computer I didn't pretend to understand all the rules, which are many and complicated. Just because he can't talk doesn't mean he's stupid. Sketch is probably brilliant.

At eight o'clock I met Mandy in the parking lot behind the courthouse. Because we had to drive relatively close to the Zuta, I dropped off Vicky, and the two of us drove her state-issued Toyota Camry to the state prison in Bennersville, about ninety miles away. When we got on the highway, she reached into her briefcase and handed me a wrapped package. "For dinner."

I hefted the package and felt pretty sure it was a trade paper book. I peeled off the wrapping and found a copy of *Fishing for Dummies*.

She flipped her turn signal on and changed lanes. "Thought maybe you could use some help."

I flipped open the cover and read the note inside, *Chase—don't quit your day job.*

I set the book on the dash. "Thank you. See if I ever take you fishing again."

All around the Bennersville State Penitentiary was a twenty-foot-high chain-link fence topped with razor wire, cornered with four guard towers—each manned with armed guards. Everything about the place screamed *You don't want to be here!*

Mandy flashed her credentials at the gate, and we waited while the guard checked his visitors list. He handed us a sheet of paper to place on the dash and motioned us toward a large brick building on our left. It was five stories, the top of which was surrounded with more chain-link—which led me to think that there might be a basketball court or something atop the building.

We parked and walked inside, where one guard passed us off to another, who took us to two more guards who frisked us, searched Mandy's briefcase, and then led us to a room with two chairs, a table, and a thick piece of glass separating us from a rather unhappy-looking fellow on the other side. Mandy sat down, flicked on the microphone button on the wall, and motioned for the prisoner to do the same. He didn't move.

She spoke into the microphone. "Is your name Reuben Maynard?"

The guy looked at Mandy, then at me, then back at Mandy. His cuffed hands rested on his lap, and the number on the front of his orange jumpsuit read *74835*. As he studied her, looking from her face to her chest and back to her face, he rubbed himself. Finally he nodded and said with no explanation, "Bo."

If Mandy felt intimidated by him, she didn't show it. She held up a picture of Sketch and placed it against the glass. "Have you ever seen this kid?"

Reuben glanced at the picture and shook his head. Mandy raised her eyebrows, reached into her briefcase, and pulled out a digital video recorder. She turned it on, pushed RECORD, aimed it at him, and handed it to me.

"Now, just so we're on the same page, I thought I'd ask you again. This kid—" She tapped the picture on the glass, then held it in front of the camera, where the lens automatically focused on it. After about five seconds, she placed it back against the glass. "Have you ever seen the boy in this picture?"

He spat beneath the desk. "Nope."

Mandy sat back. "Wow . . . that's interesting. Because when I asked the boy the same question, he said he used to live in a trailer with you just down a little dirt road from Jesup Brothers Bottlers."

Bo chuckled. "You're lying. Kid can't even talk."

Mandy crossed her arms. "I'm wondering how you'd know that if you've never met him."

Bo's brow wrinkled, and his eyes darted from her to me. Mandy didn't give him time to speak before she reached in her purse and pulled out a pair of pliers that you could buy at any hardware store. She held them up to the glass. "You ever seen these?"

Bo began to fidget and then looked over his shoulder at the door behind him. Mandy didn't back down. She held the picture to the glass with one hand and tapped the glass with the pliers in the other. "Reuben . . . have you ever used these pliers to pull the skin off this kid's back?"

Reuben broke out in a sweat, looked over his shoulder again, and then said, "I want my lawyer."

Mandy dropped the pliers and picture in her briefcase and stood up. "Reuben . . . you'd better get one." She reached into her briefcase and pulled out a file. The label read BENNERSVILLE STATE PENITEN-TIARY, REUBEN MAYNARD, NO. 74835. She opened the file and spread it across the desk in front of her.

Reuben started backpedaling. "Hey, I get out of here in seven months, and all I want to do is serve my time and—"

She shut the file and sat back, crossing her arms. "Oh, you'll do your time . . . and a lot more." She picked up her briefcase, pushed her chair beneath the desk, and headed toward the door.

I sat there, still filming, wondering when to cut it off.

Reuben sat up straight and said, "Wait!" His handcuffs rattled on the desktop.

Mandy turned, raised her eyebrows, and waited.

Reuben opened both hands, like he was making a petition. "Yeah . . . maybe I got a little rough with him." He looked at me and realized he'd just said that on tape. He swallowed. "But . . . I didn't take him from that place. And I don't know where that old woman's necklace is. Honest."

I didn't know anything about any jewelry, but the pale expression on Bo's face told me he was telling the truth. Mandy played it perfectly.

Note to self: Never play poker with Mandy. She can bluff with the best of them.

Mandy sat down, folded her hands across the desk in front of her, and tilted her head, waiting. Reuben nodded, swallowed again, and tried to talk, but his tongue had grown cottony, and he looked like he could use a drink. Mandy phoned the security guard and asked him to bring Reuben some water.

The guard sloshed the water on the table. Reuben drank like a man three days in the desert and started over. "I was working the graveyard shift at the motor pool for the Fulton County Police Department. Working on cop cars. Now tell me that ain't ironic."

Mandy spoke slowly into the microphone. "Reuben . . . you're stalling."

"And I met this girl. Sonya. She weren't no good, but she were a girl and—" He looked at me, then back at Mandy. "Anyway . . . we had this thing going, and I learned she worked at this old folks home. You know, one of them places that smells like urine. Well, she was always talking about how these old people tell her stuff. Like about the diamonds and emeralds they used to wear when they was younger." He shrugged. "We'd been seeing each other a few months when she showed me some of the stuff. Said it was easy 'cause most didn't remember having it, so they never missed it. I liked the action, so we got us a rental off the Perimeter and started living the life. Easy money, free sex. You know, Bonnie and Clyde.

"That's when we really started working the old people. Her on the inside, working their rooms and what was left of their memories, and me on the outside, working the homes they'd moved out of. Then one day, she meets this kid, and 'cause she'd drunk her insides rotten and couldn't never have no kids, her motherly instincts kick in and she starts talking about us being a family and blah, blah, blah. Whatever. She was a girl, and I needed one. So I let her talk. Anyway, Sonya kicks the bottle and starts acting all respectable, and next thing

I know she's gone and filed papers to adopt this stupid kid. Couldn't even talk. What kind of dang kid is that? I just called him Snoot. Anyway . . . I didn't care as long as . . . well, she knew this old lady had taken to the kid, and she had a rock about the size of a gumdrop. So she used him like bait, lifted the candy, and next thing I know, I'm driving Sonya and her kid in the getaway car, and she's draped in some old lady's family heirloom." He sat back and paused. "We drove to the coast and lasted about a year 'fore she drank half our money and shopped away the rest. It ain't ever enough. So I took up at the bottling plant."

Mandy sat up. "How long ago was this?"

"Two, maybe three years."

Mandy reached into Reuben's file and pulled out a mug shot of a woman who looked to be forty with enough miles to make her look fifty. She held the picture to the glass. "This the woman?"

Bo nodded. "Sonya." He laughed. "And when you see the ol' biddy, tell her she better bring back my dang Impala."

Mandy pulled a second picture out of her briefcase and looked at it briefly before she showed it to him. It was the picture of the charred and burnt body of someone driving a car—a car that had gotten so hot the rubber had burned off the rims. The driver's fingers were still wrapped around the steering wheel, but most of the skin, hair, and clothing had been burnt off.

Mandy held the picture to the glass and said, "I'll tell her, but I don't think she's going to be able to hear me . . . and you're not going to get your car back."

Bo's head turned sideways, the picture registered in his brain, and he swore. "I knew I never should've picked up with that woman." He spat again. "And that was a good car. Paid for, too."

Mandy stood, threw everything into her briefcase one final time, and walked to the door. She turned and said, "I'll be in touch."

Reuben stood up and screamed, "But I still don't know what she did with all them dang jewels! And tell that crappy kid I want my baseball card back." He banged on the glass. "Don't let that kid fool you . . . he's a better thief than all us put together."

We walked out into the sunshine, into freedom, and I took a deep breath—one I'd been needing for about twenty minutes. We drove out of the security gate, onto the highway, and I looked at Mandy. "Remind me never to do anything to make you mad."

She looked in the rearview mirror and licked some lipstick off the front of her tooth. "What?"

"You're vicious."

She smiled and adjusted the air conditioner. "In my experience dealing with the Bos of the world, if you can ask the right question and get under their skin, then get them to backpedal a bit, they'll start talking. Reuben was just like all the rest. They all live by the philosophy 'If I go down, I'm taking somebody else with me.'"

"You think he was telling the truth?"

She tossed her head. "Mostly. But we'll find out. You think your paper will let you do some research in Atlanta?"

"The question is not will they let me research, but are the Braves playing, and if so, can I submit the tickets on my expense report?"

She laughed and then stuck a finger in the air, her tone growing serious. "One thing."

"What's that?"

"The kid ought to go with us."

I smiled. "Few things are better than a ten-dollar Turner Field hot dog. Every kid ought to eat one."

"Is baseball all you think about?"

"When the Braves are leading the pennant race, yes."

She set the cruise and began tapping the steering wheel with eight fingers, telling me her mind was working. "I need to petition the judge to take John Doe outside county lines, but I think she'll go for it."

"Who's the judge?"

"Thaxton."

I shook my head. "Better not tell her I'm going."

She laughed. "Yeah . . . I read your file too." She shook her head and looked at me suspiciously. "Seems like you've been spending a good bit of time downtown in run-down and condemned buildings."

"I'm studying the architecture."

"And why is that?"

"That would be the question."

"You play your cards pretty close to your chest, don't you?"

"When I need to."

"Listen, I didn't grow up here, but I've got two ears. You'd have to be an idiot to live here for any period of time and not know the story."

"It's pretty well woven into the fabric of this place."

"Don't tell me you actually believe the rumors?"

I nodded.

She frowned. "Come on. Really? After all this time, and all the construction, if it was ever there to begin with . . . you don't really think it survived?"

"It was, and I do."

"Even with the water level just a few feet below the surface?"

"Even with."

She shook her head. "Well, you'd be alone on this one."

"Won't be the first time," I said, smiling.

"You know, if I were investigating you, I'd look at an aerial photo and begin to wonder if you weren't just casing out the ZB&T."

"I'm sure my uncle believes the same thing, which is why he owns all the property for three blocks in every direction . . . and why I'm not allowed within fifty feet of his bank."

"That doesn't make sense."

"It does if you've got something buried and you want to buy yourself a protective barrier around the grave."

"Sounds like a conspiracy theory."

"Sometimes the truth is hard for people to believe."

She nodded. "Good point, but if that's the case, you've got your work cut out for you. But don't you think somebody would have caught him by now? I mean, all those municipal bonds are no good if you don't cash them in. Wouldn't they have to show up somewhere?"

"If he cashed them in at all."

"Why would you steal a bunch of money and never spend it?"

"What if the money wasn't the goal?"

"What was?"

"You tell me. What's worth dying for?"

"Mostly, money."

I shook my head. She might have graduated law school near the top of her class and be one of the best attorneys on the planet, but I'd had a lifetime to consider. "No, he had plenty of that."

"What then?"

"What was the one thing he didn't have?"

She thought a minute. "You don't actually think he framed his brother?"

"I know that the first recorded sin in the Bible, after the Fall, was the murder of one brother by another."

"What's your point?"

"Think about it, Counselor. For all intents and purposes, this town hung William McFarland on a murder he didn't commit—which, by the way, included his wife and father—and a theft of millions in municipal bonds that they never found, can't prove he took, and have no evidence were ever cashed in. They were just looking for someone to blame, and he was the easiest to peg. Lastly, if he did take them, doesn't he have a rather funny way of showing it?"

"Okay, let's say Jack did all this to gain control. Control of what?"

"The Zuta. Twenty-six thousand acres of virgin, South Georgia real estate. The bank is petty cash compared to the opportunity at the Zuta. It's no secret that I think Jack McFarland is a murdering crook, but I never said he was a *stupid* murdering crook."

"What makes you say that?"

I shrugged. "What I know about Jack McFarland. You of all people should know that appearances can be deceiving."

"True. If this job has taught me anything, it's that people are good at hiding who they really are. But what about William McFarland? No one ever explained that pardon. A lot of people around here were mad, thought he didn't get what he deserved. A lot still do. Let's assume for a minute an underground basement, tunnel, call it what you will, actually existed at one time. What good would knowing that do you?"

"It would prove Jack had or knew about access to the vault."

"So what? The same would be true of William McFarland."

"Sure, but for so long the finger's only been pointed in one direction."

"Let's say Jack knew. What was his motive? We're starting to argue in circles."

"Welcome to my life."

"Twice you've been held and questioned about snooping around the bank's surrounding buildings."

"Those are just the times they know about," I said, grinning.

She rolled her eyes. "I didn't hear that. The third time, the judge put you in jail until she could figure out what to do with you. Which"—she shrugged—"is nothing, because it's difficult to take anything out of empty and gutted buildings."

"Yeah, my uncle is good at that."

"What?"

"Gutting stuff."

"He says he's renovating for the historical society."

"Yeah, he's preserving history all right. If you believe that, I've got a bridge I'd like to sell you."

"You really don't like him, do you?"

"What is there to like?"

"Well, for starters, he's one of the most well-respected businessmen in South Georgia. Not to mention an elder in his church and . . . the list goes on."

I studied her. "Do you have a boyfriend?"

"What kind of question is that?"

"Well, 'cause if you do this to every guy you meet, it might be kind of difficult to find yourself on a second date."

"Sorry. Too many courtrooms. I get carried away. But, seriously . . ."

"See? There you go again."

"I'm not kidding."

I looked at her out of the corner of my eye. "You don't trust people too easily, do you?"

She took a deep breath. "In my job, that's an asset."

"But what about your life?"

"It's given me some trouble before. Seriously"—she wouldn't let up, which I began to see as a strength in her character—"looking at an aerial photo of the block, I'd say you were casing out the bank."

"It's not necessarily the bank I'm interested in."

"Really? You can believe that somebody, somehow, came up through the Spanish-era basement—that no one can find—and bored through a couple feet of concrete and into the old vault, where they then stole most of the town's municipal bonds, all of which were kept in individual lock boxes that required two keys, one of which was only held by the box holders?"

"You've done your homework."

"Law school taught me that."

"Is that the same law school that taught you not to trust people?"

"No, this job pretty much took care of that."

"Did you just break up with a boyfriend or something?"

She laughed and shook her head. "Even if the basement still exists, wouldn't it flood? What about the water table?"

I wasn't about to play all my cards at one time. Not until I knew more. "Maybe, but not necessarily."

"Then how do you explain the new high-tech vault you see when you walk in the front door?"

"I don't. I'm only interested in how they got into the old one."

"Just what are you looking for? Certainly, you don't think Jack McFarland is dumb enough to keep anything of value down there."

"That depends on what you value." I looked at her over the top of my Costa Del Mars.

"Sounds like there's a story there."

"Yes . . . but I'm not quite ready to write it."

There's a lot I don't know about my life. Don't know my real name, don't really know where I came from, who my parents were, or why they dropped me off on the doorstep of a boys' home. Lastly, I don't know much of anything about the man who raised me except this: I have lived my entire life in a chasm between hope and hate, and the only man to climb down into it with me was Unc.

And that's enough.

Chapter 17

The afternoon of my man-overboard adventure with Unc, we cleaned the fish and put most of them in the freezer in Ziploc bags. Needing some cornmeal for a fish fry and horseradish for the cocktail sauce, we drove to town. Returning from the grocery store, we were driving down Highway 99 when we came upon an entire fleet of flashing lights. Eight fire trucks, six police cars, four state troopers' cars, and an ambulance were parked in a random circle around what looked like a well head out in a farmer's pasture.

Unc wasn't too welcome most anywhere in town, but when he saw all the lights, he stopped and asked the trooper who was directing traffic, "What's going on?"

The trooper pointed. "Ain't good. Little kid fell in a well. Wedged in. Can't get him out."

Unc looked at the swarming chaos, then at me. He clicked on his blinker and pulled into the pasture. We approached the crowd of professionals who had gathered around the top of the well, and he elbowed his way in and quickly put two and two together. Most farmers in and around Glynn County feed their flocks with surface water. Few wells exist because the surface of the earth is so close to the water table, but there are exceptions and this well was one of them. It was a fifty-foot seepage well, and its walls were made of coquina.

The boy had climbed down into the well much like he would a set of monkey bars. Problem was, when he neared the bottom, he was hanging upside down with his flashlight when he lost his grip and fell. Given the diameter of the shaft and complications of the bars, the men in the group were all too big to climb down, and the kid—who was upside down and only partly conscious—couldn't grab hold of anything sent to him. Lastly, they couldn't disturb the construction of the well because it had grown brittle over time. If they did, chances were good it would collapse on the boy. That meant they needed somebody small who could retrace the boy's steps, wind around the crossbars, and take a rope down to him—even tie it around him if need be. And they needed all this done right then.

That's about the time that everyone looked at me.

One of the firemen knelt down and explained this in terms I could understand. When he finished, he said, "Son, we'll give you a flashlight and tie a harness around you so that if anything goes wrong, we can just lift you out." He raised his chin and sized me up. "You think you can do it?"

Evidently, they had already chosen the smallest among them to try this very thing, because a dwarf of a man was squatting atop the well smeared with mud and dressed only in boxer shorts. He wasn't much bigger than me. If he couldn't make it, then they weren't kidding. I looked at all the people looking at me, then back at the fireman. Each forehead was framed in deep creases.

I'd already had enough excitement for one day, but I figured we were on the upside. What else could go wrong? I nodded and then slowly pointed at Unc. "But he holds the rope."

That night, after Unc and Aunt Lorna had turned out their light, I sat up and wrote a letter to my dad. When I think about the start of my writing career, I look back to this letter.

Dear Dad,

Today I almost drowned. We were fishing when I dumped the boat over. Got caught on a tree beneath the water, and Uncle Willee spent three minutes underwater trying to get my foot unpinned. He did. But his face turned real red, then blue, and tonight he's got a real bad hacking cough. I think he almost died, too.

Then later this afternoon I climbed down into a well and pulled this kid out who was upside down and turning blue. He had fallen in, broken his arm, and couldn't get out. The fire department said they're gonna give me an award and the newspaper man says my picture will run on the front page tomorrow. But I was scared. I only did it 'cause up above me Uncle Willee held the rope.

A lot has happened since I've been here.

When I got here, Aunt Lorna baked two cakes—because I didn't know if I liked chocolate or vanilla better. Until then, I'd been passed over a lot and passed around from home to home to home. The kids on the bus call me a "reject." I think that's what you are when you don't have a home.

But Uncle Willee and Aunt Lorna gave me a room and helped me paint it whatever color I liked—which changed three times in the first three months. A few months ago, I wore holes in my shoes and Uncle Willee bought me new ones. Last Christmas they took me to Disney World, and I rode Pirates of the Carry-bean seven times. And when I wanted a bicycle, Uncle Willee worked nights to buy me one. It was an all-chrome, Schwinn Mag Scrambler with knobby tires and a Bendix brake. And then, a few months later, when somebody at school stole it, he worked nights again to match my savings and help me buy a new one.

Since being here, I haven't needed nothing.

Most days I wonder if I was just a mistake. Why did God make me? Am I really what the kids on the bus say I am? And I guess I get this look on my face, 'cause when I think that way Uncle Willee puts his hand on my shoulder, and I feel something like butterflies in my stomach. Uncle Willee says that's hope. At first I thought it might have been worms like I had before at that other home. I'm not sure what it is, but I think I like it. 'Cause when he does that, I start to thinking that maybe I'm okay. That maybe there's nothing wrong with me. That maybe God didn't make a mistake with me. Uncle Willee's hands are callused, real wrinkly, often dusty, and sometimes smell like horse poop. Usually there's a cut across one of the knuckles, 'cause he says his tools are worn smooth and they often slip.

I won't lie to you. I still cry at night. I bury my face in my pillow so he can't hear me, but he's got good ears. He walks in, sits down, and when I look up, sometimes he's crying too. I never knew grown-ups did that, but his nose runs too. I guess that's why he always carries this white handkerchief in his back pocket. He's a good storyteller, 'cause he'll tell me about his daddy and how he lived. They're good stories, too. I like them. When he's finished, we go in the kitchen and eat ice cream. But we don't tell anybody 'cause I still think crying is for sissies.

When I first got here, I'd sit up late at night and look out the window 'cause I thought maybe you'd drive down here and get me. I watched the headlights on the highway. I watched them come, then watched them go, but none of them ever turned down the drive.

So I wrote this letter to tell you that tonight, I'm going to sleep, and I'm done looking down the driveway.

Sincerely,
Your son,
Chase Walker

The next morning I put my letter in an envelope, addressed it to "The Dad of Chase Walker," got Aunt Lorna to help me put a stamp on it, and then put it in the box and flipped the flag up. Then I waited on the mailman to make sure he took the letter. He did.

Chapter 18

That morning, after we visited Bo, Mandy and I stopped in at the boys' home. The receptionist was watching a reality TV show and waved me past with a potato chip. The folks in the cafeteria were cleaning up, and the air smelled like a mixture of Pine-Sol and bad chocolate cake. The janitor's yellow mop bucket sat empty, his mop was dry, and both were rolled up in the corner where the marks on the wall told me he kept it.

I pushed open Sketch's door and saw what Aunt Lorna told me I'd see—the kid was teaching Unc how to lose at chess. The board was laid out on the bed where Sketch sat Indian style. Unc sat backwards in the chair with his legs on either side like he was riding in a saddle. He was resting his head on his arms atop the backrest and chewing on his lip. That meant he was losing.

Most of Unc's pieces were laid across the bedspread at the kid's feet, and most all the kid's pieces were still on the board making a pretty tight semicircle around Unc's king.

When I walked in, he tilted his hat back and said, "It's a good thing you showed up, 'cause I'm about to die . . . again."

"Don't look at me. He beat me in straight sets."

Unc shook his head. "Buy you books, send you to school, and all you do is chew on the covers."

Mandy walked in behind me. She didn't want to see Sketch as much as she wanted to see Unc. She'd been chewing on her fingernails ever since we got back into town. She curled her finger to summon him into the hallway, and he pushed back from the bed.

"Here"—he offered me the chair—"take my place. You can't make it much worse."

"Thanks a lot. Your confidence in me is inspiring." I flipped his baseball cap with my fingers, knocking it onto the floor. It exposed the bald spot and how his hair had shaped to his hat. He stepped out into the hall, twirling his cap in his hands while Mandy talked. I tried to eavesdrop while the kid concentrated, but chances were good he heard more than I did.

In the crack between the hinges and the doorjamb, I could see that Mandy was talking a lot with her hands. "I just want to make sure you're aware of what you're getting into."

"Yes ma'am."

"I mean, it's been awhile since you two have done this."

"Yes ma'am."

"That boy's parents could show up any day, and you might not like what you see, but you've got no control. The law will literally put him in the car and watch them drive off."

"Yes ma'am."

"Here's the simple truth. . . ." Mandy lowered her voice, telling me that she didn't like saying it any more than Unc liked hearing it. "There are more than five hundred thousand kids just like him around the country, and since we're pretty sure he's older than eight, the chances of his going anywhere but to another foster home before freedom at eighteen are about 70 percent against him. Once he gets past ten, which he might already be, the chances of his ever getting adopted are close to nothing."

Unc twirled his cap and nodded, speaking softly, "Yes ma'am."

"Are you listening to me? Because all I'm getting is this 'yes ma'am' stuff that's hard to read."

"Yes ma'am."

She shook her head and put her hands on her hips. "Mr. McFarland, I admire what you're doing. You all are good people. This boy deserves a chance. And I think he's starting to make a friend of Chase in there, but . . ."

"Ms. Parker?"

"Yes."

"Your case is shiny, but it won't hold lighter fluid."

"Excuse me?"

"I appreciate what you're doing, and I understand why. I really do. Were I in your shoes, I'd do the same. And you're right . . . the possibilities in that boy's future may hurt us. May hurt a lot. But I'm no stranger to the rain." He looked back at Sketch. "It's the hurting that makes it right . . . makes it worth doing." He sucked through his teeth and put his hat on. "'Sides . . . this ain't my first rodeo. So let us do what we're good at."

She smiled and folded her arms. Through the crack in the door, we made eye contact. "Yes sir."

Chapter 19

Dressed in his apron that read *QUICHE AND FONDUE ME,* Unc shucked corn while Aunt Lorna picked off the silk. She'd given him the apron for their twentieth anniversary, and I laughed every time I saw it. On the steps, Tommye chewed on a fingernail while I wrestled an errant Confederate jasmine vine that had climbed through the railing. I wound it up the porch column as the four of us watched the phone. It's not like any of us were practiced at this. The thing that kept us going was the idea that no matter how imperfect and insufficient it was and we were, and no matter how little we knew about this kid, we were pretty sure that here beat any place he'd ever been before.

Finished with the pile at his feet, Unc stood, ran his fingers around his waistband, and looked out over the plume of dust billowing across the pasture and blanketing the backs of his cattle. He took off his hat and brushed the brim with the back of his hand. "It's so dry the trees are bribing the dogs."

It was nearly dinnertime when Mandy called. As the state's *ad litem* representative, she explained that she would drive with us to the boys' home and effect the transfer.

We'd spent most of the afternoon cleaning house and spiffing up my room. Now it was T-minus thirty. When Mandy arrived, the five of us loaded into Aunt Lorna's Tahoe and drove to Brunswick. Since none of us quite knew what to expect, nobody said much.

While Mandy and Unc handled some paperwork in the office, I wandered back to Sketch's room. The door was cracked, and he sat on the edge of his bed, one leg tucked under the other thigh, looking out the window. I watched him from a distance, and the vague feeling of familiarity fell over me. *I used to do that.*

Tommye saw me lost in yesterday and tapped me on the shoulder and tucked her arm under mine. "Come on."

Ten minutes later we drove out of the parking lot—the kid sitting between Tommye and me. Seems like passing off a kid ought to take a bit longer. Like there should be some universal ceremony where a heavenly trumpet—about the size of Italy—descends from the clouds, blows really loud, and alerts every race and nation that a child's world is getting rocked. Wishful thinking. It only takes two seconds to drop a kid on a doorstep, so our process seemed prolonged in comparison.

We drove through historic Brunswick in pin-drop quiet. No one knew where to start. The only noise was the *wop-wop* of an out-of-balance front right tire mixed with the *ting-ting-ting* of what sounded like a piece of gravel stuck between the treads.

Leave it to Unc.

We passed a Krispy Kreme, and the HOT NOW sign was lit up bright red.

In the Disney movie *The Jungle Book,* one of the characters is a snake named Kaa who is gifted with hypnotic powers. Whenever he wants to exert power over someone, he starts singing this silly song and his eyes start making circles that give him total mind control over his victim, who was, in most cases, the orphan boy Mowgli.

Whenever Unc sees that sign, his eyes look a lot like Mowgli's.

Unc crossed a lane of traffic and made an illegal U-turn across the median, bumping us around the backseat and soliciting a muted "Liam!" out of Aunt Lorna.

His only response was to point at the sign and shrug. "Hey, I'm the victim here."

Tommye laughed, and I just shook my head. We bobbed to a halt in the parking lot, where Unc turned to the kid. "You like Krispy Kremes?"

Sketch shrugged.

Unc's eyes narrowed. "What do you mean, you don't know?"

Sketch looked through the glass of the store and then shrugged again.

Unc shook his head. "We got to fix that. Come on." He held out his hand, which the boy took, and the two walked inside. By the time the rest of us got inside, Unc was halfway through his self-guided tour of how they make the doughnuts. The kid's eyes were wide with amazement, which only fed Unc.

We walked out with two dozen doughnuts and a bag of holes. I carried the boxes and turned to Tommye. "You think we got enough?"

We got in the car, Unc handed the kid a glazed and said, "Try this and tell me that it ain't the best thing you ever put in your mouth."

Sketch bit into it, and Unc added, "Uh-huh. Good, isn't it?"

Sketch looked at the box while shoving the other half of the doughnut into his mouth. Unc handed him two more—a powdered and a chocolate-covered. The kid swallowed, then bit into each, filling his cheeks like a chipmunk. Unc waited for his approval, which was to quickly inhale both of those as well. Unc turned in his seat, clicked his belt on, and looked at Lorna. "See?"

Three blocks down the street, the kid had eaten five doughnuts and was starting to eye the bag of holes.

We headed out of town and passed the cemetery where most of Brunswick either is buried or will be.

Two years ago I wrote a story about the family—now third generation—that owns it. During my interview, we were walking across one small part of the expansive lawn, talking above the constant buzz of men on mowers and boys with weed whackers. They told me it takes the lawn guys a steady week just to keep the grass down.

When I was in high school and stupid enough to think that Saturdays were reserved solely for fishing, I used to give Unc a bunch of lip about how long it took me to mow the pasture with his tractor, and how—depending on the tides—it oftentimes cost me the best fishing of the day. I took that stupidity with me to college and, because books can't cure stupid, I brought it back home again. So when I wrote my article, I was still suffering from that sickness.

Unc read my article and left it on the kitchen table with one line circled in red. In the margin he had written *Time to paint your butt white and run with the antelope.* In English that meant, "Stop arguing and do as you're told." He was right, especially when it came to hard work—Unc had known a lifetime of that—but it's hard to tell a high schooler much of anything.

A block or so past the cemetery, Unc spotted a long line of headlights approaching on the opposite side of the road. He pulled into the emergency lane, put on his flashers, and we all hopped out. Most of the rest of the cars on the street did likewise. Unc held his hat in his hands while the six of us stood quietly in front of the car. Escorted by police on motorcycles, the procession passed slowly and then pulled into the cemetery further east.

Sketch looked at the cars, up at us, back at the cars, and then back at us. When I looked down, he had a doughnut in his right hand and his notebook in his left. Noticing that both Unc and I stood with our hands behinds our backs, he did too. I caught a glimpse of both Tommye and Mandy, who were trying their best not to laugh out loud. Neither Unc nor I knew the deceased, but evidently everyone else in Brunswick did, because the line stretched for nearly a mile. After it passed, we loaded back up and merged in with the traffic. Unc caught the kid's expression in the rearview and spoke to his reflection. "Around here"—he waved his hand across the dashboard, which meant *in the state of Georgia*—"it's sort of a custom to honor people who've passed on."

Sketch nodded and finished off his doughnut.

We pulled onto our dirt driveway and started idling around the potholes. On the first pecan tree was an old hand-painted sign that Unc had posted some twenty years ago. The bottom of the board had rotted off, but it still got his point across. IF YOU STEP FOOT ON THIS PROPERTY, I WILL SHOOT YOUR A . . .

The kid read the sign and its meaning contorted his face a bit. I imagine that sign didn't make for too good of a first impression, which was probably why Unc turned around.

"That doesn't pertain to you," he said, pointing. "Back some time ago, people used to keep coming around here asking me a bunch of questions because they were mad at me. But that was a long time ago. You don't pay it no never mind."

Sketch straightened, sat back, and nodded slowly.

Aunt Lorna gave Unc a quiet stiletto finger in the ribs and said, "I told you to take that stupid thing down. He probably thinks we're a bunch of nutcases."

Unc nodded and whispered, "Well . . . letting the cat out of the bag is a lot easier than putting it in."

Tommye laughed out loud. "You can say that again."

Mandy opened the passenger door, and Sketch climbed out. He stood clutching his notebook and the chess set, staring at the world around him as if he'd just landed on Mars—his face a mixture of fear and guarded excitement.

In football, one of the defensive players is called a strong safety—
sort of a cross between a true safety and a linebacker. While linebackers
primarily defend against the run, safeties primarily defend against
the pass. Strong safeties do both. They usually line up about five
yards off the tight end on what's called the strong side. When the
ball is snapped they read, or "watch," a lot of things at once—the
quarterback, the linemen, the tight end, even the running backs.
Coaches like to say their heads must be on a swivel and they've got
to grow eyes in the backs of their heads. The strong safety's enemy is
the offensive receiver, who usually lines up outside him. Sometimes
he's a decoy, other times he's the target of a pass, and sometimes he's
a blocker. It's those times that he's a blocker that the strong safety
must watch out. When the ball is snapped, the wide receiver makes
a beeline for the strong safety, who's got an invisible bull's-eye painted
on his helmet. The strong safety, who's concentrating on the play in
front of him, can't see the receiver, who's coming at him from one
side—the receiver is counting on this. It's the reason they call this
move a crackback. A great strong safety senses the coming wide receiver
without ever seeing him. It's a feeling thing that no doubt grows out
of a survival instinct.

Watching Sketch stand in the driveway, I thought to myself that if
the kid gained 150 pounds, he'd make one heck of a strong safety.

Unc grabbed a single duffel bag from the back of the car, and we
all stood around and watched. He walked up to the kid, reached out
his hand, and offered it. Sketch looked at it, at all of us, then slowly
slipped his hand inside Unc's.

The two walked up the steps and disappeared into the kitchen,
where Aunt Lorna had set the table. She followed. Mandy, Tommye,
and I stood in the driveway quietly listening to her breaking the ice
trays over dinner glasses. A few minutes later, Unc and Sketch walked
back out again—minus the notebook and the chess set.

They walked around the yard, through the barn, up to the fence where the cows were feeding, and finally across the yard, through the muscadine vines, and into the greenhouse.

Mandy looked at the glass building and said, "Why'd he take him in there?"

I smiled. "The orchid speech."

Chapter 20

We strolled over to the greenhouse and found the light on and Sketch sitting up on a converted bar stool. His feet were nearly two feet off the ground. Unc stood off to one side, pointing out orchids and explaining how old they were, how long he'd had them, where they grow, and how they grow. I don't know how many he's got growing in that house, but I'd say it's close to two hundred.

"There are about thirty thousand species of these things, and it's not exactly right to call them plants, 'cause they don't grow in soil. Orchids grow mostly in trees or strange places. They need bark to grow, not dirt. They need water—constant water—but not too much. Too much drowns the roots, too little dries them up. They need light, but you don't want to scorch them. Shade helps, too. They need fertilizer—that's a fancy name for plant food. And they need air. You give them those things, and an orchid can grow most anywhere. Side of a tree, top of a house. Orchids can be fragile, but they can also be tough as nails."

He walked to the other end of the greenhouse and tied a small piece of rope around the stem of one that had leaned too far from its bamboo support. "All they need is a reason." He returned and leaned against the countertop. "They like mild temperatures, not extreme hot or cold." He leaned in close. "Some even smell . . . like chocolate, raspberry, lilac, or citrus. It varies."

He turned on a faucet underneath his bench. The faucet fed into a series of PVC pipes that ran around the interior of the greenhouse like a great maze. The pipes turned and twisted, hugging the contours of the house. Every so often a smaller tube ran out of a larger tube, then fed into an even smaller rubber tube that Unc had laid across the root system of his orchids. When the faucet was on, it spilled small amounts of water across the roots.

"No matter what anybody tells you, the key is water. More heat, more water. Less heat, less water."

He walked back near the door, where he had moved all those that were blooming. Around the door was a plethora of purple, red, white, and even light blue blooms in all shapes and sizes.

"If you spend some time with them, take care of their roots, give 'em a good place to live where they feel safe, and give 'em just the right amount of water"—he ran his finger along a stem with twenty or thirty blooms—"they'll burst out in color and amaze you. 'Cause that's what they do . . . they bloom. A bird in the rain forest will eat a seed, then crap as it's flying over the canopy. That will settle in the fork of a tree some hundred feet off the jungle floor below, and yet that orchid will take root. It digs in, grows up, out, and blooms for all the world to see."

He sat down next to Sketch. "Now, we need to do one thing. We don't know your name, and you don't know your name, and that's okay. We'll come up with one."

Sketch's head tilted sideways.

"But we need to come up with something other than 'hey you' or 'the kid.' What have folks called you in the past?"

Sketch opened up his pad and wrote quickly.

"Snoot? That's what they call you? Do you like that name?"

Sketch looked at the word and shook his head.

Unc agreed. "Me neither. Sounds like something you do with your nose. Now . . ." Unc pulled a pen out of his pocket and laid the sketch-pad across the potting bench in front of them. "How 'bout . . ." He paused, waiting for Sketch to write something. He read the word and nodded approval. "Michael is a good name. One heck of an archangel with that name. You like Michael?"

Sketch shrugged.

Unc looked at the page again and held his pen just inches from the paper. "How about . . ."

Sketch scribbled quickly again while Unc read along. "That's a good name too."

He looked at Unc, looked at me, and then tapped Unc in the chest with his pencil.

Unc tipped his hat back and knelt down next to the bar stool. "Well . . . William's a good name. It's the name my father gave me . . ." Unc tried to laugh, but it was a cover, he was stalling. "But when it was just us two"—he lowered his voice—"he called me Buddy."

Sketch wrote again, eyeing the page and then showing it to Uncle Willee.

Unc nodded. "Then Buddy it is." He stood up, his knee joints cracking and sweat trickling down his neck.

Sketch stared at his notebook, then closed it and hopped off the stool. When he stood up, he looked two inches taller.

Mandy nodded. "Hi, Buddy."

He turned around like he was on a carousel.

Tommye, who hadn't said much all night, squatted down, held out her hand, and raised one eyebrow. She stuttered—something I'd never heard her do—and said, "B-Buddy. It's one of my favorite names. Always has been."

The air was thick with moisture and heavy with the aroma of lilacs and raspberries the day that Unc gave me the orchid speech. When he finished, I remember opening up my lungs and taking the first deep breath I'd ever known. It filtered down into my toes and made me feel like I could have held my breath for a week.

Sketch looked around the greenhouse, eyeballed us, then closed his eyes and filled his chest like a zeppelin.

Chapter 21

Following that first summer, Unc and Lorna enrolled me in third grade. In my various tours of foster and boys' homes, I'd encountered my fair share of bullies, but this one was different. He was the son of a welder who lived farther west down Highway 99 and rode the afternoon bus with me. He began by name-calling.

"Hey, orphan-boy . . . what happened to old man McFarland? Your Uncle Willee shoot him?" He didn't let up. "And where's all the money? You all buried it in mason jars in the backyard?"

I guess with a name like Rupert he had learned to get the attention off himself.

I ignored him, but when he didn't get a rise out of me, he started slapping me on the back of the head. The bus driver saw it, but she must have been a sympathizer 'cause she did little to stop it. She hollered once or twice, but he smacked me close to a hundred times. The bus route drove past our driveway, so I was let off literally within sight of my front door. My stop was just before Rupert's. I knew things were getting bad when he forged a note instructing the driver to let him out at my stop—nearly a mile from his house.

One afternoon it all came to a head. Rupert off-loaded behind me, and about the time the bus door shut he started laying into me.

I guess he wanted the other guys on the bus to see how tough he was. He tripped me, rolled me in a mud puddle, pulled my backpack off me, and started kicking me in the ribs. I wrestled myself clear and outran him to the front door. I bounded onto the porch and nearly ripped off the door handle. I only had one problem—it was locked. And our front door was never locked. Unc always said, "Let them come. Anything I ever had worth stealin's already been taken."

Hearing the sound of Rupert's feet, I ran around the back porch to the kitchen and pulled on the screen door. Same thing. I banged on the doorframe and peered through the screen. Six inches from my face, Unc stood, arms crossed, looking back at me.

I screamed, "Let me in!"

Aunt Lorna stood at the kitchen counter trying her best not to look at me.

Unc shook his head and said, "Chase . . . you got to learn to pick your battles." He looked at Rupert coming around the back of the house. "And this is one you fight. Now get out there and stand up for yourself."

Rupert climbed the steps onto the back porch, dangling my backpack in his hand. "Hey, chicken. Time for your homework." He held it like a carrot, dancing around like a cross between a chicken and a turkey.

I had started crying, so I turned back to the screen and said, "Uncle Willee."

He shook his head.

I turned around, wiped my tears and snot on my forearm, and stepped toward Rupert. I couldn't go back and didn't want to go forward. I figured words wouldn't get me anywhere, so I gritted my teeth and made a decision. I started at him on a dead run. When I got within arm's length, I crouched, left my feet, and hit him in midair. He toppled backwards, dropped my backpack, and landed on the ground below the steps. He probably had forty pounds and six inches on me, so I sat up and started hitting him in the stomach and then the face. After I'd popped him a couple times, I jumped up, waited for him to stand up, and when he did I hit him as hard as I could in the eye. Blood trickled out of his nose and down into his mouth. The last I saw of him that day, he was running home screaming something about his momma.

As Rupert ran home, Unc sat me down on the porch step and put his arm around my shoulder. "Chase? You mad at me?"

I nodded.

He squeezed me tighter. "I want you to listen to me."

I looked up at him.

"I don't want you using this as a recipe to fight every boy in school. There's always somebody bigger." He nodded at my feet. "Best thing God gave you was two fast feet. God wasn't kidding when he said turn the other cheek, but"—he spat out across the porch and into the grass—"turning the cheek don't mean be a doormat."

It was a hard lesson to learn. It was also one of the best.

The next day, Rupert's eye was black and nearly swollen shut, but that afternoon on the bus he never said a word to me. And he got off at his old stop.

Chapter 22

Aunt Lorna fluffed up Sketch's pillows and put his few pieces of clothing away in the dresser next to his bed while Tommye and Mandy cleaned up the kitchen. Tommye was washing the dishes, reaching into the soapy water, as Unc and the kid walked through the back door.

Talking to Mandy and not really paying attention to what she was doing, Tommye slipped her hand into the soapy water and immediately jerked it back. She turned away from us, grabbed a paper towel, and wrapped it like a Popsicle wrapper around her finger. Within seconds, the blood had soaked through the tip. Trying to make light of it, she held her finger in the air and said, "E.T., phone home." She grabbed another towel, but was careful to bury the first deep inside the trash can.

Aunt Lorna pulled the first-aid kit from the cabinet and emptied the Band-Aids, tape, and gauze pads across the countertop. Unc watched with measured restraint while Sketch walked up to Tommye and pulled on her shirtsleeve. Tommye looked beneath her arm and said, "Oh, it's okay. I just cut it on a knife down in the water." She bit her lip and tried to laugh. "Sharp, too."

Sketch pulled on her arm and stretched his neck, trying to see the wound.

She held it away from him, out across the soapy water, and wrapped the paper towel tighter. "Little Buddy, I better handle this one myself."

He stepped back and dropped his head, like he'd done something wrong.

Tommye knelt down, still applying pressure, and made eye contact with him. "You're sweet. Thank you. You probably know a thing or two about stuff like this. But . . . I have cooties."

Unc stepped up, patted Sketch on the head, and said, "You all have a seat, we'll be there shortly." He peeled the plastic off the gauze and took the lid off the antibiotic ointment.

Tommye spoke beneath her breath, "You're not welcome either."

He dabbed her good index finger with the ointment, then held out the gauze while she wrapped it around her cut finger. "That might need a stitch," he said.

Tommye accepted his help, realizing she needed it, but she looked at him with disapproval. When he had her bandaged up, he wrapped his arm around her shoulder and gave her that hip hug that people do when they're familiar with one another. She shook her head. "You know, you're not too old to get cooties."

He nodded. "Yeah, but once you've been dead, everything else is gravy."

Sketch showered, Unc touched up his back with that same tube of antibiotic ointment, and then the kid climbed into bed. Lorna had bought him some Spider-Man pajamas, which he seemed to like. The short sleeves came down beyond his elbows and the shorts fell past his knees. She smiled. "You'll grow into them."

Unc turned out the light, left the door open, and pulled a brass cowbell from behind his back. He sat back down on the bed and held it in his hands. "This is a cowbell. You hang it around her neck if you want to know where she is when you can't see her." He jingled it lightly, sounding a low, brassy clang. "It also makes a pretty good midnight bell if you need either me or Aunt Lorna." He set it on the bedside table. "Just give a ring if you need us, okay?"

Sketch nodded, but his eyes were wide, and I didn't see much sleep in them.

Tommye, Mandy, Aunt Lorna, Unc, and I sat in the den talking lightly, hoping maybe Sketch had worn himself out and he'd drift off to sleep. Thirty minutes later I crept around the corner, peeked into his room, and saw him looking wide-eyed at me.

When I came back to the den and reported, Unc nodded and walked out the front door, and I smiled.

Mandy asked, "What's he doing?"

"South Georgia rain dance."

A minute or so later, we heard a faint pitter-patter on the tin roof above the porch and Sketch's room. The sound grew louder. When Unc walked back into the den and sat down, his boots were wet across the toe.

Mandy said, "What's that about?"

Tommye sat on the couch, her feet tucked beneath her, and said, "Uncle Willee can't sing a lick, so he's learned to improvise."

Two minutes later, I crept around the corner and peeked into Sketch's room. He looked like one of those kids in a stroller whose mom has spent three hours pushing him around the shopping mall. One foot was sticking out from underneath the covers, and he was drooling out of the left corner of his mouth. I pulled the covers up around his shoulders and arms, which were folded in a protective fence around both the bell and his notebook.

The next morning, Sketch woke early and found me alone in the kitchen. He shuffled in, sleep still heavy in his eyes, and sat at the table clutching his notebook. I slid the cereal box across the table and set a bowl in front of him. He poured himself some Cheerios, mixed in some Raisin Bran, and covered it with milk. Then he walked to the drawer, pulled out a spoon, and we ate in silence—which seemed okay with him.

Chapter 23

It was nearly Christmas, my first with Uncle Willee and Aunt Lorna. Because kids dream, I had spent considerable time imagining that my dad, who by now had been reduced to the voice in my memory, would appear like St. Nick carrying packages, a smile, and a one-way trip out the driveway. Unc told me they'd put ads in papers from Charlotte to Miami telling folks about me. So my dad could come get me. I just knew he'd read it. He had to.

On Christmas Eve, just before dinner, somebody knocked on the door. I was standing on a stool in the kitchen helping Aunt Lorna cut up carrots and sweet potatoes. I heard the knock, my face lit, and I tore through the den, nearly knocking Unc over. I flung open the door, eyes wide, and found an older woman, glasses hanging around her neck, carrying a manila folder and selling a pasted-on smile. I pushed open the screen and looked around her. "Where is he?"

She looked confused. She reached down to shake my hand. "Hi . . . you must be Chase."

"Where's he at? He hiding?" I ran to the porch steps and cupped my hands to my mouth. "Daddy!" When he didn't answer, I screamed again, "Daaaaaaddddd!"

"Is Mr. McFarland here?"

Unc appeared at the door. "I'm William McFarland."

"Hi, I'm . . ."

I didn't hear what else she had to say. I ran around the front yard looking for his truck, because I just knew my dad wasn't coming to get me in a yellow Buick.

They talked quietly, Unc nodding his head every now and again. I ran back up on the porch to get a bird's-eye view of the drive and heard her say the word "termination." Finally, they shook hands, and the lady stepped into her yellow submarine and disappeared out of the drive. Unc sat on the top step and patted the wood next to him. I sat on one side, opposite the folder.

He put his hand on my shoulder. "Chase . . . you know how we told you about those newspaper ads?"

"Yes sir." I craned my neck to see around the railing that was blocking my view of the driveway.

"Well"—he scratched his head and let out a deep breath—"when no one answers them . . . the state sort of becomes your parents."

"What? But . . ."

"Technically, it means—"

I knew what it meant, and I didn't want to hear it. I ran off the porch, jumped the pasture fence, and ran across the pasture and into the darkness toward the highway. When I reached the other side, I jumped up on the fence and sat like a swivel, looking east and west, but the highway was dark and the night air cool. It crept through my clothes and turned my sweat to icy fingers.

A few minutes later, Unc walked up next to me and hung his arms across the fence railing. In his hand he held an empty mason jar with holes punched in the lid. He stood there a long time turning the jar. Inside, a single lightning bug fluttered off the sides of the glass. Every five or six seconds, he'd light his lantern. Unc turned the jar in his hand. "Scientists say that these things evolved this way over millions of years." He shook his head. "That's a bunch of bunk. I don't think an animal can just all-of-a-sudden decide it wants to make light grow out its butt. What kind of nonsense is that? Animals don't make light." He pointed to the stars. "God does that. I don't know why or how, but I'm pretty sure it's not chance. It's not some haphazard thing he does in his spare time."

He looked at me, and his expression changed from one of wonder to seriousness, to absolute conviction. "Chase, I don't believe in chance." He held up the jar. "This is not chance, neither are the stars."

I was hurting inside, and the streaks shining on my face didn't scratch the surface at telling how much.

He tapped me gently in the chest. "And neither are you. So, if your mind is telling you that God slipped up and might have made one giant mistake when it comes to you, you remember the firefly's butt."

The laughter walked up behind me, wrapped around my tummy, and tickled my ribs, finally bubbling out my mouth—taking the hurt parts with it. That's something Unc was good at. He gave me his laughter and took my pain.

He walked back into the pasture and began making wide sweeps with his arms. The air above him was lit with tiny flashing orange and yellow-green stars. Every few seconds one would glisten, shoot through the air in a circular pattern, and then disappear, only to be answered by another shooting star several feet away. No sooner had one quit than another started. Unc followed the circles, running here and there, pulling the lid off and then screwing it back on. Minutes later, he returned with the heavens in his jar. He offered it to me. My single scoop of the Milky Way.

I set the jar on top of the fence post and settled back on the top rail, staring through the glass with the real Big Dipper shining through the other side. Unc was quiet a few minutes. He looked up and down the highway and in the distance, a single headlight approached—the 11:15 freighter to the ports in Brunswick. In the distance we heard the horn sound, hollow and haunting.

He pulled the folded manila folder from his back pocket and struck a match on the fence post. He held the flame to a corner of the folder and turned it so the fire climbed up and swallowed the papers inside. He put his hand on my shoulder, turning the icy fingers warm. When the folder got too hot to hold, he dropped it in the pasture, and we watched in silence as the papers turned to ash. He turned me around, set his hands on my knees, and looked at me square.

"Chase . . . technically, it don't mean a thing."

The fire burned out. The breeze picked up the flakes of ash and spun them on the air like feathers fluttering off an angel's wings.

"Absolutely nothing."

That night, I lay in bed watching my stars swim around inside the glass and light my room in flashes. Before he turned out my light, Unc squatted next to my bed and tucked me in. It was growing colder, so he wrapped me in a cocoon and pushed the hair off my face. "I'm pretty sure that if your dad had read those ads and could have answered them, he would have. And in my book, no matter what the state says or does, he still can." He tapped the lid of the jar. "If God can make a firefly's butt light up like a star, then anything is possible. Anything."

Chapter 24

To help ease the transition, I'd told Unc I'd hang around and maybe take Sketch into work with me if he'd go. I was watching him eat his cereal when Tommye walked into the kitchen, looking sleepy. She pulled the orange juice from the fridge, poured herself a cup, and sat at the table, her shoulder leaning against mine. She winked at Sketch, then laid her head on my shoulder.

She spoke to me without looking. "I like Mandy." She sat up and crossed her legs. Her face was flushed, and her eyes looked glassy.

I placed my hand on her forehead, and she pulled away. Still hot. "How're you feeling?"

She shrugged me off. "I need to go to town today and thought maybe I'd make you my lunch date. You game?"

"You gonna answer my question, or pretend like you didn't hear me?"

"You gonna take me to lunch, or do I have to ask Spider-Man here?"

The kid, whose head was on a swivel as we talked, looked at me, eyebrows lifted. He wanted to know just as much as she did.

"You like barbecue?" I asked him.

He looked at Tommye, who nodded at him and then wrote a

secret note on her napkin and passed it to him. He read the note, turned the napkin, nodded, and slid the napkin across the table to me, then tapped it twice.

I knew what it said without looking. Tommye and I had been eating at Hawg Heaven since we were old enough to drive each other to school and appreciate good barbecue. I finished off my coffee and looked at Sketch. "You like Hawg Heaven?"

He looked down at the napkin and double-tapped it again.

"Okay, okay . . . I heard you the first time."

He sat back. Tommye gave him a smile and another wink, and in less than a second his spine grew another two inches.

As we were walking out the door, Unc appeared from who knows where and said, "Hey . . ."

Sketch looked up.

"I have some work to do today and thought maybe you'd be my helper."

Sketch looked at me, asking for permission to stay and at the same time wanting to know if I'd take him to Hawg Heaven another day.

I smiled. "Yeah . . . I'll take you some other time."

Unc put his hand on Sketch's shoulder and looked at Tommye and me. "Good, 'cause I think they need to have some grown-up talk."

Hawg Heaven sits just north of the causeway that leads out of Brunswick and onto St. Simons Island. Famous for their pulled pork and breaded French fries, they're a local staple.

We sat at a booth in the back, Tommye with her back to the room and still wearing her sunglasses even after the iced tea had been delivered.

I leaned across the table. "Not too bright in here."

She nodded and said, "Uh-huh."

After we ordered, I noticed five guys in white shirts and ties sitting at the table in the center of the room whispering and looking our way.

Every now and then one of them would utter a hyena laugh. A few minutes later, the tallest and broadest walked over to the table and sat down next to Tommye, brushing his shoulder to hers. He threw his business card on the table. His voice betrayed him—he was nervous.

"My buddies bet me a good bit of money that I wouldn't walk over here, tell you I've seen most of your movies, and offer to let you star in one with me."

Tommye slid her glasses down to the end of her nose, turned just slightly, and noticed the wedding band on his left hand. She was wearing a sweatshirt but looked cold, and the dark shadows behind her eyes had only gotten darker. She looked at me but spoke to him. "There was a day when I'd take that as a compliment, but I guess that really just tells you how little I thought of myself." She tapped his wedding band with her fingernail. "Go home to your wife and burn the movies."

"Oh . . ." He turned, looked behind him, got a giggle out of the table, and then turned back to Tommye. He put his hand on her thigh. "I love it when you talk dirty to me."

She read his business card and looked at the table behind her. "Robert . . . you all got money?"

He threw a money clip on the table. The wad was thick, and Thomas Jefferson's face sat on top.

She eyed the parking lot. "You got a car?"

"At least."

She put her hand on his shoulder. "Let's go." She slid her glasses over her head and looked at me. "I'll be right back."

Robert lit up like he'd just won the Georgia State Powerball. He stood up and waved her in front of him—some sort of sick version of a Southern gentleman.

She slid off the bench, grabbed my keys, handed me her glasses, and said, "Hold this for me."

"You sure you want—?"

She waved me off. "Easy. I got this."

She slid the ignition key almost an inch through her index and middle finger, faked a practiced smile, and threw a stiletto-jab into the soft spot beneath Robert's Adam's apple. He grabbed his throat, choking, which opened him up to the vicious right that followed. One hand on his throat, the other on his groin, he doubled over and crumpled. His four wide-eyed compatriots stood up, toppling three chairs. Tommye straddled Robert like a calf roper, grabbed the guy's testicles with both hands and squeezed, using her thumbs for emphasis. The only thing louder than the waitress's scream was his—only it was an octave higher.

She leaned over him and spoke loud enough for the surrounding tables to hear. "I made a couple hundred movies, and I regret every . . . single . . . one. I don't care what you've seen, watched, or dreamed, the only thing sicker than me . . . is you."

In one violent pull, Tommye ripped her hands upward, producing an involuntary and geyserlike vomit from Robert. "Maybe you wastoids could consider for just a moment that it's all a lie. Nothing but evil. On me . . . and on you." She spoke through gritted teeth, holding back tears that I guessed she'd held a long time. "It's a sickness worse than what's floating in me." She looked out the window and shook her head, talking to the marsh and the ocean. "The only one sicker than me . . . is you."

Tommye looked around the restaurant, then kicked Robert, who had made it to his knees. The blow caught him in the stomach and dropped him. Tommye grabbed her glasses off the table and dropped back down into the booth, slid over to the wall, leaned against it, and closed her eyes. She was breathing heavily, her face was ghostly white, and she was sweating. Her lips were caked white and her tongue was blue.

Robert slithered off the carpet only to find one of the cooks standing at his table with a rather large knife, asking him if he needed an escort out. The giggle-crew left, and the waitress delivered our food. She set the plates down and said, "Lunch is on us."

Minutes passed as I tried to make sense of what Tommye had said. Between the naps, the fever, the dark eyes, skin-and-bones complexion, and fever blister that never went away, it all fell into place.

All I could do was stare at her.

Feeling the weight of every eye in the restaurant, and that maybe we'd worn out our welcome, Tommye called the waitress over and asked for some to-go boxes. We walked out, stepped into Vicky, and I sat with my foot on the clutch.

Only after I turned on the causeway, drove to the island, and zigzagged to the lighthouse did the tears fall out from behind my sunglasses and land on my T-shirt.

Tommye leaned against the seat, tired, her breathing shallow and measured, but when she saw the tears, she leaned across and wiped them with her palm. "Hey." She grabbed my chin. "Everybody dies. I'm just . . ." She shook her head and faded off.

We walked around the lighthouse to the sidewalk that ran along the bulkhead where the Altamaha met the ocean. The sun sparkled painfully on the water, and somewhere off in the distance the jack crevalles were hunting in packs and tearing into the mullet atop the water. We sat on a park bench and watched the flurry.

Lost in the horizon, I whispered, "How?"

She laughed, leaned back on the bench, and laid her head on my shoulder. "You want the truth, or you want me to lie to you?" She read my expression and said, "Okay . . . we'll try the truth." She crossed her arms, tried to breathe deep, and for the first time I heard a wheeze and a deep gurgle. "Well . . . it's pretty simple. You sleep with enough of the wrong guys and do enough of the wrong drugs with the wrong needles and do all that over a long enough period of time, and . . . it's a given."

"When were you going to tell me?"

She shrugged. "I was trying to tell you today . . . just maybe not like . . . that."

Moments passed.

"What is it, exactly?"

A long pause. "Three differing strands of HIV. Mixed with Hepatitis A, B, and C. There's some other stuff, but those are the biggies."

"How long?"

She laughed. "I'm not supposed to be here now."

"What about the doctors? Can't they—"

She shook her head. "I waited too long."

"Well . . . you're here now. Why can't we start now?"

"The virus . . . or viruses . . . that I have are too strong now. They compete with each other. By attacking one, I strengthen one or both of the others, speeding things up."

"I thought . . ."

She put her finger on my lips. "Hey . . ."

"Why'd you do it?"

"When I got to L.A., I found a place of respect and recognition— albeit a sick and twisted version—where I didn't have to hide my . . . me."

"But . . ."

She put her arms around my neck and shoulders and slung her legs over mine. She spoke softly, "Damaged souls look for other dam-aged souls. And when we find each other, we coexist. Out there . . . we were just medicating the black hole inside each of us. I found a family out there. And it took a lot of drugs to keep the family together."

Another tear ran down my face.

"Chase—" She ran her fingers along the veins in her arm. "This . . . this is a gift."

I shook my head. "Not to me."

"Chase, I'm done running. . . ." She looked north up the island. "He can't hurt me anymore. The girl you once knew . . . I sold her a long time ago on some set I've now forgotten. I've done things . . ." She shook it off. "I don't want to be her, and I don't want to live in her skin. I'm done."

"I'd have come and gotten you."

She kissed my cheek where the tear had fallen. "I know."

"Why didn't you . . ."

Another long pause. "I should have." She turned my face to hers. "Chase, I came home for you. I'm not leaving with regrets."

The sun's reflection off the water was harsh and painful.

She stood up, pulled on my arm, and said, "Come on, take me for a drive."

Chapter 25

Tommye always had a thing with numbers. In first grade she was always the first to finish the sixty-second math quizzes. In fourth grade they started her in algebra, and in high school she scored a 5 on the AP calculus test. Whereas most of us just added them together, she saw numbers like pieces in a three-dimensional jigsaw puzzle.

I grew up reading the sports page and the ups and downs of players and their teams. While I read it for the drama, Tommye read the same pages and took away a wealth of information to which I seldom paid attention. She knew batting averages, on-base percentages, ERAs, win-loss records, etc. And she could file all of it away with an uncanny ability to recall any scrap of information at a moment's notice.

At the breakfast table, I'd recount the story of a dropped touchdown pass by a league MVP, or a ninth-inning, come-from behind win on the shoulders of a home-run slugger, or who won the 100-meter dash in the Olympics. Tommye would sit Indian style, her bowl of cereal getting soggy, and whenever I'd take a breath, she'd straighten and fill in how many other passes that receiver had dropped, how many times the batter had struck out prior to his game-winning home run, and the split-times for second, third, and fourth place. Second only to her photographic memory was her excitement. Somehow, knowing that information and being able to fill it in on demand gave her the same fulfillment that the drama gave me.

Oftentimes at night, when Unc and Aunt Lorna were watching a game, they'd let us turn down the volume and pretend to call the game. I was the play-by-play commentator, and Tommye was the color man. Unc never laughed so hard.

TO some boys, Turner Field is better than Disney World. It was for Unc and me. Back then it was called Fulton County Stadium, but it's the same thing: the Braves played there. In 1991, after a long time of what Unc called "sucking hind teat," the Braves finally put it all together.

This came on the heels of most of Georgia calling for Bobby Cox's head on a platter after he traded Dale Murphy to the Philadelphia Phillies. But we quickly forgave him when he brought in Tom Glavine, Steve Avery, and John Smoltz—who would win fifty games between them. Meanwhile, things in the field had gotten pretty good too: Dave Justice, Ron Gant, Francisco Cabrera, Mark Lemke, Gregg Olsen, Sid Bream, and the league's unexpected Most Valuable Player and batting champion Terry Pendleton. The Braves started slow that year, but went 53-28 over the last three months of the season and, winning eight of their last nine, edged the Los Angeles Dodgers by one game.

After defeating the Pirates in seven games in the NLCS, the Braves found themselves facing the Minnesota Twins in the World Series. ESPN ranks that contest as the best ever played, because a single run decided five of the seven games. We watched all ten innings of Game 7 on television and mourned for a week after it ended.

Then came the miracle of 1992.

It was a Cinderella season.

The Braves had split six games with the Pirates and brought the NLCS back to Atlanta. If they won, they would earn a return trip to the World Series, and if they lost . . . well, I'd have worn black for a month.

Somehow, Unc finagled four tickets to Game 7 of the National League Championship Series. I still don't know how he did it, but I'll never forget sitting in my seat and hearing the guy next to me tell someone on the other end of his cell phone that he'd paid $2,800 for his two tickets. Unc wouldn't say how he'd got them, only that it was legal and that he didn't pay a dime for them. Which was good, because Aunt Lorna might have beat him if he had.

On the morning of October 14, 1992, I looked into the mirror, smiled like a Cheshire cat, and dressed in every piece of Braves clothing I owned. Skipping school was just the start of it. We drove through the Zuta to Uncle Jack's house and picked up Tommye. She walked out the door wearing jeans, a wrinkled long-sleeve shirt, some makeup that shaded her eyes, and a cap that didn't say the first thing about the Braves or baseball.

That should've been my first clue.

We got to the game early, bought a program, and clung to the fence during warm-ups. Just before the start of the game we climbed up to our seats, which were located about forty rows up between home plate and first. The key here is that we had a perfect view of home plate. I ate hot dogs, corn dogs, popcorn, cokes, pretzels, and ice cream—whatever came walking up the aisle on the head of the guy carrying it. By the time the game started, I had mustard smeared from ear lobe to ear lobe and was so high on sugar and caffeine that my butt hovered an inch above the seat. The buzz was incredible.

Somewhere about the fourth inning, I realized Tommye hadn't eaten a thing. At first I thought she was just taking it all in, starstruck. But as the innings turned over and I came closer and closer to jumping out of my skin, Tommye began to look like a turtle that had crawled back into its shell.

On the single greatest night of my shared history with the Atlanta

Braves, Tommye didn't voluntarily utter a single number. She wasn't spiteful or angry, and she'd answer if I asked her, but most of the time I didn't know how to ask the question to get the information. When it came time for the seventh-inning stretch, Tommye didn't sing along.

The Pirates carried a 2-0 lead into the bottom of the ninth inning under ace pitcher Doug Drabek. I looked at the scoreboard and shook my head. The Pirates were three outs away from going to the Series, and we were the same from going home. But the Braves' leadoff batter, Terry Pendleton, hit a double. David Justice—the tying run—reached base on an infield error, and then Drabek walked the bases loaded. Looking at a problem, Pirates manager Jim Leyland pulled Drabek and replaced him with reliever Stan Belinda. Belinda gave up a run on a sacrifice fly by Ron Gant but rallied the Pirates and managed to get two outs.

In the previous inning, I had bought and finished my second ice cream bar. By the time third-string catcher Francisco Cabrera walked up to the plate, I had chewed the stick into a matted web of splinters. I was not hopeful, for which I have since confessed and sought forgiveness a hundred times, because Cabrera lined a 2-1 pitch from Stan Belinda to left field and scored David Justice.

The game was tied and Sid Bream was advancing to third, and we were going into extra innings. But then an extraordinary thing happened. Sid Bream was tall, bumbly in a loosely athletic sort of way, and as Unc liked to say, could run all day in the shade of a tree.

That was, until he rounded third base.

Pirates left fielder and eventual National League MVP Barry Bonds fielded the ball as Bream put his head down and began throwing his arms, legs, and body toward home plate. The entire stadium sucked in an enormous breath of air, willing Sid homeward. Bonds's throw, unlike Sid, was a rocket. Sid and the ball arrived home—simultaneously. Catcher Mike LaValliere caught the ball, extended his arm, and Sid threw himself at the plate in a gesture that even now is known around the baseball world as "The Slide."

Braves announcer Skip Caray stood in the press box and called the play: "Swung, line drive left field! One run is in! Here comes Bream! Here's the throw to the plate! He is . . . safe! Braves win! Braves win! Braves win! Braves win!"

The place erupted. People were hugging total strangers, the players emptied the dugout, mobbed Sid at home plate, and then got tangled in a huge pile on the field. It was five minutes before either Unc or I quit screaming. Crazed fans were running across the outfield, and fireworks were exploding overhead. I had never seen more people more happy at one time in my entire life.

Except Tommye.

She was gone. Twenty minutes later she reappeared, unaffected, saying there'd been a line at the bathroom.

On the drive home I started listening to that part of me that asks questions. I had two: who in their right mind went to the bathroom at that moment in the game and, given the fact that Tommye hadn't eaten or drunk a thing since we'd picked her up that morning, what need did she have of a bathroom? I looked through the darkness of the backseat and studied her. As we passed by the streetlights, or into the light of oncoming cars, the shadows betrayed her. Between the flashes, I saw the face of the little girl who ran through the Zuta that night in her flannel gown.

Chapter 26

Tommye and I drove north up the island, through the security gate at Sea Island, and past the country club. When we got to Uncle Jack's house, she said, "I'll be right out."

I leaned against the hood while she unlocked the door, ran upstairs past the rather loud objections of a cleaning lady I didn't know, and then ran back out three minutes later. She had a duffel bag under her arm and a giddy smile on her face. She waved over her shoulder at the still-screaming cleaning lady, jumped into Vicky, and said, "Let's go."

I was sure they'd stop us at the security gate, and I was right. The guard walked out of the house, held out a huge hand, and said, "Excuse me, sir, you want to step out of the car?"

When I did, he walked around to Tommye's side and said, "You too, ma'am."

Tommye said, "Honey, you're gonna have to do better than that."

He opened the door and reached to put his hand on her. "The owners will be here shortly, as will the police, and I'm told they want to charge you with breaking and entering and grand theft."

"Oh?" Tommye smiled and shook her head. She dangled her keys and driver's license in front of him. "How can I be accused of breaking into my own house? And if I own it, then how's it stealing?"

"Ma'am?"

She handed him her license. He read the name and the address that matched her dad's. "Oh, well . . ."

She turned to me. "Chase, get in the car."

The guard stepped back, and I did as she said. He handed her back her keys and license, and she said, "Tell my dad I left a few other things. I'll be back in a few days."

"Yes, ma'am."

"You can raise the gate now."

He raised the gate, and we drove through. I said, "You want to tell me what's going on?"

She laughed and said, "Not yet. But that's coming. Let's drive to the old house."

"What, you mean . . . ?"

"Yeah, the Zuta house."

"You got a key to it too?"

She grinned. "Or something."

Uncle Jack had moved out of the Zuta not long after Tommye left. He'd built on Sea Island, and his Zuta mansion has been vacant ever since. The only things he kept there were his horses, and by now he was down to just one, an old quarter horse named Lil' Bubba. Son of Big Bubba, Lil' Bubba must be twenty years old now, and nothing about him is little. He stands nearly eighteen hands and some twelve hundred pounds on the hoof. He stays in the pasture, watches the cars drive to and from Jesup, and probably dreams about the days that Tommye and I rode him bareback across the Zuta. I don't know why Uncle Jack has kept him all this time, but I think it has something to do with Unc.

Tommye and I pulled up to the wrought-iron gate, and I touched it with the bumper. It creaked, and rust busted off the hinges as it swung open. The grass was waist-high along the driveway, mostly weeds, and the house was in desperate need of paint. Flakes were chipping off around the windows and soffits, and the front door was swollen at the bottom where it had taken on water.

"You got a flashlight?" she asked me.

I pulled one out of the center console and handed it to her.

Tommye slid it in her back pocket and stood staring at the house a long time. Without looking at me, she said, "You remember my brother?"

Peter was one more unanswered question. I had never met him, because he had shot himself in the head not long after I moved in. I used to ask questions, but nobody had any answers, only shrugged shoulders.

She pointed toward a basement window. "He died in that room right there."

Tommye wasn't talking with me as much as she was talking at me. The questions were piling up, but this was no time to be a journalist.

She walked to the side of the house and picked up an old brick buried in the dirt beneath a cracked clay pot. Then she went up the front steps, peered through the glass of the front door, and without a word, threw the brick through the glass. She reached in, unlocked the door, and walked in.

She crossed her arms and looked around. The house smelled of mildew, and there was black mold growing on the walls. The bad kind, the kind you don't want to breathe. Tommye pulled her sweatshirt up over her mouth and circled behind the steps. She opened a big heavy door, clicked on the light, and walked down.

It smelled musty, and the sump pump had apparently quit working years ago; stagnant water puddled on the concrete floor. She stood at the base of the steps and leaned against the wall. She shined the light around the room, and I heard something scurrying off into the recesses of the basement.

The racks of wine were mostly full. There must have been two hundred bottles stored in bins that tilted forward, keeping the corks wet from the inside out. She sat on the bottom step, leaned her head against the wall, and I sat down behind her. Waiting. She shined her light across the room to an old leather chair that had split. Most of the padding had either been eaten out or rotted away.

"Jack used to come down here and taste his wines. Peter was older than me by about four years. Quiet and not very healthy. Bad asthma. Jack brought him down here and made him rub his feet while he sipped some ancient cabernet or pinot noir. At least that's how it started. About three glasses in, he'd climb back up the stairs and shut the door, keeping Peter down there for quite a while. I didn't know what was going on until I was eight, and Jack brought us both down here. I hadn't even reached puberty yet."

She shook her head and gritted her teeth, shaking loose the tears. "When he tired of Peter, he turned to me. . . . That went on for about a year—him bringing us both down here together. We never talked about it. Not ever. One night, Jack brought us down here, and while he was . . . with me, Peter got Jack's pistol and shot himself." She shook her head. "The police called it an accident. The local community, church, business, everybody else, felt sorry for Jack. The headline read ONE MORE TRAGEDY IN LIFE OF HARDSHIP. Said he'd suffered so much loss in his life." She sighed. "Some lies run deep."

She turned and put her hand on my knee. "That was the night I ran across the Zuta . . ."

We climbed out of the basement and walked out through the kitchen to the back porch. The pool was green and covered in scum. Grass grew up through the cracks of the deck, and tiles had fallen off the side above the water level. Tommye looked at the barn where Lil' Bubba stood hanging his head out over the stall door, looking at us. She put her hand on my shoulder. "Hey, why don't you check on Bubba? I'll be along in a minute."

"You sure?"

She nodded.

I walked across the pasture to the barn where Lil' Bubba greeted me with slobbery kisses. "Hey, big guy. How you been?" He was groomed, brushed, and his feet were freshly shod. Unc had been taking good care of him.

I hopped into his stall, grabbed the rake, and started mucking out the manure while he nudged me around with his head. I spread some fresh mulch, poured some oats in his bucket along the wall, and cleaned out his self-filling water bowl.

Minutes later, I heard Vicky's muffler outside the barn. Tommye stepped out of the driver's seat and leaned against the hood, staring at the house. That's when the trail of black smoke caught my eye. It climbed out of the kitchen window. It climbed higher, and seconds later it billowed out of the soffits.

Tommye folded her arms, leaned back, and her shoulders arched downward.

"Did you do that?"

She nodded.

"I don't think your dad's gonna be too happy about this."

She laughed. "You haven't seen anything yet."

Just then, an explosion rocked the house and blew off the back sliding doors and windows. Glass splintered across the pool deck and shingles were slung through the air like boomerangs. A second explosion occurred somewhere deep within the house and blew out one entire side. Flames appeared, engulfing the back half of the building. Within seconds, the formerly grand South Georgia mansion was one huge fireball.

Tommye stood expressionless, unaffected by the sight or the consequences.

I'd had about enough surprises for one day. I looked up and down the highway. "Don't you think we ought to get out of here?"

"Why?"

"Well, your dad might—"

She stepped into Vicky, leaned back, and closed her eyes. "It's not his house."

Hearing sirens, I cranked the engine, pulled behind the barn, and slipped down an old logging road into the cover of the Zuta. We watched through the trees as the flames climbed higher. The wind carried pieces of ash, which flittered down on us like black pixie dust. A piece landed on Tommye's thigh. She flicked it off and stared through the trees as the second story collapsed onto the first.

"I've been wanting to do that for a long time."

With the sirens growing closer, I dropped Vicky into 4-wheel drive and we slipped off through the trees. We paralleled the main road, crossed the Buffalo, and drove aimlessly around the Zuta until night fell across South Georgia. By the time I pulled out onto the main dirt road, Tommye was asleep.

I parked beneath the barn, carried her upstairs, and tucked her into bed. As I pulled the covers up around her shoulders, her skin hot to the touch, she placed a palm behind my head, pulled me toward her, and kissed me gently on the forehead.

"I love you, Chase Walker."

I had not heard that tone before, but my heart told me what it meant. I turned down the AC, closed the door, and walked down the steps outside her room. I walked out of the barn, away from the house, and toward the pasture. Stars lit the night sky, sparkling down. Darkness had fallen, outside and in. I could hold it back no longer. I reached the fence and buried my face in my hands, and somewhere in there I hit my knees.

Minutes later, I felt a hand on my shoulder.

I wiped my eyes. Flies circled a dried cow patty a foot or so away. "Why? Why didn't you tell me?"

Unc looked up at Tommye's window. "She wanted to be the one. She knew it'd hit you hard."

"Well . . . what about doctors? All these new medicines I hear about. Can't we do something?"

He shook his head. "When I flew out to get her, the doctors said she should have died already. Clinically, they don't know how she's still alive. Her body's immune system can't fight a sniffle."

"We can't just sit here . . . I mean, Unc, think about it. We're sitting here right now waiting on her to die."

"Chase, she's a grown woman. Made her own decisions." He turned away, wiped his face with his sleeve, and turned his hat around in his hand. "And we got to live with those. The question is not when, but what do we do with what we've got left."

"Well . . . that just sucks."

"Hey . . . " Unc's tone caught me. "That's a scared girl up there. She needs us. Needs us real bad."

The Saturday morning sun broke through the window and landed on Tommye's face, but I was already awake. I don't think I'd ever gone to sleep. An hour passed, then two. Finally, she blinked and opened her eyes. Neither of us said anything for a while. She reached out from under the covers for my hand. "I should've told you."

I had to look further to find her eyes. "We should've done a lot of things."

She sat up, steadied herself, and said, "You help me to the bathroom?"

I helped her to the sink and squeezed the toothpaste while she held the brush. I put the lid down on the toilet, and she sat down to brush her teeth. When she spit, the primary color was red.

"If my life were still a movie, this is the part that would end up on the cutting room floor." She looked in the mirror. "We were all just fill-ins for a long-running soap opera. The actors changed, but the story seldom did. Certainly not the action."

She stood up and hung her arms around my neck, gathering both her breath and her emotions. She hung there, and for the first time in our complicated life, she said the one thing I, in my selfishness and own blinded pity, had never considered. "You know, you're not the only one with a hole in your chest. Girls get them too. We just fill them differently."

She wiped her eyes, held my face in her hands, and tried to smile. "Seeing as how I can't gain weight no matter how hard I try, I can pretty much eat whatever I want. And right now, I want some chocolate."

Sometimes I dream that I'm stuck down there under that stump, that black water covering up my head and all the air sucked out of my lungs—my chest about to explode. Minutes pass, but Unc never shows and no headlights turn down the drive. Just before the black hole pulls me down, I wake up, gasping, sweating, pulling at the headboard, having tied a knot in my sheets. And while I'm draped in a blanket of sweat and fear, I notice that it's there—my head coming out of the water—that the air tastes sweet. Filling. I lie there, sometimes 'til morning, sucking it in. Gorging. But it's never as sweet as that first breath out of the water.

I pressed my forehead to Tommye's, and I could see the water starting to pour in over her head. She was losing her hold.

We walked slowly, arm in arm, across the yard. She stepped lightly, almost hobbling. "Sometimes my feet feel like they're walking on broken glass."

Unc, Aunt Lorna, and Sketch sat at the kitchen table. The kid was eating a bowl of cereal and beating Unc in a game of chess. Aunt Lorna stood over the stove, hot pads in her hands. We sat down, and Aunt Lorna pulled a pound cake from the oven.

Unc caught my attention. "Mandy called. Said she's got to come by this morning." He glanced at Sketch. "State business."

I nodded. Behind me, Aunt Lorna stuck ten candles into the top of the pound cake and began carrying it to the table. Unc cleared away the chessboard, and she set the cake in front of Sketch. He looked up at her. She pulled matches from her apron and spoke as she lit each one.

"Since we don't really know your exact birthday, Unc and I have decided that it's today, August 1." She kissed him on the forehead. "Happy Birthday, Buddy."

He perked up, and his eyes darted from us to the candles.

Unc started, "Happy Birthday to you . . ." and we joined in. "Happy birthday to you . . ."

The candles lit Sketch's face, and the uncertainty grew. We finished singing and waited for him to blow them out.

I leaned forward and whispered, "You can blow them out now."

"Make a wish," Tommye added.

Sketch closed his eyes, inhaled—which spread his chest and shoulders—and then slowly blew across the top of the candles. Smoke rose from each one as he spent his lungs.

Aunt Lorna slipped the knife through the cake, slid out a piece, and placed it on a plate in front of him. The amazing thing wasn't that he had blown out all the candles with one breath, or the fact that he held Unc's hand with his; it was the smile that had pasted itself on his face. Every few seconds he would grow conscious of it, force it down, then forget about it—letting it climb back up his cheeks.

It was a great smile.

Chapter 27

In the summer between our junior and senior years, the county fair came to town for two weeks. That meant a windfall for Uncle Willee. He split his time shoeing horses for the wannabe cowboys who had come in for the rodeo, and mucking the stalls before and after the cattle auctions.

It also meant a windfall for me. Growing up on the outskirts of Brunswick, what some might call "the sticks," I didn't get out much. Excitement for me was the birth of a new cow. The fair spiked my curiosity and, in one particular case, satisfied it. Completely. Remember that scene in *Charlotte's Web* when Templeton goes to the fair at night and eats himself sick? Me, too, but it'd be good to forget it.

Friday night I waxed Vicky, and Tommye and I drove to the fair around dark. I didn't know it at the time, but Tommye was trying to drown her own demons, so we bought a five-dollar bottle of bootleg. Real rotgut stuff. We'd been listening to Don McLean's "American Pie" and thought it'd be neat to sing dirges in the dark and toast the world with whiskey or rye.

We rode the carousel, threw baseballs at the bowling pins, shot candles with squirt guns, and ate cotton candy, hot dogs, and nachos, and then stepped on the Ferris wheel. The guy working the wheel kept starting and stopping, letting people on and off and juggling with the contents of my stomach. I couldn't feel my lips or face, and judging by Tommye's speech, she couldn't either. We reached the pinnacle of the wheel, polished off the bottle, and the controller slammed the wheel to a halt.

That was the straw that broke the camel's back.

To Tommye's wide-eyed amusement, I grabbed the safety bar, braced myself, and vomited in a fantastic arc out over the front, splattering six or eight swinging buckets of fairgoers. Mind you, prior to that night, I'd never had a drink in my life. Tommye, a sympathetic vomiter, didn't have the good sense to grab the railing and keep it out of our bucket or off me. By the time the truth filtered down to the controller, people were screaming, which for some strange reason seemed really funny to Tommye and me. We laughed, vomited some more, and by the time we reached the bottom, our bucket and the ground below us was a mess in need of some diesel fuel and a match.

Somehow we stumbled back behind the tents and passed out. Just as the sun was driving an axe through the center of my head, somebody kicked my foot.

"You two 'bout finished?"

I cracked my eyes, but the sun had moved. It was sitting three inches from my face, burning a hole in my retina. I tried to nod my head, but the first wave of nausea told me I'd better not. I held up a stop-sign hand and whispered, "Please stop the world from spinning."

Unc wasn't having any of that. "You two want to live the high life, I can't do much to stop you. Probably wouldn't do any good anyway. You're old enough to make up your own minds." He looked around and shook his head at the rank smell of us. "But if you can stay up all night acting like a couple of idiots, you can work all day like honest folk. Now get up."

His tone of voice told us he was only going to say it once.

I stood up and dry-heaved from my toes. It sent me to my knees, my hands landing in horse manure. I looked at them and shook my head.

"I don't know what you're shaking your head at," Unc said. "You been sleeping in it all night. Even got it in your hair."

He took us to the stalls, handed us a pitchfork and wheelbarrow, and pointed. "Muck 'em. All of 'em. You can take a break when you finish."

I looked down the long row of stalls. There must have been a hundred of them. That's when I decided to quit being stupid.

Tommye was still too gone. Her face was crusted over and her hair was matted to her cheek. Unc walked off, she passed out, and I spent seven hours lifting manure out of fresh mulch clippings.

In my head, Don McLean kept asking for some happy news.

Late in the afternoon, I walked out of the barn to check in with my boss. He was shoeing a roping horse, the front foreleg pulled up between his knees while he filed off the tip of the hoof and scraped out the frog. With sweat pouring off his forehead, a cut on his forearm, and dirt smeared over most every square inch of his body, he looked up at me and then looked down again without so much as a word.

I was about to start reciting the apology I'd spent all day memorizing when two guys carrying brown-bagged beers walked by the stall. The first one, a dark-haired guy with a heavy gold watch, looked twice at Unc and then poked his buddy in the shoulder.

"Hey, if it isn't the murdering thief of Glynn County."

Unc looked up but didn't skip a beat. They walked closer and their voices grew, drawing attention.

"Lookee here. If it ain't the whipping post of Fulton County Penitentiary. Hey everybody, come quick! It's the cold-blooded clown of Brunswick."

The fog of last night hung on, rattling inside my head.

"Come on up, folks, step right up." They knocked his hat off, kicked it between them, and then flattened it atop a rather massive pile of horse droppings. While one fellow ground it into the dirt with his heel, the other played the role of circus announcer. Within a few seconds, a crowd had gathered.

"Step right up, folks. One free punch. No admission. If you lost your shirt, family heirlooms, or last penny in the Zuta First National Robbery, then here is your chance to feel better."

With that, the guy turned and poured beer across the face of the horse. The alcohol must have stung its eyes, because it spooked. The horse jumped, broke the reigns that had tied it to Unc's trailer, and kicked. Both feet caught Unc squarely in the chest. Think of a cannon shot. Flying backwards, he crossed the stall and landed hard against the wall on the other side. When I got to him, blood was coming out the corner of his mouth, at least one rib was poking through his shirt, and he was having trouble breathing.

People were screaming for a doctor—who would later tell us he'd broken seven ribs—but that didn't stop the guy who hit him. He walked up and jabbed me in the chest.

"Be glad you ain't his boy. Last one he had got taken, burnt to a crisp, and dumped on the courthouse steps. You don't want to be blood kin to him." After he spit in Unc's face, he walked off in the direction of the cotton candy machine.

With my head pounding, cotton filling every corner of my mouth, and no desire for another drink the rest of my life, I saw for the first time just how much and to what degree the folks around town blamed and hated Unc for every bad thing that had ever happened in Glynn County. Somehow, somewhere, somebody had twisted the truth to the extent that they couldn't see the forest for the trees.

I've often wondered—if Unc really had made off like a bandit, then what in the world was he doing shoeing horses at a county fair? Not to mention the fact that the robbery cost him his career, inheritance, wife, and son. Is it just me, or does none of that make sense? I wanted to ask the guy at the fair that, but I never got the chance, because the helicopter came and airlifted Unc to the hospital, where he spent a couple hours in surgery. It'd be two months before he could walk to the greenhouse and another before he could even think about getting back to work. To make up the difference, I filled in after school taking care of his horses, and Aunt Lorna began working doubles at the truck stop whenever she could get them.

But maybe the thing that has caused me more thought through the years, the thing I can't seem to reconcile, is that I've never seen Unc mad. It's like all the bad stuff that happened to him poured into one side of his heart and fell out the other, flowing through the hole left by the death of his wife and son.

I'm no expert, but I know one thing about anger—it's like alcohol. At some point, if you pour enough in there, it's coming back up. You may think you've built up a tolerance, but the truth is this—no man, not even Unc, can bury it so deep that it doesn't erupt at some point like Vesuvius and splatter your soul across the earth. There was a time when I wanted to be around to see the eruption, but now I'm not so sure. 'Cause I'm not sure what that would do to Unc.

Chapter 28

HIV and AIDS had never spent much time on my radar screen. Most of my knowledge involved pictures of gaunt-eyed, bald men suffering painful, hallucinogenic deaths in sterile hospital rooms. It was a disease passed among gay men, not little girls from South Georgia who liked to fish, ride the carousel, and watch baseball.

My mistake.

I got to my office early, googled HIV, and spent the morning educating myself. Finally I placed a call to a doctor in California who'd published several articles on the progression of the disease. Unlike the other countless specialists, his articles were written in language that an ignoramus like me could understand. The receptionist paged him, and I played the role of journalist.

"Hello, Dr. Myers, this is Chase Walker. I'm a journalist for the *Brunswick Daily* in Georgia. Our community has been affected by HIV as of late, and I wondered if I could ask you a few questions."

"Sure, but forgive me if I'm terse. I'm between patients, and chances are good they have less time than you."

"Let me skip the small talk. Can the disease be defeated?"

"In the short run, sort of. Long run, not yet. Least not that we know of. With drug therapy, we can eliminate any trace of the disease in someone's blood system, making old age a very real possibility. Some of my patients have had the disease fifteen years and yet are medically healthier than I."

"So it's not a death sentence?"

"Not like it was in the eighties. It used to be that the only treatment we had was AZT. We administered high doses, extended a patient's life by a few years, and the side effects were many and not pleasant. Research has since taught us that the virus enters a cell and attacks the DNA, enabling it to make more of itself. To do this, it must come out of the membrane of that cell, destroying that cell—which, in effect, destroys the immune system. This occurs exponentially, not sequentially. You remember the brainteaser where someone asks you if you would rather have a million dollars or a penny doubled every day of the longest month of the year? Well, take the penny. This research led to the development of protease inhibitors. In short, they block the reproduction of the cell within itself, thereby placing the virus in a holding pattern."

"Making it dormant?"

"That's one way to look at it. If we start early enough, we can virtually eliminate any trace of the virus within a person's bloodstream."

"What's early enough?"

"Well, that depends on the person. Some people succumb much faster. Some can hold their own for quite a while before they ever see the effects. It depends on their immune system prior to infection."

"What about when combined with other diseases of the blood?"

"Good question, but let's back up a minute. HIV today is not simply one virus. There are now several strands with differing characteristics. By attacking one, we can enable another. Add to that any type of hepatitis, and we've got trouble."

"How's that?"

He paused. "It's the perfect storm. Treat one, and you encourage the other. Leave it alone, and they combat one another, growing stronger and ravaging the host, or patient. Either way, it's the worst possible scenario."

"How long would that patient have?"

"If we diagnosed early enough, we could give them a couple years. Maybe even a decade. Assuming compliance."

"Compliance?"

"To get better, the patient has to want to. Which means they have to willingly take medication, daily, for the rest of their life."

"Can they start anytime?"

"Well, yes, but again, there is no morning-after pill. Each patient reaches a point of no return where the body has been so ravaged that no medication on earth can reverse the damage. At that point, it's a matter of time."

"How much?"

"Again, look at the patient. It can be a week, month, year. After reaching critical mass, time—or one's expected lifespan—is a function of the level of infection, multiplied by some sort of coefficient of their immune system, divided by exposure to germs—or something like that. And we're still trying to figure out that coefficient. I've had patients who've died while on their first visit to my office. Obviously, they waited too long. Others came ten years ago, we patched them up, and they're hanging in there."

"How's it end? I mean, physically?"

"It's not pretty. I wouldn't wish it on anyone. The human body can handle a fever up to about 104. Much above that, and the proteins in your body start to unravel and break down. At 105, delirium often sets in, the patients convulse, step in and out of consciousness, lose control of their internal organs." He paused. "Have you ever seen those TV shows that depict people with hemorrhagic fever?"

"That bad, huh?"

"Worse. It's called Disseminated Intravascular Coagulation."

"Say that one more time."

"D.I.C. for short. The patient's blood system begins to clot, and not just in one place. But your body only has so much ability to clot. Once you've used up that ability, exhausted those antigens, the reverse happens. From there it's a snowball. They bleed from every organ, pore, and orifice. If they're lucky, they'll suffer a clot in either the brain or lungs, which will end the misery."

"I thought research was gaining on this thing."

"It is and we are, but this disease is always one step ahead of us. About the time we think we've caught up with it, it cloaks itself and changes." He paused. "Side effects aside, it's a remarkable thing."

"You sound like you admire it."

"I respect it, I feel for those who have it, empathize with the loved ones affected by it, and I wish I could eradicate it from the planet. It's an evil unlike any I've ever studied. But there's no magic wand. In twenty years of treating this disease, I've witnessed some horrific scenes of human experience. But while it can and does kill the body, maybe the worst damage occurs in one's psyche."

"What do you mean?"

"When was the last time you thought about dying?"

I was quiet a minute.

"See what I mean? For most patients with HIV, it's a daily thought. They might not dwell on it, it might not even depress them, but for most, every time they swallow their meds, it crosses their mind. That has an effect on a person's soul."

"How do you treat that?"

A chuckle. "I'm a medical doctor. Not Dr. Phil."

I liked him. Given better circumstances, I'd buy him a beer and ask him where he went to medical school and how he got started in this area. I decided to ask anyway.

"How'd you get started treating HIV?"

He paused. "Following a routine surgery, my wife received a blood transfusion. This was before we knew about the virus. After watching what it did to her . . . well, you can probably write the rest of that story."

"Thank you, Doctor."

"Anytime."

I found Tommye sitting beneath an orange tree behind the house. In the four weeks she'd been home, she'd lost more weight. She had begun to look like the gaunt, hollow-eyed pictures in my head.

I picked a twig of grass, broke it, and stuck it between my teeth. "I had an interesting conversation this morning."

She lay down and placed her head in my lap. "Yeah?"

"Uh-huh, with a doctor in California named Myers."

"And what's he do?"

"He's a leading HIV specialist."

She closed her eyes, and I ran my fingers through her hair.

"And what'd he say?"

"He said a lot."

She looked at me. "Don't you get cross with me. I'm still one week older than you."

"Uh-huh, and you look it, too."

She smiled. "When I get to heaven, I'm gonna talk to God about you not respecting your elders. Besides, I've put more mileage on my chassis than you have."

"I'm not sure how to take that."

She laughed. "Oh, come on, one of the things you and Uncle Willee have always done is laugh at yourselves. I'm just trying to remember how."

We let the breeze push through the grass and spread the summer sun around us.

"So?"

"You want the long version or short?"

She shrugged. "I probably know the long version."

"He said he had medications that, depending upon a few factors, could give you a few more decades to—" I glanced at the house where Uncle Willee was teaching the kid how to whittle with his new pocket-knife. "To watch the orchids bloom."

She smiled. "I'd like that."

"So, why aren't we at the doctor's office right now?"

She took a deep breath. "I contracted about four years ago. The business is pretty good about testing, but it's not foolproof. Which would explain the end of my acting career." Another deep breath. "After a few years of weeklong parties, all of which included multiple needles and people, I woke up on the floor of a room I'd never seen in a house I'd never been in with people I didn't know. I walked out, checked into a treatment center, and started thinking more about tomorrow than yesterday." She opened her eyes and looked at me.

"When I got there, my immune system was pretty much gone. I was one sniffle away from no return. So we started a megadose aggressive treatment of protease inhibitors that we thought was working—but by attacking one, we strengthened the others. Sort of a sick and twisted catch-22." She closed her eyes again. "Now the medications I take just help with the pain." She sat up, wrapped her arms around me, and pressed her ear to my chest.

"How long had you been in the hospital when you called Uncle Willee?"

"Couple of weeks. They had to bring me back once. Jump-start me. You know, with those white air-hockey-looking paddles, like you see on TV? Well, don't try that at home. Take my word for it—it hurts."

We sat quietly, listening to each other hurt. Finally she lay back down, rubbed her chest where the memory must have made her itch, and placed her head on my thigh, speaking to the underside of the orangeless tree limbs above us.

"I had this dream." She chuckled. "I was standing on a stairwell inside a huge lighthouse. The stairwell spiraled around the inside of the walls of the lighthouse, and it was packed with people like me. Each stood in line, looking up toward the front where people were getting ready to meet whoever was up there. While they waited, they fussed over the pages in a book. Some looked like huge scrapbooks, while others looked like spiral notebooks. Everyone was working furiously, like kids trying to finish their homework before class. But I didn't have one.

"Every now and then we'd get to move up a step, closer to the top. I could see a man, maybe the lighthouse keeper, sitting at a desk reading the books handed to him. If he liked the story, he smiled and placed it gently on the shelf behind him. The shelves went on for miles. Pretty, gilded books. Leather bindings. Gold leaf.

"But he didn't like every book. And the ones he didn't like, he pitched down through the middle of the lighthouse. They fluttered down and landed in a huge fire that was mounded high as a house." She was quiet for a moment, then continued. "Then I felt something in my hands and looked down to find a book in them. I opened it and found the story of me. And I didn't like it. Talk about depressing. I nearly pitched it in the fire myself. But then I got to the end, and the last few pages were empty. I looked up front and the line was moving sort of slow, so I figured I still had time. And . . . I knew the story I wanted to write. So I raised my hand. Everyone looked at me like I'd lost my mind, but what did I have to lose? I'd already been dead.

"So I said, 'Sir, you're not really gonna like the story I've written, but if I could fill in these last few pages, you might.' He just looked at me, like he knew what I wanted to ask, so I went ahead. 'Can I go write these last few pages and come back when I'm done?' He studied me, then smiled and nodded. I turned to the person behind me, said, 'Hey, save my place,' and walked down the steps and out the door." Tommye laughed again. "When I left, every hand in the place was up."

She sat up, Indian style, and brushed her thumb along my eyebrow and the lines of my jaw. "Do I sound like I've lost my mind?"

I smiled and nodded slightly, earning a punch in the shoulder.

"You're not supposed to agree."

"Well . . . you do."

We sat with each other. Just being together. It was good stuff.

"You know . . . I set my homepage to the *Brunswick Daily*. In a sense, I've gotten to talk with you twice a week for the last five years."

"A conversation is always better when the other person gets to talk back."

"I know that. I'm just trying to show you that I'm not the forgetful pig you think I am. I kept tabs on you."

"You have a funny way of doing it."

She nodded, scooted closer, and put her arms around my neck, locking her fingers. "Chase, you have every right to be mad at me. I'd be mad at me too." She shrugged. "In fact, for a long time, I was mad at me, but being mad doesn't change things."

"I know that."

"I need you to do something for me."

She was turning on the charm, of which she had plenty, so I tried not to look at her. I picked another piece of grass and stuck it between my teeth. I wanted her to know that her leaving had hurt me.

She leaned in, shook her head, and waited until our eyes locked. "It's not going to be easy."

I waited.

She whispered, "Forgive me."

I smiled. "You're right, that's not easy."

"Trust me on this."

"Why?"

"Because one day, it'll all make sense."

"When?"

"Not long." She smiled again. "I've just got to write a few more pages. That's all."

"When do I get to read it?"

"I don't know, but you'll be the first."

"You left a pretty big hole in me. And coming home just opened up the wound and exposed the shrapnel left inside."

She sat back, the actress in her waking up. "Dang, did you think that up or read it somewhere?"

"Tommye . . ."

"Hey, you're not the only one with a hole in your heart from what your dad did to you."

"I know, but when you were around, mine hurt less."

"Mine too."

"At least you knew your dad. I can't help it if he was a sorry . . . a sorry whatever."

She stared at me. "You're not playing the victim, are you?"

I shrugged and smiled. "Maybe just a little. Is it working?"

She shook her head.

"I didn't think so."

"Hey, if you want me to feel miserable for going out west, for never calling, getting sick, and then coming home so I can die . . . I already do. Can't feel much worse."

"Sorry. It's just that . . . you've had a little longer to get used to the idea of you not being here."

"Whoever said I was used to it?"

"You know what I mean."

"Chase—I know that I loved you before I ever met you. I know that my heart broke when I drove out of town. I know that I dialed and then hung up the phone a hundred times from California."

"Well . . . why?"

She placed her finger on the end of my nose and tilted her head. "'Cause I didn't want you to know what I'd become. Shame hurts, Chase. And it's going to hurt a lot worse if I have to live the days I have left thinking you're looking down your nose at me."

I wrapped my arms around her, pulled her to my chest, and

squeezed. "Tommye, I'm not looking down my nose. I'm looking across a broken heart—one that only gets worse the skinnier you get."

"Chase?"

"Yes?"

"Thank you."

"I'm going to miss you."

She thumbed the tear off my cheek. "I miss you already."

She looked out across the pasture, then out across the horizon— she was lost in a gaze that looked down on the earth from another galaxy. Her tone changed. "Hey." She turned my chin to hers. "If you talked to the doctor, then you know how it ends." Her eyes searched to find mine. "When the time comes . . . no 911. No doctors, no hospital." She swallowed. "Let me go home."

Unc found me on the porch long after everyone else had gone to sleep. He walked down along the railing near their bedroom, where Lorna's climbing rose was wrapped around the chimney. He sniffed several, clipped a few, then sat down next to me, packed a pipe, and spent five minutes trying to light it.

I smiled. "When did you take to smoking a pipe?"

He coughed. "'Bout thirty seconds ago."

"You like it?"

"Not sure yet."

We sat there, him smoking and me breathing. He exhaled, his eyes burning. "You talk with Tommye today?"

"You don't miss much, do you?"

"Not when it matters." He puffed again. "Well?"

"Yes sir."

"Get your questions answered?"

I shrugged. "Yes sir."

He hung the pipe between his teeth. "Well?"

"Well, what?"

He raised his eyebrows. "What now?"

"Heck if I know. What's left to know?"

"It's not what you know. It's what she knows."

Unc was setting me up, and I knew it. I also knew I wanted whatever he was about to give me. "What do you mean?"

"My life has been real different than I thought. Ain't turned out how I hoped . . . nor dreamt. But I'm not the only man in the world to get screwed by life. Lots are worse off than me. That's life. You take the bad with the good. Rise up through it. Live in the midst of it. It's the bad that lets you know how good the good really is. Don't let the bad leave you thinking like there ain't no good. There is, and lots of it, too."

"You know they sell that same stuff down at the grocery store in those magazines along the checkout counter."

He nodded, then he picked up one of Lorna's roses and set it in my lap. "Here."

I picked it up and smelled it.

He poked me in the shoulder. "See what I mean? Thorns don't stop you from sniffing. Or putting them in a vase on the kitchen table. You work around them." He stuck a finger in the air. "Why? 'Cause the rose is worth it." He looked at me. "Think what you'd miss."

We sat a long time while Unc learned to smoke. After he got the hang of it, he smoked the ashes white, then tapped it out on the heel of his boot. "Sometimes good judgment comes from experience, and a lotta that comes from bad judgment."

"Doesn't seem right."

He nodded slowly. "Yup."

Chapter 29

We loaded up, packed the cooler and the pole, and walked outside where Unc had Lil' Bubba tied up. He helped Tommye up into the saddle and then placed Sketch behind her. The five of us walked out through the back pasture, underneath the canopy of cypress and oaks, and into the dense cover of the Zuta. Thirty minutes later, we walked out of the water and into Ellsworth's Sanctuary. The crepe myrtles were in bloom and sprinkling the ground with small pink blossoms. We walked to the north end, Tommye dismounted, and we sat down on logs to watch Unc teach Sketch how to fish.

Unc slipped the worm onto the hook, threading it from head to tail, and then tossed it into the water where the warmouth were popping bugs on the surface. He held the pole gently, raised his chin, and whispered, "Talk to me, sweet lips. I'll find you in the dark." Just then the bobber disappeared; he set the hook and handed the pole to Sketch, who started reeling furiously. A moment later, he stood on the bank watching his fish flop on the ground as Unc laughed and clapped.

Tommye bumped me with her shoulder. "Aren't you going to join them?"

I shook my head.

"Why not?"

"Only one pole."

She frowned. "Well, that doesn't make any sense."

I smiled, staring back into my own memory. "The point is not the fishing . . . the point is the kid."

We spent the morning watching the two of them fill up the stringer. Midmorning, after Sketch had the hang of it, Tommye slipped her arm inside mine and said, "Let's go for a walk."

She steered me around the Sanctuary, walking slowly, saying little. We skirted the edges, then broke through the brush to stare down on two tombstones. We stood for a moment, our eyes tracing the names on the marble. The ground around each had been brushed back, and dead flowers lay between them.

Unc walked up behind us. Whether it was the sunlight or the place, his face had changed. Normally young and vibrant, his age suddenly showed. There were wrinkles on his neck and around his eyes, and a single muscle in his cheek twitched.

We three stood looking down. Tommye hooked her arms inside ours, holding onto us as much as uniting us. Finally she spoke. She turned to Unc and said, "I want you to do something for me."

She looked at the ground next to his son's grave. Mushrooms and small ferns were reaching up out of the ground, and a caterpillar was slowly making its way across the dead leaves. She slipped her hand into his. "I want you to speak at my funeral. And I want you to bury me right here."

Unc gritted his teeth, pulled her to his chest, and nodded.

While dusk had set, it had grown dark inside the swamp. Unc slid his flashlight into his back pocket, lifted Tommye, and then handed Sketch up to her. She wrapped her arms around him, and the two held onto the saddle horn while Unc told Bubba, "Old Man, you're carrying precious cargo. Better take it easy."

Watching that picture, I was reminded that there are still things in this life that are beautiful. Tommye and Sketch were two of them. The beam from Unc's flashlight bounced off the water and lit their smiling faces as they bobbed atop the horse. Then it hit me that the reason the light bounced off the water was because Unc was pointing it behind him. And maybe that was the prettiest picture of all.

We walked out of the Sanctuary as the last rays of the sun glanced off the earth, making room for the cooler sea breeze that swept itself over the islands, across Brunswick, and down into the Buffalo. When we walked into the house, the phone was ringing. Unc answered it, spoke briefly, and hung up.

"It's Mandy. She's coming by." He looked at Aunt Lorna. "Bringing somebody with her."

Mandy's state-issue white Camry turned down the drive, followed by a blue van. The van hung back at a distance as Mandy parked. She mounted the porch and then looked at Sketch.

"Hey, I heard you had some cake today. I wonder if you could cut me a piece?"

He nodded and disappeared into the kitchen.

After the door slammed shut, Mandy's poker face returned. "You know those little flyers you get in your mail that have a kid's picture on front with an accompanying age-progression photo to the right?" She held one up, passed it around, and then pointed to the van coming down the drive. "This lady is from Tampa. She saw our classified ads in a Miami paper. She lost her son to a kidnapping about six years ago. The picture there is her son. She thinks Buddy might be him."

Tommye, who was white as a ghost and wrapped up in a blanket in the rocker, stood up and looked over Unc's shoulder.

I looked at the age-progression picture, which was the spitting image of Sketch. "How will she know? I mean, how will she know for sure?"

Mandy heard footsteps coming from the kitchen and lowered her voice. "A birthmark. She wouldn't tell me where it is. Just said she'd know him for certain once she got a chance to look at him up close."

Sketch walked out onto the porch carrying a slice of pound cake on top of a paper plate. He carried it with two hands, having stuffed his sketch pad inside his waistband behind his back.

The lady in the blue van parked and got out. Mustering her courage, she walked up the porch steps. She was in her midforties with graying hair and a bit ragged around the edges. She stepped up to Sketch, who turned and took her breath away. She covered her mouth, composed herself, and pushed her hair behind her ears. She tried to speak but could not.

Mandy sat down next to him and said, "Buddy, this kind lady just wants to look at you a moment."

Sketch nodded. The lady put her hands on his shoulders and turned him sideways. She then gently pulled back his right ear and stared at the skin. Sketch stood unmoving, still holding the cake.

The lady released his ear, shook her head at Mandy, and stood up, facing all of us. No one said a word. Unc stepped forward and extended his hand.

"Ma'am, I'm William McFarland. This"—he waved his hand across us—"is my family."

The lady nodded. "Before my son was . . . taken, we were working in the yard. He was five then. He was playing in the driveway and fell on a clay pot. It cracked and cut his ear. We had to have it sewn back on. There would be a scar."

Aunt Lorna stepped forward. "Will you stay for dinner?"

"No. Thank you." The lady turned, looked again at Sketch, and walked to her car.

He watched the van's taillights disappear out the drive, set down the cake, and walked to his room. No one had told him what was going on, but no one had to. He'd been passed over before.

Mandy looked at all of us. "I'm sorry. She . . ." She put her hands on her hips, and I saw her poker face return. "I think I've found a permanent home that will take him. Some folks out of Charlotte. Attorney and his wife. Good people. Might be two or three weeks before we get approval. Judge is on a European vacation." She walked to the railing, her back to us, and looked out over the pasture. "At least in criminal court, the guilty get what they got coming."

On my eighteenth birthday Unc and Aunt Lorna took me outside and said, "You're free to go as you like. You're also free to stay. The state put you here, now you can choose."

They gave me my freedom, but I didn't want it. Taking it would have sealed me officially as a fatherless kid. I would be no one. That's a hard way to live.

Before the driveway dust had time to settle, another set of headlights pulled into the drive. They were that bluish color that comes on real expensive cars. The black Escalade skirted the potholes and parked in front of the steps. Tommye's eyes narrowed, and Unc stepped down off the porch, standing between the driver of the car and us.

I've never seen Uncle Jack without a tie. White shirt, bluish tie, immaculate hair. His pants draped like Italian silk, and his loafers looked like soft calfskin. He walked up to within three feet of Unc. They studied each other. Jack was bigger. Barrel-chested, he stood three inches taller than Unc.

Jack spoke first. "William."

Tommye stepped off the porch and walked up behind Uncle Willee, holding loosely to his shirtsleeve.

Uncle Jack spoke to Tommye. "Heard you came by the house."

"Yeah . . . thought I'd stop in. Grab a couple of things."

He paused, thinking. "I guess you heard about the Zuta house?"

"No, do tell."

"Somebody lit a fire in the kitchen, then cut the lines to the propane tanks in the cellar. Burnt it to the ground."

Tommye stepped around Unc, but slipped her arm inside his. "Gee . . . that's too bad. All that wine . . ."

Uncle Jack looked at me. "You like prison?"

I thought about him in that house, down in that cellar, admiring the legs of his wine . . . and his daughter. Then I thought of Tommye running through the Zuta that night—her gown covered in the last remnants of little girlness. Jack had lived his entire smug life having stepped above his secret, the prize of the Brunswick business and church community. He had taught Sunday school and been an elder six times. I listened as the wind cut through the pecan trees carrying Tommye's echo, *Some lies run deep.*

I stepped in front of Unc and under the shadow of Uncle Jack. He was taller than me by six inches. I placed my face less than a foot from his and said the thing I'd been wanting to say a long time. I guess sitting in that cellar, looking backward, I found the gumption. "Keep a good watch over your shoulder, because those footsteps you hear . . . they'll be mine."

I had caught him off guard, I could tell. I scratched my chin. "You ever heard of the Freedom of Information Act? If not, you will shortly."

Unc stepped between us. "You need something, brother?"

"I heard my daughter was home." He looked at the hollow shell Tommye had become.

Her taut top lip quivered, pulling the trickle of sweat down off her face.

Sketch stared through the front door screen.

Uncle Jack saw him too. He spoke out of the corner of his mouth. "Heard you took in that boy found at the railroad track. Keeping him while the DA looks for his parents. That's good." Then he looked directly at Uncle Willee. "Every man should have a son."

Unc closed his eyes and shook his head. Then he smiled and half-laughed. He turned Tommye, ushering her into the house, and motioned for me to follow. I shook my head and hung my thumbs in my jeans pockets.

Unconsciously, he did the same. He looked again at Jack. "Thanks for coming."

Uncle Jack turned, stepped into his car, and disappeared down the drive.

I turned to Unc. "Why do you always let him do that to you?"

Aunt Lorna stood on the porch, leaning against the house. Her silence told everyone that she agreed with me.

Unc cleaned his glasses on the untucked front corner of his shirt. "You think I'm the one getting 'done' here?"

I nodded.

He looked at Tommye. "That the way it looks to you?"

"Unc, he's been walking over you all of my life and then some."

He stared at the dust sweeping over the road. "Never corner something you know is meaner than you."

I was out of line, but I'd had about enough of speaking in code. "Is he meaner, or are you just a lifelong coward?"

He chewed on his lip. "I've got more to lose."

I laughed. "Like what? He took everything you ever thought about having."

"You sure?"

I flicked a piece of paint that was flaking off the railing. "Just look around you."

He looked at all of us. "I did."

"Well . . . maybe your eyes need checking."

Unc slipped on his glasses and watched Uncle Jack turn left onto Highway 99. "Chase . . . perspective often depends on where you're standing."

Chapter 30

I had applied to every school I could think of, but while my academics weren't too bad—my high school GPA was a 3.2—my SAT was miserable. A combined 1080. Florida State flatly refused me. Unc read the rejection letter, looked at my face, and said, "Is this where you want to go?"

"Yes sir."

He looked at the letter. "Load up."

We got in the car, drove four hours, and stepped out in front of the admissions building about four o'clock. Unc took off his hat, walked up to the receptionist, eyed the bottom of my letter, and said, "We'd like to see Ms. Irene Sullivan."

The receptionist looked at us over her glasses. "And this is regarding?"

He pointed at me. "My boy here."

"Do you have an appointment?"

"No, ma'am."

"I'm afraid you'll have to make an appointment."

Unc looked through the glass at a lady sitting at her desk, talking on the phone. "When is the next available?"

The receptionist eyed the computer in front of her. "Tuesday, nine thirty AM."

Unc eyed his watch. "You mean tomorrow morning."

"No, I mean Tuesday week."

Unc said, "Well, I don't need that much time. If you'll just tell her we'd like five minutes, I'd be grateful."

She shook her head. "I'm sorry, sir."

I turned to leave, but Unc was having none of that. "You don't mind if we wait for an opening." He sat in a chair along the wall next to her desk, knees together, spinning his hat in his fingers. I could tell his mind was spinning too. I sat next to him, looking over my shoulder for a security guard.

A few minutes later, the receptionist dialed a number and turned her head, and the lady behind the glass picked up the phone. I couldn't hear what she was saying, but I had a pretty good idea it had something to do with us. She hung up, and an hour passed while the lady behind the glass saw people into and out of her office. She was busy—there was no getting around that.

About 5:30 PM the receptionist gathered up her things, closed down her computer, and left without a word. Unc didn't budge. A few minutes later, the lady behind the glass walked around the corner to the water cooler, poured herself a cup of water, and then walked into the waiting room, where we immediately stood up.

She looked at us and then motioned to the cooler. "Can I offer you two a drink?"

Unc shook his head. "No ma'am. We don't want to take up any more of your time than is necessary."

She smiled and motioned us into her office. We sat down, her on one side and us on the other. Unc's right leg was bouncing. She leaned back, looking half-amused, and said, "How can I help you?"

Unc slid the letter across the desk. "Ma'am, my name is William McFarland." He spun his hat in his hand. "For nearly half my life,

folks have called me Willee." He looked at me. "This is Chase, and"—
he eyed the letter again—"well . . . he'd . . ."

She typed something into her computer, brought up a file, and
read quietly. "Mr. McFarland. While his grades are not too bad, his
test scores are quite short of what we require. He needs another two
hundred points. I'm sorry, I can't—"

Unc stood up and handed her his business card. "That's my personal number, comes in right here." He tapped the cell phone in his
shirt pocket. "If he doesn't make straight As, or at least your dean's
list, every semester, call me, and I'll make sure. He's a good kid, a
hard worker."

I stared at him like he'd lost his mind. He shrugged in my direction.
"Mr. McFarland . . ."

"Ma'am. Can't you make an exception?"

She shook her head. "I'm sorry."

Unc twirled his hat in his hand and lowered his voice, almost as if
he were talking to himself. "Ms. Sullivan, my life hasn't turned out
exactly as I'd hoped. In one sense, I've lived two lifetimes. Please give
him a chance. Just one. If he screws it up, then he'll have to live with
that, but please don't take him out of the game before he gets his
chance at bat. You won't be disappointed. I can promise you that."

She looked at the computer, back at Unc, and finally at me. "Is he
always like this?"

I nodded and twirled my own cap in my hand. Looking back, we
must've looked like twins. "When it's important."

She leaned forward on her desk, folded her hands, and bored a
hole right through me. "Well, is it?"

"Yes ma'am."

She chewed on her lip, leaned back, and looked out the window.
Then she looked at Unc. "What do you do?"

"Ma'am, I'm a farrier . . . I shoe horses."

"I imagine you're used to hard work."

"I've known it a time or two."

She looked at me. "Probation." She typed a few sentences into her computer, then grabbed a sheet off her printer and handed it to me. "You've got one semester to prove yourself." She smiled and looked at Unc. "When he makes the dean's list, I'll be the first to call you."

Two months later Unc and Lorna moved me to Tallahassee and rented me a room in a little house just off campus. Late in the afternoon, we stood on the front porch, all three afraid to say good-bye.

Finally Unc turned to me. "You say you want to study journalism?"

"Yes, sir."

He nodded and tongued the toothpick from one side of his mouth to the other. "You can put your boots in the oven, but that doesn't make them biscuits."

I didn't need a translation. But then he surprised me by offering one.

"You can say whatever you want about something, but that doesn't change what it is." He put his hands on my shoulders, looked out over campus, then back at me. "You tell the truth . . . the first time . . . every time."

I nodded, but no words came. My throat wouldn't let them out.

Three and a half months later, Ms. Sullivan kept her word, and his phone rang.

Chapter 31

Nighttime fell across the Zuta, bringing the sound of two hoot owls shouting at each other across the treetops. I leaned against the front porch post not knowing if they were setting up to mate or telling each other to stay off their property. Eyes closed, I heard the screen door creep open. Tommye had gone up to bed shortly after her dad left, and Unc was paying bills at the kitchen table with Aunt Lorna. Sketch shuffled out of the house wearing his Spidey pajamas. He sat down next to me, his notebook on his lap. He scribbled quickly and held it up for me.

WHO WAS THAT LADY TODAY?

"She's a momma . . . looking for her son."

DID SHE THINK I WAS HIM?

"Yes."

He wrote without looking at the page. AM I?

His question pressed me against the railing. Men spend their lives asking *Who am I* when the real question is *Whose am I?* I don't think you can answer the first until you've settled the second. First horse, then cart. Identity does not grow out of action until it has taken root in belonging. The orchid speech taught me that.

Across the pasture, fireflies sparked inside the fog that had drifted in.

I shook my head. "No."

He rested his head on top of his arms, which were folded across the top of his knees. I hadn't said much to Unc since Uncle Jack left. None of us had. Supper was quiet, and Sketch had picked up on the tension.

The screen door creaked. Unc walked out in his slippers and sat down on the steps opposite me. He was carrying a white chunk of marble, about the size of a Rubik's cube. It was mostly white with a single smoke-colored vein running through the middle. Two sides were jagged—where it'd broken off the slab—and the others were smooth and flat. The topside had been polished to a high shine.

He turned the marble in his hands and rubbed at it with his thumbs. "I was working the other day at this new barn on the north side of the island. Folks there are building a house. Real nice, too. Big. From their crow's nest they can see both the ocean and the intracoastal. They've got this big trash pile out back. Sort of a place where they throw all their scraps. I found this, and the foreman said I could have it."

Sketch's interest piqued, and he looked into Unc's lap.

He handed it to the kid, turning it onto its flat end. "Careful, don't let it cut you."

Sketch ran his palm flat across the top.

Unc looked at him down his nose. "You ever heard of Michelangelo?"

Sketch shook his head.

"He was an artist."

The kid looked up.

"Yeah . . . like you, but I think you might be a bit better when it comes to that pencil. Michelangelo was also a painter." He chuckled. "Pretty good one too. Even painted the ceiling in a church." He pulled a small flat-faced hammer and wood chisel out of his back pocket and set them on the porch between them.

"But he was also a sculptor. I heard it told once that he used to go to these huge quarries where they get rock, and he'd instruct the masons to cut out a gigantic piece of marble, about the size of a Buick, then roll it back to his workshop, where he'd spend a couple of years chipping away at it. He'd cut all kinds of things from those stones. People. Horses. Even kings. He'd bang away with a huge hammer and chisel, taking off huge chunks. Then he'd come back with a smaller hammer, smaller chisel, maybe a file, then some sandpaper, and finally a damp velvet cloth.

"Admirers used to ask him, 'How did you create that out of a chunk of rock?' He'd shake his head and say, 'I didn't. It was there all along. I just let it out.' He called it 'releasing the form inside.' People used to buy his statues and then put them in the center of their house or someplace they could shine a light on them. It was special to have one, and they'd put it in a place of honor."

Sketch looked up at him, eyes curious.

Unc tapped him gently on the chest. "Inside you is a thing worth putting on a pedestal—worth putting out there for all the world to see. That piece of rock might have been knocked around, roughed up a bit, considered scrap, and thrown on the trash pile . . . but that's only because they don't know what's on the inside. They can't see like Michelangelo. 'Cause if they could, they'd know that there's something in there that's just waiting to jump out. Like there is inside you. I'm sorry for the hammer and chisel. I wish life didn't work that way." He pulled a small scrap piece of velvet out of his pocket, unfolded it, and laid it across Sketch's leg. "Just remember . . . the velvet cloth ain't far behind."

Sketch looked up at Unc, wanting more. Unc pulled him closer, but he was done. He'd said what he came to say. The three of us sat on the porch watching the fireflies dance across the pasture. Aunt Lorna, who'd been eavesdropping at the screen door, stepped out and handed me a mason jar with holes punched in the top.

I walked off the porch and began skipping across the pasture, snatching at the stars. Sketch watched me with a tilted head. Then my jar lit up like a riverboat lantern. We spent an hour running across the pasture chasing fireflies. Unc too. By the time all three of us were out of breath, we'd shoved half the Milky Way into that jar.

When we tucked him into bed, he set the jar next to his bed where every few seconds it would flash like a meteor.

Unc and I stood in the doorway. He whispered, "You want to talk to him, or me?"

"I think he needs to hear from you."

He walked into the room, squatted, and looked into the glass. I lingered outside my old room, listening, remembering.

"You ever wondered why God made light come out of a firefly's butt?"

I shook my head and smiled—laughter for pain.

I had a strong need to sit on my boat, so I grabbed my keys off the hook and headed for the door. When I reached Vicky, I heard the screen door close behind me. I cranked her up and slid the stick into neutral. Unc leaned on Vicky and waited for me to get the rest of it off my chest. I was angry, but when I looked at him—his yellowed T-shirt, red neck, freckled shoulders, and honesty painted across his face, I couldn't aim it at him. Least of all at him. "How do you know about Michelangelo?"

He smiled and pushed his toothpick from one side of his mouth to the other. "What I know might surprise you."

I didn't often get uppity with Uncle Willee. He had lived too much, through times that were too hard for me to think I knew better than him. But sometimes the pressure in the cooker needed venting.

"What's eating you, boy?"

"Honest answer?"

He nodded.

"You."

"Oh, that. What is it that you believe about me?"

"Uncle Jack took everything you had or dreamed of having. Why haven't you ever hired an attorney? Pleaded your case, struck back, hit him where it hurts?"

"So what then? What would I have?"

"Respectability."

"Then what would I have?"

"A good name."

"Then what would I have?"

"People's respect."

"Then what?"

"Some dang dignity."

"But I have all that."

"You do? How? You're a doormat, and his Italian leather shoes have left prints all over your face. Why don't you get in his face and tell him what you think?"

Unc had a way of hammering nails in the coffin of your argument when you least expected it. He stared at me, then spoke softly. His tone told me he was talking more to me than about his brother. "Words that soak into your ears are whispered, not yelled."

"Unc—I don't doubt you—or what you know. What I doubt is why you keep it a secret."

"I know. But you're gonna have to trust me on this."

"I have. My whole life. But"—I stared up at Tommye's window— "it's getting harder."

"Chase, I can't tell you what you want to know."

"Can't, or won't?"

"Won't."

"Why?"

There was a long pause where I could see him arguing with himself. Finally, the side that won spoke.

"Because . . . I love you that much."

He blinked, and for the first time in my adult life, I saw something I'd never seen.

"Always have."

Water lapped the side of the boat, which was pointing west and tugging on its two anchors. That told me the wind was out of the west and that tomorrow would be warm. Even hot.

I spent most of the night working on my article. Red said he wanted a story of life with the kid, where he is and how he's doing, mixed with the life of an orphan. Sort of a window into the orphan's plight, using Sketch's eyes as our telescope. I went over my story—reading it aloud several times—tweaked it in a few places and, at two in the morning, e-mailed it to Red.

He called me ten minutes later. I flipped my cell phone open.

"Don't you ever sleep?"

"Not much. It's too quiet here. I miss the sounds of taxis, horns, sirens, and people screaming at one another. All I've got out here is the sound of bullfrogs, owls, and the occasional cat in heat."

"You don't know how good you've got it."

I heard his screen door squeak, which meant he'd read my story on his porch.

"You've got something different going on in this story."

"What do you mean?"

"The detached, cold, hard journalist of fact has been replaced by someone with a pulse."

I wasn't sure how to take that. "You want me to rewrite it?"

He chuckled. "Not hardly."

"What then?"

"Keep looking. And yes, I'll buy the Braves tickets."

An hour later, I turned out the lights—after my computer had beat me three times in a row at chess.

Chapter 32

THE POWER OF A NAME: DISCOVERING THE IDENTITY OF JOHN DOE #117

Though mute, he is anything but silent.

John Doe #117 was moved to the Brunswick Boys' home last week following his release from the hospital. A mute boy of unknown identity—whose age is believed to be somewhere between eight and ten—was discovered nearly two weeks ago next to a railroad track. Authorities believe he had been kidnapped and thrown from the car just before the driver was hit and killed by a southbound freight train. DNA testing determined that the driver of the car was no relation to the child. Following a week's stay in the hospital, where he displayed a penchant for pizza and ice cream, the boy—who, though mute, is anything but silent—was moved to a local boys' home while authorities worked to secure a suitable foster home. Authorities are trying to find the boy's relatives, but are cautious given the many scars of physical abuse marring the boy's body. Since leaving the hospital he has proved adept at jigsaw puzzles and chess—which he seems to have mastered better than most in Glynn County.

John Doe #117 is one of more than 500,000 unadopted children living in foster care in the United States. Each, like Little Orphan Annie, lives with the inextinguishable hope that Mom or Dad will walk through the door at any moment and reclaim their baby. Yet, in truth, for every child that is adopted, three more are passed over. Their average age is eight. Most can wait three to four years to be adopted, while others reach eighteen and the wait is over. Statistically, when a child reaches eight or nine years of age, their likelihood of remaining in foster care becomes higher than the probability they will be adopted.

The emotional effects of a seemingly parentless life can plague them for a lifetime—abandonment, rejection, low self-esteem. "Adoptees suffer from a fear of loss. They see loss all over the place," stated the late Dr. Marty Hernandez, who was a psychiatrist at the University of Washington's School of Medicine and a nationally recognized expert on adoption.

Abandonment bleeds into every area of their lives, permeating their psyches and whispering the lie that others in their lives will also abandon them. Most children feel there must have been something shameful about their past and begin to feel ashamed of themselves. As a result they fear rejection, have trouble making commitments, and avoid intimacy—even sabotaging their relationships out of self-preservation in an attempt to insulate themselves from further abandonment. Why? Vulnerability costs too much. "They fear that a person they invest in will leave them, just like their birth parents," said Dr. Hernandez. "If it happened once, it can happen again."

Milestone events—such as graduation from high school or college, marriage, the birth of a child, or the death of an adoptive parent—can prove especially difficult for adoptees because they spark commonly asked questions: Why did my parents put me up for adoption? Was something wrong with me? Did I enter the world defective? What would life have been like had I not been adopted? Some rationalize their feelings with monologues such as, "My birth mother was not able to care for me, and she wanted me to have the best home possible," or, "At least they didn't abort me," but these arguments are easily worn out, and most know better.

One question commonly shared by all adoptees surrounds their name. What was/is their real name? Language philosophers such as Wittgenstein, Langer and Percy suggest two primary modes of thought on language. The first holds that language had meaning before humans got hold of it, i.e., an Edenic language discovered when Adam and Eve first entered the garden. They pulled words off the shelf as needed with the meaning inherent. The second philosophy says that words have no meaning except that which we give them. Any combination of letters can mean anything we want. Meaning is obtained through use.

So what does an ivory-towered academic discussion have to do with unadopted children? More than you might think. A name tells them not only who they are but, maybe more importantly, whose they are. Every adoptee lives knowing that at one time he or she had a real name—the one their mother or father whispered the nine months before they were born. Some were recorded on birth certificates, some not, but all were known by the parent and believed in by the child. A change in paperwork can't erase words stamped on the human heart.

Recent history records many famous orphaned, fostered, and adopted kids—Babe Ruth, John Lennon, Marilyn Monroe—but it's those from fiction that mean most to those passed over and still waiting. They carry the stories with them: Superman, Luke Skywalker, Oliver Twist, Peter Pan, Mowgli, Huckleberry Finn. They read, tell, and retell the stories of the heroic and the happy because the ending has already been written—and they know it by heart.

Chapter 33

I'd been home from Florida State just under a year when I pulled the orange crate out from under my bed and tacked my collage back up on the wall. While I had passed with honors, I still could not crack the story that had gotten me started in the first place. Too many pieces of the puzzle didn't fit. For so long I had buried it, held it at bay, closed my ears to the rumors and whispers, that finally the pressure cooker just exploded in my lap. I had grown up under the shroud of two indecipherable mysteries: I didn't know about me, and I didn't know about Liam McFarland. I figured I couldn't know about me, but I had an idea the truth about him could be found if I knew where to dig.

Have you ever been in a boat on a river or lake and been approached by people in another boat? They throw you a rope and then, in order to help, you pull the two together and place one foot on each boat, holding the two off each other but close enough so that passengers can jump from one to the other. That's what my life was like: standing on two boats, anchored to nothing, with constant waves and wind—just one wave short of going over.

Together, it was just too much static—like a radio dial that would never tune into the Braves game. While the newspaper gave me a job and put me to work writing all the stories nobody else wanted, I spent late nights, early mornings, and all-nighters obsessed with a twenty-year-old secret. Through the Freedom of Information Act, I requested old court documents, transcripts, the official pardon, and I even interviewed one of the guards who drove Unc from prison to bury his son.

Six months later, I laid it out for him. I told him his own story—at least what I knew of it. For two hours he nodded and dug his hand into a grocery sack of boiled peanuts. I think he was proud of my work. When I finished, he sat rocking, sucking the juice out of an unopened peanut, his feet propped up on the front porch railing. Throwing a shell over the railing, he sipped some water and studied the peanuts in his hand. "And?"

"What?"

"You still haven't asked me your question."

"Which question?"

"The one question you been wanting to ask me for twenty years."

I looked out through the pecan trees and watched a black fox squirrel jump from one branch to another, ferrying an uncracked nut in his mouth. I leaned against the railing and grabbed a handful of peanuts. "Well?"

"Well, what?"

"It's hard to beat the evidence."

"That's not a question."

"You were the last one in the vault."

"That's not either."

"You, Perry Kenner, and Ellsworth McFarland were the only ones with access to the bonds, because I don't think Ellsworth or Perry trusted Jack, given his affinity for both poker and leverage."

"You're still making statements."

"When I finally found and interviewed one of the guards who drove you to Brunswick from prison, he said something I've never understood. He said William McFarland did not cry. The Willee I know would have cried his eyes out."

Unc seemed lost in the memory, and if it had an impact, he kept it hidden.

"Well?"

"Well, what?"

"Unc . . ." I cracked open a peanut, which squirted me in the eye with salty juice. "After twenty years of rumors and people whispering behind your back as we walk down the street, I'd like to know."

I was in a bad place. I had tired of fighting the demons I couldn't see.

"I'll admit, guilty or not, your life has pretty well sucked, but how'd you like to be me? I grew up under the rumors. Hearing people whisper behind your back and never knowing if they were right or wrong. I didn't ask for this. I got brought into it . . . you brought it on yourself."

Even now, I wish I could take that back.

He waited a long time, then nodded.

"You mean . . . you did it?"

He shook his head.

"Then what are you saying?"

"I know that it's been hard on you." He paused. "Maybe the hardest on you."

"So?"

He sucked on a peanut and shook his head again.

"Why won't you tell me?"

He slid his glasses off his nose, wiped his forehead with his shirt-sleeve, and cleared his nose. When he sat back and put his hat back on, tears broke out of the corners of his wrinkled eyes and fell off his sun-weathered cheeks. He stood, walked to the end of the porch, and adjusted his belt. His voice was strained and weak. "Signing that release to the state to let them have my . . . my son . . . was the second hardest decision I've ever made." He sucked through his teeth, then spat.

I watched him walk away, and knew that I'd hurt him. It was self-ish, and I knew it. "Uncle Willee?"

He stopped, his back to me. I wanted to take it back. Bridge the chasm. But it was too late. His big, broad shoulders were slumped.

I wasn't mad at him. Not really. I was mad at my real dad for never driving up that road. That, too, hit me after the fact. Maybe wanting to hide my own mystery made me want to expose his. I'd lived most of my life thinking there was something wrong with me, that I was somehow defective, so I thought if I could take the attention off me . . . but it was a stupid thing to do.

"What . . . was the hardest?"

He tipped his hat back, scratched the back of one calf with the toe of the other foot, then walked off through the muscadine vines, through his tomato bushes, and into the greenhouse to talk to his orchids. I didn't see him the rest of the day.

That night, I wrote another letter to my dad.

Dear Dad,
I lied. I never quit looking out the window.
Chase

Chapter 34

I left the boat just after six and arrived at the house a little before seven. Unc, who was usually gone by now, sat at the kitchen table with Sketch. The kid's mouth was covered in syrup and butter, and half a stack of pancakes sat on his plate. He hardly noticed me when I walked in.

The chess set sat on the corner of the table—a match half-played. Unc was intently studying the board. His face told me he might as well have been studying quantum physics.

On the refrigerator, Aunt Lorna had taped three sketches. The first was a peacock, the second was Bob the Turkey, and the third was an orchid in bloom. Each looked as realistic as the thing itself.

It was Sketch's move. He shoved a forkful of pancakes into his mouth, moved his rook, and captured Unc's bishop with barely a look at the board. Unc sat back, tilted his hat, sipped his coffee, and leaned in toward the board again.

I poured some juice and stood next to Aunt Lorna, who was packing bologna sandwiches. I looked out the window toward the barn, where the lights were off. "You seen Tommye this morning?"

Aunt Lorna shook her head. "She left shortly after you last night."

"When did she get back?"

Aunt Lorna placed four sandwiches inside a large Ziploc bag and shook her head. "She's not."

She served me a plate of buckwheat pancakes, which I ate while I watched the kid beat the pants off Unc. An hour later, swimming in the sleepy buzz that follows a heavy dose of flour, sugar, and fat, I leaned back in my chair, sucked on a toothpick, and watched Unc read my story in the paper. Red must've stopped the press to get it in—with a small paper, anything's possible.

Around eight thirty, Mandy opened the screen door and waved. She looked nothing like the woman I'd seen at the table across the glass from Reuben. She wore a blue T-shirt, faded jeans, running shoes, and her hair was pulled back in a ponytail. All she lacked was a Braves cap. Aunt Lorna served her a plate of buckwheat pancakes, and she started swirling them with syrup. She spotted the newspaper folded up on the corner of the table. "I read your story."

Comments like that are two-part. Writers learn this. "And?"

She sank her teeth into the pancakes and spoke with her mouth full. "Something's different."

I grabbed a stack of cards and began shuffling them on the table. "That's what Red said."

She mumbled through the wad of pancakes in her mouth. "Good editor."

She finished her pancakes and then pulled me out on the porch for what I sensed was attorney-talk. First she looked back inside the house to make sure Sketch wasn't listening.

"I want to run back by the trailer behind the bottling plant. I'd like to take Buddy inside and watch his reaction."

I considered this. "What do you hope to gain?"

"Don't know." She shrugged. "It's just a hunch that he might show or tell us something we missed."

"Okay, but we don't need to spring it on him."

"Agreed. You want to tell him, or me?"

"I'll tell him."

"I was hoping you'd say that."

I went back inside, and Sketch met me with a deck of cards. I shuffled, dealt us two cards each, and set the deck between us. Sketch eyed the cards, did not look impressed with my challenge, and picked up his cards. He studied them, then raised his eyebrows and held them there: my move. I looked at my hand and realized I hadn't dealt myself a very good one—a pair of eights.

I slid a card from the top of the deck and said, "I'll take one." It only made matters worse. "You?"

He tapped the table one time, then laid down his cards. At first he laid down a seven and a three. Then he laid the third card—a face card—across the other two.

I laid mine down—a pair of eights topped with the face card I'd just picked up. Then I pointed at Mandy. "Ms. Parker and I think we found the trailer that you sketched in your notebook."

He listened without changing expression.

"We'd like to go back by there today on our way to Atlanta."

He looked at Mandy, then back at me.

"It's empty. No one's home." I shrugged. "Except a bunch of cats."

Surprisingly, his reaction wasn't negative. He simply nodded one time, and then looked at me as if to say *What else you want to talk about?*

"Okay, then."

The trip to Atlanta was turning into more than I bargained for. Unc got whiff of the Braves game and shook his head. "Ain't no way on earth I'm letting you go to Turner Field without me just so you can come home and tell me about it for the next three months. Especially not when they're this close to winning another pennant. Besides, I need to go along for Buddy, to explain the rules of baseball."

Being that this was now a road trip, Unc insisted on driving, and when he traveled, he liked to do so in style. He backed Sally out of the carport and drove around the front. Because a hearse is custom-fitted to carry long pine boxes, rear seating can be a problem. Backseats have to be retrofitted in if you plan to carry people who want to sit upright. Unc had taken care of this a few years back, but it did little to stem the thought that you were sitting where countless horizontal bodies had once lain.

Unc patted the black top. "Mandy, meet Sally."

"Oh, this . . . she . . . has a name?"

Unc nodded. "Ain't she a beauty?"

"Unlike anything I've ever seen." Mandy slid into the seat, hesitant to lean back, and slowly looked around.

When we pulled out of the drive, Sketch sat in the front seat devouring the scenery out the windows and listening to Unc talk about baseball while Mandy and I sat in the back fighting over the direction of the air-conditioning vents. The only trouble with leaving was that Tommye hadn't shown. I wasn't sure if that was bad, but I was close to certain that it wasn't good.

Because I knew I wasn't much competition, I placed my Apple laptop on Sketch's lap and showed him how to work the touchpad to play a game of chess. I set the computer level on novice, and he began playing the machine. Fifteen minutes later, he'd beaten the computer in three straight games.

We drove beyond the Zuta, its gargantuan pine trees spiraling up into the horizon, and then west along Highway 25. While Unc asked Mandy where she was from, where she went to law school, and just generally made small talk, I found myself lost in the rows of pines, the power lines, the telephone poles, the cypress swamps, and the yellow deer crossing signs. I didn't realize how quiet I'd been until Mandy tapped my shoulder.

"You in there?"

"Huh?"

"Yeah, you."

"Oh, yeah . . . just—"

"Don't mind him," Unc broke in, "you ought to see him when he really gets constipated." Mandy laughed, and he continued, "He can chew on an idea for days before he lets you in on it."

"I do not . . ." It was a feeble attempt.

He looked at me and said quietly, "She's fine."

"Huh?"

"She went to see your Uncle Jack."

"What? Why didn't she tell me?"

He shook his head. "She had a meeting in town and then said she wanted to get a few of her things out at his place."

"But . . . she was gone all night."

"She's a big girl."

"Yeah, but . . ."

Unc paused. "What do you do when you've hooked one that might snap your line?"

I knew where this was going. "You loosen the drag and let him run."

He nodded and looked out the window, lifting his sunglasses back over his eyes. His voice dropped almost to a whisper, like he was talking to himself. "Then you pray they don't shred your line on an oyster bed."

We arrived in Jesup about twenty minutes later and drove around the back of the bottling company. Sketch shut the lid on my laptop and sat clutching his notebook. I tapped him gently on the shoulder.

"Hey . . . nobody's here, okay?"

He nodded and pushed his glasses up on his nose, but didn't look at me. We pulled up in front of the trailer and parked. I opened his door, and he stepped out. He stood a minute, taking it in.

When Mandy walked up the steps, he followed. She pushed open the door and sent cats scattering to the far corners. Sketch stepped across the threshold and did something I'd never heard him do. He whistled.

Two seconds later, a large tabby cat with no tail came out from underneath the back of the couch. Surprisingly, it wore a collar and looked well-fed. In fact, it was huge. This one could have starred in a Disney movie. It walked up to him, and he knelt and picked it up. The cat purred, rubbed its whiskers against his face, and licked his nose. Evidently they'd done this before. After they'd said hello, he held the cat in his arm and showed me the collar. Clipped to the buckle was a round, silver nametag.

Mandy looked over my shoulder while I read it aloud. "Bones. I take it you know her?"

He frowned at me, turned the cat over and showed me its belly, among other things.

"Oh . . . sorry. I mean *him*."

He nodded.

Unc stepped around me and said, "You know, we been needing a good cat around the house."

The kid looked up at Unc as if the freedom even to make such a request had not occurred to him.

Unc rubbed Bones's head. "Oh, yeah. This is my kind of cat. Big. Tough. Got one heck of a name. He's coming with us."

I knew that Unc had never cared too much for cats, and Unc knew that I knew. He thought they were the prima donnas of the pet world. But I had the good sense to keep my mouth shut.

The kid looked toward the bedroom like he was waiting for somebody bigger, with more authority, to walk in the room and set Unc straight. When it didn't happen, he set the cat on the couch and then walked to Unc and put his hand out—another thing I'd never seen him do.

Unc smiled big as the brim on his Gus hat. He stooped a bit, gently shook the kid's hand, and said, "You're welcome. And it's my pleasure."

We walked through the trailer, following Sketch. He walked from room to room, not really touching anything, just looking in. When we got to the bedroom, I touched the handle to open the door, but he reached out, touched my hand, and shook his head.

Coming back down the hallway, he walked into the bathroom and knelt at the end of the tub where the faucet came out of the wall. He tapped on the corner board below the tub and tried to pull it back, like he wanted to open a miniature sliding glass door. When it didn't budge, he started looking around the bathroom. Not finding what he wanted, he opened his sketch pad and drew a picture of a flathead screwdriver.

I shook my head, while Unc reached into his pocket. He pulled out his two-bladed Barlow pocketknife and clipped open the smaller blade. He passed it handle-first to Sketch and said, "Careful. It'll cut you."

The kid inserted the tip in the crack, pried slightly, and the piece of wood budged just far enough to get his fingers inside. He carefully closed the pocketknife and handed it back to Unc, who held his hands out like a stop sign.

"No, no. That's bad luck. Always hand a knife back the way you got it."

The kid put his fingernail in the groove, reopened the knife, and passed the handle back to Unc.

"You got one of these?"

Sketch shook his head.

Unc squatted on his heels, eye-level with him. "You mean to tell me you don't own a pocketknife?"

Sketch looked at me, then slowly shook his head.

"Well, that ain't right. I reckon you better keep mine."

Sketch looked up, surprised.

Unc twirled his hat in his hands. "Yeah, long as you're a guest in my house, you better hold onto that. It'll cut most fishing line and clip orchids, and you just never know when you might need it." He poked me in the stomach. "Just ask him."

I smiled, reached into my pocket, and pulled out an exact copy of the one he'd just given away. Sketch studied both, his chin lifted almost an inch, and then he slipped it into his pocket.

Kneeling on the floor, he pulled back the board and then reached his arm as far as he could back underneath the tub. We heard something clank a few times, then he slid his arm out, pulling an ivory-colored plastic box with him. It rattled like it was full of marbles. He sat Indian style on the floor, unlocked the little brass clasp on the box, and flipped it open. When he did, both sides met squarely in the middle and turned into a travel-sized chess set. With all sixty-four squares staring up at us, he slid open one of the two drawers and pulled out a baseball card. He rubbed it against his chest, shining the face side, then handed it to Unc.

Unc flipped it over, and his eyes grew big as half-dollars. "Whoa . . . where'd you get this?"

Sketch shrugged, pulled one of the bishops from the box, and shined it on his shirt. He studied a few other pieces, then closed the lid, locked it, and tucked the box under his arm.

Unc handed the card back. "Well, don't lose it. By the time you get there, it might pay for half your college education."

The kid shook his head, slid the card into Unc's shirt pocket, and tapped it twice.

Unc said, "No, son, I can't . . ."

The kid poked Unc in the stomach, pointed at his shirt pocket, nodded, and walked out of the bathroom.

Unc looked at me. "Well, I'll be . . ."

"What?" I said.

"He just gave me a Hank Aaron baseball card."

I watched Sketch walk down the hall, pick up the cat, and walk out the front door, the cat in one arm, the box in the other. "Well, I'd say you got the better end of that deal."

Mandy pulled Unc aside. "Mr. McFarland?"

"Yes ma'am."

She smiled, crossed her arms, and rubbed the toe of one running shoe across the shag carpet. "You really think it's safe to give the boy a knife?"

"Ms. Parker?"

"Yes sir."

"Sooner or later, somebody somewhere is gonna have to trust that boy with something." Unc looked through the jagged edges of the trailer window. "Becoming a man don't happen overnight. It's something that's passed down. That boy's behind. But he can catch up." He stuck his thumbs in his pockets and waited.

"But sir. Don't you worry that—"

"Aw, I been cleaning horses' hoofs with it all week, and it's duller than a round ten-penny nail. Probably won't cut a wet noodle."

I knew this, too, was not true, and Unc knew I knew. But I also knew that this was one of those cases where he was right and what she didn't know wouldn't hurt her.

"You realize that if he cuts himself, and you take him to the emergency room to get stitched up or cleaned up or whatever, child services will be knocking on your door before the Betadine dries."

"Well, then . . . looks like I'll just have to doctor him myself."

I laughed, and Mandy looked at me. "What?"

I held up my right hand and showed her the faint outline of a twenty-year-old scar on the first knuckle of my thumb. She shook her head and turned to walk out, pulling her sunglasses down off the top of her head. "I don't even want to know about it."

I turned to follow her and Unc stopped me, whispering, "He cuts himself . . . even nicking a hangnail, and I'm holding you responsible."

"Thanks."

Chapter 35

Uncle Willee taught me how to fish from the first summer I came to live with Aunt Lorna and him. We'd fish off the pier in Brunswick, in the tributaries of the Altamaha or the Little Brunswick, in the pools around the Sanctuary, and anywhere else we thought fish would bite. If he wasn't working, and I wasn't in school, then chances were good that we were somewhere wetting a line.

In high school I bought a used kayak, put in at the harbor amongst the shrimp boats, and slipped out through the grass where not even the guys in flatboats could go. That took me along the shoreline for miles. I caught trout, drum, reds, and even hooked up with a tarpon or two. This produced a lot of good dinners during high school.

After my sorry attempt to tell Unc his own story, I needed to clear my head, which is often the point of my fishing. So I woke before daylight, loaded my kayak atop Vicky, and drove to Brunswick. I put in near the Brunswick harbor and started hugging the coastline, wanting to fish the first of the outgoing tide.

Maybe a half mile downriver—still well in sight of town—my paddle struck something in the weeds that was hard but not necessarily rock, and it certainly wasn't an oyster bed. The marsh grass had grown up around it and the mud flats had mounded over it. I dug around and uncovered what looked like a coquina drain. Nearly three feet square, with a two-foot opening, it came out of the hill upon which some of the town sat—including the ZB&T. The mouth was blocked by a tic-tac-toe of crude iron bars.

Given the Spanish influence, forgotten coquina structures lie scattered all over these islands, so it was not entirely unusual, but it was the bars that really piqued my interest. They were hinged. Meaning they would swing out, but not in. And they were locked. Somewhere further up that two-hundred-year-old "pipe" was a mechanical release that triggered the lock to allow the bars movement. After two centuries in salt water, the bars literally crumbled when I applied pressure. Twenty minutes later, I wrestled the spindly remainders out of the coquina.

Scratching my head, I looked around. Something didn't make good sense. High tide covered up the drain completely. But I also knew that the tidal fluctuation ranged from four to six feet. The reds were circling the schools of shrimp, so I fished a few hours and paddled back in as the tide was halfway out. What I saw answered my questions. While the incoming tide filled the pipe, and high tide covered it up, the outgoing washed it out and allowed it to empty.

I'd heard of Spanish and Moorish forts using this very "technology" to drain the latrines of their coastal forts and castles both stateside and in Europe. So I timed the tides, and knowing I had a couple of hours before the water returned, I strapped on a headlamp and belly-crawled through the pipe. It snaked uphill for what must have been a couple hundred yards. About the time I was totally and completely freaked out and starting to wonder how in the world I was going to crawl out backwards, the pipe turned straight up. More iron bars covered the opening. They, too, were hinged but in working order. I flipped the latch and swung the bars up and open.

I climbed up into a coquina cavern, maybe twenty feet wide and sixty or so feet long. Two rows of columns, maybe ten feet apart, supported the ceiling, which was some twelve feet above my head. The ceiling above me was a twentieth-century combination of steel support beams, rebar, and poured concrete. Again, I scratched my head. Certainly, whoever poured the concrete floor above my head knew the coquina was here. Whether or not they knew about the drain was another matter.

The walls were covered in names and dates carved into the coquina, starting in the 1800s. Most were from the mid-1800s. Some quoted Scripture, while others listed their names and those of their family. On the wall just above the entrance of the drain, someone had carved the word _FREEDOM_ and drawn an arrow toward the drain.

I, like everyone else in Brunswick, had grown up hearing rumors of the underground railroad that freed slaves from nearby plantations. But with the passage of time, no one ever really knew where truth ended and rumor began. Looking around, I had a feeling that the truth had been buried pretty close to where I stood.

I checked my watch, gauged the tide, and spent some more time studying the walls. In the southeast corner I found a spiral staircase that led up to a wooden trapdoor. I tapped it, but it didn't budge. It was solid wood, and judging by the sound of it, thick. I pressed my back against it and shoved with my legs. It moved. I did it again, and it broke free, scurrying roaches along the wall and covering me in dust. The door must have been six inches thick and weighed seventy-five pounds. Finally, I lifted the hinged door and slammed it against the concrete wall. A small shaft led upward, maybe two feet, to another piece of wood. This one was thinner and looked like plywood. I pushed, and it, too, lifted upward this time more easily. I pulled upward, felt carpet on my hands, and looked around.

Nothing could have prepared me for what I saw.

I stood up and found a light switch on the wall. I clicked it on and found myself in a bank vault, maybe ten feet long and eight feet wide.

It took me maybe a nanosecond to figure out which one. Unc had never talked much about it, but between the newspaper articles, town gossip, and what I could dig out of him, I'd put together a pretty clear picture of him spending the night in here during the storm that changed his life forever.

Two walls were lined with individual safety deposit boxes, while the opposite walls were lined with much larger ones. At the far end, opposite the door, sat a chair and single table. One last thing caught my eye. A small oriental rug lay crumpled above the carpet-covered door I'd just climbed through. I spread it out over the trapdoor and realized that it was there less for decoration than to cover the cut lines in the carpet. Between the poor lighting and the rug, you'd never know the door existed. Add to that a power outage, and, well . . . I left with one question.

Did Unc know about the trapdoor?

I wanted to snoop around some more, but I knew the tide wouldn't let me—unless I wanted to spend the next nine to ten hours in the basement. I stepped into the basement and finally down into the drain, where I heard the echo of water lapping against the coquina. It was time to go.

I crawled quickly, scared a few fiddler crabs in the process, and slid out the mouth of the drain just as the tide was rolling over the lip. I slipped back into my kayak just as the shrimp boats were idling out to sea.

I don't know why I discovered the drain that particular morning. I'd paddled by that spot more than a hundred times since junior high, and why my paddle never banged against the coquina before is beyond me. Proximity to shore, water level, how far I was inserting the paddle on each stroke—all of these things played a part, but that still doesn't explain the mystery of why then and there.

That night, I sprung it on Unc. I was mad, and he could tell from the tone of my voice. "I found something today."

He looked at me over the top of the newspaper. "Yeah?"

"I did some digging today in the basement . . . the bank basement."

He raised his eyebrows.

"Yeah . . . until today, I thought it was just a cool piece of slave history. How come you never told me about the door under the carpet?"

My question caught him off guard.

He set the paper down and tilted his head, studying me. "Chase, I didn't steal those bonds."

I crossed my arms. "Then you're saying you knew about it?"

" 'Course I knew about it. Jack and I found it as kids."

Pieces started falling into place. "So you knew all along that he took the bonds?"

He nodded.

"Why?"

Still he said nothing.

"Unc?"

"Some things are worth more than money."

I studied him and for the first time, understood that he was hiding something. Something close. "What're you hiding?" Then it hit me. "Oh, I see. He's got something on you, and you both know it."

He didn't move.

"What's he got on you? What's he been using all this time to keep you quiet?"

Unc just nodded and smiled. "You're gonna make one heck of a reporter someday."

"Let me get this straight—you lost your dad, your wife, your son, your job, most everything you ever owned . . . heck, even your name." I looked around. "Now what on earth is worth that?"

He studied his fingernails and chewed his lip. "I heard about this guy one time who, back in the fifties, went off into the bush and tried to convert the natives. He got off the plane, and they surrounded him and shoved about eight spears through his chest." He shook his head.

"Seems like a waste, don't it? Before he left, somebody asked him why he was going." Unc walked toward the edge of the porch and talked to me over his shoulder. "He said he gave up what he couldn't keep to gain what he couldn't lose."

Unc stepped off the porch, looked around what little world he had left, and then turned and looked at me. "I've tried to remember that." He smiled. "And some days I do."

In the five years since that conversation, I've written over a thousand newspaper articles—several of which have been syndicated nationally. Readers say I have a nose for the truth. Red would be the first among them, which is good because he's my boss. That may be correct, except for the one story where it really matters. Now, when I look at the collage on my wall, I can only scratch my head. Like the Scarlet Pimpernel, the truth is elusive. I know the who, the what, the when, and the how, but I have yet to crack the code on the why.

I've crawled back up that drain many times and spent hours in the vault. Despite this, I can't prove what happened in the summer of 1979. My nose tells me only one man can do that, but for some reason he's not talking. When he does, he quotes dead people or says something that only he understands.

Discovering the basement and the trapdoor in the vault didn't help my case any. By giving him access, it only added nails to Unc's coffin. By keeping it a secret, he's thrown dirt on it. By admitting he's known all along that Jack stole the money, he etched his own tombstone. Contrast that with my college philosophy class—my professor said there are five ways of "knowing": personal experience, revelation, empirical evidence, logic, and hearsay. Given those methods of knowing something, I *know* this—and I'd stake my life on it: William "Liam" McFarland willingly took the fall for something he didn't do.

I have lived my entire life in a chasm, pulled between two polar tensions. On one side stands the entire town, what they believe, what history has recorded and suggests. And at the front of that crowd is Uncle Jack, confirming everyone's belief. Helping him out is Unc's silence, which only makes matters worse.

But on the other side stands Unc. Battered. And unbending.

Somewhere in the middle, scratching my head, is me.

Chapter 36

Due to some beltway traffic, an overturned car, and a bypass around Spaghetti Junction, Mandy, Unc, Sketch, and I arrived at Turner Field just a few minutes before the game started. Unc left the windows cracked, giving Bones a cross-breeze as he curled up in the backseat. Scurrying across the parking lot, we were intercepted by a one-legged man in a wheelchair. His hair was matted, and he reeked of alcohol. He spun around in front of us, slurring his words, his lips thick and numb, and spit across the asphalt. "Chhhhhangggge?"

I walked past him without a second glance. As did Unc and Mandy, who had turned her head and was breathing into the wind. About the time I took a deep breath, a small hand tugged on my back pocket. I turned to find the kid standing with his hand out and palm up. I pointed toward the stadium. "Wait 'til we get in there, and I'll get you whatever you want."

He shook his head and jerked his hand.

"What?"

He pointed at the man in the chair.

"Sketch, if I give that man money, he's going to wheel himself out of this parking lot and down to the corner liquor store."

The kid stomped one foot and jerked his hand a second time.

"I'm not giving that man money."

The kid opened his notepad and wrote in dark, bold letters, GIVE TO ALL WHO BEG FROM YOU.

I put my hands on my hips. "Who says?"

The kid looked up, then back at me, expressionless.

Unc and Mandy stood behind me, trying to decipher this round of charades.

I looked up and behind me. "Who!?"

He flipped a page, drew a cross on a hillside and the words MATTHEW 5 beside it, and held it up for all three of us. By now, the man in the wheelchair had rolled himself up behind the kid.

"You're quoting scripture?"

He opened his notebook and pulled out a single wrinkled page that had been torn from its binding.

I turned it over in my hands. "You've got to be kidding me."

The kid shook his head.

Unc stepped in front of me, pulled five dollars from his pocket, and stuffed it into the man's shirt pocket. Looking at me, he said, "I should've raised you better. Come Sunday, you're front and center. You been spending too much time fishing."

We walked into the stadium, up a couple ramps, and out into the stands. Our seats were down past first base, about thirty rows above where the clay meets the outfield. We bought a program, sat down, and I took a long look around. The park had changed, the roster had changed, the music was louder, and the food and drinks were twice as expensive, but it was still magical. Sketch's face told me that he thought so too.

I studied the program and looked at all the new faces and talent. Terry Pendleton was now the hitting coach, and Chipper Jones was in the fourteenth year of his career and a shoo-in for Cooperstown. I counted—it'd been fifteen years since "the slide." I looked over toward where our seats would have been in the old stadium and tried to remember being there with Tommye. I caught Unc's eye and realized I wasn't the only one who remembered.

We bought food and drink from most every vendor who walked past our seats: popcorn, cotton candy, peanuts, hot dogs, cold beer, pretzels, a couple slices of pizza, cokes, water, ice cream. By the sixth inning, the kid's stomach looked like a little Buddha's. Mine too. We had to slouch in our chairs just to make room for them.

I looked around the stadium at all the fathers and sons sitting side by side, gloves ready to catch a foul ball, rally caps turned up, and smiles spread earlobe to earlobe. Despite the multimillion-dollar insanity, the steroids, and the egos, baseball still does that. It brings them together.

Then I thought about Sketch's life and what lay ahead. Since the means of terminating parental rights was a public process, the DA's office had placed ads in nearly twenty papers around the Southeast. That's like waving a sign that reads, "Hey, come pick up your kid." And —no matter what I thought of them—they might read that ad, show up tomorrow, throw him in the backseat, and disappear. Forever. 'Course, they'd live under some close scrutiny for a while, but if they kept their noses clean, they'd keep him. They could be the worst, most abusing white trailer trash in the country, and yet neither Mandy nor I could do anything about it. The law protected the parents.

Sketch's right arm rested next to mine. He slid his arm down the armrest, rubbing his elbow along my forearm. The skin was thin, tough, and felt like it'd been run through a cheese grater.

When I was about his size, Unc had me working in the greenhouse. One night after dinner, we went out there to check on his plants. He clicked on the light, sat me down, and slid a purple orchid with a three-foot stem close to my nose. "Pretty bloom, isn't it?"

I nodded.

He tapped it. "The bloom doesn't come from up here"—he brushed away some crushed bark and loose dirt from around the roots—"it comes out of here." He held the orange clay pot in both hands. "Care for the roots, and the flower will bloom all on its own."

Unc then took a slender but strong bamboo shoot, about four feet long, and slid it into the dirt along the stem of the orchid. Then he loosely tied the stem to the shoot. "That's to guide the stem. Otherwise it'll bloom too much, and the weight of the blooms can break the stem. So, let it bloom all it wants, but give it something to lean on."

Mandy caught my eye and the look on my face. "You okay?"

"Yeah . . . just . . . taking in the game." It was a pitiful lie.

I watched Sketch study the field, follow the path of fly balls, read the scoreboard, and saw how his feet dangled from the seat when he leaned back. Mandy watched, too. He was no longer just an assignment to either one of us.

I thought about my story, the last in the three-part series, which Red wanted on his desk in a few days. He said our readers would tire and lose interest if we didn't reach some resolution, so "find it . . . because it's out there." Resolution? *How can an orchid bloom if the roots have been twisted off with pliers, burnt with Marlboros, and drowned with beer?* Where's the resolution in that? Where's the happy ending?

Sketch was watching the batter at home plate, intensely trained on the movement. His right hand—sticky with sugar—unconsciously sketched lines and shades in the thin air, showing that the pencil was tethered to his brain. To his left, Unc was feeding him a constant stream of information, telling him about the batters, the players, who was good at what and why. For once Unc got to play the role of color man. Not surprisingly, after thirty years of following the Braves, he was good at it. But listening to him, I missed Tommye.

With two outs in the middle of the seventh, the batter hit a high pop fly to center field, where Andruw Jones caught it for the third out. The Braves ran in, ground crews pulling screens across the field ran out, and the music began to play. On cue, Unc and I jumped up out of our seats, took off our caps, crossed our arms around each other, and sang at the top of our lungs with the rest of Atlanta. "Take me out to the ball game, take me out with the crowd. . . . "

Mandy laughed, and Sketch pulled both feet up on his seat, watching us with a mixture of curiosity, odd amusement, and maybe a little bit of shock. Unc and I raised our caps and sang louder.

The seventh-inning stretch is almost as entrenched in baseball as the baseball itself. Several theories about its origin exist, but truth be known, we have no idea where and when the custom began. One suggestion involves President William Howard Taft, another a Brother Jasper of Manhattan College. While Unc gave Sketch this lecture, I climbed the steps and went to the restroom.

Everywhere I looked, I saw Tommye. Little girls clutching pink cotton candy, their faces painted with tomahawks, floated around like ballerinas high on the clouds where their fathers placed them. I could hear Tommye's straight-faced commentary, watch her laughter, soak in her little-girl-ness—and yet the woman at home, draped in shame and bad decisions, walked beneath a rain cloud rather than floating atop one. When I reached the walkway overlooking the parking lot, I dialed my loft apartment. It was nearly nine thirty, and chances were good she was asleep under the snowfall of my window unit.

The phone rang seven times, but she never answered.

The Braves were down by two in the bottom of the ninth. Things were not looking good for Sketch's first game. Unc looked worried. The Braves' batter was down in the count and inched in to guard the plate. With two men on, the pitcher came from the stretch and sent a wicked slider at about ninety-four miles an hour. The batter took a wide swing, tagged it poorly, and sent it arcing high and to the right. The first baseman ran back, and the right fielder ran up, both in foul territory, but the ball spun further foul, dropping in the stands some twenty rows below us. It landed smack in the middle of the steps, bounced hard, spinning sideways, and climbing further foul.

Every boy enters a baseball game wanting a souvenir. A pennant, a cap, a program. These mark the moment; they're proof that we went, we watched, we were a part of the greatest game in the world. And once we leave, we hold them like brittle eggs, guard them, brag about them. For with them, we are the envy of every other boy who's ever thrown a baseball. But in all the history of baseball, there's really only been one souvenir that mattered. And to us who worship the winds of baseball, it's the Holy Grail.

Every boy and man around us was trained on that ball. The noise of it spinning sounded like a miniature tornado or drill bit, and it was radar-locked on Sketch's head. I knew it was coming fast, but I reached too slowly. The ball nipped my fingertip just a few feet from him. The speed of it froze him. His eyes crossed, and the veins in his neck popped out. Inches from his face, Unc's huge, knotty hand spread across the space in front of his nose. The ball struck Unc's hand square in the palm with a loud smack and his fingers wrapped around the ball like a vise. Men and boys around us let out a collective, deflated breath of air. Unc slowly opened his hand, palm up, and held the ball in front of Sketch like the Hope Diamond.

Unc's eyes were as round as Oreos. He shook his head, his smile wide. "In one day, I got a Hank Aaron baseball card and a foul ball." He looked out over the crowd. "When we leave here, I'm buying a lottery ticket."

Next, the pitcher sent a blistering fastball, high and slightly inside, which is about where the batter struck it. The ball took off like it was attached to the back end of a plane. It passed over the center field wall maybe seventy feet in the air, clearing the bases, winning the game, and clinching the pennant race. Unc sat back like he'd just eaten a really great meal. He took off his hat, wiped his brow, and looked out over the center field fence. "Yep, I'm definitely buying a lottery ticket."

I looked at the ball. "You know, it's customary, as you get older— being the patriarch and all—"

Unc flashed me an *Oh boy, here it comes* look.

"—to give . . . you know . . . your fishing buddy . . . any foul balls that you catch at a pennant race game."

He stood up and hefted the ball. "Why don't you spit in one hand and wish in the other."

Mandy laughed while Sketch held out both hands, palms up, eyeing one and then the other trying to figure out which one would get fuller the quickest.

We drove out of the parking lot with the kid still looking at his hands. His face was the closest thing to a smile I'd seen since his birthday. That's not to say the ends of his lips were turned up, but his eyes looked amused and excited.

'Course it didn't compare to the stretcher pasted across Unc's face. With Bones sitting in his lap, helping him steer, we hopped on I-75 North, pulled off at Tenth Street, and rolled into The Varsity a few blocks later. Unc pulled into one of the full-service parking spaces and rolled the window down. Driving a hearse always raises a few eyebrows. Now was no exception. People kept looking in the back to see if we were carrying a casket.

Sketch looked out the window and stared up at the buildings climbing into the night sky all around us. A minute later, he sat up on his heels and corkscrewed his face sideways, trying to frame what he saw through the rear window of the car. Finally he lay down across the seat on his back and stared through the top corner of the window. His calves were resting on my thighs, and he kept pushing against the door to get a better view.

"Sketch"—I tapped him—"you okay?"

Not satisfied, he unlocked the door and began jogging across the Tenth Street bridge. Unc was in the process of saying, "You better go with him" as Mandy and I hopped out of the car. He would jog a few steps, look over his shoulder, then turn and jog some more. We followed close enough, but not so close that we hampered whatever he was doing.

We jogged two blocks through the Georgia Tech campus up along the side of the football field to the top of a hill, where he stopped and took another compass reading with whatever coordinates he was using in his head. He was sweating and breathing heavily, but wasn't tired. Mandy ran alongside me, but I think I was in the worst shape of all because I'm not real good at running in flip-flops.

Mandy pulled up alongside him and said, "Buddy? You looking for something?"

He eyed both of us, then sat down on a curb and sketched on his notepad the picture in his mind. He was looking through a window frame at a city skyline. The buildings looked further away than we were now, but in the right-hand corner was one unmistakable building. It was that blue, mushroom-like building with the rotating restaurant on top that looks like it came straight out of a *Jetsons* episode. He tore out the page, handed it to me, and then started jogging again.

I turned to Mandy. "He's trying to match the picture in his head with what he's looking at now."

"Well, let's follow him."

Unc followed along behind us, spotlighting us with the headlights, while Bones stood up on his hind legs and leaned against the dash. We jogged another three blocks, but Sketch seemed to be getting more frustrated with every block. Two more, and the trees began to obstruct our view of the skyline. He found a magnolia tree and started climbing, so I shimmied up after him. Thirty feet in the air, he sat on a limb and pulled back a branch. He shook his head and started to climb back down.

"Sketch? Do we need to be closer or further away?"

He pointed over my shoulder, away from the city, in a westerly direction. We climbed down, and he started off on foot again.

I said, "Sketch, let's do this in the car. You can sit up front, and we'll cover more ground. Okay?"

He looked at the oozing blister on my right foot and nodded.

We zigzagged a few blocks toward the highest ground we could find, then stopped the car and lifted the kid onto the hood. He stared at the city, then back over his shoulder and pointed again. This continued until after midnight, while we drove a Pacman route around town. By one o'clock he'd drawn two more pictures. The first showed an elderly lady sitting in a La-Z-Boy chair, looking out her window. She was dressed in a long gown and slippers, and the room looked rather plain. Not real homely, but also not a hospital. On the table next to her sat a picture of a man in military dress uniform and a tattered Bible.

I held up the picture. "Do you know this lady?"

He shrugged and nodded.

"You sort of know her?"

He nodded again.

"Is she in her home? In a house?"

He shook his head.

Mandy knelt down next to him. "Buddy, are there other old people with this lady?"

He nodded.

"Lots of them?"

He shrugged and then nodded again. Mandy dialed 411 and asked for the address of any retirement homes near us. The operator gave her two: Sherwood Villas and Cedar Lakes Community. Sketch read the names and shrugged. Unc studied his road atlas and located Sherwood Villas two miles away.

We pulled into the poorly lit parking lot and let Sketch out of the car. He looked around, bit his lip, and shook his head. Unc handed him the atlas, and they navigated another ten or twelve blocks to Cedar Lakes. We pulled onto a long driveway with green ryegrass, lined with magnolia trees, and the kid's legs started bouncing like the puppeteer had awakened. We reached the parking lot of an upscale retirement home with several buildings—some even looked like condominiums—a parking garage, and bright lights everywhere.

Unc hadn't even come to a stop before Sketch was jumping out of the car. He ran across the parking lot toward the front door, but before he got three car lengths away he skidded to a stop, ran back to the car, grabbed his chess set, and tucked it under his arm like a football, and then went running back across the parking lot. We followed a few feet behind.

He ran up to the front door, but it was locked. A security guard stood up from behind a desk just beyond the door. He punched a button and waved us in. Sketch ran past the desk and headed down a long carpeted hallway to his left. The guard came around the desk and hollered, "Hey, you're not allowed on the hall at night."

The three of us chased him down the hallway, which was lined with doors like a dormitory. The guard hustled along, his large ring of keys clanking against the radio clipped to his belt. The only thing louder was his squeaky shoes. Sketch jogged right, then left, up a flight of stairs and down another long hallway.

The guard began wheezing and slowed to a stop. He mashed the transmit button on his radio and said, "Greg . . . Bert here. I've got a crazy kid running down Seattle West."

Mandy and I left him in the stairwell and followed Sketch onto the second floor. He was sprinting now. At the end of the long hallway he stopped, turned the knob on the last door on the right, and pushed it open. I walked in right behind him. In front of me sat a large chair looking out through an enormous window that overlooked the city skyline.

Sketch flicked on the light and walked over to the bed. The fluorescent light flashed once, then lit the room and a tall figure in bed whose feet were sticking out from the covers on the other end. An elderly man with thin gray hair, bushy eyebrows, and big ears stared at us through eyes the size of saucers. The kid studied the man, who was studying us. Not satisfied, he lifted the corner of the sheet and looked beneath.

The guard rushed in behind us, coughing, and shined a flashlight in our faces. He was trying to speak, but couldn't catch his breath. Sketch turned around, walked to the window, then sat down in the chair and looked down at the floor. The old man sat up in bed and took a deep drag on an inhaler.

The guard finally caught his breath. "You people can't be in here. Everybody out, now."

I held out the picture of the old lady sitting at the window and whispered to Sketch. "Is this the room?"

He nodded and looked back at the floor, chewing on his lip.

I turned to the guard. "Sir, I'll explain in a minute." I turned to the old man, who was looking at each of us but had yet to formulate any words. "Sir? Have you been in this room very long?"

He stuttered, "'B-b-b-b-out a year."

I turned to the guard. "Do you know if there used to be a woman in this room?"

He shook his head and began mother-henning us out of the room. He spoke to the man in the bed. "Mr. Tuttles, I'm real sorry . . ." He pushed us out into the hall, where we were met by another guard along with Unc. "You people are in trouble."

"Please, sir, just give me a minute and I'll explain."

For the first time, he really looked at Sketch. He studied him a minute, then said, "Ain't seen you in a while."

"You know him?" I asked.

"Sure, he used to come see Mrs. Hampton all the time when he lived down yonder at Sparks."

"Sparks?"

"Uh-huh. Boys' home few blocks down the road."

"Is Mrs. Hampton still around?"

Bert looked at Greg and raised his eyebrows.

The second guard shrugged. "It's not like she's sleeping."

Bert, looking empowered, walked past and waved for us to follow.

We took the elevator down to the first floor, then walked to a second building that required a key-card for entrance. This wing looked more like a hospital. Nurses sat at a station when we walked in, watching fifteen or so monitors along the desk above them.

"This is San Antonio," Bert said. "Name don't mean anything other than it's the Alzheimer's wing." He pointed back behind us. "When they get too sick to live on their own in Seattle, we bring 'em to San Anton'." He held up the key-card that was tethered to his waist via a miniature plastic slinky. "You can't get in or out without a key. Some of these folks like to wander, but they're not too good at getting back."

He looked down at Sketch. "You've grown a bit. What's it been? Two years?"

He shrugged and shifted his chess set from one arm to another.

Bert pointed. "Looks like you're still playing. She doesn't play anymore."

Sketch's eyes narrowed, and he followed Bert down the hall.

The guard stopped at the nurses' station and said, "Gretta, how's Mrs. Hampton?"

She pointed to a monitor. "She ain't sleeping."

We walked down the hall to room 108, and Bert stepped aside. Sketch pushed open the door and walked in. An elderly woman was sitting up in bed. Her hair was thin, and most of it had fallen out. She was chewing on a fingernail, and her eyes seemed glossed over. When she saw Sketch, she smiled and patted the side of the bed. He pulled up a chair next to the bed and climbed up. He sat down, Indian style, facing her. She reached for his hand and sat looking at him. She tried to speak, but no words came out.

The nurse whispered behind Mandy and me, "Missus Hampton's been in here 'bout a year. She hasn't spoken the whole time."

Sketch opened his chess set and set up the pieces. Mrs. Hampton stared at the board, then slowly moved a pawn one space forward.

Bert nodded. "He used to come see her most every day. She taught him how to play."

"Who is she?"

"She's a true Southern belle. Must be close to a hundred. Lived in an antebellum home downtown, not far from the Margaret Mitchell house. Used to tell some of the best stories." He pointed to the picture beside her bed. "That's her husband, Colonel Hampton. He died some twenty years ago now, but she keeps that picture and—"

As he was talking her left hand would move the chess pieces while her right hand came up just above her gown and began searching her neck for something that wasn't there.

"Oh . . . there she goes again. She's looking for it now."

Mandy whispered, "Looking for what?"

Sketch had yet to move. When Mrs. Hampton's hand began searching her neck, he pulled on one of the drawers of his chess set and dug his fingers into the back of it. He pulled out a piece of tissue paper and began unrolling it. Mandy and I stepped close enough to see. Sensing us over his shoulder, he looked up at us.

"It's okay," I said, "go ahead."

Sketch unrolled the tissue and spread it out across his hand.

Bert eyed the chain lying across the kid's palm and said, "That."

Sketch picked up a long silver necklace. Held it up with two hands and offered to slip it over the lady's head. She saw it, eyed the diamond at the bottom, and leaned forward. He slipped it over her hair net and hung it gently around her neck where the diamond fell between her lonely fingers. He slid his sketch pad from beneath the chess set and quickly wrote, MRS. HAMPTON, I'M SORRY ABOUT YOUR DIA-MOND. I DIDN'T TAKE IT. I KNOW YOU'VE BEEN MISSING IT. SORRY I DIDN'T GET IT BACK SOONER.

He laid the note on her lap and turned it around so she could read it. The nurse slipped between us and said, "Child, she can't really read anymore." She held the note and read it quietly to Mrs.

Hampton, who was looking out the window, her fingers reading the facets of her diamond.

"Shook this place up pretty good when that thing got stolen. We all had to take lie-detector tests. Then Sonya didn't show up for work, and that's about when everybody started pointing fingers at everybody else."

Mandy and I looked at him in amazement. He liked knowing something we didn't, so he didn't mind talking.

"Yeah, reporters, news crews. Lots of people." Bert pointed. "The Colonel gave her that diamond after he returned from his North African campaign. He was shot down over there."

Buddy and Mrs. Hampton sat in silence, understanding each other perfectly.

Unc stepped up to the bed and said, "Buddy, let's let this sweet lady get some sleep. We'll come back tomorrow. Okay?"

Mandy pulled Bert aside. "Don't you have some sort of policy where you encourage family members to remove a resident's jewelry when they come here?"

Bert nodded. "We do, and we tried with Mrs. Hampton. Only we ran into two problems—she didn't have any kin, and even if she did, she wouldn't willingly take that necklace off."

I opened my wallet, pulled out Sketch's torn page, and walked around to the corner table and the picture of the colonel. I tried to open the Bible to the fifth chapter of Matthew, but it wasn't there. I spread the binding, found the tattered edge, and placed the single page up against it. It fit perfectly.

Sketch nodded and slipped off the bed, but she didn't let go of his hand. He gently patted her with his other, and she let go. We walked out into the hall, where Unc talked with Bert. Sketch tugged on my pant leg and pointed to his sketch pad. His note read, AM I GOING TO JAIL NOW?

I showed it to Mandy, who knelt down and shook her head, "No,

Buddy . . . you're not going to jail." She ran her fingers gently across his head. "If anything, we ought to give you a medal."

Because I figured Red was never going to believe this, I put us up in two adjoining rooms at the Ritz Carlton on Peachtree. Mandy in one, the three of us in the other. Four if you count Bones. Sketch wouldn't hear of him sleeping in the car, so we smuggled him up the back stairs, bathed him, and ordered room service.

Unc watched the cat lap up the milk and whispered over his shoulder, "This could get expensive."

We slept late and then gorged on the brunch buffet. While Mandy and I communicated with our respective offices, Unc and the kid played chess in the lobby. And I was right, Red didn't care.

By lunchtime we were sitting in the office of Chester Buckley, the CEO of Cedar Hills, apologizing for last night. He didn't seem too upset, given the fact that Mrs. Hampton had her diamond back. After we finished explaining how we got there and he worked through his list of questions—which was long—Mandy and I asked a few questions of our own.

He explained that Starks was a city-funded boys' home three blocks down the street. Several years ago they began bringing some of the boys in to spend time with his residents. "The kids were allowed to come if they were of the right temperament, which Stuart is."

"Stuart?" I asked.

"Stuart. Stuart Smoak."

"That's his name?"

"If it's the same boy, which I think it is. He's mute, right? That'd be Stuart. He used to come see Mrs. Hampton most every day."

"What happened?"

"Don't really know. About three years ago, the diamond disap-

peared, and so did one of our orderlies. A woman by the name of
Sonya Beckers."

Mandy slid a picture of the crumpled Impala across the desk.

Mr. Buckley pointed at the burnt figure. "That's her?"

Mandy nodded.

He turned up his lip. "Guess crime really doesn't pay."

We thanked Mr. Buckley and, with his permission, left Unc and
the kid with Mrs. Hampton while Mandy and I drove Sally to Starks
Boys' Home. Located a half mile from Cedar Hills, Starks stood as an
Atlanta staple. An enormous, factorylike brick building, eight stories
tall, it stood down near the railroad tracks that had been taken over
by MARTA since the day that the garment factory pulled out. The
sign out front read simply "Starks. Est. 1946."

Sherry Quitman met us at the door with a smile, a handshake, and
a native Georgian accent. A handsome lady, midfifties, her presence
and the confidence with which she carried herself told me she could
be CEO of a Fortune 500 company. Reminded me of a Dixiefied
Margaret Thatcher. That told me she took this job because she wanted
it. I liked her from the moment she said hello.

She led us to her office and shut the door behind us. With little
small talk, she slid a file across the desk and opened it for us. There
before us lay what she could piece together of the life of Stuart Smoak.

Sherry leaned back in her chair and recited the folder from memory. "Stuart came to us when we thought he was about four, maybe five."

"You thought?"

She nodded. "Not much paperwork. He came to us from a foster
home in South Georgia, and they got him from another foster home
who got him from somewhere in Tennessee."

"What do you know about his speech?" Mandy asked.

"We got him that way. As best we can figure, one of the foster
moms tried to strangle him after he peed in his pants. Crushed his
voice box and damaged the muscles that control it."

"How'd he start spending time with Mrs. Hampton?"

"We developed this visitation policy with the folks at Cedar Hills. Stuart spent a lot of time down there because he could do what he was good at. Listen. I'm afraid that no matter how hard you try, kids will make fun of kids who are different. And Stuart is different. So he spent most of his afternoons down the street."

"Who taught him to draw?"

She smiled. "Pretty amazing, huh? That's something he picked up on his own. When he found he couldn't talk, he just started slipping the words out his fingers."

Mandy needed specifics, so she continued to probe. "What legal steps did you take?"

"Well, he was so young that I thought his chances of being adopted were still pretty good. So we did what you're doing right now—tried to find out more about him. I backtracked as far as I could, and the trail went cold in Tennessee. Seems there was a fire in the facility there. Records destroyed. Computers, too. The folks there told me that if we were talking about the same child, then he was a true foundling. Dropped on a doorstep in a basket. But we can't be sure." She shrugged. "We couldn't determine where he came from, who his family was, or even what part of the country he was born in. If one ever slipped through the cracks, it's him. When I figured all this out, we started the process to terminate parental rights—assuming there were any. Then we worked to find him a home, but it's hard enough to place children without disabilities.

"A few months after he started going to Cedar Hills, a lady came to us and said she wanted to adopt him. We followed protocol, she checked out—no criminal record, home inspection went off without a hitch. She seemed real good with people, and the folks down at Cedar Hills gave her textbook references. We were elated. Thought we'd beat the system and the statistics. That's the last I'd heard of him until now."

Mandy nodded and leaned back. Her face told me she was putting the pieces together faster than I. "Guess I can cancel those newspaper ads."

"Why?"

"Because there's nothing to terminate."

"But can't we keep looking? We can't just quit. What if he's not a foundling? What if he's got some real parents out there somewhere? What if somebody's looking for him? I mean, somebody gave birth to the kid. That's got to mean something."

Mandy shook her head. "Chase, I know you probably understand this better than both of us put together, but . . . nobody's coming to get this kid."

Sherry agreed.

I pressed her. "What happens to him now?"

"The state will resume custody. Given his past, his abuse . . . chances are good he'll remain a ward of the state until he reaches maturity."

Sheryl Crow sings a song about how the first cut is the deepest. She's right. Only she ought to add a verse to that song. Because people who cut the heart of a child ought to have that same knife shoved up their spine and broken off at the hilt.

I thought about Sketch playing chess with Unc, holding Mrs. Hampton's hand, eating a MoonPie, shuffling across the floor in his Spider-Man pajamas, wanting to stop the bleeding on Tommye's hand, standing in the street watching the funeral procession with his hand across his heart like he was reciting the Pledge of Allegiance. In a short time, he'd given me a lot of pictures.

In a short time, well . . . the kid was no longer a story I was writing.

I remember the story of Jesus sitting there surrounded by kids— maybe one or two sitting up on his lap. He said something about woe be to those who steer a child wrong. Something about how it'd be better for them to have a millstone hung around their neck and be thrown into the deep. In Sketch's case, I'd like to line them all up, tie them to the bumper of a Peterbilt, and pull them like beer cans down the highway.

My mind raced. What was I going to tell him? How do you explain to a kid that nobody was ever going to turn down the driveway? What hope is there in that?

The one thing I wasn't going to do was start calling him Stuart. Stuart was the name of a mouse in a movie. An underdog that tugs at your heartstrings. A kid with no chance. Not a kid who sketches like Norman Rockwell. Not a kid who gives Hank Aaron cards to salivating old men. Not a kid who's been passed over, passed on, passed up, beat to hell, and who . . . who reminds me of me.

Chapter 37

I'd only been asleep about an hour when Tommye knocked on the hatch of my boat. I lifted it and studied the water around us. "You know what time it is?"

Strangely energetic, she grabbed my hand and looked at my watch. "Yeah, just a little after midnight. Guess I'm still on California time. Not that we slept at night much anyway. The 'family' has a way of turning most people nocturnal."

I sat down in the galley and hung my head in my hands, shaking off the sleep.

She threw a shirt at me. "Come on."

I was dead on my feet. Only she looked worse than I felt. "Where to?"

"I want to show you something."

"What could you possibly want to show me at this time in the . . . morning?"

"Can't you just let me show you one thing before I get so I can't?"

"Why you gotta be so morbid all the time?"

She put her hands on her hips. "'Cause I can look in the mirror and recognize the face. Now . . ." She rolled her eyes. "Chase, shut up and get in the car."

I pulled on a T-shirt, backwards and inside out, and paddled her back to shore.

With no vehicle in sight other than Vicky, I raised an eyebrow. "How'd you get here?"

She stuck her thumb in the air and lifted her sweatpants above the ankle.

"You've got to be kidding me."

She smiled smugly, and I just shook my head. Tommye was never afraid of much.

We climbed into Vicky, and I eased off on the clutch. "Where to?"

She pointed, so we followed her finger to town. With little to no breeze, the air was warm, muggy, and stuck to our skin. I'd like to think that was the cause of the sweat on her face, but I knew better. Every few minutes, she swigged from a water bottle that she clutched in her hand.

Vicky bumped along the bricked streets and eventually rolled to a stop a block from the ZB&T. Tommye pointed to the parking spots along the road. "Anywhere is fine."

I eyed the bank, then her. "You trying to get me arrested?"

She laughed and shook her head. "For all your education, sometimes you just miss the boat."

"What? You read the papers. I'm not allowed to set foot within fifty feet of this place."

She laughed. "I guess Jack just doesn't want your business."

She walked to the front door, where the three different security cameras captured our every move.

"Tommye . . ." I pointed at the cameras.

Hands on hips again, she shook her head. "Tell me"—she punched several buttons on the security pad—"why would I arrest you for walking into my bank"—the security system beeped three times and four lights turned green—"when I invited you?"

"Your bank?"

She chuckled, punched a few more keys, and the electronic lock sounded inside the door. She pushed it open, flipped on a light switch, and welcomed me into the lobby. "Come on in."

Against my better judgment, I stepped into the bank. To my surprise, I heard no piercing shrill exit the speaker of the security system. As for a silent alarm, well, I figured I'd find out soon enough.

Tommye walked through the lobby and up the stairs, and pushed open the door that read PRES. JACK MCFARLAND.

"Have you lost your mind? We need to get the heck out of here while we still can."

She flicked on the light in her dad's office. "Anyone ever told you that you're kind of uptight? You need to relax."

I stepped into the room. "Tell me about it."

The office was enormous. It took up most of the second floor. The walls were twelve feet high and lined with oak shelves stacked full of leather-bound books that looked designed more for show than go. The hardwood floors were covered in six or eight oriental rugs, and two leather chairs and one enormous leather couch dominated the center of the room. I found a personal bathroom off in one corner, matched by a wet bar in the other where a hundred or so bottles of wine were stacked from bar top to ceiling.

The centerpiece of the office was a giant desk, maybe nine feet long and four feet wide, ornately carved from oak. I'd heard Unc talk about it. Ellsworth McFarland had it custom-made from oaks cut off the Zuta about the same time that they built the Brooklyn Bridge. Unc said he and Uncle Jack used to hide under that desk, playing cowboys and Indians.

I walked around behind it. "May I?"

The rolled and engraved edges were worn and darkened by time. It was truly the most magnificent desk, table, or piece of woodworking I'd ever seen. The desk was stacked with rolled architectural and engineering drawings detailing his plans for the Zuta.

I looked out the window and saw a pair of headlights turn the corner. Atop the car, I saw blue lights. The officer parked his car, slid his nightstick into the loop on his belt, and strode to the front door. I pointed. "Fun's over."

Tommye pushed down the blind and smiled. "Be right back."

I followed at a sensible distance as she walked down the stairs and opened the front door for the officer—who, by the way, was the same one who had arrested me as I came out of the thrift store across the street just six weeks earlier. She cracked the door to the lobby and stuck her head through, acting friendly, but not letting him in.

"Oh . . . hi, Miss Tommye. Everything okay? I got a call saying that someone had entered the bank. No alarm or anything, but you know how Mr. Jack is."

She waved him off. "I'm fine. Couldn't sleep. Still on California time. Just making some copies for Dad. Thanks for checking." She looked out at his car on the street. "Feel free to hang out awhile. I feel better knowing you're around."

He ran his fingers along the insides of his belt and hoisted his Glock above his hip. "Yes ma'am. Will do."

He pointed at Vicky. "Your cousin know you got his mistress? He's pretty partial to that ratty old thing."

She laughed. "Yeah, he knows. I won't be long." She pointed to the coffeemaker in the lobby. "You want me to make you some coffee?"

He shook his head. "No ma'am. Had my fill. I'll be in the car if'n you need me."

"Thanks."

Tommye climbed back up the stairs and to her dad's office while I trailed behind, wide-eyed and amazed. She laughed and redid the two buttons she'd undone on her way down the steps.

"You want to tell me what on earth is going on here?"

She pushed the blind down again and watched as the officer stepped back into his car. "Years ago, Dad made me a director."

"What? I thought you two weren't exactly on speaking terms."

She smiled. "He had to, since I own 49 percent."

"Get serious."

"Think about it." She waved her hand across the room. "What else was he going to do?"

I sat down in the desk chair, my head spinning. "What do you mean?"

"Don't you know anything?" She sat on the couch, propping her feet on the coffee table. "One thing about Jack McFarland you need to know: while he may have one foot in the river, he's still got one foot on the bank."

"I don't have any idea what you're saying. You're as bad as Unc."

She sat up. "He did it to protect himself. He's got no other heir. No one else he can"—she put her fingers in the air, making imaginary quotation marks—"'*trust*.' So, with me gone to California and promising never to come back, he protects himself by transferring assets." She smiled and lay back again. "Yeah, I'm probably the second richest person you know. 'Course, I can't get to it or spend any of it. He's not stupid."

I frowned. "How'd you know all the codes?"

She walked around the desk and pulled out the retracting table that slid into it just above the top drawer. A small piece of paper was taped to the rear of it. "Jack's never been too good at memorizing stuff."

"But anybody would know to look there."

"Yeah, but they wouldn't know that all the numbers are backwards and multiplied by two. So you cut each in half and reverse them. Also, you've only got one shot with the system. Mess up once and it'll lock you out. And he changes them every month."

I looked around the room, trying to juggle all the puzzle pieces in my head.

She leaned on her elbows next to me and smirked. "What do you hear?"

"Right now? My heart racing."

"Close your eyes."

"Tommye . . ."

"Chase. Close your eyes."

I obeyed.

"Now, heels together."

Again, I did as she told me.

"Now, listen." She tapped the floor behind me. "Sounds pretty solid, doesn't it?"

I nodded.

"Now you do it."

I did, and the sound took my breath away. I pushed back from the desk and knelt beneath it. She laughed and handed me a small flashlight. "You'll be needing this."

I ran my fingers along the lines of the carpet beneath the desk and found a small latch. I released the latch, pulled up on the knob, and shined my light. A ventilation shaft, complete with a small ladder, led straight down. I stuck my head into the hole, shined the light to the bottom, and saw a coquina floor.

I sat back up and leaned against the inside of the desk, my head spinning. I shined my light at her. "You better start talking right now."

"When I was a kid, I heard Uncle Willee talking about playing up here. So I did the same. Didn't take me long to find the latch. And I've never been too afraid of the dark."

"Where's it go?"

She pointed. "Go ahead. I'll wait on you."

I stuck the light in my mouth and climbed down without a second's thought. The shaft was made out of brick, maybe a ventilation shaft or an old chimney. Whatever, it led to a coquina floor, which turned into another small shaft, large enough to crawl through. I crawled maybe fifteen feet, scaring the cockroaches, and came out into the far end of the Spanish basement, behind the ladder I'd climbed up a dozen times. The shaft I was in exited in a small cleft of space just above the support beam. From the other side, the side I'd always been on, it looked like nothing. Like a shelf. I hung on the ladder, looked up, and saw the oak trapdoor that led into the vault.

A lot of questions were answered in that second.

I crawled out, turned around, and then climbed back up to Jack's office, where Tommye sat smiling and twirling her hair between her fingers.

"Why didn't you tell me?"

"I was asked not to."

"By who?"

"Uncle Willee." She looked down, rubbed the back of her calf like she had a cramp, and swigged from her water bottle. "Chase, I can see it on your face. You've lived a long time not knowing. It's eating at you, and you won't let it go. Further, I can feel the tension between you and Uncle Willee." She pointed. "I showed you this because I don't want you ever to doubt Uncle Willee."

"What are you not telling me?"

The sun cracked the skyline, and daylight broke through the windows. Downstairs, we heard somebody coming in the front door, pocket change rattling as he climbed the stairs.

Tommye's eyes lit up. "Come on."

We shut the office door and began walking down the steps, where we bumped into Uncle Jack. Obviously, he had known we were there, but what could he do? Tommye laughed as she passed by, but said nothing.

He put his hand on my chest and raised his chin. "You miss jail?"

I've always had a fear of Uncle Jack that I never could explain. Something in me, deep down, got the heebie-jeebies whenever he was around. I think he knew this, too, because he always had this air about him that said he knew he had the upper hand.

I ducked around his hand, leaving him to point at my shadow.

When I got to the bottom of the steps, I turned around. He stood, his head on a swivel, looking up at his office and down at us. I smiled, because I read the uncertainty filling his eyes. It was an unusual feeling, knowing something he didn't want me to know and knowing it before he knew that I knew it.

I spoke slowly, "Uncle Jack, I'm reminded of something your brother once told me while we were eating breakfast: The truth is a lot like the milkman's bucket."

Tommye put her hands in her back pockets. "This ought to be good."

"The milkman can scrape that milk, cut it, even shake it 'til it's nothing but bubbles, and then sell it as whole milk, 2 percent, or nonfat, but sooner or later, the cream is going to rise to the surface and be known for what it is. And when it does, he's going to have to explain to his customers why he's been holding out." I looked him in the eye. "You may be good . . . but I doubt that even you are that good."

I turned my back on him, grabbed a mint off the receptionist's desk, and dropped my wrapper on the floor as I walked out. When I stepped into Vicky, Tommye was leaning against the seat back, eyes closed, fist clenched.

We pulled onto 99 and she began rubbing her leg.

"You okay?"

Tommye's always been a good liar. She could charm the devil himself. For most of her life, she did. She nodded and tucked one leg beneath the other. The only thing different here was that I knew she was lying.

Chapter 38

Some journalists make a big deal about the muses, and how they've got a direct line and write best when the muses are moving. In my experience, the muses are seldom on time and even less seldom do they tell the truth. When they do, they only tell half of it. With this in mind, I got to my office and forced my butt into the seat. Stories don't write themselves. Besides, Red had pushed up my deadline and didn't like excuses. Funny how that has a way of moving the muses.

I had a decent draft and was in the process of e-mailing it to myself when the phone rang. While in college I lost three weeks' worth of thesis work due to a school-wide virus. It was a difficult lesson. As a result, I created several dummy e-mail accounts to which I send drafts of articles while I work on them. Now, in the event of an office fire, the theft of my computer, or another sadistic virus created by some latchkey fourteen-year-old with too much time on his hands, my stuff is relatively safe in cyberspace. Provided I can remember where I sent it.

I flipped open my phone and pinned it between my ear and shoulder while my fingers worked the keyboard. "Chase here."

No one spoke. Cell reception was routinely poor in and around my office. I stood up next to the window and tried again. "Chase Walker here." I heard some shuffling, short quick breathing, and then two taps. "Sketch?"

A single tap.

"You okay?"

One tap.

"Tommye okay?"

Silence.

Maybe that's a hard question to answer. Thought I'd help him out. "She sleeping?"

One tap.

"Unc home?"

Two taps.

"Aunt Lorna?"

Two taps.

"She run to the store?"

A single tap.

"Is it something else?"

One tap.

"Tommye?"

Silence, followed by a single tap.

"Hold tight. Sit with her and tell her I'm coming."

The phone clicked dead. I finished e-mailing myself the article and jumped into Vicky.

While in the car, I called Unc and Aunt Lorna. Twenty minutes later, the three of us nearly collided in the driveway. I ran up the steps, unprepared for what I saw. Sketch was kneeling at Tommye's bedside, holding her hand.

Running in behind me, Unc looked at Lorna. "Take Buddy into the house."

Tommye lay in bed. Her eyes were nothing but slits, her face was flushed in places and gray in others, and the room smelled of human waste and vomit. I placed my hand on her forehead and looked at Unc. "She's on fire."

He knelt, sliding his hand beneath hers, and I dialed 911. I placed the phone to my ear, but she grabbed it and flipped it shut. She shook her head and motioned us both closer. Her speech was labored. Her mouth was cottony-white, her tongue swollen, and blood oozed from her mouth, nose, and around her eyes. She placed her hand on Uncle Willee's chest and closed her eyes, catching her breath. "Do something for me."

Uncle Willee nodded.

She opened her eyes, and they danced around the room and finally focused on him. She lifted her head off the pillow. "Baptize me."

"But I . . ."

Her breathing was short and shallow. She shook her hand. "I can't hold on much longer."

He pulled the sheet back, and I almost turned my eyes. Tommye had lost control of her insides, and the sheets were soaked—front and rear. Unc scooped his arms beneath her, lifted her off the bed, and turned to me. "Crank Vicky."

He carried her down the stairs and climbed inside, holding Tommye in his lap.

We drove through the Zuta and pulled up to the landing where the water level averages from knee-deep to waist-deep. Uncle Willee nodded at my four-wheel-drive stick. "Are the hubs locked in?"

I knew what he meant. I stopped, locked the hubs, shifted into four-low, and eased down into the water. The water level came up above the top of the wheels, then spilled into the cab, covering up our feet but stopping short of rising above our knees. I eased her across the sandy bottom, the slight current of the water washing over us. We steered around stumps, between trees, through holes, and Vicky never stuttered. It was as if she knew.

We drove the half mile across the swamp bottom, then pulled up to one of the small streams that fed into the Altamaha—the stream where Unc and I had done most of our fishing. I knew it was deep. I also knew I couldn't leave Vicky. I downshifted her into Granny gear—my hands below the level of the water—and eased down into the deeper water. The water rose over the hood, pushed against the windshield and up to my shoulders. Midway across, we bumped into something too big for Vicky to push out of the way. Her tires spun, dug into the sand, and I shook my head. We were ten yards from shore, but she would go no further. I didn't know how long she could continue to run under water. As long as she kept running, the exhaust would force the water out of the engine, but I wasn't sure about her plugs, distributor, or anything else.

We swam out of her, and I helped Uncle Willee get Tommye to shore and keep her head above water. Her eyes were closed and her body limp. Uncle Willee picked up the pace, nearly running through the trees. Five minutes later, winded and wheezing, we reached the swimming hole on the far side of the Sanctuary.

There was no moon. Clouds covered the sky and threatened rain. Uncle Willee stepped into the water at the edge of the swimming hole where we'd spent our summers, and Tommye opened her eyes. "Wait."

He knelt on the sand, her body spilling around him. She tried to lick her lips, but her mouth was mostly blood. She swallowed, caught her breath, and looked at Unc. "One last thing." She focused on him. "Speak at my funeral . . . please."

He choked back a sob, then nodded.

She pressed him. "Say it."

He whispered, "Okay."

"Lastly . . ." She choked and coughed, gasping. Her chest rose and fell. She recovered one last time. "Tell him."

Tears broke from his eyes.

She poked him in the chest. "Promise me."

He nodded. Her head bobbed backward, and her body went limp. Unc stood, and her breathing grew more shallow. He tried to stand, but stumbled. "Help me."

I held her head as we waded in. Waist deep, we stood holding Tommye, her arms and legs floating limp.

Unc tried to speak but couldn't. I put my hand on his shoulder and stood alongside him. He tried again, but still the words wouldn't come.

Finally I said, "Unc . . ."

He held Tommye's head in his huge, tender palm, kissed her forehead, and whispered, "Baby . . . in the name of the Father . . ." His voice broke as he gently slipped her body beneath the water. He pulled her up, his muscled shoulders shaking. ". . . and the Son . . ." Again he pressed her down into the water, only to pull her back to his chest and hug her. He held her, crying loudly now, the moans coming from deep down—some place that daylight never saw. He kissed her cheek and said, "and the Holy Ghost . . ." and laid her back down in the water.

The water swallowed her face, wrapped around her head, and flowed across her, pulling bubbles from her mouth and nose. Unc stumbled. I stretched my arms beneath his, and we lifted Tommye from the water. Her head tilted toward me and her eyes flickered. She was half here and half there.

She placed her hand behind my head and pressed her forehead to mine. "Your book . . . it was already on his shelf." She inhaled and tried to speak again, but the words were all gone. Her last breath floated off, carried to the sea by the ripples on the water.

Her absence hurt. I wanted to be mad at her, thinking it might lessen the hurt, but every time the anger bubbled up, I heard her laughter, felt her soft touch, and saw the light that once sparked behind her eyes.

In truth, I was mad at me. I felt responsible. Somewhere in the second day, the guilt set in. Yes, I'd called and written dozens of times with no response over the years, and yes, she was the one who left, but how hard had I tried? I wasn't naive enough to think I could've changed the course of her life, but I could've . . .

Well, see what I mean?

After two days staring off the bow of my boat, the self-doubt and second-guessing drove me away. Before I knew it, Sally had bounced against the curb and delivered me to my office. But while my geography changed, the view did not. Tommye was everywhere I looked.

Given enough research, details, and time to let the story percolate in my head, I can write a couple hundred, even a thousand, words in fifteen minutes. Tommye's seventy-five-word obituary took me the better part of a day.

Sometime after supper, Red sat on the edge of my desk and pressed PRINT. He read the page that slid out and raised both eyebrows. "You're done. Go home."

The obit ran the following morning.

MCFARLAND, TOMMYE LYNN, born April 17, 1976. Friend, actress, memorizer of baseball trivia, lifelong Braves and Bulldogs fan, Miss Brunswick High 1993, singer of Don McClean songs, unselfish, tender, and compassionate, died Sunday, August 27. Tommye was sexually abused by her father, Jack McFarland, when just an innocent girl. She went west to fill the gaping hole he left in her chest. When she did, it killed her. She died surrounded by her family, having found peace and knowing love. Weather permitting, outdoor funeral services will be conducted at the home of William and Lorna McFarland at 1:00 PM Wednesday, August 30, followed by a private burial in the family cemetery.

I knew Jack wouldn't be too happy with me, but I really didn't care. Red, of course, did, so he cut the three sentences that would have gotten both him and me sued.

But writing is cathartic, and I felt better. Maybe that's what Sally was thinking when she drove me to the office.

Chapter 39

Fog blanketed the water the morning of the funeral. No breeze stirred the surface, so my boat sat oddly still. Even it was reverent. I threw on some shorts, bought a couple bags of ice at the store, and got to the house after breakfast, where I cut the grass and coordinated with the rental company to set up chairs. We didn't know how many people to expect, but Unc said, "People ought to have a place to sit, even if it's just for a few minutes," so we rented fifty. We set them up beneath one of Ellsworth McFarland's pecan trees that was bordered by a wild muscadine vine that Unc had trained along an arched arbor years ago.

Aunt Lorna had spent the previous day cooking Tommye's favorite chili, which she intended to serve to anyone who wanted it following the funeral. Sketch and I set up tables on the porch and turned the ceiling fans on low to keep the flies off. It was hot and muggy, and his glasses kept fogging up and sliding off his nose. We set out paper plates and bowls, plastic spoons, a couple of boxes of Saltines, and some iced tea, and Unc threw in three dozen MoonPies for good measure.

About lunchtime it turned overcast and gray, threatening rain. Because Unc had been removed as an elder and kicked out of his church some thirty years ago, our funeral locations were limited to the house, but we figured Tommye would like it that way.

When the mortician delivered Tommye to the house, he told us that Uncle Jack had identified the body at the morgue, but he never contacted us to talk about the funeral. If he had plans, he didn't express them. We carried her coffin to the front of the chairs and set her on top of a stand made just for that purpose. The box was simple, like Tommye. Stripped of any pretension.

The mortician asked me, "Open or closed?"

I looked down at the box, then shook my head. "Closed. If somebody wants to look, they can open it."

A few minutes later, a delivery truck pulled down the drive. Unc spoke to the driver, then directed as he backed up to the coffin. They lowered the tailgate, set down a heavy, tarp-covered object on the grass, and drove off with a handshake from Unc. He straightened any wrinkles, then took a long walk around the house before climbing back up the porch.

At twelve thirty, Unc walked out of the house dressed in his best and only suit. By the looks of it, he had not worn either the blue suit, the white shirt, or the striped tie in at least two decades. Looking uncomfortable and self-conscious, he walked across the drive and disappeared into his greenhouse. A moment later he reappeared carrying a single purple orchid. It was about three feet tall and covered with maybe a hundred little white-tipped blooms. He set it on top of her coffin and then sat down in the front row.

I—dressed in shorts, flip-flops, and a T-shirt—studied his getup, and got caught looking. Sketch did too. As the minutes passed, Unc kept fidgeting with his pants and tie and then pants again. Suddenly he got up, walked back into the house, and reappeared a few minutes later wearing faded jeans, muddy boots, a denim shirt, his Gus hat, and his Costa Del Mars.

When he sat back down, I whispered, "You feel better?"

He nodded.

"Good, you look better, too. Not as silly."

At a quarter to one, a single car drove down the drive. It was that Lincoln Continental again. I shook my head. Couldn't he have picked a better day?

Pockets stopped, left the car running, and walked over to Unc, who saw him coming and just shook his head. Pockets handed Unc an envelope and said, "William . . . I've done all I can. You've got thirty days."

Unc took the envelope and nodded. "Thank you, Pockets. I don't doubt your abilities."

"After all this time, I sure as hell do." He turned, walked to his car, and looked around. The house, the pasture, the orchid house, the chairs set up for the funeral. Just before he stepped back into the car, he spat, swore, and looked back at Unc. "William, I really am sorry."

When he'd left, Lorna tugged on Unc's sleeve. "You going to open it?"

Unc shook his head. "I know what it says." He turned the envelope in his hands. "We lost the appeal." He looked around and then spoke quietly, "We're losing the Zuta. Losing the Sanctuary." After a deep breath he said, "He finally got everything."

By ten minutes to one nobody had showed. Aunt Lorna, Unc, Sketch, Mandy, and I sat alone in the chairs, listening to the cows. Sketch held Bones in his lap, and every few minutes one of us would look over our shoulder or rub the cat between the ears.

Five minutes later, three stretch limos pulled into the drive. A young guy about my age rolled down the window and asked, "Is this the funeral for Tommye?"

I nodded.

He waved to the other cars and they parked along the drive. When they stepped out, it didn't take me long to figure out who they were. I'd never seen more beautiful people in one place in my whole life.

The guys were all fit, muscular arms, tight T-shirts, sideburns. Several of them had close-cropped beards. Half the women were blonde, a few brunettes, a few jet-blacks, some tall, but all seemed just as fit as the men. Evidently most had visited Tommye's plastic surgeon. Most wore sunglasses or had them propped atop their heads, holding back their hair.

The group, all twenty of them, walked quietly across the grass. Some of the girls took their heels off and walked barefoot. If this was the partying crowd Tommye had talked about, they didn't look it.

At 1:05 Unc checked his watch. He looked at me and nodded to the back row. I knew what he meant, so I walked down the center aisle and spoke to the group as a whole.

"Hi . . . I'm Chase. Tommye's cousin." I paused, looking at each one. "I don't know if she'd be mad at you or want you to sit up front where she could be near you . . . so because I can't figure it out, and because she's not here to straighten me out, why don't you all come sit up front with us."

They nodded and followed me single file up to the front. Once they were situated, Unc stood up next to Tommye's coffin. He had some note cards in his hands, which he kept shuffling like a card dealer. He tried to start, shook it off, then stood studying his cards and chewing on his lip for a minute. Finally, he dropped the cards on the grass, took off his hat, walked in front of the coffin, and began to speak.

"I'm William McFarland, Tommye's uncle. She come to live with us . . . back some time ago."

Three peacocks flew up into the branches of a pecan tree behind the house and began squawking.

"At one time I was mad at God 'cause my son got took, and I had a hard time forgiving him. Then Tommye come to live with us, and I seen it as God's way of easing my pain. 'Cause she did that." He held his hand out to the side, level with his waist. "When she was just a kid, I used to call her my Band-Aid—'cause she stuck to me and healed all my hurts."

The crowd on the front row seemed to take a collective deep breath, and a few smiled or laughed.

"And I've told God that on more than one occasion. Told him I was grateful and that I was sorry for being mad. 'Cause if any man has ever known anger . . . known pain . . . I reckon it's me." He looked off across the pasture, sniffled, and then set his hat on top of Tommye's coffin while he blew his nose into a white handkerchief.

"Tommye left us . . . went out west . . . when she was twenty. Trying to outrun her demons. I tried . . ." He looked at Lorna and me. "I guess we all tried to help her battle them, but . . ." He faded off, then looked at his hands. "I'm a farrier by occupation. Us farriers, we read horses by looking at their shoes. How they wear tells us a lot about how they walk. You can read people the same way. Their shoes don't lie. The other night my wife and I were packing up a few of Tommye's things, and I started looking at her shoes. They were running shoes. The heels were worn at an angle . . . far too worn for someone as light as Tommye. It looked like she'd been carrying the weight of the world on her shoulders."

He turned and faced the coffin, tried to speak to her, but couldn't. He turned back around and looked out across the pasture. "I can't quite figure this life out. Mine's had its ups and its downs. Some would say more downs than ups, but . . ." He shook his head. "I quit screaming at God a long time ago, 'cause I reckon he knows a thing or two about hurt. When things get bad . . . when I think I've hit bottom . . . that's where I go." He nodded toward the Sanctuary. "And he knows—I've been there many a time. That's what gets me from there to here . . . and to there."

While he spoke, I heard myself humming *So leave me if you need to, I will still remember.* . . . Tears trickled off my face. Willie Nelson had it right. I wiped them away, but it didn't do any good. Mandy put her arm around me and leaned in closer, pushing more of the hurt out of the corners of my eyes.

Unc talked with each of us. Not at us, and certainly not to us, but with us. The California crowd felt the difference. If I'd have been in their shoes, I'd have been tempted not to come—too much condemnation—but they had shown up, and that said a lot. They seemed to feel at ease with him. Some leaned forward, others half-smiled, but all were listening, and nobody's leg was bouncing around. Not even Sketch's.

Unc continued, "When I was in prison, I had this dream that my life was a rolling canvas. Every day it rolled off the sheet, bleached white, onto the beach of my life. Come sunup, I'd begin to paint it with my thoughts and actions. My breathing, my living, and my dying. Some days the pictures pleased me, maybe even pleased others, pleased God himself, but some days, some months, even some years, they didn't, and I didn't ever want to look at them again. But the thing is this . . . every day, no matter what I'd painted the day before, I got a new canvas, washed white. 'Cause each night the tide rolled in, scrubbed it clean, and receded, taking the stains with it. And in my dreams . . . I just stood on the beach and watched all that stuff wash out to sea."

Several of the girls were dabbing their eyes, and one of the guys put his sunglasses back on.

"Nothing more than ripples on the water." He waved his hand out across the pasture. "No canvas is ever stained clean through." He looked at Tommye. "Not one."

One of the black-haired girls in the second row let out an audible whimper, which embarrassed her so she tried to cover. Unc stopped, uncertain what to do. He handed her his handkerchief, which she took, but that only forced more tears out. Sketch stood up, walked down the second row, and handed the woman his tabby cat. She laid it in her lap and tried to smile. The blonde-haired lady next to her scooted over, making room for Sketch, so he sat on the edge of her folding chair in between the two. A few seconds later, she picked him up and just sat him on her lap.

Unc continued, "One of my favorite musicals is *The Man of La Mancha*. It's based on a story written a long time ago, somewhere in the 1600s." He looked at me. "For those of you who just chewed on the covers while you fished your way through school, that'd be the story of Don Quixote."

A few of the jet set looked at me and laughed.

"Old Don, he saw things a bit different than most. Lot of folks thought he was just flat crazy. Maybe he was. He saw windmills as evil giants. He once turned a barber's basin upside down, pulled it down like a baseball cap, and called it a golden helmet. Saw his old horse as a trusty stallion. Thought the old inn was a castle and its innkeeper a lord. Lastly, he saw Aldonza, the inn's prostitute, as a virtuous lady. Pure. Unblemished. Radiant. She protests, tells him that she was born on a pile of crap, what she calls a dung heap, and she'll die on one too." He hung his thumbs in his jeans. "Old Don doesn't hear a word she's saying. He just shakes his head and calls her Dulcinea. Her real name. The name he gives her.

"Don Quixote saw things as God intended them, not as what they'd become. He said, 'I come in a world of iron, to make a world of gold.'" Unc shook his head and spoke, almost to himself. "I like that."

He looked out across us. "'Cause he never gave up, Aldonza began to see not only herself differently, but the whole world too. Aldonza, like a caterpillar, became something new and different. Something clean. A butterfly . . . Dulcinea. All because some crazy windmill fighter convinced her that the mirror don't always tell the truth."

Unc wiped his eyes, chewed on his lip, and kicked at the grass. He reached behind him and pulled the tarp off the granite tombstone that stood next to her coffin. It read:

TOMMYE LYNN McFARLAND
1976–2006
MY DULCINEA

Unc looked down the drive, beneath the canopy of pecan trees. "'Tween now and whenever I get home, I'm gonna paint my canvas, and come sundown, I'll lie down in the water, let the waves wash me clean, and leave the rest to God. . . ." His voice cracked, and he shook his head and wiped his nose on his shirtsleeve.

Most everybody was crying—their eyes draining out the inside pain. The woman holding Bones was using the cat's back to dab her face. Finally, Unc sat down. We all just sat looking at the coffin, wondering what to do. Somewhere near the foot of that simple wooden box it hit me—her wing had healed, she'd flown away.

Aunt Lorna looked at me, so I stood up and took Unc's place. The grass beneath me was green, but crushed down from his boots. "We closed the coffin 'cause . . . well, we just closed it. But, if you want to say good-bye, you can open it. She'd probably like that. Sometimes it helps.

"Unc and I won't take her to the cemetery 'til after lunch." I pointed to the porch. "Tommye liked chili, so Aunt Lorna made that. We got some crackers, iced tea, Tabasco sauce, and . . . you all can stay as long as you like."

We sat there a long time. One by one they stood, walked to the coffin, and paid their respects. Some touched the top, a few opened it, and some even kissed her on the forehead. Finally, Lorna started serving plates, and pretty soon the porch was filled with people. Unc walked off toward the greenhouse and closed the door. I sat on the front row trying to make sense of the box in front of me.

While I sat there, one of the girls walked over and sat down. She carried a folder, thick with clippings and other papers. She handed it to me and whispered, like she didn't want to wake Tommye, "She'd want you to have this. I lived with her for a time. She talked about you often."

I opened it up and found most every article I'd ever written. She'd scribbled on many of them, underlined sentences, and written things like, "Sounds just like you." "How'd you know that?" Or "Come on, tell the truth."

Sketch appeared at my side. His glasses had slipped down onto the end of his nose and chili stained his shirt. He was carrying his chess set. He walked over to the coffin and looked like he wanted something.

"You want me to opcn it?"

He blinked, then nodded. I lifted the lid and watched him slowly look over the edge. He sucked in a short breath, then forced himself to exhale. He opened his chess set, pulled out a single piece, polished it on his pants leg, and then laid it gently on her chest. He touched his finger to his lips, pressed it to hers, then slowly stepped back and walked to the porch. I closed the coffin, but not before eyeing the chess piece.

It was his queen.

Chapter 40

By midafternoon, Tommye's friends thanked us and then disappeared as quietly as they'd arrived. I don't know if she would have liked knowing they were here or not, but something inside me tells me she would have. Around five o'clock Unc appeared carrying two shovels. Lorna and Mandy kept Sketch at the house while we slipped Tommye into the back of Sally and pointed her bumper toward the Buffalo. We drove slowly to the edge of the water, slid her coffin into Unc's canoe, and waded into the water. We pushed her across and because she was light, she floated easily. We floated her around the northern end of the island and beached the canoe not far from the gravesite. Two hours later, as darkness fell around us, Unc lit a lantern and we finished up the digging by its light. We worked slowly, neither of us needing to speak. Sweat trickled off our faces and dripped onto the black soil below. A few feet to our left lay the graves of Unc's first wife, Suzanne, and his young son.

Around nine o'clock we lowered her body into the hole. Unc held one side of the rope and I the other. I thought it fitting—Unc was holding Tommye's rope one final time.

Leaning on our shovels, we stared down. The lantern flickered low, several bugs circled in characteristic frenzy, and in the darkness, the tree frogs and crickets sang a final lullaby. Unc looked like he wanted to say something, but every time he opened his mouth, no words came. Finally he looked at me. "I'll be 'long directly."

I nodded, slid my shovel over my shoulder, and walked out through the Sanctuary. I slipped down into the water, waded through, and passed Vicky sitting waterlogged and at an angle. Water was flowing across her seats and bubbling up under the hood and out the grill.

I left Sally for Unc and walked home. A high moon lit the road and cast shadows across my feet. I thought of Tommye, eight years old, running through the Zuta, bloodstained and scared, her innocence stolen. Then I thought of Uncle Jack, and my anger swelled.

I got to the house, climbed up on the porch, and slipped down into the swing. Mandy's car was gone and Sketch's light was off. Across the pasture, fireflies lit the air. I looked for comfort, but found none. Instead, the emptiness blanketed me.

At three in the morning, Lorna shook my shoulder to wake me. "He's not back."

"Unc?"

She nodded. "I think you'd better go get him."

I jumped off the porch and ran barefoot down the dirt roads and back into the Zuta. The moon was still high, and my shadow stretched out before me. I reached the headwaters, and Sally was right where I'd left her. I slipped in, chest-deep, where the warmth of the water surrounded me, patted Vicky as I waded by, and climbed up the bank on the other side. That's when I heard the screaming.

I stopped and tried to listen above the sound of my own breathing. I could make out no words, but what I heard scared me. It was the sound of pain. I ran through the ferns, the dirt soft beneath my feet and the branches tearing at my chest like the arms of a jealous lover. The further in I ran, the darker it became. Dark rain clouds had moved in fast, covered up the moon, and the temperature had dropped maybe ten degrees. I shivered as the breeze wrapped around me. I got my bearings, turned right, and headed back toward the grave site and the sound. I cleared the magnolias and palm trees, ran through the heart of Ellsworth's creation, around our fire pit, and out the other side. In the darkness, a man stood over the grave, arms raised high, fists clenched, and head angled up. I crept forward just as the rain came down. Big drops that soon drenched me in a torrent. The sheet of rain drowned out the screams, but I could see his body shaking in the dim light of the flickering lantern. I slipped around the other side and hid myself in the bushes.

Unc stood over the three graves, screaming at the top of his lungs. His face was contorted, painted in pain. He paced back and forth, first to his wife's grave, then his son's, then Tommye's—now mounded with dirt. Every few steps he'd stop, lift his hands high, clench his fists, and shake his head. He'd torn off his shirt, and his jeans were soaked clean through. Noise, unintelligible words, poured out. The indecipherable tone of a broken man. Lightning crashed above us, thunder spread across the sky, and the rain puddled at my feet. Soon it ran in trickles across the roots and drained off into the Altamaha—carrying our sweat and Unc's tears.

As quickly as it had come, the rain stopped. Huge drops cascaded off the trees above and landed on my shoulders, chilling me from the outside in. Fog rose off the water and swirled into the trees above.

The lantern burned low, casting an eerie light on Unc, who seemed to grow up and out of a black hole in the earth. Having either exhausted himself or reached his limit, he crumbled and hit his knees, then began falling backward. I cleared a few tree limbs and reached him just as his head and shoulders swayed backward toward the graves. I caught him in my arms and laid him in my lap. His eyes looked at me, but they were focused somewhere out beyond the Milky Way. His body was rigid, every muscle a bowstring. Vesuvius was erupting, and a lifetime of pain was exiting Unc's body. For minutes, I just held him. His body was quivering, and every few seconds he'd let

loose a gutteral moan that echoed off the trees above and then
spread out over the water that surrounded us.

Unc was breaking.

I wrapped my arms around him, cradling his head in my hands.
Everything in me hurt, but every time his teeth ground together, I
knew that my pain didn't compare with his.

After the lantern had burned itself out, we sat beneath the canopy
of the Sanctuary, wrapped in the ripe smell of freshly turned earth
and angry sweat. Somewhere in there, he drifted off, and I laid his
head down on Tommye's mound. I watched his body slowly relax.
The only sound was the grinding of his teeth. An hour later his fist
opened, and his big hand lay limp on the ground beside me. The
moon had reappeared and shone down, bringing out the blue in his
veins and the white of his palms.

I studied his hand. So many times he'd placed that same hand on
my neck and chased away my demons. Now I sat helpless, unable to
stem the tide of the demons that tried to kill him. I wanted badly to
swing back, to return to the battlefield and rescue the wounded—but
comfort was not to be found or offered.

Sometime later, he stirred and opened his eyes. He stared at the
underside of the trees, studying the leaves and the sky that shone
between. Finally he spoke. "We were just kids. Jack was a senior, and I
was a year behind him. We were driving back at night, don't remember where we'd been, but we were in Daddy's Cadillac, and Jack was
driving. Going too fast. Somewhere 'round a hundred. This mangy
old dog, a long-eared beagle, got caught in the headlights and decided
to cross the road. I remember it was limping, nose gray, hobbling
across. Jack floored it, swerved out of his way to hit it. The bumper
caught it square. It spun sideways through the air, landed in the ditch,
and lay there wailing.

"I got to it first. Remarkably, only its leg was broken. I picked it up
and carried it to the car, but Jack appeared from behind the trunk

with a pistol. He never even asked. He just walked up, stuck the bar-rel to the dog's head, and pulled the trigger. He'd been waiting for me to pick it up so the target would be still. The dog went limp, a huge hole in its head. I looked at Jack, and he was smiling. Enjoying it. Evil down to his core." Unc paused.

"I don't know how he got that way. Same dad, same mom, same town, same life. I used to think I had something to do with it, that maybe I could bring him back, but then . . . well, I couldn't. The next day I buried that dog and promised myself that I'd never forget that night. Never forget that old beagle." He looked at me. "And every time I bury somebody I love, I remember."

An hour later we walked up the porch steps, where Lorna met us with a tearstained smile and a cup of cold coffee. He wrapped his arms around her, kissed her, and said, "Honey, I've got to do some-thing. Something that's been a long time in coming. I've got to bury one more person." He pressed his forehead to Lorna's. "You wait on me 'til I get out?"

She nodded. "Only if you're right."

Unc toweled off his face and said, "I've been right my whole life. I'm not about to change now."

We loaded into Sally and backed out. Sketch stood in the drive, arms folded, blocking the car. Scared but unmoving.

Unc rolled down the window and studied him. "Well, if you're gonna hang around here very long, you might as well see what you're getting yourself into. You coming?"

He nodded.

Unc pointed at the scars on his arms. "You might not like what you see."

Sketch shoved his hands into his pockets and shrugged.

Unc opened the door. "Well, I won't stop you."

He climbed in and clicked into his seat belt. We drove to town, where the streets were heavy with morning traffic. Unc drove around the bank once, saw Uncle Jack's Escalade parked outside, and then drove right up onto the sidewalk, knocking over the newspaper bin and parking in front of the door.

The security guard ran out, saw Unc, and pointed. "You can't park—"

Unc ignored him, walked into the bank, and began climbing the stairs. Behind me, I heard the security guard get on his radio and say something about calling the police. This promised to be a short visit.

Unc topped the stairs just as Uncle Jack was walking out of his office. He held some papers in one hand, a cup of coffee in the other, and his reading glasses were down on the end of his nose.

Unc never even paused. He took three steps, reached thirty years back into the past, and caught Uncle Jack with an uppercut that lifted him off his feet, rocked his head back into his spine, and sent him back through his office door. His secretary screamed and started fumbling with the phone. Before Uncle Jack could move or moan, Unc was on top of him. He picked him up by his tie and hit him with another vicious right that sent him stumbling backwards into the great oak desk. He bounced into it and spit out several teeth, his mouth and nose spilling blood. He lifted a hand in front of his face while bracing himself on the desk with the other, but Unc tagged him a third time before he could see straight. The last blow caught him square in the chin and shot him backward across the desk, where he spilled on the ground like a corpse. Unc walked around the desk and sank a knee deep into Jack's rib cage.

"Brother, enough is enough. I spent my whole life being afraid of what you might do rather than living it. This ends today. All of it." He shoved Jack's head beneath the desk, flipped the latch on the trapdoor, and threw it open.

Jack's eyes grew wide.

Unc sat him up and pointed. "I know, brother. I know a lot. There's some I can't prove, but some I can . . . some I will."

The State of Georgia and those who work for its governing municipalities have always believed in massive firepower when it comes to the handguns that their law enforcement officers carry. The two officers who walked in, guns drawn, were no exception. I could've stuck my pinky up the barrel. I know this because both were about a foot from my face.

One was screaming at Unc, "Hands on the desk!"

The second turned to me and pointed his Glock in my face. "You too, paperboy."

"What for?"

He didn't like my response, so he body-slammed me onto the oriental rug, carpet-burning my face.

Unc obeyed and smiled as they smacked his face onto the desk and zip-tied his hands behind his back with all the speed of a calf-roper. A half a second later, they hog-tied me and then lifted me off the carpet, cutting the circulation to my hands. About then Lorna ran through the door and grabbed Sketch.

Unc stopped and looked at her. "Better call Mandy. Oh, and send me an RC Cola and a MoonPie. I'm hungry." He turned to me. "You want anything?"

I tried to say something cute, but the officer lifted my wrists into my armpits, and I decided not to be stupid.

They tried to shove us through the door, but Unc was bigger and stood his ground. He turned to the officers. "Guys, I'm going. But I'm walking." He turned to Uncle Jack and shook his head. "You never should have shot that beagle."

Uncle Jack kicked the trapdoor and shouted at his secretary, "Get me a doctor!"

Unc laughed and walked out the office door. Sketch and Lorna stood in Jack's office, the kid's eyes round.

Jack wiped his mouth on his shirt and screamed at me, "What're you looking at?"

"Funny . . . we didn't really miss you at the funeral."

He picked up a paperweight and heaved it across the room, but it missed me by a few feet.

We walked down the steps. Unc's hand lay flat across the lower part of his back. The middle knuckle was cut deep, and blood covered his fingertips. If it hurt, he didn't seem to mind.

They shoved us into the back of a squad car, but then the guy driving looked into his rearview mirror and said, "I got a better idea." He opened the door; they grabbed each of us and paraded us like a couple of circus elephants two blocks down to City Hall. We passed an old lady coming out of Jack's First-something-or-other church. She recognized Unc, shook her head, and turned away, muttering.

Unc turned away, nodded, and said, "Afternoon, Ms. Baxter."

Several steps down the sidewalk, he turned to me. "Don't mind her. She's a good woman, she just don't know no better. You live with a lie long enough, and pretty soon it starts to sound true."

I looked behind me as she waddled to her car. "Why didn't you get in her face and tell her what you think?"

He shook his head and smiled. "Remember . . . words that sink into your heart—"

I watched him walk—his wet boots sloshing as his feet slid up and down inside the heels that had not dried from last night.

"I know, I know . . . they're whispered, not yelled."

He nodded. "You're learning."

Chapter 41

After some routine niceties, they gave me one phone call. Mandy's voice mail picked up, so I left her a message. Then they walked us downstairs and threw us into my home away from home. I walked over to my concrete block, scratched through TWICE with the side of a quarter and wrote 3x in big block letters.

A few minutes later Mandy showed, a digital voice recorder tucked in her shirt pocket. She sat down outside the cell, crossing her arms and legs and raising her eyebrows. "You two have been busy."

I was about to open my mouth, but Unc beat me to it.

He sat back, took a deep breath, and closed his eyes. "Jack always did like to gamble. To say it was in his blood wouldn't be fair. It was hard-wired into his DNA. We used to kid about it when we were young. Then he got older, things changed, and what was a hobby became an addiction. The night of the storm, I knew he was down cutting the cards, but . . . well . . ." He turned to Mandy. "Ain't you gotten us out of here yet?"

"You in a hurry?"

He nodded and looked at me. "Yup. First time in a long time."

She probed. "What's the holdup?"

He chewed on a hangnail and spit it across the cell. "Been trying to get my nerve up."

Mandy laughed. "For how long?"

"Nigh on to three decades."

Lorna walked in, leading Sketch by the hand. "You 'bout done?"

I was starting to get aggravated. "You guys are talking in code, and I don't understand a thing."

Lorna gave Mandy a receipt. "Five thousand dollars." She looked at Unc. "Bail bonds are expensive."

Unc fingered the receipt. "Bonds. Can't live with them, can't live without them."

An hour later we walked out into the noontime sun. Mandy tapped me on the shoulder and said, "I've got to get to the office. Things will heat up this afternoon."

Unc shook his head. "Not if you want to be my attorney."

She held up his hand, eyed the cut across the middle knuckle, and then looped her arm inside mine. "I'm not sure I want to be *your* attorney."

Unc drove all five of us through Dairy Queen, where he ordered lunch and five dipped cones. Sketch slammed a cheeseburger and French fries, then went to work on his cone, which was dripping down his hand, but he didn't seem to mind. Absent was his chess set. Present was a smile covered in vanilla and chocolate.

We drove into the Zuta to find a television news truck parked along the highway, the transmitter telescoped forty feet into the air. The reporter was giving an update as we drove in. He stuck the microphone in Unc's face, but Unc ignored him and drove slowly by. Sketch waved, then pointed to the NO TRESPASSING sign.

Unc stopped at the barn, grabbed two shovels, and drove us further back into the Zuta. The only two people who seemed to know where we were going were Lorna and Unc, but neither was talking. When we got to the water, I threw Sketch up on my shoulders and waded in.

Mandy balked. "High heels and a skirt don't exactly work here."

Unc waved her on.

Lorna turned and smiled. "Trust me. You don't want to miss this."

Vicky sat right where I left her. The water level had receded some, but her floor wells were full and the hood still bubbled. I patted her on the bumper. "Hang in there, girl. I'm coming."

Unc threw a shovel over each shoulder and led us through Ellsworth's Sanctuary. By the time we reached the grave sites, his shoulders looked like each shovel weighed a thousand pounds.

I set Sketch down and stood next to Unc, who stood over his son's grave. To our right, the ground above Tommye's grave still lay mounded, covered in shale and loose rocks that had been uncovered in the rain. Unc looked at me. The right side of his face was twitching, and his eyes were blinking a lot.

After a few minutes, Lorna patted him on the shoulder. "Liam . . ."

He nodded, licked his lips, which were cottony-white, and whispered, "What kind of man are you?"

"What?"

He stepped closer. "I said, 'What kind of man are you?'"

"Unc, what's that supposed to mean? What's this . . ."

He pointed at me. "Don't call me that. Not anymore. I don't want to be your uncle anymore." He handed me a shovel and said, "Dig."

I looked down, eyes wide. "Where?"

He sank his shovel into the ground above his son's grave and didn't say a word.

I leaned on my shovel. "Have you lost your mind? I'm not digging anywhere around here."

Unc paid me no mind. He just kept digging. In ten minutes, he was shin-deep and reaching further. I looked at Mandy. She shrugged and mouthed the word, "Dig." Sketch sat on the ground, sketchbook tucked up close under one arm. ·

I jumped down into the growing hole and gently stepped on my shovel. An hour later, we were chest-deep and winded. Unc had taken his shirt off, which was good 'cause between yesterday, last night, and this morning, it was starting to stink.

We dug another thirty minutes when I said, "You know, these things are usually encased in concrete."

He didn't even look up. "Who said anything about concrete?"

A few minutes later, my shovel tip struck wood. Unc hit his knees and began shoveling off the dirt with his hands. When he had the lid uncovered, he stood up on top of it, his head and shoulders just clearing the top of the hole. He wiped his head on his forearm and filled his chest with salty air. Then without another word he knelt, grabbed the handle, and lifted one half of the lid. I closed my eyes and waited to hear a sucking in of air as the seal was broken, but none came. Not wanting to see a worm-eaten body or bag of white bones, I opened my eyes slowly. Sketch was leaning over the hole, peering in. Mandy too. Only Lorna sat back, not looking. Unlike the others, she was looking at me.

Unc propped open the lid with his shovel, reached in, and grabbed a green trash bag wrapped in duct tape. It was about the size of an Igloo cooler but only half as deep. He climbed out of the hole, sat Indian style on the ground, and began searching his pocket for his knife, but the kid beat him to it. Sketch opened the smaller of the two blades, held it out handle first, and Unc took it gently. He slit the tape, slid off the bag, and pulled out a plastic storage case. He flipped open the latches, popped off the lid, and pulled out something about the size of a legal folder that was maybe three inches thick. Then he began cutting what looked like an inch worth of plastic wrap and tape. Whatever was inside had been protected and made as watertight as it could get with plastic.

Unc pulled off the remainder of the plastic wrap and exposed a large, black, legal-sized notebook stuffed with yellowed, but dry, papers. Curious, Sketch scooted up next to him and looked across his lap. Unc stared out through the cypress trees rising up out of the Buffalo, and it looked like his lips were struggling to make words.

Sketch looked over his lap and down into the casket, searching for the body. But there wasn't one. When he was satisfied that a mummy was not about to rise up out of the earth, he pointed and raised his eyebrows.

Unc shook his head. "Ain't no body." He pointed downriver. "I dumped it out there, long time ago."

I spoke first. "You dumped your own son in the river?"

Unc shook his head and looked at me like I was the one who'd lost my mind. "'Course not."

"Well then, who got ditched in the river?"

He shrugged. "I don't know. He was dead. I didn't know him."

Mandy's face was sheet white. "Mr. McFarland, I think you might need an attorney."

Unc paid her no mind. "When they took me to the morgue and pulled back the sheet, I knew right away. It was a close match, real close, but the body on that table didn't belong to me. He was no relation of mine."

"How'd you know?"

He smiled. "Ear lobes. His were connected. My son's were not."

Mandy looked at him, then me. Sketch reached up and started fingering his ears.

I wasn't following him. "What do you mean?"

He pulled on his own ear. "Like this. The bottoms are loose, not connected down on the jaw line."

"Well, then . . . who was the kid on the table?"

"Heck if I know." He shrugged. "All I knew was that I didn't kill him, and more importantly"—he paused and rubbed his hand across the cover of the notebook—"that meant my son might still be alive."

When I'd interviewed the driver of the prison truck that drove Unc back from the funeral, he had told me that Unc looked mad, not sad. And that he had not cried. I had never made sense of that. The Unc I knew would have cried his eyes out. "Why didn't you say something?"

He shook his head. "What did I have to gain? Yes, I was real sorry for whoever was looking for that kid on the table, but when I started putting the pieces together, I doubted anybody was. I figure he was dead long before he got burnt. I kept my mouth shut, because if I had said anything, I would have let whoever took my son know that I knew the body wasn't his. If I said nothing, and my son was still alive, I could help keep him that way by keeping my mouth shut."

I shook my head. "Well . . . what if he's still alive?"

"He is."

"Well, where? Why don't you go get him?"

Unc looked at Lorna, then Mandy, then me. "I did."

The questions swirled. "But? What about the . . . the ransom note? It was a fake?"

He nodded and smiled. "Keep going."

"How'd you know?"

"I grew up playing cards with my brother. I knew when he was bluffing long before he could."

"But you went along with it?"

He nodded again.

I sat back, the video of our life flashing across the backs of my eyelids. I described what I saw. "He knew that you knew he'd taken the bonds, and he needed something to keep you quiet." I turned to Sketch, then back to Unc. "Well . . . what was it?"

He pulled a single sheet of paper from the notebook, then reached up, touched my ear, and looked across at Suzanne's grave. "Your mother wanted to call you 'Junior.'"

I looked at the sheet of paper. It was a birth certificate. Across the top it read, WILLIAM WALKER MCFARLAND JR. BORN MARCH 31, 1976.

Unc put his hand on the back of my neck and held me as if he were afraid I'd escape. He swallowed. "I told you once that the second hardest decision I'd ever made was signing those papers and letting them take my son. Making him a ward of the state. That's 'cause the hardest . . . the hardest thing I've ever done has been living every day, watching him grow into a man that I'm danged proud of, and not telling him. Of living that lie my whole life.

"But I couldn't risk losing you a second time. Dying was hard enough once. I'd rather not do it twice. Then by the time you got old enough, and saw how the town saw me, what they thought of me, the story that has dogged my past, I was afraid you wouldn't want me." He nodded at the birth certificate, pulled me toward him, pressed my forehead to his, and tried to laugh. "I told your mom I wasn't about to call you Junior. Told her I was giving you the most valuable thing I had. So I gave you my name." He lifted my head and whispered, "Told her we were gonna call you . . . Liam."

The name bounced off the insides of my head, rattled down my neck, circulated through me, and hovered above my chest.

He looked at me, his lips tight. He nodded. "Liam." The whisper jolted the word loose, flipped it a few degrees, and then it slid down into the hole in me where it echoed like a gavel.

"But . . . why didn't you . . . ?"

He shrugged. "Wasn't worth it."

"Wasn't worth it? But you lost everything."

He shook his head and smiled, his lips quivering. "I gained everything."

"What?"

"You . . ." He put his hands behind my head. "You're my inheritance."

"But . . ."

"Son . . ."

The word stopped me.

He filled his chest. "'Cause nothing"—he poked me in the chest—"not one single thing . . . compares to you."

For the first time in my life, I'd heard the word *son*. Aimed at me.

"But . . ."

He held up a finger. "Before the trial, Jack produced Ellsworth's last will and testament, which I knew was fake."

"How?"

He reached into the notebook. "'Cause I had the original." He pulled out a document that was several sheets long. "The reason Dad had Perry Kenner at the house that evening was because of this." He handed it to me. "Dad didn't trust Jack. He loved him, but he said he was 'akin to meanness and a close cousin to downright nastiness.' So he wrote up this, which splits everything down the middle. He'd told me about it the day before. Unlike the one Jack produced, it gave me—the younger brother—managerial control of all Zuta Properties." He shook his head. "He knew Jack would never go for that. But neither Dad nor I thought he'd kill over it. My guess is that Jack stumbled upon Dad and Perry, they told him the truth, and he shot them both, then Suzanne, leaving the gun in Perry's hand. He must've stolen the bonds some-where shortly after we exited the vault, coming up through the tun-nel beneath."

"Well . . . what about . . ."

"One thing at a time. I got out of prison, came home, and started secretly looking for you. I knew Jack wasn't saying something, so I swam back up the drain, into the basement, and crawled up under his desk. I did that for months. Just listening. Sure enough, he slipped. Made a phone call and started talking about 'moving him someplace out west where he'd disappear.' He left his office, I crawled up and inside, pressed redial, and talked to the voice on the other end of the line. It was my second break."

Mandy broke in, "And the first?"

He looked at Lorna. "The pardon. Lorna used to work in house-keeping at the governor's mansion. Worked the night shift. Responsible for the guesthouse. Seemed the governor was having more guests than his wife knew about. He started coming on to Lorna, she refused him, he started talking about firing her, so she took some pictures for safekeeping, filed them away in a safety deposit box . . . and resigned to go to work with the department of corrections. Guess they had better benefits. She didn't tell me about the pictures until I'd been in prison a couple of years." He looked at her. "Still not quite sure why she pulled them out of hiding. She mailed copies off with a real sweet note and told him that William McFarland deserved a pardon. And that if he didn't get one, the next set of copies was going to his wife and the media."

I looked at Lorna, who smiled and shrugged.

Unc continued, "Next thing I knew, this big guard who was always picking on me unlocked my door and walked me outside into the clean air." He laughed. "We still got those negatives, too."

Mandy just shook her head. "Kind of a lucky break."

"I was due one." He looked back at me. "Once you got old enough, and I knew that Jack couldn't try anything even if he found out about you, I tried to tell you . . . a thousand times. A man ought to know his own story. I owed you that. But you grew up with people spitting on me and screaming at me from across the street and I . . . I just figured that . . . well, maybe you were better off not being related. At least on the surface. Then I got scared that if I told you, you'd get hacked, take off, and never look back."

Mandy sat up. "I'm not sure any of this will stand up in court."

He shook his head. "I'm not going back to court."

Her eyes narrowed. "Why not?"

"Don't have anything to prove."

She waved her hands across the notebook. "What about . . ."

He shook his head, looking from Lorna, to me, and finally to Sketch. He sat the kid in his lap and said, "I got everything I need."

"But we can't let him get away with . . ."

"Mandy, darling . . ."

Mandy still had her attorney's face on. "You know, Jack's not going to just let you waltz into his office, take a few swings at him, and forget about it."

"He will when I show him this." He looked at Lorna, held out his hand, and she placed an envelope in it. He handed it to me. "Tommye wanted me to give this to you."

I slid my finger under the flap of the envelope and tore it open. I unfolded the single sheet of paper.

Unc laughed. "I'd like to see his face the next time you show up at a shareholder's meeting. He's gonna crap a brick." He looked at Sketch and put his hands over the kid's ears. "Oops, sorry. You weren't supposed to hear that."

Sketch smiled as if he'd snuck in on one of the better-kept secrets of life.

I read the letter out loud: "The Last Will and Testament of Tommye McFarland. I, Tommye Lynn McFarland, being of sound mind but infected and dying body, do hereby leave everything I own, or possess, in any way, shape, or form, to Chase Walker, formerly . . . and hereafter . . . known as William 'Liam' Walker McFarland Jr."

On the bottom, the letter had been notarized and signed by three witnesses—a notary I did not know, Lorna, and Unc. Across the bottom she'd written in cursive, *Chase/Liam, visit Dad's new vault, safety deposit box #1979 (fitting, don't you think?). Try the keys around your neck. You'll like the paper trail. You owe me. But you can pay me when you get here. I love you—Tommye.*

I stared and reread the letter. "She knew? I mean, about you and me?"

"Yeah, she figured it out a long time ago. Said you had my eyes."

"Why didn't she ever say anything?"

"I asked her not to."

I thought back over our lives together. "That explains a lot."

Unc looked at Tommye's will. "I imagine he'll contest this, but . . . he knows as well as I do that it's akin to a royal flush."

I interrupted him. "I thought you said you didn't like to play cards."

"I don't. But I never said I didn't know how." He shook his head. "Funny thing, too. Jack's the one who taught me."

I stared again at the birth certificate, doing the math in my head. "You mean I'm already thirty?"

"Yeah."

"I just lost two years of my life."

He looked at me, his eyes wondering. "You mad at me?"

"You mean for making me live a lifetime, wondering, not knowing . . . and you keeping it a secret the entire time?" I looked out across the swamp, Tommye's grave, and the black water flowing some hundred yards away, floating out to the sea. I shook my head. "I've spent most my whole life looking down a dark driveway. Hoping to see headlights. My whole life I've envisioned my dad driving up, hopping out of his truck, and taking me home—a shiny new bike in the back. And every time my dreams lasted long enough to let me see his eyes, he had your face."

Unc—my dad—dropped his head to his chest, set the kid on the ground, and wept, his tears dripping into the black soil below.

We stood up and started walking out of the Sanctuary, Ellsworth's creation rising up all around us. Sketch walked alongside the man who'd always been my dad, holding his hand. All at once, he stopped and tugged on the hand, and Dad knelt down. Sketch's eyes narrowed, and a wrinkle appeared just above his nose. His lips grew tight, and then he opened his mouth, his neck growing red and his shoulders rising.

The vein in his neck swelled, and I could see his pulse quickening. He looked at Lorna, Mandy, me, and then the big, callused hand next to him. He gently placed his inside. Finally, a whisper cracked. "A-r-e—" He took a deep breath and spoke slowly, taking his time, making possibly the most beautiful sound I'd ever heard. "A-r-e w-e a f-a-m-i-l-y n-o-w?"

Dad scooped his little body up in his arms and pressed him to his chest. He wrapped his arms around the kid and laughed like a man who had returned from the battlefield to find his family sitting on the front porch, a yellow ribbon wrapped around every tree for a mile. Finally he wrestled the word out of his mouth. "Yes." Then he threw Sketch over his shoulder like a sack of potatoes and tickled his ribs. "Yes, we are." He laughed a deep belly laugh. "And you can take that to the bank."

Mandy stopped him and looked at Sketch. "You can talk?"

He shrugged.

She put her hands on her hips. "Why didn't you?"

"D-i-d-n-t w-a-n-t t-o."

I put Sketch on my shoulders and waded back through the swamp. He sat atop me, pulled on my ears, and snatched at the fireflies buzzing around his head. When the water reached my chest, it hit me—after a lifetime of wondering, I finally knew the story of me.

Love does that. It names the nameless and gives voice to the voiceless.

Chapter 42

I was in my office polishing my article when Red walked in and said, "You 'bout finished?"

I clicked SAVE, pressed PRINT, and handed it to him.

He leaned against the window that faced the jail and began reading. When he finished, he laid it on the desk and said, "Jack know about this?"

"Not yet."

He laughed. "Might catch him off guard."

"I hope it's not the last time."

He raised an eyebrow. "How you coming on that other article?"

"Which one is that?"

"The other one."

"Still missing a few pieces."

"Got any leads?"

I shrugged. "I think I know what happened, I just can't prove it."

He walked to the door. "Keep digging."

I put my computer to sleep and grabbed my keys.

"Where you going?"

"Taking my little brother fishing." I shrugged. "Well . . . sort of."

"What's biting?"

"Vicky, I hope."

Because of the restraining order, Mandy had asked the court to allow her to accompany me to the bank. She and my shadow met me downstairs. He was wearing flip-flops, cutoffs, and one of Tommye's Georgia Bulldogs T-shirts.

I squatted down and said, "Nice shirt."

He smiled and jumped up on my back. While I piggybacked the kid, Mandy escorted us to the bank, where an expressionless manager met us, assisted by one of the police who'd arrested me. Without a "Hello" or a "Would you like a cup of coffee," he led us through the lobby and into a private sitting room adjacent to the bank's high-tech vault.

I showed him the number, he retrieved the box, we turned our keys, and he walked out, closing the door behind him. I lifted the lid, pulled out a stack of papers, and laid them on the desk. They were old and yellowed, but they smelled of Tommye's perfume, which told me she'd been here. Most of the sheets were deposit receipts from 1979 and 1980. One set came from a wholesale brokerage house in New Orleans, and others from an offshore bank in the Bahamas. The dollar amounts were staggering. I picked up the first, reading and rereading it several times. About the third time, the numbers added up and the truth sank in.

"Holy sh—" I looked at Sketch. "I mean, smokes!"

Mandy leaned in and we stared, shoulder to shoulder.

Tommye had arranged the receipts according to date, so I spread them across the desk and tried to make sense of the bigger picture. It didn't take either one of us very long.

Mandy's eyes grew wide, and her jaw dropped. "And to think this has been sitting under his nose the entire time. This could ruin him. How'd she get it?"

If there ever was such a thing as a paper trail, we were looking at it.

"No telling. Tommye could get into anywhere." I looked at the puzzle pieces in front of me and, in my mind, began writing the story I'd been wanting to write for most of my life.

At the back of the stack I found two pictures. The first was a picture of Tommye taken in high school. She stood between Unc and me, her arms around our shoulders. It was the Tommye I wanted to remember. She must've known this.

The second picture was one that Lorna had taken on the front porch just after Sketch ate his birthday cake. Dad and I stood on either side, while Sketch sat in Tommye's arms wearing an icing mustache. Her hair was thin, eyes dark and sunk deep into their sockets, and pain had wrinkled her forehead. I studied the picture and noticed something I'd not seen that night. Printed in small black letters across the bottom of her T-shirt were the words AMERICAN PIE. A yellow sticky note was attached to the back of the picture. On it she'd written, *The three men I admire most . . . they caught the last train for the coast. . . .*

I could hear her voice, see her sly smile and the look behind her eyes. I held the picture while the edges grew cloudy and my insides began to ache.

Mandy put her hand on mine. Quiet comfort that felt no need to speak.

Sketch looked at the picture and then at me. He'd been practicing, but we were still a long way off. His face grew red as his mouth tried to remember how to form the words. The whisper was broken and raspy. "Y-o-u m-i-s-s h-e-r?"

"Yeah . . . I do."

He held the picture, tried to speak, but then just smiled and tapped himself on the chest.

I make a living with words, but sometimes words can't say what needs saying. Sketch taught me that. I slid the picture into my shirt pocket and then shoved all the papers back in the box, locking it and hanging the keys around my neck. "Might as well let him keep it safe for us. Leastways 'til we can get the FBI down here."

Mandy nodded, pushed the box away, and sat back. "Ironic, don't you think?"

"Yeah . . . but sometimes the thing you need the most is right there under your nose."

We walked out of the vault, Sketch's hand in mine, the sound of our flip-flops echoing off the shiny steel walls. We stood on the sidewalk, where a September breeze met us after it had stirred on some foreign continent, swept across the sea, and filtered through the marsh, carrying with it the smell of home and moments worth remembering.

JOHN DOE #117 ADOPTED

John Doe #117 was given a permanent home this week, as he was adopted by William and Lorna McFarland of Brunswick. The State of Georgia, along with the help of an independent investigator, determined that John Doe #117 was a foundling—abandoned since birth. Parental rights were terminated five years ago in Atlanta and, in an effort to place the child in a permanent home, the child was named Stuart Smoak.

Two years ago he was adopted by Sonya Beckers, a Certified Nursing Assistant at Cedar Lakes Assisted Living Facility. Shortly thereafter, Sonya and Stuart disappeared. The two reappeared three months ago when Ms. Beckers dropped Stuart off at a railroad crossing south of Thalmann on Highway 99 just before her car was struck by a southbound freight train. Authorities did not speculate if the death was a suicide, as no note was found. Stuart was placed in Brunswick Boys' Home, then transferred to the McFarlands' home until a permanent living situation could be arranged.

Last week Mr. and Mrs. McFarland filed a petition with the courts to permanently adopt the child. Yesterday, in a private ceremony before the judge, the couple officially adopted John Doe #117. At the child's request, he changed his name to Tommye Chase McFarland. When asked what he wanted to be called, he scratched his head and said, "T.C."

When asked why he would adopt at the age of fifty-five, William McFarland said, "Every boy is born with a hole in his belly. If his dad don't fill it, it festers and becomes an aching black hole—one that he'll spend his waking hours trying to fill. Mostly with things that do him more harm than good.

"Lord knows I'm not as young as I once was, and I've made my fair share of mistakes, but . . . well, I ain't that old, and if I got to put a square peg in a round hole, well . . . That boy might not have been born of my loins, but he's been born of my heart. And I reckon that's good enough."

Mr. and Mrs. McFarland first became foster parents some twenty years ago when they accepted the placement of then seven-year-old Chase Walker. When asked why he chose to adopt Stuart, but hadn't adopted Chase more than twenty years ago, Mr. McFarland smiled, shook his head, and asked, "Why would I adopt my own son?"

Afterword

Since I met him at the hospital, my new little brother had known six names: "the kid," Snoot, Sketch, Buddy, Stuart, and finally, T.C. The first five seemed like impostors, or stand-ins until the real thing could be located. But when we finally started calling him T.C., well, the name was like an old shirt. It draped across his shoulders, hung loose around his neck, and the sleeves weren't too long. Besides, he seemed to like it. The more difficult transition occurred when I tried to insert "Dad" where "Unc" had once been. Problem was, when I tried to do so, I found they both meant the same thing.

T.C. and I watched from the porch steps as William "Liam" McFarland stepped out of Sally and walked beneath the pecan trees to the mailbox. His boots were muddy, shirt stained with salt and manure, and his hat was tipped back, shading the falling sun off his neck. He reached the end of the drive, flipped open the door, pulled out the mail, and pitched the junk into the trash can. He flipped through the bills, slid them into his shirt pocket, and meandered back toward us.

He climbed the steps, patted T.C. on the head, knocked my Braves cap on the floor, and sat between us, letting out a deep breath. "Phew, my dogs is tired." He tilted his hat back, leaned on his elbows, and stared out across the pasture. After a few minutes, he reached into his shirt pocket and handed me a small slip of paper.

It was a picture—yellowed and wrinkled from time. It looked like it was taken somewhere in the seventies. A small boy sat on a man's shoulders. The boy was smiling, pulling on the man's right ear. The man had sideburns, one leg in a cast, and was leaning on a single wooden crutch. The other hand supported the boy's foot, but also kept him from falling backward.

I held up the picture and studied it. The boy wore a pair of cut-off jeans, cowboy boots, no shirt, and a summer tan. The man was a mixture of faded denim, snap cuffs, and a smile that spoke of contentedness.

In the distant background, I saw a brick building with a dark shingled roof and clock tower. It stood at the end of a long drive lined with trees. I extended the picture at arm's length and compared it to the driveway that spread out before me.

I flipped it over. On the back it read *Liam and Me, 1979.*

Unc slid a dirty finger underneath his nose and wiped his hand on his jeans. He spoke out across the porch steps. "That's us just a few days after you got caught on the tracks and took fifteen years out of my life . . . which I couldn't spare."

T.C. laughed, pushing out a hoarse whisper.

Dad calculated. "That's about six months before the storm hit, and we found we weren't in Kansas anymore."

"You kept it all this time?"

"Sometimes . . . when I reached my bottom and felt lower than a snake's butt in a wagon rut . . ."

T.C. smiled. I just shook my head.

"And needed to remind myself that I wasn't some hallucinating lunatic, I'd pull it out and imprint the image one more time onto the backs of my eyelids." He sucked through his teeth and twirled the brow of his hat through his hands. "That picture got me through a lot of bad times."

"What's with the cast?"

He rubbed his leg. "Trains ain't gentle. And they ain't quick to slow down neither."

"The train actually hit you?"

"Well, of course it hit me. How you think I got you off that track? I jumped off the platform thinking I was Superman, tried to drag you off with me, and when I did, the front of that thing nearly tore my leg off. Spun us both through the air like a helicopter."

I studied the pictures in my head. "I have no memory of that."

"Probably just as well. It wasn't too pretty."

"The leg ever bother you?"

"Not really, but I can predict the rain or a coming cold snap better than that fellow on Channel 11."

I stared again at the picture. "What's the building?"

"Oh, that . . ." He laughed. "That was the train depot that used to sit at the end of our driveway."

"Right down there?"

"Yup. Once your mom heard about your little escape—which, by the way, was the third time I'd found you down there—she contacted the city, said it was some sort of rat-infested hazard, and petitioned to have it torn down. So . . . no more depot."

"That explains a lot."

He smelled of manure, sweat, and honesty.

"You got any more secrets?"

He raised his eyebrows, the laughter rising up from his belly. "That's probably enough for one lifetime."

There it was again. Laughter for pain.

T.C.'s hands were blazing across his sketchpad, and the puppeteer was warming up for a tap dance. We leaned in and studied his sketch. From a track-level perspective, his picture depicted a train that had come and gone and was now fading off into the distance—a black trail of smoke dissipating in its wake.

Dad put his hand on T.C.'s neck and patted his shoulders gently. T.C. shut his book, slid his pencil over his ear, and rested his head across the tops of his arms. If manhood is passed down, if it is a mantle cut from the cloth of one and draped across another, it is not done so using titles or accolades. Not hardly. It occurs there—in that spout now resting neck-high—pouring down the spine and into the belly in a language that has never been transcribed, but that every boy on the planet understands and has always understood.

I tucked T.C. into bed and promised him we'd go fishing tomorrow. He whispered, "It's dark in here." I clicked on the closet light and pulled the door behind me.

Because Vicky was sitting on blocks in the barn and weeks away from drivable, Dad let me drive Sally. Darkness blanketed the pasture, stars lit the atmosphere, and the first hint of a gentle and nearly-cool easterly breeze swept across my face. Headlights off, I idled down the drive, stopping in front of the mailbox. I cut the engine, folded the letter, stuck it in the box, and raised the red metal flag.

I lifted my nose, smelled the marsh, and closed my eyes. I heard the distant sound of booted footsteps jumping off hollow porch boards. When I opened my eyes, I saw a man wearing pants and no shirt running figure eights through the pasture, waving his arms in the air. With every swipe, he'd pull down a star, place it in the jar, and then run wildly in search of another. Trailing not far behind him came a giggling, skinny boy, the moonlight bouncing off his glasses.

I shook my head and slipped through the fence, where we spent the next hour filling up that mason jar—and the kid who would carry it.

Oh, yeah, the letter read:

Dear Dad,
I was looking the wrong way.
Your son,
Liam

It was the first time I'd ever written my name.

On Uncle Willie

I was eight. Maybe nine. Still in that magical age where hope and sweat dripped from the same pores. My neighborhood was filled with rough and tumble boys. If we were not throwing a football, or hitting a baseball, then we were riding our bicycles, terrorizing the neighborhood. Everybody had a dirt bike. Everybody but me. My bike, if you can call it that, was a hand-me-down, via my sister, and about two sizes too small. It was yellow, had a banana seat, and little white plastic tassels hanging from the grips which, all total, made me the laughingstock of the neighborhood. Further, the crank arms were so short and it was geared so low, that I had to pedal twice for every one of my friends' revolutions. Riding around the neighborhood, my legs looked like a spinning blur of tennis shoe over tube sock.

Over the next year, I saved my allowance and every penny that the tooth fairy brought in hopes that I could afford a new bike and throw my sister's in the river. The object of my lust was a Schwinn Mag Scrambler. I still get goose bumps. Chrome frame, black five-spoke mag wheels, it came decked out with a Bendix brake and knobby tires.

Problem was I had sixty dollars to my name and the Scrambler cost $119. Easy math. One year down, one to go. But, a month before

Christmas, dad surprised me and told me he'd match my savings. I could have kissed his feet.

Dad drove me to the Schwinn store. We walked in and I pointed. We rolled her to the register, and the young guy at the counter upsold us into getting all the pads. By the time we walked out, I had promised the next four months of allowance to make up the difference.

Dad loaded her into the car and we drove home. I wanted him to make a few loops around the neighborhood so all the guys could see the handlebars sticking out the trunk. We unloaded her and then he rolled it into the house and leaned her against the wall next to the tree—no self-respecting dirt bike came with a kickstand.

A week later, Christmas daylight broke through my window. While my sisters were rubbing the sleep out of their eyes and shuffling down the hall in their slippers, I came running out of my room wearing a football helmet and knee pads. Mom and Dad laughed, opened the front door and I rode across the threshold.

Over the next several months, we built ramps, learned how to jump incredibly stupid distances, rode way too fast without helmets and traveled places our parents never knew about. If there is one word that described that bike, it was *Freedom*. Because that's what it gave me. I've often said I lived a Huck Finn childhood and that bike was a big part of that.

I rode to the movie theater, to Peterson's Five-and-Dime, to the firehouse where the firemen let me slide down the brass pole, to Stand-n-Snack for a slaw dog, and when I needed air in the tires, I rode up to Mr. West's gas station and he'd fill them for free.

Eventually, I learned to cat-walk—which is nothing more than an extended wheelie. We compared ourselves and measured our progress by counting the number of parking spaces we could pedal on one wheel. Anything over five was good. My number was forty-seven.

Three years passed, I turned eleven and hit a bit of a rough period. I'd started picking on some of my friends, maybe *bullying* is a better word—and I couldn't quite tell you why other than I was a "tweener." In size, I found myself "between" the bullies and the runts, so when the bullies turned on me, I turned on the runts. I'm still sorry about that. Because of this, Mom and Dad had been working with me—if you can call it that—on sharing, and something about loving your neighbor as yourself because evidently I wasn't.

The school bus dropped me off, I threw my books on the floor of my room, ate a snack, and then headed out for San Marco to hook up with my buddies. I made it down Arbor Lane, across Sorento Road, past the Saltmarsh's house, and onto Ballis Place that ran between the movie theater and Peterson's before intersecting San Marco Boulevard. Approaching the intersection of Ballis Place with the alley that ran behind the theater, a kid I did not know and had never seen, flagged me down. He was likable enough. Had a good smile, offered to tell me a few jokes, and his shoes were worn and had holes in them. He leaned on my bike, his hands gripping my handlebars, and we talked a minute. Then he asked to ride my bike.

Somewhere in the prior week I'd bullied a buddy—I can't quite remember the details but my butt would if you asked it—and so when this guy leaned against my bike and asked if he could ride, a lightbulb went off, *Hey! This is what Mom and Dad must be talking about. Here's a chance to share, and I don't even know this guy. This is probably worth double points. Why can't stuff like this ever happen to me when they're looking.* So I hopped off and said, "Sure, but just"—I pointed with my finger—"right here."

That kid hopped on my bike and started smiling like I'd given him a Moon Pie and an RC Cola all at the same time. He made a few feeble attempts to cat-walk, so I said, "Hey, I can teach you to do that." I just knew God was happy about me being all kind and unselfish. I had turned over a new leaf. Nothing but the straight and narrow for me. And I think my butt was happy about that.

He swung another loop around me, which made four, and then

arced a bit out into the dirt. He said something about liking the knobby tires and I said, "Yeah, they really grip." He looped again, smiling wider, white teeth brilliant—heaven smiling on us both—then he stood up, jumped on the pedals like a BMX racer, and I never saw him again.

I stood there a few minutes, staring at an empty dirt road. Then I walked to the end of the alley, thinking his excitement just got the better of him. I don't know how long I stood there.

I walked home crying. Afraid to show my face. *How was I going to explain this?* Mom saw me coming up the street and her eyes narrowed, "What happened?" I was crying so hard, I couldn't tell her. I walked inside, sat on a chair in my room, and cried an angry, bitter cry. I remember my shoulders shaking, rubbing my snotty nose on my shirtsleeve, and being unable to catch my breath for a long period of time.

I just could not understand why.

I sat in that chair, my feet dangling off the floor, and asked God to help me forgive that boy 'cause I knew I needed to, but I also knew I wasn't about to do it on my own. Then Mom prayed for his soul which I didn't care too much about but in hindsight was probably a good idea. Finally, she asked God for a new bike for me which was good 'cause I had a feeling he listened to her.

That night, Dad got home, Mom told him, and I remember seeing pain on his face. Not anger pain, like he was mad at me or even that boy but deep-down parent pain. If you have kids, then you know what I'm talking about. That night, alone in my room, I prayed that God would kill the devil. And for all I cared, he could stay in hell and I hoped it was hot, too.

A few weeks later, I was standing in the driveway, shooting hoops, bored to tears and growing in my hatred of the devil. Somewhere after five, Dad pulled into the drive. The trunk rested half-open, oddly canted. He stepped out of his car, smiling, tie loosened. It's almost like he knew. Boys at age eleven have graduated from jumps and cat-walks to pure, unadulterated speed. He untied the trunk and lifted out a polished, midnight-black, Schwinn 10-speed.

It was after dark when I finally got home. Normally, I'd have been grounded. My eyes and the sweat pasted on my forehead told the story: the boundaries of my life had just widened exponentially.

It may seem silly, but that bike was indicative of something much bigger going on.

As I got older, grew taller and outgrew that 10-speed, I watched a lot of my friends rebel against their dads. Some fought and punched holes in the Sheetrock, others screamed and threw chairs or car keys, while still others shook their heads and cursed them behind their backs. That always struck me as odd. I'm not saying that Dad and I didn't have our disagreements, we did, but a disagreement is one thing. Hatred is another.

Having been born one, and now trusted with three, I know this about boys: we are all born with a dad-sized hole drilled in the center of our chest. Our dad's either fill it with themselves, or as we grow into men and start to sense the emptiness, we medicate it with stuff. Usually addictions.

Uncle Willie bubbled up and out of a place down inside me that my dad filled up. He filled it with that 10-speed, by baiting my hook, coaching my t-ball team, helping me crank the mower, shining his flashlight behind him, popping the tab on my first beer, finding me when I was lost in West Virginia, standing beside me the day I married, spending three weeks with me in Africa, anointing my head with oil . . . I could go on.

Last week, our youngest son Rives turned four. Until now, his bicycle has been the rusted, bald-tired, split-seat, hand-me-down that has survived eight years of punishment thrown at it by his two older brothers and the rear wheels of Christy's Suburban. A week before his party, I drove to my local bike shop, pointed at what I wanted and paid my friend, Scotty, $120 for a shiny chrome dirt bike and all the pads we could find to fit it. (By the way, if you bought this book then you paid for a portion of Rives bike, so thank you.) On the day of his party, I drove Rives to the bike shop, they rolled it out of layaway, and he lit up like a spark plug. Then, without pause, he jumped on me, pressed his face onto my thigh, and said, "Thanks, Dad."

Listen. Did you hear that? There it is. That sound, that *Thanks, Dad*, that's the sound of me filling him up. In contrast, the boy who stole my bike thirty years ago, he was empty, running on fumes.

There is a much larger conversation here and it has to do with the role of the father in the life of his son. Uncle Willie is my best attempt at joining that conversation. If I need to restate it then you weren't listening the first time, but I can sum it up in two words: *nothing compares*.

Reading Group Guide

1. What is your favorite Uncle Willee "ism"?

2. What do you think is the significance of the title, *Chasing Fireflies*?

3. How would you describe Chase's relationship with Unc? With Tommye?

4. Each character in this story is, in some way, profoundly touched by abandonment. How does this affect Unc, Tommye, Chase, and Sketch?

5. Though Lorna is often a silent character in the story, she plays a significant, nurturing role in the lives of Unc, Tommye, Chase, and Sketch. How does she care for each of them?

6. How do you think Mandy influences Chase's life and his search for the truth about Unc? Have you ever had someone come along-side you with encouragement and assistance in a difficult situation?

7. The Sanctuary is an important place of refuge and peace for Unc, Tommye, and Chase. Do you have a place like it?

8. Why do you think Willee took the fall for the crimes he didn't commit? Have you ever taken the blame for something to protect someone you loved?

9. Unc says, "Kids are like a spring, or a Stretch Armstrong. No matter how many times they're passed around, passed off, and passed on . . . they snap back. Hope . . . it's the fuel that feeds them." Do you think this is true?

10. Which character in the book do you most identify with? Why?

11. In an article, Chase quotes a psychiatrist: "Adoptees suffer from a fear of loss. They see loss all over the place." How does this perspective affect Chase? How do you think it affects the way he sees and understands Unc's story?

12. Why do you think that Willee continues to use his "prison name" after he's released?

13. Unc says, "Words that sink into your heart are whispered, not yelled." What do you think he means? Have you found this to be true in your own life?

14. Chase often refers to the "hole in his chest." What happens to that hole once he finally discovers his true identity?

15. Discuss Unc's story of the firefly in Chapter 23. How does this story speak to you?

16. What do you think is the significance of names and who gives (or doesn't give) them to you?

17. There are many cases of mistaken identity in this story. What are they and how do they affect each character?

18. Everyone in the book has a defense mechanism. Is this true in real life?

19. Value—Unc puts value on people, which is profoundly affecting. When he saves Chase, he says, "'Cause, Chase, nothing . . . not one thing . . . compares to you." What value do you put on the role that people play in your life?

Also available from
CHARLES MARTIN

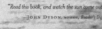

AUTHOR OF
The Dead Don't Dance

CHARLES MARTIN

WHEN CRICKETS CRY

A NOVEL of the HEART

"Read this book, and watch the sun come out."
—JOHN DYSON, writer, *Reader's Digest*

Wrapped in Rain

A NOVEL OF COMING HOME

CHARLES MARTIN

author of THE DEAD DON'T DANCE, *a future Hallmark Hall of Fame movie*

Martin's writing is strong, honest and memorable...an author to discover now."
—CAROL FITZGERALD, Bookreporter.com

the
Dead
don't
Dance

CHARLES MARTIN

A NOVEL OF AWAKENING

THOMAS NELSON, INC.
Since 1798